"I could hardly leave you to fend for yourself, now, could I?"

Jordan's light murmur belied the snarling ferocity he felt toward anyone who would dare harm her.

Mara stepped back from him, her wary gaze searching his face. "I suppose you are still a gentleman, even if I am not a lady, hm?" She smiled ruefully when she said it, but he stiffened nonetheless at her gentle rebuke.

"I'll check on thc coachman." Hc pivoted and marched slowly toward the door, burning with thwarted desire for her alone.

"Jordan?"

He cast a wary glance over his shoulders as he reached the door. "Yes?"

"I didn't know you could fight like that," she said.

He cast her a cool half smile. "Darling, you have no idea what I can do."

By Gaelen Foley

MY IRRESISTIBLE EARL
MY DANGEROUS DUKE
MY WICKED MARQUESS

GAELEN FOLEY

My Irresistible Earl

AVON

An Imprint of HarperCollins*Publishers*

This is a work of fiction. Names, characters, places, and incidents are products of the author's imagination or are used fictitiously and are not to be construed as real. Any resemblance to actual events, locales, organizations, or persons, living or dead, is entirely coincidental.

AVON BOOKS
An Imprint of HarperCollins*Publishers*
10 East 53rd Street
New York, New York 10022-5299

ISBN 978-0-06-173396-3
www.avonromance.com

First Avon Books mass market printing: April 2011

Printed in the U.S.A.

10 9 8 7 6 5 4 3 2

Love, that releases no beloved from loving,
took hold of me so strongly . . .
that, as you see, it has not left me yet.

—Dante's *Inferno*, Canto V. ll. 103–105

England, 1804

Being born into a secret, centuries-old order of chivalry sworn to the fight against evil was not a destiny for the faint of heart.

As a newly minted agent, twenty-two years old, Jordan Lennox, the Earl of Falconridge, had just completed years of rigorous training at the Order's remote, military-style school in the wilds of Scotland.

There, with his brother warriors, he had mastered all sorts of dangerous fun. He could scale sheer rock faces with naught but ropes and pulleys, had already swum the English Channel, could devise explosives out of a little saltpeter and random everyday objects found at hand. He was fluent in six languages, could navigate by the stars, and was so much at one with his smooth-bore rifle he could hit a bull's-eye at fifty yards blindfolded.

These were basic requirements for any young knight of the Order about to be deployed on his first mission.

Jordan, however, more prudent, sensible, and cautious than his headstrong teammates even at the start of their illustrious careers, had already made up his mind about how he did *not* want the life of a spy to affect him in the long term.

After years of observing the grim demeanor of their handler, Virgil, he had made a pact with himself not to end up like *that*.

Too many of the older agents had that same dark look: cynical to the point of bitterness, hard-edged, stony.

Ice-cold.

What was the point of taking the Order's blood oath to protect the Realm and everyone he loved—friends and family—if a man ended up as dead inside as an old, blackened hunk of petrified wood?

And so, wherever his future missions might take him, he vowed, he would not let his work for the Order become the only thing that he had in his life.

The key, as best he could figure, was not to lose touch with normal people, normal life, as silly and trivial as it sometimes seemed compared to the high-stakes shadow war that he and his brother warriors had pledged to fight.

Max and Rohan preferred to scoff at the oblivious people in Society, but Jordan, with his wonderful parents, adoring siblings, and countless cousins, found a certain quaint charm in ordinary goings-on.

Participating in all the social rituals helped him keep his balance—and it was for this reason that he accepted the invitation to the country-house party.

He probably wouldn't be able to stay the full month of

July, he supposed, for any day now, he expected to receive his first assignment to one of the foreign courts presently under threat.

With Napoleon running amuck across the Continent, every agent was needed, especially those of high birth who could be given entrée into places and meet with people to whom common folk had no access.

But all this was a care for another day.

For now, there would be picnics, outdoor games, strawberry picking with the delicate young ladies, quadrilles with debutantes, perhaps a home theatrical at their hosts' elegant country estate.

It was all so deliciously normal, the sort of pursuits in which any highborn young gentleman might while away the long, lazy weeks of summer. Jordan relished the chance to pretend for a while that he was no different than any of the other, well-fixed young rakes, aside from having already come into his title.

He was even prepared to let the other lads win most of the athletic contests. What he was completely unprepared for, however, was meeting Mara Bryce . . .

Chapter 1

London
Twelve years later

"There is a gorgeous man over there staring at you," Delilah drawled under her breath as the two fashionable young widows sat amid the wealthy crowd amassed at Christie's grand auction rooms in Pall Mall. "Mmm, he's very fit. Blond, with a smoldering look. Impeccable clothes. Go on, have a look. I'll take him if you're not interested."

"Sh! I'm concentrating!" Mara, Lady Pierson, ignored her friend's mischievous efforts to distract her and kept her attention focused on the auctioneer, who was smoothly managing the sale of the Old Master from his raised podium at the front of the long, high-ceilinged chamber.

"Seven hundred fifty, do I have eight hundred pounds? Eight hundred fifty . . ."

"You don't need another painting, darling," Delilah opined. "What you really need to do is take a lover, as I have long advised."

"That, I assure you, is the last thing I require."

"Prude."

Mara snorted, barely paying attention to her as the bid was raised again. "Another arrogant male to come along and lord it over me? No, thank you. I've just got rid of one."

"A lover, sweet, is different from a husband."

"Well, you would know."

Delilah smacked her arm lightly for this bit of insolence. Mara shot her a wicked, twinkling look askance, then returned her gaze to the front of the room. "No, my dear, I assure you, I can do without a man. I'm nearly thirty years old, and I've only just *now* got my life the way I want it. Why should I give some randy male the chance to wreck it for me?"

"Well, that is a good point. But randy males have their uses, darling. I daresay you will learn to enjoy them in time."

"I doubt it. I have no talent for such things, just ask my husband." She cast her worldly friend a cynical glance.

Delilah smiled sympathetically. "All the more reason for you to find a man who actually knows how to satisfy a woman."

"Is there such a creature?" she murmured, watching the auctioneer attentively.

"To be sure! You could borrow Cole—but, no. Then I'd have to scratch your eyes out."

Mara laughed softly. "Don't worry. Your Cole is safe from me. The only male I care about right now is two years old."

"That may be, Mama bear, but be warned, now that you're out of mourning, you're going to find yourself considered fair game."

Mara shrugged with a restless glance around the auction

hall at her competition for the painting. "Whoever tries will only be wasting his time."

"Do I hear nine hundred?"

She quickly raised her numbered paddle again.

Delilah let out a bored sigh. "Why are you spending a fortune on this gloomy old portrait of some Dutch merchant's wife? She's ugly, anyway. She has a bulbous nose."

"There's more to art than prettiness, Delilah. Besides, the painting's not for me." Mara winced at the climbing price as the auctioneer proclaimed: "One thousand pounds!"

"Who's it for, then?" Delilah asked in surprise.

Her friend waited expectantly; Mara hesitated before answering the question.

"Well?"

"It's for George," she conceded at last in a low tone, flashing her paddle again.

"George?"

"Do I have eleven hundred?"

"Who is George?" her friend whispered eagerly.

Mara sent her a cautious, meaningful look, trying to be discreet.

Delilah's eyes widened. "Ohhh, *that* George! You mean the Prince Regent!" She gasped in scandalous delight. "Oh, you *are* having an affair with Prinny! I knew it!—oh, but darling, he's so *fat*! Then again, he will be king. Hold on! Is he in love with you? Good God, you could get diamonds as big as your fist—"

"Delilah!"

"How is he in bed?" She laughed with wicked glee. "Oh, I'll bet he's terrible! But no worse than other heads of state—I wonder. What about King Louis of France? He's also fat, and very old. At least he's not Napoleon, poor little thing." The merry widow's meaningful laugh was pure deviltry.

"For heaven's sake, keep your voice down!" Mara scolded

in a whisper, trying not to laugh. "Listen to me, you mad-woman. I am *not* having an affair with the Regent. We are *friends*. Friends, do you mark me?"

"Mm-hmm."

"His Royal Highness is my son's godfather, as you are well aware. That is all!"

"Tell it to the ton, love." Delilah folded her arms across her chest and studied her with a knowing eye. "With all your visits to Carlton House, there has been *speculation*."

Mara let out a sigh. *I know,* she thought wearily. What a perverse world it was. Why did people always assume the worst?

"Eleven hundred! Do I hear twelve?" The auctioneer scanned the sprawling room. "Eleven hundred fifty?"

Holding her paddle high, Mara bit her lip with another quick glance around. "I think I've just bought . . ."

"Sold! To the lovely lady here." With a polite nod to Mara, the auctioneer banged his gavel.

"Well, bully for me." When Mara turned to grin at Delilah, her friend was staring quizzically at her. "What?"

"Eleven hundred pounds? Darling, I just furnished my entire beach house at Brighton for that much. Why else would you spend such a huge sum on the Regent unless he is your *cher ami,* hmm?"

"Because," she answered ever so reasonably, "Gerrit Dou is his latest collecting craze. And—" Mara stopped herself, unsure how much she was allowed to say.

"And *what*?" Delilah leaned closer.

"And . . . I happen to possess certain information that a happy royal occasion is about to be announced. Now you see how frightfully clever I am?" she teased. "I'll already have my gift picked out, while the rest of you will be left to scramble when the big announcement comes."

"What big announcement?" Delilah prompted, tugging at

her arm. "Are they finally going to let him have his divorce? Because, just think, then you could—"

"No! Sorry, my lips are sealed." Mara chuckled at Delilah's imploring huff.

"You're really not going to tell me?" she exclaimed with a wounded air.

"I can't, love. They'll throw me in the Tower."

"Right."

"My dear, I dare not. It's not my news to *tell,* you see. But you'll hear it soon enough. It should be made public within a sennight."

"You are wicked."

"Look who's talking! So, where is this gorgeous man you were talking about, anyway? What did you call him—impeccable and smoldering? I rather like the sound of that."

"I thought you didn't want a man."

"Well, I don't mind looking." Mara followed her gaze as Delilah glanced around.

"Oh. He's gone now. I don't see him anymore." Then Delilah sent her a small pout. "Honestly, you *would* tell me if you *were* sharing a bed with the Regent, wouldn't you?"

"With the way you gossip? Absolutely not," she answered mildly.

"But, my dear, that's why you love me!"

"True. All the same, there is nothing to tell. His Royal Highness is my son's godfather and my friend."

"Your friend."

"Of course! He's been altogether gallant to me and to Thomas ever since my husband's death."

"I wonder why," Delilah answered dryly.

"Well, you know, he is married," Mara pointed out with an evasive shrug.

Delilah scoffed. "And your point is?"

"Come, everyone knows the prince has always preferred

older women. He's kind to me, that's all." *And I owe him in ways that you don't understand.* "What more can I say? I genuinely care for him."

"Well, that's very sweet, darling. But you may be the last person in England who feels that way."

"I don't care what anyone says about him. I adore our Prinny. He has an artist's soul."

"Just what the country needs. Can we leave now?" Delilah complained. "It's stifling in here, and it smells like my grandmother's attic."

"Fine with me. I accomplished what I came for. I'm anxious to get home to Thomas, anyway. He woke up yesterday with a bit of a sniffle. It has me rather concerned."

"Horrors, a sniffle! And how many physicians have you had to the house in the past twenty-four hours to tend our little viscount?"

"Delilah Staunton, you know nothing about children."

"I know enough to stay away from 'em, don't I?" she retorted, her eyes twinkling.

Mara gave her a severe look in answer.

Delilah laughed blithely. "Come, I'll send for our carriages if you want to go settle up for your painting and make the arrangements for its delivery."

She nodded, then the two ladies rose from their seats.

As they maneuvered their long skirts with care, climbing as discreetly as possible past the row of still-seated patrons, Mara reflected on the pesky rumor that she was the Regent's newest ladylove.

Obviously, she did not want to risk insulting the future king by too vehemently repudiating the tale, as if the thought of him as her paramour disgusted her. Not for the world would she ever wish to wound the extremely sensitive royal George's feelings. He was so conscious of his weight, so tenderhearted, so easily made to feel rejected.

Thanks to her parents' methods of raising her on a steady diet of barbed criticism and disparagement, Mara knew firsthand the difficulty of trying to live when one's foundation, as it were, was built on complete uncertainty about oneself. Constant attacks on one's worth and value tended to fill a person with a hopeless sense of failure, no matter how one tried.

That was why she could sympathize with the poor Regent. For him, there had never been any real chance of living up to the expectations of his father, the King, let alone the expectations of his countrymen. They had wanted a Wellington combined with a royal Adonis, and instead they had received an insecure, portly dilettante who had quickly become a nervous wreck.

The pressure on the Regent was beyond enormous, and he was not the sort of man built to carry that kind of load. Mara knew he needed friends, actual friends, not two-faced toadies around him, and after what he'd done for her and her little boy, she was happy to stand by him with stalwart loyalty even if doing so did some damage to her reputation.

What did it matter? She was no longer a girl of seventeen, anyway, obsessed with others' opinions, trying to please everyone.

With the Prinny situation, the wisest course in her view was simply to laugh off the rumor and protest it only mildly—in a way that would not bruise the royal ego.

After all, a monarch's friendship was not without hazard. If Beau Brummell himself could fall out of favor after one too-sarcastic jest, anyone could. The Prince Regent might be unpopular of late, but he still had the power to sentence anyone to *social* death.

In the meanwhile, Mara assured herself, the Regent did not really want to bed her. He had only dropped a *few* hints, no more than a light, unserious flirtation. The thought that he might be serious in any degree was too terrifying to contemplate. No, his Royal Highness merely enjoyed her company—which was more than she could say for her late husband.

Besides, the whisper of her supposed tryst with the Regent worked like magic to keep all the other lecherous lords of the aristocracy at bay. They dared not poach on what might be considered royal territory.

Delilah was right. Widows who still owned a share of youth and beauty were often the most hotly pursued women in the ton, fair game in the eyes of London's many highborn seducers. There was a time when Mara would have savored so much male attention, but that was long ago. Her brief career as a coquette seemed another lifetime.

Her priorities were very different now. She was no longer an insecure young debutante, desperate for a husband—any husband—in order to escape her parents' loveless home, but an independent woman who had fought hard to come into her own. Two years ago, the birth of her son had changed everything. For Thomas's sake, Mara had grown strong.

Reaching the aisle along the gallery wall, Delilah and she walked toward the back of the crowded auction room, where people were milling around, quietly coming and going. Delilah nodded to various acquaintances along the way, while Mara, following, gazed at the rain tapping at the high, arched windows along the opposite wall.

The flat gray light of winter-weary March did little justice to these sad masterpieces so unceremoniously put up for sale. Dozens of oil paintings crammed the gallery wall, along with watercolors and sketches of all shapes and sizes.

Most of these Old Masters had changed hands many times over the ages, she supposed, but still had not arrived at their true home. There was something so poignant about seeing them hanging there, as if they were just waiting for someone to come along who might finally see and appreciate their subtler beauties, not just buy them for the sake of others' envy or for some haughty sense of self-congratulation.

She thought of her supposed lover with a wry smile.

The Regent would have probably bought them all if the country were not already outraged at his spending.

Her gaze trailed wistfully down the gallery wall to the long tables where statues, vases, jewelry, and other objets d'art were displayed, awaiting their turn on the auction block alongside rare old books and a few ancient, illuminated manuscripts.

Glancing forward again to mind her step, Mara unexpectedly locked eyes with a man leaning against the back wall a few yards ahead.

She stopped in her tracks.

Stunned recognition nearly knocked the breath from her lungs. She knew him at once though it had been years.

Gorgeous, impeccable, and smoldering, just as Delilah had said . . .

Jordan—?

Jordan Lennox!

He was staring at her, but he did not smile.

But, how—? What on earth was he doing here?

Pain gripped her as she held his stare, a sudden surge of anguish that came without warning.

Delilah walked on ahead, oblivious to her halt.

Mara floundered in a state of shock.

Of course, her logical mind had known it was inevitable she would run into him sooner or later, but to see him standing there after all these years . . .

He narrowed his eyes in aloof curiosity, watching her.

Mara stiffened though her mouth had gone dry, and her heart was already pounding.

Treading water in a flood of buried hurt and long-nursed anger, she saw that she would have to walk right past him.

There was no other way out of Christie's unless she went all the way round to the other side of the room. And she did not intend to give the ice-cold bastard the satisfaction of her doing that.

Perhaps he won't even speak to me. I meant so little to him in the end, after all. It's been so long, he probably doesn't even remember who I am.

Since there was no point in trying to pretend she had not seen her former suitor, the one she had naïvely thought might be her true love, she masked the tumult of her emotions, steeled her spine, and proceeded forward with a haughty lift of her chin.

She felt naked, however, before the earl's cool, steady stare. He did not look any more pleased by their little reunion than she was.

As she approached, still defiantly holding his gaze, refusing to show any intimidation, quite unlike the first time they had met, she thought that his ice blue eyes looked even shrewder, more piercing than she remembered.

Not as kind.

He was still terribly handsome, that austere face with a hint of Nordic blood, all chiseled planes and angles. But he did not look like a happy man.

Good, she thought fiercely. If she'd had to suffer in the years that had passed since they had parted, it was only fair he should've done the same.

Everything she had gone through in nine miserable years of marriage could have been avoided if Jordan had not abandoned her. If he had really been different from the rest of the young men who had once vied for her hand.

Oh, he was different, all right. The others were merely shallow. He was worse, crueler, in his way, than her rough-mannered husband.

Tom had been a club, but Jordan was a scalpel.

"Mara." He condescended to a dutiful nod when she was right in front of him, the crowd jostling her closer to him than she had any desire ever to go again.

The sound of her name on his tongue made her flinch.

How dare you speak to me?

"Lord Falconridge," she replied in a frosty tone. She meant to keep going without so much as slowing down, but he spoke again—as if he could not help himself—his words polite, his tone slightly goading.

"Congratulations on the Gerrit Dou."

Mara paused, turning to him with a guarded stare.

He flicked a rudely approving glance over her figure. "You're looking well."

Gracious, this bold appraisal from Lord Holier-Than-Thou quite astonished her! He had always been—or pretended to be—the model of knightly virtue when they were young.

Perhaps he'd changed. Perhaps he'd given up the act of chivalry at last. *Good.* The world did not need any more hypocrites.

"Thank you," she clipped out. Again, she meant to walk away, and again he stopped her with another comment—seemingly in spite of himself.

"I did not know you collected art."

There's a lot you don't know about me, you prick. "I don't, my lord. Good day."

"Mara—"

"Lady Pierson," she corrected him in sharp reproach, but she, too, could not help turning back in spite of herself. Folding her arms across her chest, she subjected him to the same rude perusal that he had just enjoyed of her.

It did not help her peace of mind to see that he still looked good. Very good. Actually, to her dismay, the false-hearted cad looked even *better* than he had twelve years ago. He must be what, now? Thirty-four?

The years had hardened the comely, golden youth into a man. He was still clean-cut, his sandy hair cropped short and neat, while the careful discipline of his dress had matured into effortless elegance. But no wonder that, she thought in disdain, as this was a man who spent his time lounging around European palaces.

Leaning by the oak-paneled wall, casually winding his fob watch, the worldly diplomat earl wore a bottle green riding coat, its stand collar framing his neat white cravat. His waistcoat bore a discreet herringbone pattern; tobacco brown breeches disappeared into black top boots with buff turnovers.

That was Jordan for you, she thought with an ache that had never quite gone away. Nothing extreme. Coolly controlled, the consummate gentleman. All subtlety, precision. A model of exacting, pitiless perfection.

Years ago, she had heard one of his friends call him "Falcon," short for his title, Falconridge, and indeed, the nickname fit him well. A fierce, beautiful, and solitary creature flying over all, out of reach, looking down on the rest of the world from a distance, his most private thoughts known only to the wind.

He had always fascinated her. Even now, to her complete exasperation, she felt the heated pull toward him in the core of her body, a womanly yearning for a completion with this man that had been too long denied.

He just watched her with a hawklike detachment, both very close and yet, so far away. That piercing stare made her think he could read her as easily as a street sign, but for his part, he was still a mystery to her, unknown and unobtainable.

At least now, in her widowhood, she had an inkling of the freedom he enjoyed as a male, with the money and time to do as he liked, having to answer to no one.

Perhaps that was part of why he had walked away from her all those years ago. She had thought she understood back then that the thing he cared about most was friends and family, the connections that wrapped a life in comfort; but instead, to her bewilderment, he had become a rootless wanderer.

Well, but it did not signify. Their history together was as dead and gone as Tom.

Mara advised herself to leave. Now. And yet, caught in his gaze, she remained.

"Back from the Continent, are you?" she asked begrudgingly, remaining aloof. "Or do you merely condescend to honor England with a visit, my lord?"

Jordan put his watch away again, looking amused by her hostility. "Back to stay, as far as I've been told."

The news shook her. *Oh, perfect. So now I'll have to deal with you on a regular basis in Society?*

Delilah had stopped ahead but pivoted upon finding herself alone, then returned the few short paces to Mara's side. She smiled at the earl with admiring interest, then turned to Mara in curious expectancy. "Shall I wait for you?"

"No need. I'm coming," she replied, but Jordan, damn him, dazzled her companion with one of his most devastating smiles.

"Won't you introduce me to your friend, Lady Pierson?" he asked very deliberately, his tone silky-smooth.

Mara gritted her teeth. "Mrs. Staunton, the Earl of Falconridge."

"Mrs.?" he asked, a teasing twinkle of regret in his pale blue eyes as he took her friend's offered hand.

"Alas, Lord Falconridge, my poor husband has gone on to be with the Lord," Delilah purred.

"What a shame," he murmured with a frown full of sinful intent. He dipped his head and kissed her knuckles. "Pleasure."

Mara clenched her jaw harder.

Delilah's stare devoured him. "I marvel that we have not met before, Lord Falconridge."

"The earl spends most of his time abroad," Mara interjected, studying him in disapproval. "England is far too small for the likes of him. Provincial, I'm afraid."

"I say!" Delilah laughed, noting Mara's razor tone. "Where have you been wandering, my lord?"

"Yes, where, Jordan, pray tell? The nine circles of Hell, perhaps?"

"Not all nine yet. So far, I've only seen a few. Here and there," he added, answering Delilah's question with a smile. But he sent Mara a sardonic frown at her pointed reference to the scandalous Inferno Club, of which he was a longtime member.

All London knew that only very bad boys with fine bloodlines and deep pockets were admitted into Dante House, the headquarters of that exclusive and rather mysterious society of rakehells and highborn libertines.

Years ago, Jordan had charmingly assured her that he was the club's token "good boy," the one responsible fellow who made sure the others got home unscathed after a night of riotous drinking and wenching, or whatever other violent mischief his mad friends got up to in the middle of the night.

At seventeen, she had been naïve enough to believe him. Now she understood this was just his line.

It had certainly worked on her.

"Provincial or not," Jordan added lightly, watching Mara, "I am back in London now."

"How fortunate for the entire Realm," she drawled, unnerved by his presence and this news. "Come, Delilah. I must get home to Thomas. Good day, my lord."

"Thomas, yes, of course. How is your charming husband, my lady?" he challenged her.

Mara looked at him, taken aback. "Lord Pierson has been dead these two years. I was referring to my son."

"Ah." Jordan looked not at all surprised. "I'm so sorry," he added with a polite nod and an utter lack of sincerity.

She realized he had known of Pierson's death.

For whatever reason, he seemed to have asked merely as an experiment to find out her reaction.

Mara eyed him warily, then turned away, but alas, Delilah lingered. "I say, Lord Falconridge, considering you've only just returned to Town, why don't you and Lady Falconridge come to my dinner party tomorrow night?"

Mara whipped around, aghast, hearing this.

"You mean my mother?" he drawled.

Delilah's lashes fluttered. "Oh, you are not married?"

"Most assuredly not, last time I checked." The air crackled with furious tension after that remark.

He did not look at Mara, and she could not possibly look at him.

In that moment, she was paralyzed with the memory of their final night together at the country-house party, when she had risked her reputation and her mother's wrath to sneak away and join him in the garden, as he had asked.

Running out to him through the flowery garden paths glimmering in starlight, she had been so sure he meant to propose, and she already knew that her answer would be yes, yes, yes.

Every hour since she had met him had been magical.

But as it turned out, that was not the reason for his summons, as she had soon learned when he had taken her hands gently in his own.

"I wanted to see you privately so I could say good-bye."

Stunned disappointment nearly stole her voice. *"Good-bye?"*

"I must go." He had searched her eyes soulfully. "My orders arrived this afternoon from the Foreign Office."

"Well, w-when do they want you?"

"Immediately, I'm afraid."

Mara had struggled to absorb the blow. "W-will you be gone long?"

"Six months, at least. Maybe as many as eight."

"Eight months! Oh . . ."

"I'm sorry."

Her head was reeling. The thought of having to stay even longer in her parents' house made her wince, but if there was hope they could be together eventually, she had to admit he was worth the suffering. "C-could I at least write to you?" she ventured.

"Oh—I don't know yet where I'll be."

Being in shock made it hard to know what to say. "If you let me know the address when you find out, I'll write you every day. You can write back to me when you're able."

"I'm not sure that will be possible, Mara," he had said, searching her eyes with such sincerity. "But I will try." He had lowered his gaze. "Miss Bryce, I know you're anxious to change your situation. But if there's any way you could delay making your choice for a while, then in a few months when I return, perhaps we could see each other again, and if we still feel the same—it's just, I've never met anyone like you—"

"Oh, Jordan!" Without warning, she had thrown her arms recklessly around his neck and kissed him on the lips.

He had seemed as surprised by her sudden advance as she was.

A moment later, he had cupped her face between his hands and kissed her back with such reverent restraint.

"Take me with you!" she had whispered breathlessly, as soon as his lips stopped caressing hers.

"I can't," he breathed, shaking his head.

"Why not?"

"It's too dangerous, Mara." He closed his eyes. "The

whole Continent's a battlefield right now. I'm not dragging you into the theatre of war. You'll be safe here."

"Don't go! I'll die if anything happens to you!"

"Nothing is going to happen to me. I'm just a diplomat. I have to go, sweeting. People are counting on me. It's the right thing to do. And besides, it is my duty," he said, though the look in his eyes was anguished despite his conviction.

Mara had gazed at him adoringly. How beautiful he was! How noble! she had thought in awe, staring at him. How could a silly thing like her ever have attracted a golden-hearted hero like him?

If he left, he was sure to come to his senses once they were apart. Trembling, Mara had lowered her gaze to the ground for a long moment. Everything in her said, *Don't let him get away.* It was obvious how and why she needed him. But some small voice inside her heart warned her, illogically, that somehow, Jordan needed her, too.

Rising panic made her desperate enough to dare whisper the boldest question of her life: "Could we not marry before you go?"

At least then she'd have her own house and the guarantee that he'd come back to her eventually.

He had gazed at her in tender regret and tucked a lock of her hair behind her ear. "Mara, try to understand. I do care for you. But this is all so sudden. I have—responsibilities. We mustn't let our emotions run away with us. A person can't fall in love in three short weeks. That's just the moonlight talking."

She had lifted her head and stared at him. Did he really doubt what she knew they both were feeling?

She nearly blurted out her doubts, but she was already embarrassed that she had just more or less proposed to him and been rejected.

"Please. I have no choice," he had whispered to her with

an imploring gaze. "We have to be adults about this. When I come back, if things still feel the same between us, if you want to, then we can . . . oh, don't look at me like that, sweeting. I'll be back before you know it! You won't forget me, will you?"

"Oh, Jordan, I could never forget you."

"Then you must be strong."

"And you be safe," she had countered, tears rushing into her eyes.

He had winced, pulled her closer, and pressed a kiss to her brow. "Don't worry about me. You just behave yourself like a good girl, and I will see you soon." He had kissed her hands, then released them, gazing reverently into her eyes as he backed away, bowing to her when he reached the edge of the grove.

Mara had choked back a sob as he pivoted and marched off into the shadows.

That was the last time she had seen him until this very day. No wonder she could barely draw her next breath of air in past her corset.

But Delilah had no knowledge of their painful past, still prattling on. "You must come and let us entertain you, my lord!" Her friend was sidling closer to him and looking altogether pleased to discover that he was a bachelor. "I'm famous for the excellence of my table—and Lady Pierson will be there! I see you two are acquainted. You'll want a chance to catch up, no doubt. And given that you've been away, we'll both be happy to introduce you around again to everyone. *All* the best people come to my soirees," she added, preening.

Mara's heart was pounding. She stared at her friend, discreetly hiding her wrath, but Delilah paid no heed, exuding charm.

"How very generous of you, Mrs. Staunton," he replied.

"No, no, Delilah, please," she pooh-poohed him. "So, would you like to come, my lord?" she asked in a decidedly wicked tone.

The handsome blackguard looked delighted by her naughty innuendo, but before he could answer, Mara spoke up through gritted teeth. "I don't think that's a very good idea."

She willed Delilah to notice her warning glare, but the merry widow could not tear her gaze off the worldly earl.

"I'd be honored," he said smoothly.

"Excellent! I live at 16 Chesterfield, off Curzon Street."

"Ah, nice and close to the Park," he purred with a stare that practically caressed her friend.

If he was ogling Delilah for the express purpose of irritating *her,* by Jove, the childish trick was working.

How unlike the Jordan Lennox she remembered!

"Come at half past seven, and we shall dine at eight," Delilah instructed him.

He nodded politely. "I look forward to it. Thank you for your kind invitation, madam. Ladies." He taunted Mara with a sly, sidelong glance, then sketched a bow. "If you'll excuse me, they're about to introduce my item. Wish me luck."

With that, he sauntered back into the bustling main auction room, leaving both wide-eyed women gazing at his broad shoulders and his compactly muscled derriere.

Mara turned to Delilah with a severe look when he had disappeared into the crowd. "You should not have done that."

"Why ever not?" Delilah beamed and clapped her gloved hands in jubilation. "Oh, Mara, he's perfect for you! What an utterly delicious specimen! Just the sort of lover you should start with—"

"Oh, God, don't make me ill!" She pivoted and immediately began marching toward the clerk's station to pay for the Gerrit Dou.

"What's wrong?" Delilah exclaimed, hurrying after her.

"I despise that man!"

"Don't be absurd."

"I do! I hate him—he hates me—we hate each other—couldn't you tell?" she asked rather frantically.

"Right." Delilah folded her arms across her chest. "That would explain why neither of you could stop staring."

"Nonsense, it was you he was drooling over!"

She cocked an eyebrow. "Darling, you sound jealous, and yet you hate him? Now, here's a mystery!"

Mara scowled at her impossible friend, but her heart was pounding as she joined the short queue to pay for her Gerrit Dou. "Well," she announced in a businesslike tone, tugging off her gloves, "I cannot possibly come to your dinner party now."

"Of course you can."

"No. The sight of him would more than ruin my appetite," she declared with a shudder.

"Not mine." Delilah glanced admiringly in the direction the earl had gone. "He is quite the robust entrée, if you take my meaning. Good English beefsteak. Bit of tenderizing, and I'd put him on my menu any night."

Mara rolled her eyes heavenward at Delilah's familiar brand of irreverence. "Are you going to flirt with him like that tomorrow night in front of Cole?"

"Perhaps. What does it matter to you since you cannot abide him? Anyway, Cole and I do not pretend to have an exclusive understanding."

"Oh, really? Is Cole aware of that? In case you haven't noticed, the poor man is in love with you."

Delilah shrugged in studied nonchalance. "That is his problem, not mine. So, why this aversion to Lord Falconridge? He seems entirely charming to me."

Mara shook her head and looked away. Though she was fuming, she finally conceded: "We had a falling-out a long time ago."

"Over what?"

"It does not signify!"

"Well, if it was long ago, maybe it's time to let bygones be bygones?"

She shot her a glare. "No, it's not. And I *don't* wish to discuss it," she added, before Delilah could ask again.

Her friend frowned. "Well, at least tell me what he's been doing out of the country!"

"I don't know; something to do with the war," Mara mumbled, moving forward as another gentleman finished his transaction with the clerk. "Now that it's over, it appears the bleeder's back."

"Is he an officer? He looked rather dangerous to me." Delilah elbowed her. "Did he ever show you his *sword*?"

"Would you behave? He's in some branch of the diplomatic service. Foreign Office or some such."

"How intriguing! Where was his post?"

"I don't know, and if I did, I wouldn't even care!" she declared a little too emphatically.

Delilah scowled at her. "Very well. I'll go and tell the boy to bring our carriages."

"Please *do*."

"Touchy!" Delilah muttered, but lifting the hem of her skirts a bit, she glided off to fetch their transportation.

Reaching the front of the line, Mara shoved Jordan Lennox out of her mind with a vexed huff; but as she reached into her reticule and wrote out a cheque to pay for the painting, her hands were still shaking from their brief encounter.

Handing over her payment, she set up a time to have the Gerrit Dou delivered to her home. She would present it to her royal friend in person when he returned from Brighton. The arrangements made, she smoothed her reticule over her wrist and went to the entrance, where Delilah waited.

She realized she had been rather vehement with her friend and approached with a chastened attitude. "I'm sorry for being short with you, darling. It's just that seeing that, that *person* again was—a trifle upsetting."

Delilah gazed at her. "He meant a lot to you?"

"Once, he did. Until I realized he's just a fraud. Too good to be true," she said with a sigh.

"Perhaps he's changed since you last knew him."

"Oh, I'm sure we both have. For the worse." Gazing down Pall Mall as she waited for her driver to bring the coach, Mara shook her head. "I don't know. I once imagined he and I shared something . . . beautiful and sweet, and so innocent . . . but obviously, it was all a girlish delusion. He left without a backward glance, and that was how I ended up with Pierson."

Delilah's eyes widened. "Pierson was your second choice even from the start?" she whispered.

Mara nodded wryly. "And once he realized that, he never forgave me for it."

Her friend studied her with a thoughtful frown.

"What is it?" Mara asked.

"Mara, Pierson's gone," Delilah said. "You are free to do as you choose. Perhaps destiny has given you and Lord Falconridge another—"

"No. He had his chance," she cut her off. "He's not going to hurt me again, I can promise you that."

"All the same, that's the biggest reaction I've seen out of you toward any man—well, ever."

"That's because I despise him, as I told you."

"You know what they say, my dear. Hatred is but the other side of the coin to love."

She snorted. "Not in this case."

"Very well, then. Maybe you're just saving yourself—for George."

Mara scowled at her.

Delilah laughed. "Here's my carriage. *Au revoir,* darling." She gave Mara a peck on the cheek, then nodded to one of Christie's footmen posted by the door; he opened it for her onto the busy, windy avenue. "Remember, tomorrow evening, seven o'clock!" Delilah called. "Come early so we can make fun of everyone else before they arrive."

"I told you, I'm not coming anymore."

"Of course you are!"

"No, I'm not. Not if *he's* there."

"Very well! Since you clearly have *no* interest in that lovely fellow, I'll make sure to entertain him *personally.*" With a pointed glance over her shoulder, Delilah paraded out the rest of the way to her waiting carriage, where her liveried groom handed her up.

Before her carriage pulled away, she looked out the window with a knowing smile and an arch wave farewell.

Mara was left stewing on the pavement. *I know what she's trying to do, but it's not going to work.*

Delilah could have the cad for all she cared.

A moment later, her trusty driver, Jack, brought her coach gliding to a halt before the entrance. At once, her footman got the carriage door and knocked the step down for her.

Mara climbed in, assuring herself again that she did not give a fig if Delilah seduced Jordan, or the other way round. It mattered not the tiniest iota.

All *she* cared about was getting home to Thomas. Her pride and joy, the center of her world.

Whatever capacity for love she possessed, it was reserved for her child and him alone. Her baby deserved all she had to give. Besides, a creature so pure and innocent, so full of love, would never betray her, never hurt her like everyone else had. Even if by some wild chance, Jordan were interested in her again, it did not signify. Her decision was already made.

She was Thomas's mother now, and that was all that she desired to be.

2

Sometimes things just didn't work out the way you planned. Missions ran long, and sometimes the people you counted on lost faith, gave up on you, and moved on with their lives. When that happened, the correct, the honorable thing to do was not to put up a fuss but to bow out like a gentleman, no matter how it hurt . . . just to let them go with one last, lingering wish that they might find a way to be happy.

How many love letters had he crumpled up and thrown into the fire rather than send them, knowing the enemy could follow his communications straight to her?

Not for the world would he have ever put her in danger. Even if it meant losing her to someone else.

Well, it scarcely mattered anymore. Stalking back into the auction room, Jordan eluded pain with the sardonic anger that had become as much a part of his defenses as his favorite smoothbore rifle.

But a cold, private smile tilted one corner of his lips, for he was still rather smugly pleased at Mara's appalled look when he had accepted her friend's invitation.

How could he resist such a golden opportunity to make the lady squirm? Might as well enjoy her discomfiture, he mused, as this was likely to be the only satisfaction he'd ever have of Mara Bryce.

Ah, but, of course, she wasn't Miss Bryce anymore, he thought acidly. She hadn't been called that in years.

She was Lady Pierson now, a wealthy, widowed viscountess, newly out of mourning.

Yes, of course, he knew. Knew more about her than he had let on. Far more, indeed, than he even liked admitting to himself.

He had spotted his former darling in the crowd long before she had noticed him—today, of all days.

Naturally. It would have to be today—just when he was knee deep in a mission for the Order. The day's operation had been weeks in the planning, but that was Mara for you. She had always been the most damned inconvenient female on God's green earth.

At least by glimpsing her first, he'd had time to absorb the shock of this unexpected encounter.

Though he had feigned nonchalance, in truth, a flood of tangled emotions had rushed through him at the sight of her—a shock in itself, considering he had been numb for so long it was actually starting to scare him.

Now the vortex of feeling she had left churning in his breast compelled a moment's starkest honesty. For twelve years, he'd been pretending he did not give a damn what that woman did with her life.

But if this were true, his meticulous brain would not have filed away so many details of her existence. Like the date she had been married. The date of her idiot husband's death, the location of her country house in Hampshire and where she lived in London—37 Great Cumberland Street, to be exact.

He would not know that she had one small son, called Thomas, after his loud, vain braggart of a father. Nor should it still make him vaguely nauseous to think of her carrying another man's child.

Jordan would've liked to claim that his knowledge of all these varied Mara facts was nothing but an occupational hazard. Information, after all, was an agent's stock in trade. But clearly he still harbored some morbid fascination with the woman.

Very well, he conceded as he wove his way through the crowded aisle toward the front of the room. So he was not indifferent to Mara Bryce.

But what he felt for her could not be called affection.

On the contrary. He bloody well despised her.

The loss of all that might have been was bearable that way. If only she could have been strong enough to wait a little longer. If only he hadn't been so sensible, so cautious in the first place—so *him*.

He shrugged off the memory of how her startling offer of marriage had nonplussed him that night in the garden—the bold young agent, afraid of nothing! A beautiful seventeen-year-old with her heart shining in her big, dark eyes had unnerved him with a kiss. Indeed, she had scared the hell out of him.

Well, Virgil had never trained them in what to do in the face of *that* particular calamity—falling in love!

Jordan had been so taken off guard by it all, so much out of his element, it had been all he could do not to go tearing out of there like he'd had the devil at his heels.

At the very least, he was not about to trust that his crazed attraction to Mara was real until it was tested by a sensible absence. As much as she tempted him, he had not been willing to throw aside the duty of his line to serve the Order, as every Earl of Falconridge had done before him.

Above all, he had refused to let his friends down; he would not tell Mara his secrets when she could, in all innocence, let slip one wrong word in the right ear and get people killed—his brother warriors, his handler, and himself.

Difficult as it had been—even knowing what he knew now, how duty would conspire to keep them apart until she had settled for Pierson—Jordan held grimly to his conviction that he had done the right thing. And for someone like him, he told himself, that was enough.

To Hell with happiness. Honor was all that really mattered at the end of the day.

As for now, he was merely thankful that Mara and her highborn harlot friend had left Christie's. He did not need the headache of protecting two daft Society ladies added to his already-long list of duties and details for this mission.

There was unseen danger in this room that an idle observer would never have suspected, but today's ruse should soon lure out the hidden enemies lurking in their midst.

The operation would begin shortly.

Jordan made his way to a spot near the front of the soaring auction hall, from where he'd be able to see everyone who might bid on the Alchemist's Scrolls.

Assuming a casual pose, he leaned against the wall and folded his arms across his chest, exchanging a few taut, communicative glances with his men posted at various points around the room.

He had fanned them out to monitor the exits and to keep a close eye on particular persons of interest.

Each man's subtle nod in answer relayed the message back to him: *All clear.*

So far, so good. They would not have long to wait.

For the moment, the auctioneer was smoothly urging on both sides of a grand battle between parties vying for a pair of ancient Roman vases. But next up, according to the catalogue, was the extraordinary item around which the day's operation revolved.

Even now, one of Mr. Christie's staff members carried the ancient wooden case containing the scrolls up to the display table near the podium.

Scanning the crowded rows of chairs, Jordan watched the numbered paddles lifting. Aristocratic buyers leaned an ear to their slick art agents, who whispered advice on when to quit and when to press on to capture a worthy prize.

His survey moved on restlessly, assessing the clientele. Pomaded dandies, rich men's pampered wives in elaborate hats. A few bookish types—archivists from the British Museum as well as the Bodleian Library.

His glance skimmed past all these. *Where are you? Show yourselves, you twisted bastards . . .*

He could feel the enemy here, somewhere in the crowd—but who, exactly? Who among the rich and powerful in London had become secret adherents of the Prometheans' dark cult?

Patience. The bidding on the Alchemist's Scrolls would soon reveal them. But in reality, it should not be too difficult to pick them out of the crowd.

In his experience, the Prometheans had a look to them, something slightly off, something missing from the eyes—a spark of soul, perhaps, that the evil they dabbled in ate away.

Biding his time, Jordan's scanning gaze happened back to the row where Mara had been sitting. The seat that she had occupied was still vacant, just like the place in his life she could have held if she had been someone he could have trusted with the truth.

But he hadn't dared. As much as he had wanted her, she

was too impulsive, reckless, fragile, immature. There was no way he could have placed the lives of his brother warriors in the hands of a seventeen-year-old girl who had still had a lot of growing up to do.

Staring at her empty chair, he could still see her in his mind, having watched her there for a quarter hour in a potent brew of lust and loathing.

The woman he had nearly made his wife had been dressed for today's late-winter afternoon in a charming chocolate brown ensemble, a shade no doubt that flattered her famously sparkly dark eyes. Her rich sable hair had been pulled back in a casual knot at her nape, so dramatic against the silken luminescence of her pale, exquisite skin.

The years, he'd had to admit, had not done the lady any harm. If anything, the passage of time had only made her more interesting to his worldly tastes.

Yet he had ached a little as he watched her.

God knew she had failed him.

He had often wondered how different his own life might have been today if he had had a home and a family, some shred of normality to return to in between his bloody, brutal missions. A good, steady wife to embrace him and a few children to justify the future, give him a tangible reason for putting himself through all this.

That was all he had ever really wanted from life, but his simple dream had lost its glamour after her defection.

He smirked away any hint of self-pity, but at the same time, couldn't help wondering if the charming brown-eyed coquette had ever bothered to grow up. Perhaps she would merely use her widowhood to keep collecting men.

That's what they all did, he thought cynically, all those fashionable, independent widows. He and his brother warriors had bedded many of them. Hell, they practically passed them around.

Of course, if that was what Mara intended to do with her newfound freedom, it could provide him with a *very* interesting opportunity tomorrow night to satisfy his long-standing curiosity about what it would be like to make love to her, at last, this one woman who had haunted him to the ends of the earth . . .

"Sold!"

The gavel banged, jarring him out of his distraction.

The Roman vases went to a portly fellow who was being congratulated by his art agent. Then Jordan could feel the tension escalating, a lightninglike electric charge hanging over the whole crowd. His outward demeanor did not change at all in response, but his vigilance intensified.

"Ladies and gentlemen," the auctioneer addressed the opulent crowd. "Next, we have for you today, from an anonymous seller, an extremely rare set of medieval documents. Just recently discovered, they have never, in all their five hundred years, been made available before."

The only sound in the grand hall was a gust of the March wind that brought a burst of raindrops spattering against the glass panes of the high, arched windows.

"We place before you six scrolls, circa 1350, in excellent condition, attributed to the colorful court astrologer known as Valerian the Alchemist. Medieval enthusiasts will recall that, according to legend, Valerian was behind a plot to assassinate Edward the Black Prince—for which he was hunted down and duly punished by a group of loyal knights sent by the king. So the story goes."

The crowd chuckled at the auctioneer's wry tone.

"For this, he met a rather nasty end."

Never cross a Warrington, Jordan thought wryly, thinking of his brother agent, Rohan. For generations, the Dukes of Warrington had produced the Order's fiercest killers.

The Earls of Falconridge, by contrast, had usually been

the thinkers of the lot, superior strategists, code-breakers, linguists, but as good with a weapon as any of the rest.

"Sepia and oxblood on parchment, the scrolls are written in Latin and Greek, with many odd runes and alchemical symbols and other notations of an unknown nature in the margins. They are presented in what we believe to be the original hardwood case: oak with kingwood veneer and mother-of-pearl inlays. The case, still in very sturdy condition, is velvet-lined, with sterling silver hasps."

Rows of elegant onlookers craned their necks to try to get a better view of the find.

"In all, we feel the Alchemist's Scrolls represent a truly rare opportunity to own a piece of England's history. This treasure would make an excellent addition to any serious scholar's library, or for collectors and private antiquarians with an interest in the folklore of the occult, or any other aficionados of the current Gothic craze. The bidding today will begin at three thousand pounds."

The crowd gasped at the dizzying sum, but to the Prometheans, Jordan knew, that would be a pittance to give up for such an acquisition, especially if the secret cult members believed that Valerian's bizarre spells and dark rituals actually worked.

Then the bidding began, fast and furious.

Jordan scanned the crowd continuously with all his acute concentration, mentally sorting, memorizing the numbers on the paddles of all those bidding on the Scrolls, stacking up long strings of figures in his head.

He would check the names later in the registry book and determine from that point if they warranted further investigation. Of course, Mr. Christie would not like the invasion of his clients' privacy, but he'd have no choice. Such was the reach and power of the covert organization Jordan served. The Order of St. Michael the Archangel answered directly to the Crown and did not take no for an answer from anybody else, at least not when it came to the defense of the Realm.

Still watching everything with fierce intensity, he mentally discarded a few of the bidders from the outset. Not all the interested parties were necessarily villains.

The representative from the still fairly fledgling British Museum. A pair of archivists from the Bodleian Library at Oxford. A few eccentric foreigners acting on behalf of their distant princes, and one pasty-faced author of gory gothic novels whom the Order had once suspected but had soon cleared.

He saw no sign of James Falkirk, the Promethean magnate they knew to be holding their captured agent, Drake Parry, the Earl of Westwood. No matter. Word would travel back to Falkirk soon enough—which was the point of all this.

Before long, the bidding on the Scrolls had reached the dizzying sum of seven thousand pounds, to the amazement of all. Jordan doubted the bids could go much higher.

Time to end this ruse. *Now.* Meeting Sergeant Parker's gaze across the room, he gave his eyebrow a casual scratch.

He did not look over again, but from the corner of his eye, he saw Parker note the signal; the sergeant turned and went immediately to one of Christie's employees near the back of the grand room.

Parker discreetly passed the Christie's man a note that Jordan had earlier prepared; the employee read it and looked up with a blanch.

Parker withdrew, leaving the premises, as ordered, to protect himself from being identified in the future.

The Christie's employee, in turn, hurried up the aisle toward the front of the room, looking rattled by this unforeseen turn of events.

Meanwhile, the suspected Prometheans were so engrossed

in getting their hands on the Alchemist's Scrolls that none of them even noticed the worried-looking fellow approaching the podium.

The employee went to the auctioneer's head assistant, posted beside the display table, where the Alchemist's Scrolls were arrayed.

The auctioneer's helper looked at him in question, took the note, and read it; Jordan saw his face turn grim.

It was now this fellow's unenviable task to slip the note to the auctioneer, who was in the middle of raising the bids to a stunning eight thousand pounds.

"Oh!—oh, dear," the auctioneer stammered, once the note was in his hand. He whispered a question to his helper, who nodded in reply. "This is—most unprecedented."

They both glanced at the note again, then the auctioneer turned back haplessly to the crowd.

"Ladies and gentleman, I-I regret to announce this item has just been unexpectedly withdrawn from auction."

Outbursts immediately erupted from several points around the room.

"The owner has had a change of heart and no longer wishes to sell!" he cried.

"What is the meaning of this?" someone shouted.

"Ladies and gentlemen, this is entirely unanticipated. We sincerely apologize for this inconvenience. We beg your pardon, truly, but I'm afraid this is a-a circumstance beyond our control! I, er, I am being told," he hastened to add, "that anyone wishing to inquire further about the Alchemist's Scrolls may contact the seller through Mr. Christie's offices. A private sale may yet be entertained."

"Altogether irregular!" one of the Bodleian archivists cried.

"I say! This is an outrage!"

Jordan watched the crowd shrewdly, taking note of every fuming face in the room. His men also watched the clients' reactions and shadowed those few who stormed out.

He longed to follow them himself, to track down and expose every last one of the evil bastards. But given his high visibility as a member of the peerage, Jordan had to be careful about preserving his cover.

Instead, he let his men follow the people who were quickly slipping out. The lads would watch where they went and what they did from here on, reporting back to him later with any information. Then all of those individuals would be investigated further.

The poor auctioneer, meanwhile, was beside himself. "Again, my dear ladies and gentlemen, I am so very sorry. Perhaps another of the rare and ancient manuscripts on offer today may capture your interest. The next lot is also of medieval vintage, er, a richly illuminated Book of Hours, mid twelfth century, from a monastery in Ireland . . ."

Jordan took a small pencil out of his breast pocket and began quickly jotting down in a blank part of the catalogue the numbers of the paddles he had memorized.

Anyone looking at him would have thought he was simply making a note to himself about the various items in the sale, but he was just being careful to get all the numbers down before he should begin to forget them.

Though it took all his self-discipline to remain where he was, leaning idly by the wall, he made himself appear all the more innocuous by joining in the bidding on the Irish Book of Hours.

Hours later, when only Christie's staff was left at the auction house to clean up and sort out their business, Jordan packed up the scrolls and left in an unmarked coach to return them to the vault at Dante House. Three of his armed men rode in back and on top of the carriage in case the Prometheans tried to take the scrolls by force.

No such threat materialized, however. The roaches had fled back under their rocks and into their dark corners as soon as the scrolls had been withdrawn from the auction.

By now, most of them probably realized they had walked into a trap. They'd be hiding in trembling expectation of a lethal visit from the Order.

Darkness had already fallen, though it was only six o'clock; Dante House looked particularly sinister in the moonlight that late-winter evening as his carriage arrived.

To the rest of the world, the darkly eccentric Tudor mansion on the Thames was the home of the debauched Inferno Club—but this was only a façade designed to keep the outer world at bay.

In reality, the three-hundred-year-old Dante House was a compact fortress in disguise, with an elaborate underground lair where the Order could carry out its covert business unseen by prying eyes. The old stronghold was full of hidden passages, false doors, and mysterious hiding places. Built right on the Thames, it allowed for stealthy comings and goings, thanks to the small, hidden rowboat dock behind its secure river gate.

When Jordan went in, the pack of mighty guard dogs greeted him.

Virgil, his handler and head of the Order in London, appeared quickly, hearing his arrival. The old Highland warrior took the enemy's medieval treasure from him with naught but a terse greeting. "I trust it all went smoothly."

"Yes, sir. I collected a considerable list of leads. We had quite a showing."

"Anyone I'd know?" Virgil asked dryly.

Jordan shrugged. "Not Falkirk, unfortunately."

"No, I don't suppose he'd show his face in such an open forum. But word will travel back to him ere long, and then we'll see. What about Dresden Bloodwell?"

Jordan shook his head. "No sign of him. Not surprised. The man's an assassin. He's too canny to walk into a trap."

Virgil nodded. "It would seem he's gone to ground ever since that night you and Beauchamp nearly had him."

"That was weeks ago," Jordan agreed, nodding. "I still can't figure how he slipped through our fingers that night. Or where he's been ever since."

"In due time," Virgil assured him. "Give your list of leads to Beauchamp, by the way. Lad needs something to occupy his mind."

Jordan furrowed his brow. "Still no word from his team?"

Virgil shook his head grimly, then said, "I'll take these down to the vault. Well done, lad. Your full report by morning."

"Is Rotherstone here, sir?" Jordan asked, as Virgil turned away to take the scrolls below.

"What, the lovesick husband?" The Highlander snorted. "Of course not. He's at home worshipping the Divine Daphne."

Jordan's lips twisted. To be sure, life had turned rather strange ever since his deadly fellow agents had become married men. Max, the Marquess of Rotherstone, was enraptured with his lovely Daphne and their newfound domestic bliss.

As for Rohan, the Duke of Warrington had recently been summoned to the Order's base in Scotland, called before the Elders to explain how one of their star agents could have possibly married a young lady with Promethean bloodlines.

Jordan didn't envy his rugged friend the interrogation, but no doubt, for Kate, Rohan would have gladly endured far worse.

"Afraid you're going to have make do with this one," Virgil added, nodding toward the hallway as Beauchamp strolled into the room.

"Make do?" the younger agent retorted. "I'd say he's improved his lot!"

Sebastian, Viscount Beauchamp, the Earl of Lockwood's heir, was the leader, or Link, of his three-man team. He and his mates were only about twenty-eight, but Jordan had already seen the younger warrior prove his mettle.

Beau's breezy attitude and all that cocksure roguery disappeared in the face of danger. He was a damned fine fighter, thoroughly cool and competent under fire.

Reminded Jordan of himself a bit.

But even a rake like Beau would have known better than to let Mara Bryce get away.

Tossing his guinea gold forelock out of his eyes, Beauchamp came to stand near Jordan, arms akimbo, his feet planted wide. "Enjoy your auction?"

"Invigorating," Jordan replied with a wan half smile. "What have you been up to this evening?"

"Not a blasted thing. Fancy a call at the Satin Slipper?"

"Didn't you just go there last night?"

"So? You like the blondes, right? They have this new girl you really ought to—"

"Gentlemen," Virgil interrupted, arching one shaggy orange eyebrow. "Falconridge has to write his report, and as for you, my lad, you will start work on the list of suspects he collected at the auction."

"What, tonight?" Beau protested.

"You've got something better to do?" Virgil inquired.

"Not anymore, it would seem," he said with a harrumph, then he plucked the list of names out of Jordan's hand. "Fine!"

Virgil eyed Jordan in sardonic amusement. "That should keep him out of trouble for a while, eh?"

Beau glanced up from the list with a wicked look. "Don't count on it."

Jordan shook his head, but in truth, the older fellows had come to view Beauchamp as a sort of rascally younger brother—just so long as the rogue obeyed their one command and kept his hands off Miss Carissa Portland, Daphne's best friend.

Max was not about to let one of their own agents toy with his wife's alluring young companion.

Carissa Portland was adorable: red-haired and feisty, loyal to a fault. The petite redhead buzzed around London like some sort of opinionated little fairy queen. Even Jordan had been tempted by her brave nature and sharp mind, but he had soon realized it was useless.

His doomed obsession with a certain brunette conspired, as always, to wreck his dismal love life. Carissa Portland could be no more than a sister to him; but then again, she gave Beau no encouragement, either, looking daggers at him every time they met.

At least her open loathing seemed to take the younger agent's mind off his cares.

Jordan was concerned about Beau. Indeed, they all were.

Despite the fact that the viscount wore the same devilish glint in his green eyes as always, Jordan could sense the coiled tension in the man even as the wait for his missing teammates dragged on.

No one had heard from Beau's team in months. They'd been given an assignment in the Loire Valley, and they should've at least checked in weeks ago.

Beau was trying to hide the fact that he was beside himself with worry. Thus his recent visits to the Satin Slipper, that dreadful, low whorehouse that was all the rage of late among fashionable gentlemen of the upper class.

Jordan had gone along with him once or twice just to give

the younger agent some moral support. He could understand the man's need to blow off steam.

Of course, Beau's arrival at that place had nearly started a riot among the girls.

"Just let me know how much detail you want on these bastards," Beau murmured as he scanned the list.

"The usual who, what, where should suffice until we can home in on the likeliest subjects," Jordan said. "I'm sure some of these names are aliases, but at least it'll give you a place to start."

"Lucky me." Beau slid the list into his waistcoat pocket. "So, with your auction concluded, what now?"

"Now we wait," Virgil answered grimly.

Jordan nodded at Beau. "We expect James Falkirk to contact us soon. After the auctioneer's announcement, he'll know how to get in touch with us through Christie's offices. Then, hopefully, Virgil will be able to set up a trade—the Alchemist's Scrolls in exchange for Drake."

"Or whatever's left of him," Beau muttered in a dark tone.

"Don't you worry about Drake," Virgil grumbled though he did not quite manage to hide his pain at the thought of one of his boys being captured and tortured like a dog for months on end, until he barely remembered his own name. "Lord Westwoood is one of the shrewdest, hardest men this organization has ever recruited. If he can just stay alive and keep his mouth shut a little while longer, we will get him back."

"Yes, sir," Jordan offered in a low tone of assurance to his handler.

But the situation was indeed dire. The latest indications suggested that Drake had been so badly tortured by his captors that the Prometheans had damaged his mind—particularly, his memory—and might have even driven the poor man mad.

If any lunatic possessing Drake's deadly skills as an agent were not worrisome enough, they now had reason to fear that Falkirk might have actually turned him.

According to their sources, Drake's first prison had been in a Promethean dungeon in the Alps, but he had been moved. To the best of their knowledge, the more gentlemanly old Falkirk was currently in charge of him, and this gave them hope that at least Drake's treatment had become more humane. But even kindness could serve as a weapon in the hands of a Promethean master.

If Falkirk stepped in as savior, he might manipulate Drake into revealing the Order's secrets more effectively than the torturers could ever have done through pain.

Just a month ago, Rohan had seen Drake with his own eyes and confirmed that their brother warrior had become so far estranged from who he was that he had actually shielded Falkirk with his own body when Rohan had had a clear shot at the old man.

Still, Drake's damaged memory could be a blessing in disguise. If the Promethean torturers had not scrambled his wits, he probably would have exposed them all by now.

In short, they had to get him back, and soon. If Falkirk wanted the Alchemist's Scrolls in exchange for Drake, that was a price the Order was willing to pay.

"Good night, lads," Virgil muttered. "Considering these are meant to buy us back Drake's life, I'd best go put them in the vault, where they'll be safe."

"Aye, sir."

"Good night, Virgil."

After the old Highlander had stomped off down the hallway, Beau and Jordan also parted ways.

Frankly, Jordan was damned tired, having been up for two days putting everything in order for the mission.

A short while later, he was driving his phaeton home

through the dark streets of Town and reflecting on the day's events.

Every mission held its wild card, experience had taught him—the thing no one could plan for, no matter how meticulous one was. That was why he had to be ready for anything. And he'd thought he was.

But finding himself face-to-face with his old flame had shifted the earth beneath his feet. He had managed to put her out of his mind in order to finish the job, but now . . .

Somehow he found himself on Great Cumberland Street, taking a restless detour on his journey home.

Past Mara's house.

He slowed his carriage, rolling to an uneasy halt across from the elegant terraced crescent where she lived, even as he told himself this was a bad idea. *What the hell are you doing?*

He thought of parking on the street and going up to her front door, knocking on it, going in to see her. To smell her, to touch her . . .

Don't be absurd.

He should not even be there; he chalked this foolish error in judgment up to plain fatigue. Yet he stared in the darkness, waiting for just one glimpse of her through the bright, warm windows of her town house on the end of the crescent, its shining fanlight over the door and three bays of windows, where empty flower boxes waited for spring to bloom.

Suddenly, he spotted her breezing past the upstairs windows, laughing. Jordan furrowed his brow and leaned closer. *Music room?* He could just make out the edge of a pianoforte.

As he watched in curiosity, he saw her catch her little son and sweep him up in her arms like a doll. In the silence of the dark street, he could just make out her merry words to her child, her voice muffled through the closed window: "I got you!"

The toddler screeched happily as she held him aloft in sheer, adoring pride.

His throat tightened. Jordan looked away even before she had drifted out of sight with the boy on her hip.

He looked again, but she had disappeared, and for his part, he could feel the darkness closing in around him.

He could barely think what to do for a second. The despair that washed over him was blacker than this winter night. He steadied himself with a deep inhalation.

He let it out again, a cloud of steam.

At least it appeared she had found a way to be happy. That was all that counted. He was happy, too, Jordan reminded himself. Well, perhaps *content* was a better word for it. Not too desperately uncomfortable.

Who the hell are you fooling?

"Should have gone to the whorehouse with Beauchamp," he informed himself aloud.

His horses' ears swiveled at his voice, but he was merely talking to himself.

Shrugging off the emptiness, he gave his horses a light slap of the reins, urging them into a trot.

But the echo of Mara's laughter and her child's followed him home to his stately columned palace in Grosvenor Square—formal, spacious, well-appointed in every regard—and as silent as a tomb.

His sigh rebounded in the marble entrance hall when he walked in, handed off his hat and coat to his butler, and wearily climbed the curving staircase to the dark and cavernous master chamber.

He had a glass of brandy as he peeled off his clothes for bed. But his head had no sooner hit the pillow and he closed his eyes, exhausted, than he was right back in that damned country house . . .

Order agents traveled light and usually alone, but young

earls on holiday came with an entourage of servants who carried their luggage for them, as a rule. Upon his arrival at his hosts' sprawling country manor, Jordan allowed his valet and footmen to lug his traveling trunks to the wing of the house he'd been pointed toward, then, to the luxurious guest chamber he had been assigned.

Leaving his servants to unpack his things, he had exited his room a short while later and wandered off to find the Breakfast Hall, where the guests had been instructed to gather at their convenience for afternoon refreshments, introductions to everybody else, and to learn what amusements were planned for the next few days.

Strolling down the wainscoted, art-hung hallway toward the main block of the house, he had been musing in anticipation over which British ambassador he might be assigned to when he was soon sent off abroad, when suddenly, he heard the most damnable ruckus coming out of a nearby room.

Jordan paused, raised an eyebrow, and turned to study the door. Barely muffled by the walls, he could hear a woman's angry voice berating whatever poor, unfortunate souls were in the room with her. He knew he should not eavesdrop, but after all, he was a spy.

Curiously, he cocked his head, listening.

"You stupid gel, you really are the most useless thing! What good is this gown if you did not bring the gloves?"

He frowned. People of Quality ought not to abuse their servants with such tirades.

"God, Mara, you are such a trial to me! Why can't you do anything right? I knew bringing you here would be a disaster. I would've left you at home if I were not so kind-hearted—and this is my thanks?"

"But Mama, the other gloves will match—"

"Don't you dare talk back to me!"

Crack!

Jordan's jaw dropped.

"That's for your insolence, you little hussy! Do not contradict me again, or we are going home."

Jordan was staring at the door in astonishment. Armed foes were one thing, but an attack from one's own family?

"I'm sorry, I'm sorry, Mama."

His stare deepened to a scowl. *Sorry for what, bringing the wrong gloves?*

"Please, l-let us stay, Mama. I won't cause you any trouble."

"Humph." A haughty sniff was all the girl got in exchange for her humiliating grovel.

It seemed to be expected of her.

"See that you don't. I came here to visit with my friends. Try being rude to me again, and I'll send you home to explain yourself to your father."

"No, ma'am, please. I am sorry, Mother."

Jordan was now glaring at the door. It would not do.

It would not do at all.

With righteous anger throbbing in his veins, his first thought was the Rohan approach. Kick the door in and grab the offending party by the throat.

But he was supposed to be the civilized one.

Strategy. Masking his fury at the injustice taking place on the other side of the door, he donned a carefree expression; as he reached for the doorknob, he heard the older woman's muttered vow. "Believe me, I'll do aught in my power to find you a husband while we're here. God knows I'm eager to be rid of you."

Jordan threw open the door with a sunny smile, then froze in feigned shock. "Oh! Oh, dear me—I'm terribly sorry—I thought this was my room! Forgive me, ladies! Blazes, how embarrassing. I must have taken a wrong turn."

Before him stood a thin, very-refined-looking lady whose eyes narrowed. "No, sir, this is our room."

"Ah, right. My apologies. You, er, would not happen to know the way to the Breakfast Hall, by chance?"

The lady folded her arms across her chest with an irritated sigh. "Down the hallway, to the left, and down the stairs."

"The left . . . um, which hallway?"

You're not very bright, are you? the woman's impatient look replied as she tilted head. "Just outside the door."

Well, she's pleasant.

"Forgive my manners," he said abruptly, ignoring her obvious vexation. "I should introduce myself since we are all guests here." He flashed his best smile. "I am the Earl of Falconridge."

"Oh! Well!" Her entire expression changed.

Jordan had rather expected it might.

"Are you, indeed? I daresay I have heard of you, Lord Falconridge."

At twenty thousand a year, he'd bet she had. It was a scheming mama's duty to keep track of Society's best catches.

"I am Lady Bryce. My husband is Sir Dunstan Bryce, Baronet, and this is our daughter, Mara."

"Miss Bryce." Jordan bowed with courteous restraint to the slim, dark-haired demoiselle who was sitting on the ottoman, her head down.

"Mara, do show the earl some courtesy!" her mother snapped.

Only now, for the first time did the girl raise her gaze slowly to meet his, her dark eyes full of wretched innocence beneath the black fringe of her lashes. Those soulful eyes were so deep a brown they were almost black, like her glossy hair, though her skin was pale—one cheek still rosier than the other from her mother's slap.

Jordan looked at her, and something inside of him was dealt a sweet mortal wound.

"How do you do," she whispered barely audibly.

He could not even speak for a heartbeat.

He had to get her out of there. All of a sudden, he was completely obsessed with rescuing her. "Ahem! Perhaps Miss Bryce would be kind enough to show me where this, er, fabled Breakfast Hall is. I understand it's where we're all to meet."

"By all means!" Lady Bryce now beamed at him as though she thought him the cleverest thing in the world. "Mara, why don't you show His Lordship to the Breakfast Hall, my dear?"

"Yes, Mother." She rose and toward the door, keeping her head down. "This way, sir."

He stepped aside with a gallant gesture to Miss Bryce to go ahead of him. When she did, he stepped behind her, placing himself between her and the simpering witch. He pulled the door shut behind him in her mother's face.

As they proceeded down the hallway, Miss Bryce barely responded to his friendly attempts at conversation. "Where are you from? Have you had a chance to meet the others yet? Fine house, isn't it? Beautiful gardens, as well. I'm sure we'll have a very pleasant stay."

She stopped at the top of the stairs and turned to him all of a sudden; before they went any farther, she stared into his eyes. "You heard the whole thing, didn't you?"

Her blunt question took him off guard. "Er, sorry?"

She knitted her dark brown eyebrows together impatiently.

He hesitated, trying to spare her pride, but she seemed to prefer the truth. He shrugged and abandoned the thought of lying to her. "I heard enough to know you didn't deserve that. Are you all right?"

She stiffened and looked away. "I'm used to it. You weren't really lost at all, were you?"

He shook his head with a rueful smile.

She glanced at him again, searching his eyes rather wistfully. "Thank you for what you did."

"Anytime." Then he shook his head, still unsettled by Lady Helen's barbarity. "Why does she treat you like that?"

She shrugged. "She's always been that way. She doesn't really need a reason."

He stared at her. "I'm so sorry."

"It's all right. I don't expect to have to listen to that much longer," she murmured as she turned toward the stairs and led on toward the Breakfast Hall.

Jordan followed, watching her in fascination. Her earlier air of defeat had turned to a posture of resolve the farther they went away from her mother. "What do you mean by that?"

"Hm? Oh, nothing." She cast him a hardened, little smile askance quite at odds with her youth.

He had seen smiles like that before. From Virgil. It was the grim, brave smile of a survivor.

Miss Bryce gazed straight ahead as they went down the hallway. "Will you do something for me?"

"Anything." The word escaped him rather more fervently than he had intended.

She paused and turned to him once more. "Don't tell anyone about that."

He looked into her eyes, realizing there were depths to this young beauty he had never encountered in a girl before. "Of course not," he whispered. "Don't worry, your secret's safe with me. You have my word of honor."

The smile of grateful relief that broke slowly over her face could have lasted any young man through a war. "Thank you." Then those lush, seductive lashes lowered, and she turned gracefully toward the corridor. "Here's the Breakfast Hall, my lord."

Jordan couldn't take his eyes off her as he escorted her into the room. All signs of the hurt and humiliation she had suffered upstairs had vanished completely by the time she paraded into the Breakfast Hall, where she was instantly greeted, nay, thronged by a crowd of young gentlemen to whom she had already been introduced.

Gone, or rather, hidden, was any trace of the fragile vulnerability in her that Jordan had witnessed upstairs.

Miss Bryce had transformed into the very picture of girlish vivacity, laughing, flirting. And while the other girls in the room looked daggers at her, every eligible bachelor appeared as dazzled as he—including the tall, loud idiot, Viscount Pierson.

Jordan was extremely intrigued but was not quite sure he liked what he saw. He realized what her cryptic comment had meant when she had said she would not have to listen to her mother's tirades much longer.

This was a girl on a mission. Not that he could blame her. As though she could feel him watching her, she glanced past her crowd of admirers; looking through them, she caught Jordan's eye.

He arched a brow at her; she smiled back with a wry little shrug.

He had snorted to himself. Then he forced himself to turn away and was soon introduced to many more young ladies, but as much as he tried to pay attention to them, Mara Bryce had already staked some mysterious claim on his awareness.

Indeed, as the days unfolded, he kept a discreet eye on her at all times, an ear tuned to the sound of her voice, just in case she needed rescuing again . . .

Chapter 3

By the next evening, all signs of Thomas's cold had evaporated, thanks to a long nap and his old nurse's favorite home remedy: a broth of boiled barley sweetened with Turkish figs and raisins.

To Mara's relief, the tiny viscount was himself again, curious and energetic as ever, building towers with his toy blocks in the drawing room and merrily knocking them over.

He was now as content as the family cat serenely seated on the windowsill, swishing its tail like a pendulum and gazing out at the evening's frigid rain.

Mara turned and gazed at the mantel clock, gnawing her lip in indecision. Life had ebbed back to normal once she was convinced anew of her son's continued survival. Now she realized there was just enough time to dress and go to Delilah's dinner party, if she was game. The chance to see Jordan. What to do . . .

She wished she were not tempted, but she reasoned if she did not go, she would likely become a topic of conversation.

If everyone was going to gossip about her at table, she jolly well ought to be there to speak up for herself, no?

As the clock ticked on, Mara begrudgingly admitted an irresistible curiosity to hear from Jordan's own lips what he had been up to these past years.

Perhaps if she went to the party and had a chance to observe him through the eyes of a grown woman, not a naïve girl, she might form a whole new opinion of her former dream man.

Lord knew, from that first moment he had come bursting into her life, distracting her mother from yet another oppressive rant, Jordan had seemed to Mara some sort of golden Prince Charming sprung to life—chivalry incarnate.

But she had no sooner looked into those sky blue eyes and beheld his air of shining gallantry that in her heart of hearts, she had instantly concluded, wistfully, that she could never have someone like him. He was too far above her.

It was not merely that he outranked her family by several degrees of the peerage. It went much deeper than that. He was better than she as a person—or so she had thought then. Handsome, kind, good; intelligent, amusing; at ease in every situation; good at everything; intimidated by no one. In short, he was a dream, and she was, well, a walking disaster, as Mother liked to say.

Someone as flawed as Mara Bryce could never be worthy of a man as close to perfection as she had ever seen, a veritable knight in shining armor.

Of course Jordan was kind to her. A man like him was kind to everyone. She had judged him innately goodhearted, a true gentleman in every sense of the word. She, on the other hand—! If even a fraction of what her mother said about her was true, then Jordan would want, indeed, deserved someone far better than herself.

With all those assumptions firmly set in her head, Mara

had spent most of her time at the country house enjoying every moment in his company but refusing to get her hopes up that he might have any real interest in her.

If he had given her certain signals, she had either not taken them seriously or been blind to them because he had seemed too good to be true. If sometimes he had an enticing look in his eyes when he spoke to her, she was sure it was just her imagination. He couldn't want *her,* especially after learning her humiliating secret.

He'd seen for himself how her own family had no respect for her, and they knew her best. Why should a paragon choose a girl who must have so much wrong with her that her own mother could not seem to love her?

Knowing that Jordan had witnessed the secret of her pain made her feel so strange being around him, wavering between uneasiness and an unfamiliar sense of safety with him. She kept waiting for him to use it against her somehow.

But he never did. He kept his promise, and that was part of why she had thought that she could trust him. Still, feeling that he was unobtainable, she had tried to check her fluttering heart and striven to think of him only as a friend—until, being seventeen, she could no longer hold back her feelings.

As it turned out, she had been right to be cautious, for she had learned that night in the garden that her feelings weren't returned.

He wouldn't even agree to let her write to him, nor would he write to her. But at least he didn't lie, she conceded as she leaned in the doorway. Well, in hindsight it was obvious that in her girlish innocence, she had wildly overidealized him—and had undervalued herself.

She knew better now. Jordan was not perfect. He was not a demigod, not an invincible hero, but a man. Even knights in shining armor had their weaknesses. This night could be a chance to get a clearer, grown-up picture of who he was, or at least who her young Prince Charming had become.

More importantly, for herself, she had finally got it through her head that she was not and never had been anywhere near as bad or stupid as her parents had taught her to believe.

She *had* worth, talents, virtues. She was good at any number of things. She was a good mother to Thomas. A far better mother than the one she'd had.

And maybe, just maybe, she actually did deserve love.

Her heart fluttered just like in the old days at the thought of him, but as she toyed with the idea of going to the party, she couldn't help wondering how a flawed, world-weary Jordan and a stronger, grown Mara might affect each other now, twelve years later. As much as time had changed them both, would they still be drawn to each other? Could they still fall in love?

Dangerous thoughts, Mara warned herself. After all, the opposite could be true. If she went tonight, she might come home again with a newfound peace of mind, only wondering what she had ever seen in him.

Then she might finally be free of him at last.

God. She shut her eyes.

Her guilty conscience enjoyed tormenting her from time to time, reminding her of the night she had conceived her son, how she had lain beneath her drunken husband, shut her eyes, and thought of *him.*

She only doubted Lord Falconridge would ever be that clumsy, rough, and inconsiderate with a woman . . .

She flicked her eyes open again, shaking off the disturbing memory.

Thomas was having a chirpy little conversation with his blocks, to the staff's amusement. Several servants had gathered to watch the tot at play. Mara didn't mind. The servants' genuine affection for her boy only endeared them to her more.

Oh, blazes, she thought, watching the whole household dote on her son, *he'll be well taken care of if I go to Delilah's just for a little while.*

To try to deny her cautious interest in finding out what Jordan had been doing all this time would have to make her as obstinate as her two-year-old, whose favorite word was "No."

She glanced uncertainly at the mantel clock again.

Other than her own stubborn refusal of yesterday, there was no real reason not to go.

She could not even claim she had nothing to wear. Her modiste had just delivered a new, lush purple satin gown. She considered her mink stole for warmth. High black gloves. She still had those from her mourning. Her pearl choker . . .

She'd *have* to look her best, just on principle, of course. Show her former dream man she had gone on with her life quite happily without him, thank you very much.

Thomas suddenly squealed with delight as he knocked down his tower of blocks for the umpteenth time there in the informal, multi-use room they simply referred to as the parlor. His old nurse, Mrs. Busby, continued praising the young builder.

Mara smiled. There was something inspiring in the way the boy immediately began constructing his little tower again. Unfazed by failure. Undaunted by the wreck of all he'd built.

Try, try again.

Right, she thought, suddenly resolute. With Pierson dead, she had to be both mother and father to Thomas, and she would not set a cowardly example for her son by hiding at home, too weak to face someone who had hurt her.

"Mary." She turned to her freckled maid with a business-like air. "Tell Jack to ready the carriage." She lifted her chin, and announced: "I am going out."

Delilah's guests had congregated in the drawing room in anticipation of the feast. The summons to the dining room was imminent, and still, Mara hadn't appeared.

Well, this was a fine thing! Jordan thought in annoyance, surreptitiously watching the door. He had only come here tonight for her sake, and the blasted hussy could not be bothered to show up. It seemed she did not even have the nerve to come and face him.

All the other guests had arrived, leaving him in a roomful of strangers and casual acquaintances. While his new friend, Delilah, kept prattling on, Jordan could only scoff at his own disappointment. Would he never learn?

Meanwhile, Delilah's tall, strapping lover, Cole, was watching him with eagle-eyed suspicion from over by the fireplace. *Don't worry, mate. I have no interest in your mistress.* He half listened to Delilah's chatter, rather wishing he had stayed home to work on deciphering some new code.

Then, all of a sudden, he saw the butler step into the room. His heart sank as he expected to hear the familiar summons, "Dinner is served."

She's not coming.

Instead, the butler announced: "Lady Pierson."

His whole body tensed as Mara walked into the drawing room. *My God.* Every man present stared, but Jordan, for a few pulsations, suffered a sheer, fleeting agony of desire.

Gone was the playful seventeen-year-old coquette, masking all her insecurity behind coy flirtation. Into the drawing room glided a devastating woman who carried herself with worldly confidence and cool poise.

Even the way she moved proclaimed her the most powerful sort of female, in his experience. The type who knew exactly who she was.

Brava, bella, Jordan thought in riveted admiration as the truth hit him. Mara Bryce had come into her own.

The candlelight slid beguilingly over the deep purple satin of her gown, the dark tone of the bodice hugging her round, glorious breasts and making the pale skin of her chest shimmer like distant starlight.

Her shadow-dark hair was wound up in a fetching knot atop her head with Classical tendrils trailing down. His gaze followed one of those fetching spirals that framed her face, gently grazing her cheek, still rosy from the cold outside, until it came to rest upon her lips; these were stained a deep rose shade with some cosmetic the ton seductresses favored.

He could not take his eyes off her, nor could any other man in the room, except for Cole, whose full attention did not stray from Delilah.

Mara had entranced the rest of them merely by crossing the room—but that was no change from when they were younger. Getting close to her had never been easy, surrounded as she had been by beaux and admirers.

"Darling! I'm so glad you came!" Delilah sailed over to greet her friend with a careful embrace, mussing the perfection of neither lady.

"Sorry I'm late. I wanted to make sure Thomas was feeling better."

"Ah, of course. No worries. I had a place set for you anyway—just in case."

Jordan noticed the wry look the women exchanged and wondered what it meant.

All of a sudden, they both looked over at him.

He felt taken off guard, caught staring.

He smiled ruefully and offered a courteous nod, which Mara returned warily from across the drawing room.

In the next instant, she was thronged by her acquaintances. They blocked her from his view. Which was just as well. For he was suddenly in a terrible state, his heart pounding; he tightened his stomach muscles to try to ward off an absurd tickle of butterflies.

Good God, what was wrong with him? She was a jolt to his system that had made his entire body tingle. He tugged discreetly at his cravat, wondering when the room had suddenly grown so hot. His clothes seemed to chafe—too constraining, his white shirt and cravat, his black formal attire. He longed to be rid of it all, in his bed with her, both of them wearing nothing but the moonlight and a lover's sweat and making up for lost time.

She caught his eye through the crowd with a faint blush, as though his sentiments were written on his face.

He dropped his gaze and swallowed hard, cursing himself for the wild, unsteady joy that now pounded in his veins. This, he observed, was one hell of a foolish reaction. He thrust his hand into his pocket and took another swallow of port, using all his discipline to bring his reeling senses back under control.

Then dinner was served.

The guests repaired to a dainty pink-and-blue jewel box of a dining room, where gilt figurines held up the candles, plaster flower garlands wound about the ceiling, and rich rose valances festooned floor-to-ceiling windows. They took their seats in lyre-back chairs at a table draped in snowy white damask. Jordan found himself two seats down and across from Mara, close enough to keep a watchful eye on her.

Soon, a parade of liveried footmen in powdered wigs began bringing in the food on gleaming silver trays. A large epergne of soup helped ward off the night's chill; but as the first course was revealed beneath the silver warming lids, Jordan skipped the calves' ears in favor of the chine of mutton.

As the first half hour passed, Jordan enjoyed merely listening to the others' banter, savoring the idle back-and-forth of normal people who did not have the weight of the world on their shoulders.

As a younger man, he had always made a point of keeping in touch with friends and acquaintances who had nothing to do with the Order. It had helped him maintain sanity. He had tried, at least back then, not to let their deadly shadow war against the Prometheans take over his whole life. He dreaded to end up like Virgil.

But somehow he had let that wise practice slip away from him over the years.

Now the idle chatter of these carefree aristocrats made a dark corner of his heart angry, or at least scornful.

Their air of bonhomie should have cheered him, restored his flagging spirits, but instead, he found himself resenting how easy they had it. Bloody hell, they would not last a day in *his* life. They lived for pleasure, without any kind of pressure on them at all.

He felt so distant from them, detached.

The only other guest at the table as silent as he was the Peninsular War hero Delilah had invited, some red-coated major about his own age who walked with a crutch, having lost his leg at Waterloo. Jordan had taken pleasure in shaking the officer's white-gloved hand back in the drawing room. Fine man. Not a hint of self-pity. The sort that made one proud to be English.

Meanwhile, the company gossiped about expected parties coming up this Season at the homes of people Jordan did not know. When the second course arrived, he chose roasted pigeon and the prawns stewed in white wine, and still, he had barely said a word.

He was trying not to stare too much at Mara; but when

he ventured another glance in her direction, he caught her studying him, the faceted chandelier speckling her with tiny chips of light.

He gazed somberly at her; she looked away. But with her face in profile to him, he could see the blossom rising from that beautiful sweep of her neck up to her cheek.

"So, Lord Falconridge," Delilah spoke from the head of the table. He tore his gaze away. "It's so nice that you could join us tonight. Lady Pierson tells me you have been in the diplomatic service."

"Yes." He set his fork down politely, sensing an interview coming.

"Where was your post?"

"Various courts in northern Europe, Mrs. Staunton. Prussia, Sweden, Denmark. Most of my time abroad, however, was spent at our embassy in Russia."

"Dear me, that must have been dangerous, considering half the time, the Czar could not decide if he was with us or Napoleon!"

He nodded with an urbane smile. "Sometimes, yes, quite, I'm afraid."

This topic roused the Peninsular veteran's interest. "Were you in Russia during 1812, sir?"

"Indeed, I was, Major."

"Did you get to see Napoleon's retreat amid the Russian winter? They say he lost a hundred thousand men just from the cold alone."

"Horrible," one of the ladies murmured.

Jordan nodded. "Yes, from a distance, I could see their columns in retreat, and before the French army arrived, I also saw the Russians burn Moscow themselves rather than let Napoleon take it," he added. "Even Boney must have realized he could not defeat a people willing to do that."

"I'm just glad the war's over," Delilah declared, "and we can all finally get on with our lives."

The major sent her a quick, cynical look. *Easy for you to say.* Jordan glanced at him in wry sympathy as the others discussed their eagerness to travel to the Continent on holiday once the bombarded cities were rebuilt; when he raised his glass to the man in a silent toast, the major gave him a grim smile and a grateful nod.

"I want to see Italy! It's been ages since even a proper Grand Tour was even possible."

"I hope all the fighting didn't harm the Roman ruins."

"What of the Alps? I've seen paintings of Lake Como that make me want to move there," one lady said with a sigh.

"Lots of people are doing just that, I hear. The Continent is supposedly easier on one's purse."

Jordan listened to their idle banter, feeling more isolated from them by the second as he marveled privately at how small their world was.

Their talk of holidays in distant lands merely seemed to emphasize the fact that, aside from their country homes, they rarely ventured beyond the well-marked boundaries of Mayfair.

"What about Russia, Lord Falconridge? Should we include St. Petersburg in our tour?" another lady asked, fluttering her lashes at him.

"Absolutely," he replied. "It's very elegant."

"Russia and elegant?" the red-cheeked, portly chap beside her grunted. "Never thought I'd hear those words in the same breath, what?"

Jordan smiled, recalling the Russians' opinion of the English in return, but he did not think it politick to point that out just now. "St. Petersburg is highly refined, my lord," he said idly. "You must be thinking of Moscow. That's where you go if you want an adventure."

"Oh! What sort of adventure?" the lady asked.

An image flashed through Jordan's mind of the three Promethean spies in the Kremlin he had hunted down and dispatched before they could make their move against the young, fickle, and vexingly impressionable Czar.

He merely smiled. "More of the true Russia, I'd say. A taste of the Eastern influence."

"Hmm, that sounds very intriguing," Delilah purred.

"Well, I think it sounds abominably cold," Mara spoke up all of a sudden, entering the conversation. "But then, you must have been right at home in that frosty climate, Lord Falconridge. Was it cold enough for you, hmm?"

Jordan turned to her, slightly startled by her soft but pointed mockery.

She brushed her lower lip tauntingly against the rim of her wineglass as she waited for his answer.

He spoke with care. "It is true the climate runs toward snow, Lady Pierson. But the Russians have devised several intriguing ways of keeping warm. Shall I describe them for you?"

"Do, do!" Some of the men who were already getting drunk laughed at his obvious innuendo.

"If you'd rather, I could show you." He moved as if to rise from his chair.

"Hear, hear!"

The other fellows thumped the table with their hands while the ladies tittered.

Mara narrowed her eyes at him. "No, thank you," she answered primly, losing the game.

He returned her scowl with an angelic smile.

Well, she had earned that poke after her impertinence.

"I feared the cold was going to keep *you* at home tonight, my lady, when we did not see you earlier," he remarked.

"No, as you can see, I was merely detained." She glanced

around the table. "I apologize again to everyone for arriving late—"

"Nonsense," Delilah scolded fondly. "You were here in time. Besides, it's understandable. Her child has been ill."

"I am sorry to hear that," Jordan spoke up in an easy tone, though he waited in amusement for some opportunity to poke at her again. "I hope it is not too serious."

"Just a cold, but he is on the mend now, thank you," Mara answered. "Thomas is a strong boy."

"How old?" Jordan already knew the answer, but he welcomed a change of subject other than his years abroad. He was an excellent liar; he just didn't like having to exercise that particular talent.

Besides, after seeing Mara doting on her child last night through the window, he suspected that this might be the one topic that could draw her out.

And he was right.

For a full five minutes, thanks to a few leading questions, he got Mara to speak, nay, to sing her boy's praises. Then—adorably, he thought—she realized the rest of the worldly guests were growing bored to the point of yawns to hear her recounting the particulars of Thomas's daily routine.

Even Jordan was not so very interested in what the tot liked for breakfast.

She was suddenly blushing. "Oh—forgive me. How I have been rambling on!"

"Not at all," he said with a fond look. "Obviously a favorite subject of yours."

"Delilah says I am the world's most doting mother."

"As much as you adore him, I'm surprised you only have the one," Jordan said.

But instantly, he realized his mistake.

Her sudden pallor told him too late that this was a highly sensitive subject. She dropped her gaze. "If it were up to me,

I would've had many more, but, you see, my husband died before we could be blessed a second time."

"Forgive me, Lady Pierson. I meant no disrespect. I beg your pardon. Again, I'm very sorry for your loss."

Recovering quickly, she looked around with a taut smile. "It does not signify. You did not know."

The trouble was, he did.

Delilah cleared her throat. "So, Cole, darling, is your prize colt going to be ready for the spring racing season?" she asked pertly, smoothing out the awkwardness that had come over the table. "What's his name again?"

"Yes—Avalanche. All of you," her consort assisted amiably, "be sure and place your bets on my horse this year at Ascot . . ."

As the conversation moved on, gratefully, to the safer topic of horseflesh, Jordan chastised himself in silence for his blunder. *What the hell is wrong with me?*

Did he not have years of training in the art of drawing people out through conversation in order to learn their secrets?

Did he not at least have eyes? Unfortunately, he saw now, he had let his long-nursed anger blind him to the obvious. Given that it was not uncommon for healthy wives to produce a child a year or at least every other year, Mara should've had four or five little ones already. Lord and Lady Pierson must have had some sort of problems with their fertility—and Jordan had just called this fact to the attention of the entire dinner party.

He lowered his head in self-directed fury, then glanced again across the table at her in apologetic compassion, realizing now why she doted so much on the one child she had.

Mara's only answer was a cold, accusing stare.

He dropped his gaze, fuming at himself. He could not believe that he, of all people, could have blurted out such a barbarous remark without thinking first. It was utterly unlike him. Putting his foot in his mouth was not something agents with years of diplomatic experience *did.*

So, why had he said it? Had he become such a cold, unfeeling bastard, so detached from the rest of humanity, that he could no longer grasp what a painful subject this would be for any woman?

Or was that precisely *why* he had said it—because a part of him wanted to hurt her in some small way after she had let him down so bitterly?

How many children might *they* have had together by now, after all, if she had been married to him all this time, the way it should have been? Ghostly sons and daughters whose chance to exist had already come and gone . . .

But that wasn't Mara's fault at the end of the day. It was his. It was the Order's. And it could not be undone.

Jordan promptly lost his appetite.

The evening lumbered on. Another course was served, but he had nothing to say for the rest of the meal.

The wine continued flowing, and soon his rude question seemed forgotten by the others—though not by Mara.

Then a snippet of conversation from Delilah's end of the table drew his attention. "Lady Pierson told me a happy announcement is soon to come from the Regent," their hostess was informing the guests closest to her with an arch smile.

"What is it?"

"I don't know! The stubborn creature wouldn't tell me!"

"Then we must prevail on her on to reveal it! Lady Pierson, what news from your friend at Carlton House?"

"Yes, tell us what's afoot!"

Mara looked over innocently. "I have no idea what you are talking about."

"Delilah said you told her that some big announcement from the Prince Regent was imminent!"

"Well, Delilah lies, as everybody knows," she shot back in studied amusement.

They laughed, while Delilah raised an eyebrow, but Jordan looked at Mara in surprise.

"You know you said it," their hostess chided her friend.

Mara shrugged. "I cannot recall any such conversation, darling."

"Come, please!" others whined.

"No, no, I cannot!" Mara laughed. "I'm sure you'll hear it as soon as His Royal Highness returns from Brighton."

"When will that be? The *Times* said he's there recovering from another attack of the gout," someone said.

"Maybe you should go and help take care of His Royal Highness, Lady Pierson."

"Now, now! He has his daughter to look after him," she said.

"Princess Charlotte also went to Brighton?"

"Yes, and the *Times* said she's under the weather, too, poor gel!" a bejeweled lady chimed in. "A nasty cold."

That, Jordan knew, was the official story. But thanks to the Order's daily intelligence briefings, he was well aware that there was another reason the Regent and his unpredictable daughter had both gone to stay at the Brighton Pavilion.

It was not to recuperate from their pet maladies. That was merely what they told the papers. In fact, the royals were there on the most serious business, negotiating the engagement of Princess Charlotte to Prince Leopold of Saxe-Coburg.

With one previous near betrothal already soured between Princess Charlotte and the Prince of Orange, the Regent wasn't taking any chances on another public debacle. But this time, according to all reports, the match was sure to take.

Those who had observed the smitten young couple together reported that the serious, sensible German prince was exactly what the exuberant, irrepressible princess needed in a mate. Prinny had no son; therefore, his only daughter would inherit the Crown one day, and Leopold's tender, steadying influence should help to rein in the girl designated as England's future queen from her flightier moments.

It was not that different from how things could have been between him and Mara, come to think of it. *Ah, well.*

The more important question that came to Jordan's mind was: How could Mara know what the royals were really doing in Brighton?

The betrothal had not yet been announced to the world. Only the Cabinet ministers and a handful a castle insiders were aware of this new development in the royal household.

Jordan doubted Mara was personally close to Princess Charlotte, given their age difference. The girl had just turned twenty, while her portly father, the Prince Regent, was in his fifties.

Well, here was a mystery. As soon as the meal ended, Jordan made it his mission to learn more. When the last cardoon was eaten and everyone had had their fill of fruit tartlets and cheesecakes, the gentlemen stood as the ladies rose and gracefully paraded off to the drawing room.

The men remained in the dining room, taking up considerably cruder language as they lounged a while at table over cigars and port. A few got up to relieve themselves at the piss-pots that had been discreetly left beneath the gilded mahogany sideboard for that purpose.

The liquor had been flowing all night, and because of that, Jordan quickly found he did not even have to resort to his spy skills to gather the intelligence he sought.

A three-bottle man who had turned his back to them to stand before the chamber pot first broached the subject. "Do you suppose Lady Pierson would mind if I whisked her off to some dark corner here and had my way with her?" he asked the others in a wistful tone—rhetorically, Jordan surely hoped.

"She might not, but I daresay His Royal Highness would," another answered with a laugh as he turned around, buttoning his trousers.

"Our Prinny always did have an eye for beauty," a third said with a smirk.

"Damn, but she is tempting, ain't she? I, for one, shall never mourn her husband."

Obviously, these men knew nothing of their past together. "So, what's the gossip, then?" Jordan spoke up, idly flicking a bit of ash off his cigar. "I've been away, chaps. You must fill me in. Is the lady spoken for, or is she fair game?"

"Word has it she's the Regent's pocket Venus, Falconridge," a tipsy man informed him with a rueful wink.

For all his training, Jordan could barely hide his shock. "You are jesting."

"No, no, it's true! Cole, didn't Mrs. Staunton say Lady Pierson bought a painting for her royal 'friend' yesterday at Christie's? Spent more than a thousand pounds on 'im."

"A thousand pounds!" someone cried.

All of the men were amazed at this news. But only Jordan was horrified.

"I thought His Highness was attached to Lady Melbourne?" one dandy chimed in, polishing his monocle.

"Well, there's enough of him to go around, if you haven't noticed."

The others laughed at the jest alluding to the Regent's ever-growing girth, but for his part, Jordan was hard-pressed to mask his astounded fury. Mara was the Regent's mistress? Could this abomination actually be true?

She was sleeping with the man that he was honor-bound to

serve? Jordan felt as though someone had clubbed him over the head with the butt of a musket.

The news sent him reeling. Yet he had indeed seen her buy that painting yesterday. That much was fact. And at dinner, she had known the real reason that the royals were in Brighton. How else could she know unless she was close to the Regent?

Very close, if this gossip were true.

As the other men began drifting out to join the ladies upstairs in the drawing room, Jordan happened to meet his own stunned glance in the pier glass.

He looked a trifle pale. He lowered his head, dazedly crushing out his cigar, but he let the others go on ahead while he remained behind to try to gather his thoughts.

He could hardly believe it . . . but then again, perhaps he could. Especially when he recalled the shameless flirt she once had been. *Good God. She must deny this.* He needed to see her again immediately; he would study her right now in the drawing room as closely as if she were one of his enemy targets. He would discern the truth.

With that, he strode out of the dining room to the foyer, but then he saw the one-legged major standing at the bottom of the stairs. Leaning on his crutch, the veteran was gazing grimly up the long, marble staircase.

Jordan curbed his impatience and went over to the man. He knew better, of course, than to offer outright help to any proud British officer. But for honor's sake, the least he could do was to keep the man company on his way up the mountain.

The major sent him a grim smile askance. "You don't have to wait for me, Falconridge."

Jordan nodded discreet encouragement and gestured toward the stairs. "Shall we?"

"Right." The major let out a sigh, then braced himself, struck out with his crutch, and started the climb with a wince.

Jordan kept him talking about politics to take the major's mind off the pain and fury that he was obviously feeling behind that stiff upper lip.

But by the time he and the stoic war hero reached the drawing room, Jordan saw that, for his part, he'd paid a bit of a price for arriving late.

Mara was already surrounded by mostly tipsy, overeager men, each waiting for his turn to shower her with compliments.

Jordan took one look at her, and that was all he really needed to see. It was not proof that her affair with the Regent was true, but the rumor certainly fit the coquettish Mara he had once known. And likewise, seeing her surrounded by beaux just as she had been at seventeen persuaded him this night had been a waste of time.

She was never going to change. She'd never be the woman he wished for, needed her to be. Perhaps she couldn't help what she had become, after the way she had been raised. Of course, he had always known she was a survivor, above all.

Like me.

Their kind held on thanks to a certain steely core, a ruthless streak that tended, by necessity, toward selfishness. Twelve years ago, he had done the selfish thing, unable to handle the pain of being so torn—falling in love just when he had to leave for the first time to serve his country. It had been easier to walk away from her with vague notions of coming back. He had lost her but he had preserved his sanity and, more importantly, had been there for his brother warriors.

As for Mara, he supposed she had waited for him as long

as she could, until she, too, could not stand the pain of her situation anymore, accepting Lord Pierson in order to escape it. Now that she had her widow's freedom, however, he considered it highly unlikely she would ever put herself in that position again. From here on in, with the possible exception of her son, it was all self-interest with Mara, her own advantage, and what could be more advantageous for any Society lady, Jordan thought angrily, than a seat on the knee of the future king?

Truly, a match made in heaven, he thought acidly, for the Regent was a famed collector of beautiful things.

Jordan could barely manage to hide his disgust.

Mara spared him a glance after a time, her dark eyes guarded and rather hostile.

But she did not extricate herself from her admirers fast enough for him.

Ah, the flirt and her stupid games. Punishing him, he supposed.

He glanced at the mantel clock, then mentally gave her two more minutes to get away from her devotees and cross the room to him. Whatever happened, he was sure as Hell not going over to her. A man had his pride.

While he waited, his mind drifted back to another time, years ago, when he had also had to grit his teeth and watch her holding court like this.

Back at that infamous country-house party where he'd lost his heart, he had tried to warn her to be careful not to get in over her head . . .

"My, my, Miss Bryce," the younger Jordan murmured in amusement when the belle of the evening finally joined him at the edge of the ballroom, having separated herself at last from her band of suitors. "It would seem you've conquered the room."

"Pshaw," she replied with droll modesty, the merry twinkle in her dark eyes brightened by champagne. She took another sip and leaned against the wall beside him.

He watched his fair young friend in amusement. "I daresay I'm beginning to feel a little left out."

"Whatever do you mean, sir?" she had asked innocently, those sultry lips parted slightly, wet with champagne.

Jordan could not stop staring. "Must I watch you enchant every other man in the room before you finally get around to flirting with me?"

"Flirt? Who, me?"

"Ah, don't deny it," he chided with a soft laugh. "I know very well what you're up to."

"I doubt it," she replied with an airy toss of her sable curls.

"You mean to land yourself a husband before the month is out." He shrugged. "Not that I can blame you."

She glanced at him in alarm.

"Don't worry. I won't tell anyone about your little scheme," he murmured with a smile.

A look of relief eased the worry that still lurked just beneath her playful surface. "Very well, so you have unmasked me, my lord," she conceded in a confidential tone. "But honestly, I can't take it anymore. I have to find a new—situation."

He noted she couldn't even call it a home. "Believe me, I sympathize. Just be careful," he advised gently. "Marriage is a permanent arrangement. Make an overhasty choice, and you may find you've only escaped the frying pan for the fire."

She shook her head. "It can't get any worse."

"Of course it can. Come, you don't need these fools," he tried to encourage her. "All you have to learn is to stand up for yourself against—Lady Beelzebub." He nodded discreetly toward her mother.

Mara smiled ruefully, but shook her head. "It's a waste of breath. I learned a long time ago that fighting back only stokes her wrath. She does not back down, and she is never wrong. Why even try? It's easier just to placate."

He shook his head. "You've let her defeat you in your mind. You mustn't give up, Mara. You're stronger than you know. You certainly needn't rely on any of these fools to save you," he added with a glance toward her devotees. "You're smarter than them. They don't even realize what sort of game you're playing."

She bristled slightly. "It's not a game, Lord Falconridge. It's a matter of survival. But I don't suppose you would know too much about that." She shrugged, avoiding his raised eyebrow.

He hid his amusement, considering he had been trained to survive in a wide variety of dangerous conditions.

"All the same," she continued with a nonchalant air, "I am sorry that you disapprove of me."

"It's not a matter of disapproving, Miss Bryce. I just don't want to see you get hurt. And I fear you will if you put your faith in someone weaker than yourself to save you. I mean, honestly—look at them."

Her witless beaux were picking pieces of fruit out of the punch bowl and throwing them at each other amid raucous laughter.

She heaved another rueful sigh. "Well, you may have a point. But if you're so strong and wise, why don't *you* save me, then? You've already proved once you're very good at it." The challenge she issued with a bold look askance at him sent a thrill as hot as a volcano racing through his body.

Willing himself not to get hard in the middle of the ballroom, he somehow played it cool. "But I only just met you, Miss Bryce," he answered casually. "And ever since we arrived, all you've done is flirt with every other fellow here."

"Maybe I'm only trying to get your attention."

Jordan's thoughts were anything but gentlemanly as he stared at her teasing smile. "Don't play with me, my girl."

"You said you wanted me to flirt with you."

"I think—" He had lifted the glass gently out of her hand. "Someone had better leave off the champagne punch."

"What sensible advice you give! Were you born grown-up?"

"Yes."

"Well, I wasn't. And one must do what necessity requires." She turned away, lifted her chin, and surveyed the ballroom like some fair lady general assessing the battlefield. "In the meanwhile, if you have a better idea, you are welcome to throw your hat into the ring."

"Perhaps I shall."

At that, she looked at him over her shoulder in feminine speculation; Jordan had to shake himself out of her spell. Good God, what was he thinking? He'd come here to pick strawberries, not a blasted wife—and this one was sure to be a hell of a handful. With his orders coming any day now, he should not even be entertaining such notions.

Somehow he managed to retrieve his idle tone. "Thanks for the invitation," he said lightly. "For now, it's rather amusing, watching you work. You're very good, you know. Most of these fools don't even know what's hit them. Do try to behave," he added, as she pushed away from the wall and sauntered back toward her suitors.

"But if I did that, wouldn't you lose interest?"

He could not take his eyes off her. "Save me a dance, Miss Bryce."

"For you, my lord, I should gladly save them all."

He laughed softly. "How many men have you said that to tonight?"

"Lots," she whispered, her dark eyes sparkling. "But I only meant it once."

He shook his head at her, half in aggravation, half delight, then he savored the pleasure of watching her walk as she returned to the center of attention.

In the next moment, she had been surrounded by admiring males . . . just as she was now, in Delilah's parlor.

Thirty seconds left for her to make the first move.

Jordan kept his taut smile welded into place, folded his arms across his chest, and pretended to listen to some drunken idiot telling him a tedious story about a recent foxhunt.

The two minutes he'd given Mara to join him came and went, a total of ten from the time he had walked into the drawing room. *Well, then,* he thought tersely, *that's that.*

He went over to Delilah and made an excuse. Thus, after the shortest possible stay in the drawing room, he took leave of their company with thanks to the hostess, polite farewells to the other guests, and naught but a cold glance over his shoulder at Mara.

Little did she know it was a wordless good-bye—for real, this time, he swore. As the butler showed him down the stairs, Jordan did not even know why he had gone to the dinner party.

He felt like a fool—duped once again by his own star-crossed desires. His slight hope that she had grown up while he was gone was all for naught. If anything, she was even worse now—the Regent's latest doxy!

Good God, how could he have been so stupid, letting this woman rule his thoughts for all these years? There was only one thing to do: forget her once and for all and find somebody else. By God, he would. He meant it this time. He'd marry a wooden spoon before he'd ever think of involving himself with that woman again!

With a brooding stare fixed straight ahead, he stalked across the foyer. What was she, after all—a disease that, once contracted, a man was doomed to carry for the rest of his life?

No, he vowed. As of tonight, he declared himself officially cured of Mara Bryce. Then he strode outside, seeking solace from his anger in the cold black emptiness of the winter night.

Chapter 4

What is that man's problem? Several days later, Mara still found herself shaking her head to herself over Jordan's churlish exit from Delilah's dinner party.

She could not believe he had left without making the slightest effort to speak to her. Beyond those few brief and mostly unpleasant exchanges over dinner—nothing.

But why should she be surprised?

Leaving without explanation was what Jordan Lennox did, she thought cynically as her carriage rumbled onto Knightsbridge. She and Thomas had just come from their dutiful, twice-monthly visit to her parents' manor in South Kensington, and she was thoroughly drained, as always, after seeing them.

The warmly bundled baby on her lap was a comfort to her after the poisonous atmosphere at her parents' house.

Thomas cooed away, shaking his rattle and chewing on it by turns, but she stopped him gently when he started trying to take off his hat. "Keep it on," she chided. It was warmer today than it had been lately, but she was ever vigilant in keeping him snugly warm. He had just recovered from a cold and did not need another.

When Thomas turned his attention toward his shoes instead, her anger snaked back toward the earl.

Arrogant . . . stubborn . . . judgmental . . .

Had the poor fellow become jealous because she did not immediately throw aside her other male friends and go running over to worship at his feet?

Well, that was rather amusing. She was gratified to know she could trigger that much of a reaction from the aloof world traveler. But what did he expect after the way he had embarrassed her at dinner, asking why she only had one child. What an utterly barbarous question!

And how painful a subject—though, begrudgingly, she could admit he had probably not intended any malice. It was just that the question had plucked at hidden shame in her that Jordan probably did not even know existed.

Her late husband's difficulties below the waistline had not been her fault, Mara reminded herself. Even the physician had told Tom that all his drinking was making him unable to perform.

Why her husband could not be persuaded to join the marriage bed in a sober state was a question to which Mara never had received a satisfying answer. All she knew was that it was a crushing blow to be rejected in bed by a husband she had never really wanted in the first place.

When she recalled how Tom had blamed her for the problem with his manhood, it made her loath to risk "taking a lover," as Delilah advised. She could not bear to be shamed like that by a man ever again.

Perhaps she should've heeded Jordan's warnings that a bad match could indeed make her life worse than it had been under her parents' roof. She had thought she had chosen well. Tom had chased her so hard and charmed both her parents in his campaign to win her; but once she was his, he had quickly lost interest.

In their new home, his courtship fervor soon turned to sarcasm and irritability. And when he was drinking, he sometimes turned downright dangerous.

Pushing away unpleasant memories, Mara turned her thoughts back to Jordan as her carriage rumbled on. She still could barely believe how much he had changed.

Gone was the tender young Galahad whose smile had warmed her starry summer nights. The beautiful man at the table had been so cold and distant, closed within himself behind his hard, worldly veneer.

The only person he seemed to relate to at Delilah's party was the poor wounded major, who had surely been through Hell on earth. But goodness, she thought, the life of a diplomat could not be all that bad.

Thomas's babbling drew her from her musings as he asked an incoherent question, banging his rattle cheerfully on the carriage window. He was learning language by fits and starts, and though clear words and even full sentences occasionally popped out, sometimes his baby babble puzzled even her. Especially when she was distracted, thinking about Jordan.

"Yes, Master Thomas, you know that place, that's Hyde Park, clever boy!" Mrs. Busby exclaimed, fondly watching her charge. His faithful old nurse sat across from them wrapped in her cloak.

Thomas repeated his mysterious remarks more insistently, pointing again at the window, and both women suddenly grasped his request.

"He wants to feed the ducks!" Mara exclaimed with a sudden laugh.

Mrs. Busby clapped her hands at the baby. "Do ye want to feed the duckies, Master Thomas?"

He reacted with a full-body wiggle, babbling eagerly and kicking both legs. Both women chuckled.

"Stop squirming, you little imp!" Mara chided, pulling him more firmly onto her lap. "Very well, you were such a good boy at Grandmother's house, you deserve to have some fun." Mara nodded to Mrs. Busby, who dutifully lowered the carriage window.

"Take us into the park, Jack!" Mrs. Busby called to the coachman. "His little Lordship wants to feed the ducks!"

Mara smiled, hearing her trusty driver's rumble of laughter. "Aye, ma'am!"

Mrs. Busby hastily closed the window again, knowing her mistress's tendency to fret over any cold drafts that might menace her child. But Mara was not alarmed about the weather that day. The sun was shining. The air was healthy and clear. A spot of exercise outdoors was good for the constitution as long as one stayed warm, and Thomas was well protected from the mid-March chill by several layers of warm clothes and mittens and the colorful jester's hat that she had knitted for him herself.

As Jack turned the coach into Hyde Park, Mara saw signs of spring already returning. Every week brought more changes to see. Most of the hedges were still russet brown, but now buds peeped out on the lilacs.

The trees' spindled branches stood stark and bare against the delicate blue sky, but the sap had begun to flow in their trunks. Soon would come the flowers. Closer to the ground, the crocuses and snowdrops were in full bloom. The sweet narcissus, too, had burst into color before the retreating patches of snow. Bright tulips still were tightly bundled, awaiting their cue like opera dancers watching from behind the stage curtain. Mara smiled at the fanciful thought as her carriage rolled to a halt beside the shimmering, wind-tossed waters of the Serpentine.

Thomas had spotted the ducks and was already bouncing with excitement on her lap when her driver came and helped the ladies and their little lord down from the carriage.

"Careful, milady. The ground's a bit muddy," he warned.

"Thank you, Jack." Mara nodded and carried her son over to the finely graveled walk beside the ornamental lake, where she set him down to play.

With Mrs. Busby on one side of him and Mara on the other, Thomas screeched happily at the waterfowl and managed to scare them off a bit, but not for long. The hardy tribe of London Mallards and Mute Swans and assorted geese knew better than to stray too far when a free meal might be forthcoming. Having Thomas so near the water jangled Mara's nerves a bit, but she told her overprotective side that between Mrs. Busby and herself, her boy was perfectly safe.

The ducks were nearly as tall as the two-year-old as he went toddling back and forth among them. His approach sent them waddling noisily out of his way, but they swarmed back when Mrs. Busby shook the tin of grain and seeds they kept in the carriage for this favorite activity. All the tension from visiting her parents was forgotten as Mara watched her son exulting in this taste of freedom.

While she kept a close eye on him, the chorus of songbirds filling the air charmed her ears. There was no surer sign of spring to revive one's spirits. Throstles called gaily to each other from across the barren meadows, larks no doubt exchanging gossip from their winter travels.

A flutter of black and yellow swept past—a small party of goldfinches on the hunt for a suitable nuncheon. The food for the ducks must have lured them. Then a little dandyish male linnet alighted atop her carriage, smartly dressed in his bright red waistcoat and cap in the hopes of attracting a wife.

She no sooner pointed the cheeky visitor out to Thomas

than the linnet flitted away like a proper Town gentleman off to his club. It was then, as she glanced after the linnet's speedy exit, that she spotted Jordan.

She straightened up from bending to steady her son and went still, staring across the faded grass at the rider on the white horse.

She wasn't sure how she knew it was he from a hundred yards away, but her recognition of the man was immediate and visceral.

As his horse galloped closer, thundering down the gentle ridge, Mara's heart fluttered at the sight of the magnificent horse and rider.

Both man and steed were tall and powerful, beautifully muscled, lean and sure. Jordan's white hunter was flecked with mud and so was he, from his black boots to his elegant dun riding coat billowing out behind him.

When his mount's aggressive gallop suddenly slowed to a rocking canter, Mara realized he must have seen her.

It would have been hard to miss her. The park was not crowded; it was not yet the fashionable hour. There was no way for her to pretend she had not seen him, either.

Oh, how awkward. Her heart was pounding. Would he snub her and just ride on? she wondered, but then, with a trace of irony, she realized that dutiful Lord Falconridge was too civilized a gentleman ever to do that.

It was easy to see his reluctance in the halfhearted way he began to turn his cantering horse on an arcing path toward her parked carriage and her little group.

Well, it wasn't necessary if he did not wish to trouble himself, she thought crossly, but she braced herself as she realized he was indeed coming over to pay his respects. She expected no more than a polite tip of his beaver hat and a short "Good day." That would have been enough to satisfy courtesy, even for him.

And yet she could not deny that his approach lit a strange awareness in her body like a small, steady flame.

He curbed his horse's pace from the lively canter to an easy, posting trot. Her carriage horses tossed their heads and craned their necks in curiosity, trying to peer past their blinders at his white hunter.

Standing next to Thomas, Mara held on firmly to her son's mittened hand, but she offered Jordan a taut smile as he reached the edge of the graveled path and reined in to a walk. He stopped his blowing horse a few feet away from them. Resting his gauntleted hands on his horse's withers, he studied her and Thomas for a long moment without a word.

The boy had gone silent, too, staring back at him uncertainly.

"Lord Falconridge," Mara greeted him at last with a wary nod, nervously breaking the silence.

"Lady Pierson." Jordan seemed torn about coming any closer, but his tone was carefully controlled. "So, this is the young fellow to whom your heart belongs." He nodded at her son.

Mara smiled ruefully in spite of herself. "It is."

"Well." He cleared his throat. "I won't bother you. Just wanted to have a look at your young lad here, after hearing you sing his praises the other night. You were right to brag," he added softly. "You have a fine boy there."

"Thank you, my lord." Mara lifted Thomas up and set him on her hip, eyeing Jordan warily. Well, he was a diplomat, all right, she thought.

He certainly knew what to say to get into *her* good graces. Nevertheless, she was pleased with his compliment to her son.

It also occurred to her it would not hurt Thomas to get a look at a grown man of Jordan's quality, in turn. With his own father dead, so far her boy had had little exposure to first-rate men of his own class. His future lack of a strong male to look up to already worried her. Thus, she told herself, it was only concern for her child that made her speak up.

"Would you care for a—proper introduction, my lord?" she ventured just as Jordan started to turn his horse back toward the green.

He glanced back at her, considering. Then he shrugged and clipped out, "I'd be honored." His expression was guarded as he swung down off his horse and sauntered toward them.

Mara lifted her chin as he approached, but Thomas stared at him in wonder, particularly intrigued by his black beaver hat.

For her part, she could not look away from his handsome face. The clear pale blue of his eyes matched that of the afternoon sky; the color was high in his cheeks from exercising his horse.

"Lord Falconridge," she said, shaking off her daze, "allow me to present Thomas, Viscount Pierson."

"Pleased to make your acquaintance, my lord. I look forward to your maiden speech in Parliament." Jordan sketched a bow to the baby; Mara fiercely fought a smile. Thomas pointed at Jordan's hat and uttered something in his own peculiar language.

"Oh, you like this, do you? Here you are, and may I say you have excellent taste, young man." Jordan swept off his hat and perched it atop the baby's head.

Thomas laughed, though the man's top hat promptly slipped down over his eyes. Jordan smiled, glancing over to acknowledge Mrs. Busby and Jack with a courteous nod.

"We are feeding the ducks," Mara informed him, warming to him slightly after the unpleasantness of the other night. "You may join us if you like."

He dropped his gaze, hesitating. "My horse will need a walk to cool, but, ah, I suppose I can stay for a moment."

"He's a beautiful animal."

"Thank you. He's as weary of being cooped up inside as I am. Fine day like this is a welcome foretaste of spring, don't you think?"

"Oh, yes—I agree." She winced to hear them speaking in such stiff tones of the weather when they once had been so close, but she supposed they had to start somewhere.

She set Thomas down and laughed as he pushed Jordan's hat up again so he could see. The boy craned his neck to peer up at the earl.

"He has your eyes," Jordan said softly, studying her son.

"Yes." Mara smiled.

"Why, you barely come up to the top of my riding boots." Laughing softly, Jordan bent down to steady the tot, taking hold of his wrist as Thomas attempted to eat a piece of gravel he had clutched. "Not wise, my lad."

"You like children," Mara observed as she pried the pebble out of her son's hand.

"I have two dozen nieces and nephews, my lady. Learning to manage them was a matter of my own survival." The warmth in his eyes belied his sardonic tone.

"Two dozen," she echoed softly. "Your siblings have been fruitful."

"To be sure. At least the title's in no danger if something untoward were ever to happen to me."

"Your family is well?"

"They are, thanks. Yours?"

Mara gave him a wry look. "You know my parents. They are not happy unless they have something to gripe about."

He sent her a warm, rueful half smile. "I remember."

"We were just visiting them," she added, then let out a sigh. "After that, a trip to the park was definitely in order. And perhaps a large brandy."

"No doubt," he murmured with a soft laugh. His knowing

look was exactly what she needed after the day's always-difficult visit.

But the wary smile they exchanged shook her. Her pulse leaped; she looked away. Watching Thomas chase the ducks, she was keenly aware of Jordan beside her, the worldly, hardened man he had become, and for a moment, she ached for all the lost years when he had vanished from her life.

Suddenly anxious that he might leave again in a moment, ride off on his fine blood horse, never to be seen again, she realized he had made the first move, coming over to see her, and that meant it was her turn to respond.

Indeed, this might be her last chance to reach out to him. Her heart pounded. Keeping her gaze fixed on her son at play, she spoke up at last with the utmost caution. "You left too soon the other night."

She sensed him stiffen, but his tone was dry. "I wasn't aware you had noticed."

"Of course I did." She held her cool smile in place, staring straight ahead. "We didn't even get a chance to talk."

"And what is there to talk about, exactly?"

At his dull tone, Mara eyed him in question.

"Let's be honest. You didn't want me to come to Mrs. Staunton's in the first place. You said it was a bad idea." He glanced casually at his horse. "I should've listened. You were right."

"So you did not enjoy yourself at all?"

He turned and looked at her for a long moment. "I did not go to the party to enjoy myself, Mara. I went to see you."

She was not sure how to take that.

The ducks clacked in the background while Thomas laughed, guarded over by the ever-vigilant Mrs. Busby.

"For your part, it was rather plain you almost didn't come, knowing I'd be there," he pointed out.

"But I did come," she protested softly. "Just a little late."

When he raised a knowing eyebrow, she gave up her effort to seem nonchalant. "Very well, I admit it. Seeing you at Christie's was a-a bit unnerving after all this time. But I changed my mind and came so that I could see you." Searching his face, she shrugged. "Then you barely spoke to anyone and slipped out at the first opportunity."

His lips flattened to a narrow line; he, too, kept his gaze fixed watchfully on Thomas. "Well, I apologize for my lack of conversation. But if you had really wanted to chat, you should not have surrounded yourself with half a dozen other men. Did you expect me to fight my way through the crowd for the privilege of speaking to you? Just like old times, eh?"

She was taken aback by the edge under his smooth voice, but she checked her anger. "Gracious, if I didn't know better, I would say that you sound jealous."

"Well, my dear, that was your intention, was it not?" he replied. "You must have forgotten, I never played those games, even when we were young. You, on the other hand, used to take great delight, as I recall, in inspiring all manner of wild reactions in all the poor, stupid males around you."

She stared hard into his gleaming eyes. "That was a long time ago," she informed him, but he would not give an inch.

"It was just a few nights ago, actually," he answered with a cool smile.

She scowled. "What girl isn't a bit of a flirt at seventeen?" she exclaimed. "I might have encouraged a few of my beaux, but it's a jolly good thing I did! Because, clearly, I couldn't count on you."

He winced and scoffed softly but shook his head and avoided her gaze.

Mara glared at him. "At any rate, we both know making you jealous is beyond my power, my lord. You made it plain long ago that you couldn't care less if I live or die."

He snorted quietly, looking at the water. "If you say so."

His cool detachment rattled her. She fought to hold her tongue, but as she shook her head, the resentful words spilled from her. "If you cared, you would not have left like that the other night—but that's what you do, isn't it, Jordan? You judge someone not worth the bother, then walk away without a backward glance."

"You have no idea what you're talking about," he informed her in a lower tone, glancing into her eyes.

"Then tell me! Whatever it is you have to say to me, by all means, let me hear it! I've waited twelve years for *some* kind of an explanation from you!"

"*You've* waited?" he bit back, keeping his voice low, for Thomas's sake. "I left—*Mara*—to fulfill my duty, hoping in my absence you might leave off playing the coquette and grow the hell *up*! I thought perhaps when I returned, you and I could've—" His words broke off in frustration. He dropped his gaze. "But it was not to be. You married good old Tom while I was away."

She searched his face, unsure how much store to put by these words. "Then—you *did* care for me?"

"If you can doubt it, then I don't know which of us is the greater fool."

"But you were gone so long!"

"Gracious, one whole year," he mocked her softly.

"You never even wrote to me!"

He narrowed his eyes with a withering look. "I was a little busy."

She dropped her jaw, outraged. "Busy?" Had he no idea how many times she'd cried herself to sleep? "Too busy to spare me one little line to let me know if there was hope for us or not? How, how could you do that to me?"

He opened his mouth, but no sound came out. He shut it again.

Mara shook her head, trembling. "No. I don't believe you. You never meant to return for me. That cannot be true."

"I'm afraid it is."

"You forgot all about me. That's why you didn't write! I meant nothing to you."

"You can believe that if it makes you feel better."

"How could that possibly make me feel better?" she cried, shaking by then.

"Because the truth is worse," he answered grimly. "The time's lost, and it was all for nothing."

She stared at him with a lump in her throat.

Then she turned away. She had to blink back the threat of tears before she could speak. "Very well, is that why you never came back, then? You were angry at me because I married Tom?"

"I did come back, actually, Mara, I just didn't come back to *you*. For, you see, unlike the rest of this town, I don't dally with other men's wives."

She narrowed her eyes, outraged once more at his frosty insolence. "You assume I'd have been willing!"

He shrugged. "No offense, darling, but I've never quite thought of you as the model of virtue. Besides"—he sent her a searing glance—"it's not as if it matters anymore."

"No, of course. You're right. It's in the past," she said. "Where it will stay!"

He dropped his gaze, the set of his wide shoulders stiff and formal. "I could not agree more. Good day, Lady Pierson. I shall not trouble you again. Congratulations on your child," he added, but he could not seem to resist one last barb as he began walking away. "Do *try* not to turn him into a vain, selfish schemer *like his mother*!"

"How dare you?" She stepped after him in fury.

"What are you going to do, send your lover's army to arrest me?" he shot back.

My . . . lover's army?

Her eyes widened with sudden understanding.

The rumor!

So, that's why he's being so horrid!

"You think the prince and I—"

"Please, spare me the particulars!" he said vehemently, holding up his hand. "I heard quite enough the other night, believe me. Frankly, I don't care what you do with whom. I just don't want to see you get hurt."

"Oh, really?" She folded her arms across her chest and glared at him.

"Be careful, Mara," he said, still as supremely arrogant of his superior judgment and wisdom as he had been when they were young. "I've spent enough time in royal courts to know how easy it is to get in over your head in that environment. Mind you don't unwittingly become a pawn in other people's schemes."

She shook her head at him. *He really must take me for a fool.* Well, if he was so very eager to believe the worst of her, if even he thought she was the Regent's mistress, then who was she to bother him with the truth? To hell with him. "Thank you *so* much for your sage advice, Lord Falconridge."

His eyes narrowed at her sarcasm. "Anytime," he replied in kind. "Enjoy your place of privilege while it lasts, my dear. Just don't come crawling to me when you're cast aside for the next royal trinket!" he growled.

"My God, Jordan, what has happened to you?" she exclaimed, bewildered by this sharp edge in the man who had once been the very flower of chivalry. "What is this cold and bitter thing you have become?"

His lips twisted. "Believe me, you don't want to know." He offered a rather rude bow, pivoted, and stalked back to his horse, swinging up into the saddle.

The parting glance he shot her seethed with rage and a

world of buried hurt. Then he wheeled his towering horse around and rode off at a restless canter.

He had even forgotten to take his hat.

Mara stared after him until tears blurred her vision.

She covered her lips with her fingers to stifle a small sob as she watched him riding away, exiting her life yet again and dissolving her hopes before they had even taken shape. *Would she never know love?* Right there in the middle of Hyde Park, her composure was suddenly hanging by a thread.

Somehow she managed to find her voice to summon her servants back to the carriage. "Jack! Mrs. Busby!" She swallowed hard, steadying herself. "We must be going! Thomas needs his nap."

"Aye, ma'am." Her coachman got the door and lowered the metal step.

Thomas waved good-bye to the ducks at Mrs. Busby's prompting, then the sturdy old woman carried her charge back to the coach. Mara waited for them there. Jack handed them up, then went and retrieved Jordan's hat. He started to ask if she wanted it in the carriage, but when he saw her face, he swallowed his question and simply went and put it in the boot. They could return it to Jordan later.

She had fallen silent, in fact, was fighting not to cry in front of her child. If she did that, it would be only minutes until Thomas was bawling with her, and once the tears started flowing, she feared they'd never stop.

As soon as Thomas and his nurse were seated safely across from her, Jack resumed his place on the driver's box, and the coach rolled into motion.

With a lump in her throat, Mara barely listened to Thomas's cheerful babbling, determined to hold on to her composure until the sting of Jordan's words abated.

Mrs. Busby looked at her in questioning worry. Mara shook her head discreetly, then looked out the window, counting the minutes as Jack headed the carriage homeward by the usual route.

Traveling along the Ring, the neat main carriage road through Hyde Park, they would exit at the northeast corner gate, just as they had a hundred times before.

There were several stately, wrought-iron gates that gave access to the hundreds of acres that made up the sprawling greenery of Hyde Park.

The nearest one to her home let out onto busy Oxford Street—but as they neared it, an unexpected obstacle ahead forced Jack to slow the carriage.

"Oh, not again," Mara murmured, frowning out the window at the crowd that had assembled all around the northeast corner of the park.

It was becoming a favorite spot for the lower orders to gather in protest against the government's various policies. These unlicensed demonstrations had grown more frequent since the end of the war. England had won, but as the dust settled, they realized the twenty-year war had left them nearly bankrupt.

Throughout England, unrest was on the rise: Riots over the Corn Laws, another round of taxes on foodstuffs casting the poor into desperate fear of starvation.

Then there was the Navy's failure to pay many thousands of sailors, now understandably angry over months of wages being held in arrears. Luddites breaking machines in the factories up north. Radical broadsheets circulating, making wild accusations against the government and giving rise to a new wave of fears among the citizenry that there might indeed be Jacobins lurking in their midst, not off in France, but right here on English soil, trying to whip up their own version of a bloody revolution.

The Prime Minister, Lord Liverpool, threatened suspension of habeas corpus if things did not settle down.

Though ladies of Quality were not expected to have opinions on such things, it did not seem to Mara, well, quite *English* to be able to lock a person up without certain cause or explanation. Still, they weren't Frenchmen, she thought as she gazed nervously out the window at the unruly crowd.

How ever angry he might be, John Bull could speak his piece without resorting to violence. She gathered her son closer in her arms and tried not to think about aristocrats and guillotines.

At present, a few hundred citizens had gathered to cheer yet another fiery orator bellowing the people's list of grievances.

Usually, these impromptu rallies were quickly dispersed without incident by a contingent of the Household Cavalry from the garrison at the southern edge of Hyde Park. So far, the elite dragoons had not yet arrived, but Jack did his best to steer her carriage slowly through the crowd.

"Who does 'e think 'e is, our fine Lord Liverpool? Threatenin' to take away our rights? The mass of men in want of bread, and what do they give us? More taxes!"

The orator ranted on against the Prime Minister and all Parliament, the Exchequer, the Admiralty, and "that brute" Lord Sidmouth in the Home Office, as well—but the name that drew the crowd's fiercest hisses and boos was that of the Prince Regent.

Mara gulped.

"As for His Royal Highness, he grows fat while these poor children starve!"

Mara furrowed her brow, irked by the hyperbole.

Of course, they were within their rights to complain, but did they not know how little power the Regent actually wielded these days?

England's stand-in ruler was surrounded by advisors with dubious agendas of their own, and if he attempted to do more than obediently sign his name on the bottom line of some new bill or policy, as his ministers instructed, he was chided with oily lectures and told he did not quite grasp the finer points of statesmanship, as if he were some giant baby. They insisted His Royal Highness was still too inexperienced to make the big decisions. And, of course, they were fond of reminding him that, so long as his mad old sire remained alive, he was not yet the real king. Those were the words that could always make him back down from challenging his counselors.

It was not in Prinny's nature to put up a fight, and his own self-doubt allowed his advisors to convince him they knew best. So their dilettante-artist prince went along with his ministers' wishes—but somehow, he was always the one who ended up taking the blame.

Unfortunately, his royal blood made him too proud to attempt to defend himself in public or to blame somebody else. Stoically, he just took it but withdrew from his people ever more pronouncedly. The populace then thought him indifferent; in reality, he was merely hurt by their complete misunderstanding of his nature and rather at his wits' end about how to make his people like him.

His estranged wife's constant scandals in the papers did not help his cause. Caroline of Brunswick had a talent for gleefully making her husband look even worse.

The royal cuckold, some of the satirists called him. *How can he manage a kingdom if he can't even control his own wife?*

Mara felt for him. From his boyhood, the prince had been surrounded by false friends, toadies, and all manner of people he knew he couldn't trust. And now demagogues like this, popping up out of their holes to make firebrand speeches bordering on sedition.

She feared that such dangerous talk could one day lead to her royal friend making his own terrible march up the bloodied stairs to the guillotine, just like his fellow king across the Channel more than twenty years ago.

"Rabid dogs," Mrs. Busby scolded under breath. "Where are the soldiers? Surely this has gone on long enough."

Mara sent her a grim look. Meanwhile, she could hear Jack shouting at people to get out of the way so he could bring the carriage through.

Unfortunately, the crowd was in no mood to be told what to do by a liveried coachman at the helm of an elegant town coach with an aristocratic coat of arms emblazoned on the door.

The speaker's audience was milling about in disorderly fashion, choking the road and only moving aside after casting her coachman surly looks. They inched forward by fits and starts until a few lads decided to challenge him.

"Why should we move for you? Go round the other way!"

"Step aside!" Jack thundered.

"Don't worry, we're almost to the gates," Mara murmured in reassurance to Mrs. Busby, but Thomas looked frightened, so she cupped his head against her chest and softly whispered nothings in his ear.

In truth, her heart was pounding; at least having her son in her arms, she could protect him.

All of a sudden, someone in the crowd must have recognized the Pierson coat of arms.

"'Hoy! Look! It's the Regent's doxy!"

Mara turned white.

Out the window, scores and scores of ordinary Londoners turned to gawk at her. The speaker heard the announcement and made a rude jest at her expense. She could not make out his words, but the crowd roared with mocking laughter. She suddenly found herself being pointed at and jeered by some two or three hundred people.

"Pardon, Your Ladyship!" the orator cried in raucous

hilarity. "Won't you deliver a message for us to your royal lover?"

She did not hear the words the orator wanted her to convey to the Regent, but the sentiment was plain as the jeering crowd swarmed around her carriage.

Jack cracked the whip to drive the people out of the way so he could bring the coach through while the throng went on mocking her as the Regent's mistress.

She was too terrified to be humiliated at the moment, sensing a menacing ugliness beneath their air of fun.

She stifled a shriek as several low ruffians, goaded on by the ugly cheers, jumped up on her carriage and began rocking it violently, laughing, their dirty faces leering at her through thc window.

Thomas began wailing.

"You got the Regent's by-blow there, ma'am?"

"Get off my coach! How dare you?" she shouted.

"The House o' Lords is parasites!" one man bellowed.

Thomas bawled louder, but the coach had now come to a halt except for its wild bouncing on its springs.

Mara clutched the boy to her chest, while up on the driver's box, someone hurled a stone at Jack and knocked his hat off. He responded with a furious lash from his long driving whip.

Mrs. Busby, ashen-faced, pulled down the carriage shades, then looked over at her mistress in terror.

Mara stared back at her, completely at a loss.

Oh, what now? Jordan thought in annoyance, as the disturbance in a distant corner of the park drew his attention.

Still roiling with anger after their fight, indeed, driven half-mad by all he could not tell her, he had been cantering his horse eastward through Hyde Park, intent on exiting by the Park Lane gate. From there, it was only a few blocks' ride to his home in Grosvenor Square.

But something made him glance back, some vague sixth sense for danger that years in the Order had honed in him, and it was then that he spotted the throng gathered in the distance.

Though it was many acres away, off in the northeast corner of the park, it struck him as most irregular. Certain spy instincts in him began to tingle. Filled with curiosity, he slowed his horse, turned the animal's nose to the north, and rode closer to see what was afoot.

A few hundred people had gathered before a scruffy

orator who was shouting to the crowd from atop the stump of an old tree.

Jordan could only make out a few words over the people's cheers of agreement and their angry jeers of shared indignation at the mention of certain names.

Lords Liverpool and Sidmouth.

"Tar and feather the lot of 'em, I say!"

Jordan's eyes narrowed. Carefully, he studied the crowd. While the Home Office wrung its hands about the threat of sedition, the Order was more concerned about Promethean meddling in the underground circles of the Radical movement.

The Prometheans, after all, had long been masters of ferreting out the malcontents in a society, offering them full backing, then slyly inciting them to violence. Whatever brought on chaos and set opposing groups at each other's throats aided their cause. He scanned the crowd for any known Promethean faces—and he received a number of surly glances in return.

This was not a crowd to welcome an obvious gentleman of wealth and breeding into their midst. Even his horse could sense the foul mood permeating the mob. The white hunter snorted, tossing his head at the unkempt rabble in lordly disdain. "Easy," Jordan soothed, reining in to a walk.

He had barely arrived at the edge of the gathering when he heard the eruption of raucous jeering at the far end of the crowd, several acres away.

He guided his horse past a stand of trees for a clearer view of the scene unfolding on the Ring.

I'll be damned. The impudent savages had stopped somebody's carriage.

Then his gaze homed in on the familiar Pierson insignia on the carriage door, and he felt his blood run cold.

A swarm of men had jumped atop her coach and were rocking it violently, amid brutish laughter, banging on the roof, as if they meant to knock the whole thing over.

Mara!

Others had grabbed the horses' bridles, holding them in place with bullying hilarity. They were throwing things at the coachman.

Good God, Jordan thought as the blood drained from his face, Mara and her child were in that coach. The old woman, too.

In the next second, he was spurring his horse toward the besieged carriage. His galloping hunter's hoofbeats thundered over the turf.

Sweeping along the edge of the crowd, he sent a few people diving out of his way, ignoring their curses in his wake.

In the next instant, he charged into the rabble surrounding the carriage, crashing into their midst with all the mass and power of his angry horse scattering the men. Some fell back, shouting as they found themselves nearly trampled under his gelding's hoofs. From inside the coach, meanwhile, he could hear Thomas crying.

He gritted his teeth, homing in on his first target. An unkempt young man was climbing up onto the roof of Mara's carriage, eager to join his whooping, stomping mates there.

Leaning out of the saddle, Jordan grabbed the lad by the back of his coat and threw him onto the ground. He rolled clear of the gelding's hooves with a startled yelp.

Jordan did not wait for him to get to his feet but immediately sought his next target. Whirling his horse around, he plucked another blackguard off the back of Mara's coach.

This one had planted himself on the groom's standing bar at the back of the vehicle. Jordan likewise knocked him back to earth while the crowd turned to mayhem, people hollering, Mara screaming his name from inside the coach.

His horse reared up, nearly bashing in some fellow's face as Jordan vaulted nimbly out of the saddle and landed atop the halted coach.

He caught his balance easily between the two ruffians dancing an insolent jig on the carriage roof.

These now greeted him with their fists; he ducked a blow and sent the one who'd dealt it flying off the side of coach.

The second, larger man laughed at him. Jordan smiled none too kindly, then punched him hard—a solid sock in the jaw. The big fellow absorbed the blow, looked at him in wrath, and then returned the favor.

Jordan staggered back but planted his feet to keep his balance on the slick black surface. While they continued trading blows, Mara craned her neck out the window to try to see what was happening up on her carriage roof.

"Jordan!"

She distracted him just for a fraction of a second, but it was enough to allow the large, smelly man to grab him in a headlock.

"Unhand that gentleman!" she ordered his opponent. "You happen to be assaulting a peer of the realm, you brute!"

"All the more reason to hit 'im!" the hefty rebel vaunted, to the crowd's cheers.

Jordan scowled at Mara, as he grappled to pull the thick arm free from around his neck. "Get—back—inside!" he ordered her, straining for breath.

He had been trying not to actually hurt anyone among the populace he protected, but he suddenly lost patience.

Throwing his weight forward, he ducked down and flipped the man over his shoulder. The big ruffian sailed to earth and landed in the gravel with a thud.

Panting, Jordan looked over his shoulder at her bloodied coachman. "Drive!" he clipped out, then he leaped back onto his horse from atop her carriage.

He could not tell if the crowd was roaring *at* or *for* him, but he ignored them either way, urging his hunter up toward the lead horse of her coach's wild-eyed team.

"Easy," Jordan murmured to her horses. But when another man shouted a taunt, describing the panicked lady inside the coach with highly indecorous language, Jordan drew his sword. "*Enough!*" he bellowed. "Fall back!" He brandished his weapon, letting the rabble know he would not tolerate further mischief. "Out of our way!"

Finally, the heaving sea of humanity around them parted.

While Jordan held the angry mob at bay with his sword, Mara's driver cracked the whip. The trembling horses leaped forward in their traces, tearing off toward the park gates.

Still warning the miscreants off with his blade, Jordan heard a distant shot as someone fired into the air.

The whole throng looked over.

A collective gasp arose at the line of elite dragoons riding toward them in the distance, the sun glinting off their plumed helmets as they advanced across the muddy green.

A tenfold pandemonium instantly broke out.

The hundreds of onlookers watching the fray and listening to the speaker made a sudden stampede for the gates to avoid arrest.

In the crush that by then resembled a riot, Jordan did not care if he had to trample his countrymen to reach Mara. His horse whinnied piercingly at the surging mob all around them, but Jordan did not relent until he had brought his animal up alongside her carriage.

While the fleeing crowd flooded into Oxford Street, he yelled at her to keep the shades closed and to stay down. Then he quickly escorted her carriage across the famed avenue and straight into Great Cumberland Street.

They did not slow their pace until they reached the grand stuccoed crescent where she lived.

Her driver stopped the coach in front of the end unit, and Jordan sprang down off his white hunter even as the door to her town house flew open. A butler stepped out with a look of alarm; Jordan yanked open the carriage door and took the crying child from her.

Mara gestured toward her front door with a trembling hand. Jordan sped the boy up the front steps while her ashen-faced driver quickly helped the ladies down.

He handed Thomas over to the startled butler, then turned back to steady Mara and the nurse. As soon as the ladies were safely inside, he slammed the door behind them and turned the locks.

"Milady, what happened?" the butler cried, but Mara could not manage a response. She merely shook her head, helping the old woman into a chair by the wall in the entrance hall.

Then she reclaimed her crying son from the startled butler's arms. While she kissed and rocked the tot, trying to hush his sobs, Jordan prowled to the bay window that overlooked the street.

Brushing the curtain aside, he peered out but saw no evidence that they had been followed. Still, he wouldn't put it past the mob to persist in harassing her.

The Regent's doxy. He clenched his jaw.

On the street below the window, a few of Mara's stable hands had rushed out of the mews behind her town house to help her driver put the coach away. Thankfully, one of the lads had had the sense to collect Jordan's white hunter.

All the horses were walked back around to the mews; with the coach and horses out of sight, there was less danger that the miscreants might still track them to her house.

Scanning the men below, Jordan furrowed his brow when he saw that her coachman was bleeding from his forehead.

More than just knocking his hat off, that rock must have

struck him, after all. It reminded Jordan that his own jaw was a bit sore after his round of fisticuffs. He had taken a few good blows but was still too riled up to feel it.

"Reese, send for the doctor," Mara was saying to her butler over in the foyer.

"No need." Jordan pivoted from the window and marched toward them. "I have some medical training. Is somebody hurt?"

Mara turned to him in surprise. "You do?"

He nodded as he stalked toward them. Battlefield medicine was a part of every agent's basic training, along with the use of many different weapons. In his line of work, such skills were required for self-preservation.

"Will you check Thomas over?" she asked, stepping forward to present her child to him.

"Of course." He nodded, but as his gaze touched hers, Jordan realized that she was entrusting him with no small favor. Her son was the most precious thing to her in all the world.

"Will you please remove his bonnet?" he asked in a cool tone. "Let's make sure he hasn't bumped his head, all right?"

At once, she started to oblige, but her hands were still shaking so much that she fumbled with the ribbons.

Jordan gently pushed her hand away, then untied the baby's parti-colored hat himself, some sort of playful jester's cap with little bells on the ends of each soft point.

"He's going to hate you for making him wear that in public when he's older," he offered softly, trying to snap her out of her needless panic with a brief attempt at levity.

She frowned at him. "I made it for him myself."

"Er, right." Jordan dropped his gaze. So much for his attempt at humor.

Thomas was still crying in loud, full-throated displeasure

at his ordeal in the park, the tiny white buds of his new teeth on display with every deafening wail.

"That will do, young man," Jordan murmured as he lifted the funny jester's cap away.

He ran his cupped hand gently over the tot's downy head, feeling for any areas where there might be swelling. He also checked the boy's neck with a gentle squeeze.

"Is there anything amiss?" Mara asked anxiously.

"No. Did he fall at all inside the carriage?"

"No, I held him on my lap the whole time."

"Good." Jordan quickly concluded that Thomas was perfectly fine, especially when the boy stopped crying presently, distracted by Jordan's inspection. Thomas batted away Jordan's gently probing fingers with a tiny hand.

Jordan smiled in amusement as Thomas studied him in babyish indignation, those big brown eyes scowling at him as if to say, "Don't touch me! You're not my mama!"

"No worries here," Jordan confirmed to the boy's worried mother, but her agitated look informed him she was not going to rest easy until he had checked the boy from head to toe.

Jordan did not argue. With Mara still holding Thomas, he felt along the toddler's arms and legs until Thomas began giggling at what he took for a game. Rather charmed in spite of himself, Jordan tickled his tummy. "No, my lady. This little fellow is just fine."

At the sound of her child's laughter, Mara apparently realized at last that the end of the world was not at hand. She heaved a huge sigh. Then she gazed at Jordan with such utter relief and gratitude that he half feared she might collapse. "God bless you," she uttered.

He reached out and steadied her by her elbow. "Are you all right?"

"I think so." As soon as she bent and set Thomas down, he pattered off after the cat, trailing a stream of cheerful babbling in his wake.

Jordan studied Mara. "Maybe you should sit down."

She shook her head. "I'm fine. Would you see to Mrs. Busby?"

He nodded and went to ask the old woman how she was. She rubbed her chest. "I never felt my heart pound so," she admitted. Jordan took her wrist and checked her pulse, but soon concluded she was more shaken up than anything. "You should get some rest, ma'am."

Behind him, Mara nodded at her. "Please, take the rest of the day off. Mary can look after Thomas."

Mrs. Busby clutched both of Jordan's hands. "Thank you for rescuing us, sir. I beg your pardon—I don't even know your name!"

"This is Lord Falconridge, Mrs. Busby," Mara informed her. "Jordan, this is Tommy's nurse. She knows more about children than ten books on the subject. Thirty grandchildren!"

"Really?" Jordan smiled at her. "I'm sure the boy is very lucky to have you, ma'am. Let me help you up."

The old nurse bowed her head modestly and accepted his hand in rising from her chair. He escorted her over to the stairs, where she thanked him again. Before leaving them to go lie down, Mrs. Busby paused and glanced at Mara in kindly concern. "Are you sure you're all right, milady?"

Mara nodded at her with a forced smile. "Thank you. Now, you go rest for a while. Let my maid know if you need anything."

The old woman gave her a grateful smile. After Mrs. Busby had disappeared up the stairs, Mara and Jordan looked at each other for a long moment.

An awkward silence filled the bright, airy foyer.

"W-were you hurt at all in that fight?" she ventured at length.

"No."

"You were brilliant, Jordan."

A nonchalant shrug. "All in a day's work." He was unsure why his heart had started pounding. He could not seem to tear his stare away from her.

Mara dropped her gaze, and Jordan suddenly sensed she was about to launch into some heartfelt speech, probably thanking him for his display of derring-do and heaping praise on him that he did not deserve.

Not after the cold and cutting things he had said to her at the park a short while ago.

Though he had felt fully justified at the time, his words now filled him with scalding remorse. He suddenly saw himself as no better than that rabble, attacking her. Who was he to judge her, anyway? *Self-righteous bastard.*

"Jordan—"

He cleared his throat, cutting her off before she could reward him with her thanks. "I'll go check on your coachman. He was bleeding from his forehead, you know."

"What?" Her eyes widened. "Jack's hurt?"

"Someone in the crowd threw a rock at him."

"Oh, no!" The awkwardness thankfully passed with this change of topic. "Let's go out to the stables and see how he is!" she said at once.

"No. You stay here. I'd rather you stay out of sight for a while. I'll take care of him for you."

She paled anew, her eyes as dark as night. "Do you think that mob might still come after me?"

"Well, no. I wouldn't think so, necessarily. But just to be safe, I mean to send for a few capable men to keep watch here at your house in case they do. They are ex-military, trained in security." He was thinking of Sergeant Parker and his mates, of course, but Mara's look of renewed panic at the thought that the ruffians might be back brought his immediate reassurance. "I'm sure you have nothing to worry about, but if you'll indulge me, it would make *me* feel better if they were here, that's all. I'll post two or three of them around your house for a day or two to keep watch—unless you have any objections?"

She shook her head dazedly.

But she looked so scared, he could not help himself. He went to her. "There, sweet. It's going to be all right."

Heart pounding, he watched as though outside himself as he carefully drew her into his arms and held her.

The feel of her in his embrace and the scent of her perfume made his senses throb; his lips grazed her brow, barely skimming the dizzying silk of her warm, pearly skin.

Mara had closed her eyes and had gone quite motionless, as well, perhaps as amazed as he at the blissful shock of their fleeting closeness.

"Thank you," she whispered with a shudder of what he assumed was belated fear.

"You are welcome," he answered in a measured tone.

"I-I didn't expect you to come back."

"Well, when I saw them bothering you, I could hardly leave you to fend for yourself, now, could I?" His light murmur belied the snarling ferocity he felt toward anyone who would dare harm her, but Mara had tensed in his arms.

"After the things you said, I can't figure why you'd bother." She stepped back from him, her wary gaze searching his face. "But I suppose you are still a gentleman even if I am not a lady, isn't that right?" She smiled ruefully when she said it, but he stiffened nonetheless at her gentle rebuke.

"I'll see to the coachman."

"He'll be in the back," she replied, as he pivoted and marched slowly toward the door, still stung with chagrin at his own outburst back in Hyde Park and still burning with thwarted desire for her, and her alone.

"Jordan?"

He cast her a wary glance over his shoulder as he reached the door. "Yes?"

"I didn't know you could fight like that," she said.

He cast her a cool half smile. "Darling, you have no idea what I can do," he murmured wryly. "Lock this behind me," he added. Then he stepped outside and pulled the door shut behind him.

Pausing on her doorstep, he took a deep breath and strove to clear his head. Shaking off his agitation as best he could, he surveyed the genteel street in both directions for signs of trouble. Nothing struck him as out of place.

The yielding arc of the grand, terraced crescent gave him an excellent view of the surrounding area. Fashionable folk coming and going. Handsome equipages passing to and fro. Across the street, the windows of the flat-fronted buildings reflected the tranquil, cloud-studded sky. Young trees lined the lane but offered no cover to any lurking villain who might have followed them from the park. Not even a bird could have hidden in their leafless branches.

Satisfied, he strode around the building and down the narrow, cobbled mews. The rhythmic ring of his bootheels rebounded off the brick and stone surfaces boxing him in; the familiar scents of horse and hay grew stronger.

When he reached the stable, Jordan found her driver more humiliated than wounded. The coachman's tricorn hat, lost in the fray, had protected him somewhat from the rock thrown at him. The cut that the missile had left on his forehead would not require stitches. It had stopped bleeding, and Jordan did not see any signs that the driver had suffered a concussion.

He announced to the anxious stable staff that Coachman Jack was going to be all right. The grooms gave him back his hat, then thanked him profusely for saving Her Ladyship and the child.

Jordan smiled and checked his horse to make sure the animal had not been injured in the melee. After determining that the white gelding was unscathed, he asked if one of the stable hands might carry a note to Sergeant Parker for him. This was quickly done. He jotted a few lines to Parker to come at once to Mara's address—armed—with however many men he had at hand. Then the young groom who had volunteered to act as his courier mounted one of the ponies and rushed off to deliver his summons posthaste.

Jordan figured they'd be here in less than half an hour. They were very efficient, and trained to be ready at a moment's notice. In the meanwhile, he sat down with the bruised and chastened coachman to get his version of how that startling row in Hyde Park had unfolded.

Jack's account comported with Jordan's own experience. "It's my fault, sir," the weathered fellow said in a heavy tone. "When I saw the crowd ahead, I should have known to go the other way."

"You had no cause to think they would turn violent," Jordan offered. "Besides, it's no mean trick to turn a coach-and-four around on that section of the Ring."

"Aye, sir," the man said gratefully. "But with His little Lordship in the coach! I would never forgive myself if he'd taken so much as a scratch."

"The boy's all right, and so are Lady Pierson and Mrs. Busby, too. They're shaken up a bit, but you're the one who got the worst of it," he said, nodding at Jack's forehead.

He pursed his lips grimly. "Nevertheless, I must go now and offer Her Ladyship my resignation. If you'll pardon, sir."

"I'm sure she won't accept it, but do as you see fit," Jordan answered, and Jack took leave of him with a slight bow. Clearly, the man felt terrible, but Jordan doubted that Mara would let him resign. She'd be a fool to cast aside such an obviously loyal servant.

Jordan remained in the stable so Jack could speak to his employer in private. But by the time he came out again wearing a look of relief that confirmed he had kept his position, Sergeant Parker was just arriving with three of his men.

The stableboy who had delivered the summons led the soldiers into the mews. Jordan walked out to meet them in the stable yard. He was pleased to see that Parker had brought Findlay, Mercer, and Wilkins with him, all good men.

"The Highlander's been looking for you this morning, sir," the sergeant informed him at once as he jumped down from his horse. "Seems your ruse at Christie's last week has already brought in a nibble from the big fish."

"Has it? Excellent news!" he murmured. Virgil must have received some sort of message from Falkirk.

"Master Virgil is waiting to give you the details in person," Parker added.

"Then I'd best get to Dante House without delay."

Jordan quickly explained what had happened in the park. "Understandably, Lady Pierson is quite shaken up by her ordeal. I sent for you lads to keep on eye on things here for a day or two in case those unruly bastards come looking to cause any further trouble."

"Right," Parker said tersely. The other men nodded, scowling at the barbarity of a mob attacking a lady and her child.

Jordan led her temporary bodyguards around to the front of the crescent, making a few suggestions for their patrol. "Don't forget to put the staff and stableboys to use, as well," he added. Every friendly pair of eyes and ears at their disposal would be helpful. They were experienced men, however, so he did not waste his breath belaboring them with his advice. Rohan himself had finished their training; they knew what they were doing.

For his part, knowing they were on duty, Jordan could now put Mara out of his mind—at least in theory—and get on with the Order's business. He was very keen to find out what news Virgil had for him. With any luck, they'd have Drake back in the Order's care by morning.

"Right, any questions?" he prompted.

The men shook their heads.

"Then come inside, and I'll present you to the viscountess. Once she meets you and sees that you're here, she will hopefully begin to feel a bit more secure. Then I can get over to Dante House and see what Virgil wants."

"Aye, sir."

Mara's butler let them in the front door. Jordan escorted them into the parlor, where he introduced Lady Pierson to his associates.

Seated in a yellow brocade armchair in the same front parlor where he had left her, she set aside the brandy snifter from which she had just taken a sip, no doubt to steady her nerves. Studying the new arrivals with caution, she was plainly still on guard after her ordeal, but he tried to put her mind at ease with a few references to the past loyal service of these brave men and so forth.

They bowed to her, in turn, and offered their regrets about the unpleasant events that had made their presence necessary. "We will try our best not to get in your way, milady. You won't even know we are here."

Parker turned to Jordan with a question in his eyes.

"What is it?" he asked.

"I'll want to check the first floor for possible entry points, sir, make sure everything's locked up properly. Also, I'll need to count the household staff and know in advance who'll be coming in or going out, at about what time."

Mara seemed to like what she heard. At the note of expertise in Parker's gruff voice, the tension in her face relaxed a bit. "My butler can assist you with all that, Sergeant." She gestured to the servant, who was standing attentively nearby. "Reese, show these able fellows around the house as they require. Gentlemen, I am grateful for your help."

The soldiers bowed to her, and after seeing the dark-eyed beauty they had been assigned to protect, they leaped to their task with all the more determination, Jordan wryly observed.

When the men had marched out after Reese to begin making sure her home was secure, Mara turned to him with a guarded look. "You're sure they're all right?"

"First-rate. Capital fellows. Why?"

She shrugged. "Giving four armed men the liberty of one's house is a tad disconcerting."

"If it's any consolation, their last assignment involved keeping watch over a duchess."

"Really? Anyone I'd know?" she asked in surprise.

He smiled. If Rohan had trusted them to mind Kate, he could certainly trust them with Mara. "I am not at liberty to say," he replied. "But I'm happy to report that Her Grace is in perfect health today, thanks in part to their vigilance."

"How exactly do you know these men?" Curiosity glimmered in her dark eyes. "Foreign Office fellows?"

"More or less. You know, we always need trained bodyguards to help look after visiting dignitaries and such. Important personages."

Still looking rather shaken, she cast him a wan smile. "I'm hardly that."

"You are to me." The utterance slipped out before he could stop it.

She lifted her eyebrows.

Jordan dropped his gaze to the floor and cleared his throat. "Well, I should be going. The excitement seems to have died down outside. You've got Sergeant Parker and his men here now on the off chance there's trouble. But I have to say, it really seems unlikely. I can ask around about that speaker and his circle, if you like. The Home Office is sure to have information—"

"No, thank you," she interrupted, shaking her head with a shudder. "I'm just glad it's over. Given that Jack's all right, and nobody else was hurt, I'd rather the whole nasty incident was forgotten. It's already going to be enough of a scandal as it is." She sighed. "I'm sure it'll be in all the papers by tomorrow."

Jordan absorbed this. "Not necessarily."

She tilted her head in question, but he was not at liberty to speak of the Order's discreet influence over London's major newspapers.

"Don't fret over it, my dear," he murmured, making a mental note to pay a little visit to the editors. "I'm sure they've got more important things to write about."

He'd make certain of it.

He was not above leaning on the newspaper chiefs to protect a lady's reputation—even if the crowd's salacious charge against her happened to be true.

Refusing to dwell anymore on her affair with the Regent, he realized he'd best be moving along, given all he had to do. "I shall bid you farewell, then." He nodded courteously to her, then headed for the door.

"Jordan—wait."

He turned around as she rose from her chair and took a step toward him.

"There's something I have to tell you." She gazed into his eyes, her own wide and dark. "I'm actually not the Regent's mistress," she confessed. She shook her head, holding his gaze. "We are only friends."

Holding his breath, he searched her face for a long moment. "Is this true?"

She nodded slowly.

"But why didn't you say so?" He furrowed his brow. "In the park, when I confronted you, you didn't deny it."

Her lovely shoulders lifted in a shrug. "What good would it have done? I could see you had already made up your mind about me—and you're always so sure you're right. Begging you to believe me seemed, I don't know. Distasteful."

Jordan stared at her, uncertain what to think.

"The truth is, the Regent has done me a kindness I can never repay. That is why I have not been very adamant in trying to put down the rumor. I don't wish to offend someone who has been such a good friend to me. Ever since my husband's death, you see, His Royal Highness has rather styled himself my chivalrous protector—but not in *that* sense. I'm sure as a diplomat, you've noticed how sensitive royal egos can be," she said. "Until today, there seemed no real harm in letting the gossips talk."

Jordan considered her words intently. "May I ask what the Regent's done to earn such gratitude from you?"

She drifted closer with a nod. "After my husband died, his relatives tried to take Thomas away from me."

"*What?*"

"The Piersons felt entitled to take charge of my son, the better to groom him for his future role as the family's title-holder. They never much cared for me," she admitted in a lower tone, eyeing him ruefully. "Pierson, well, he was always the man-about-town, and in his youth, he was one of the prince's boon companions. He died several months before my son was born." Mara lowered her gaze to the marble floor. "Poor Thomas . . . he came into this world without a father. I had only my servants and the midwife with me when I gave birth to him at our country house. Not that my husband would've been much consolation in my labor, knowing him."

Jordan stared at her, struck by the thought of her as a young woman alone in her moment of greatest need, going through the agony of childbirth alone. Or at least, without her husband to protect and comfort her.

"At any rate, when Thomas was born, the Prince Regent agreed to stand as my son's godfather as a tribute to his old friend. That's why His Royal Highness has taken an interest in Thomas from the start. When Pierson's relatives began putting pressure on me to try to take the baby, I fought them as long as I could, but I was alone and afraid. At last, I could not think what else to do but to throw myself on the mercy of my child's royal godfather."

Jordan reached out and touched her elbow in wordless consolation.

She met his gaze warily, folding her arms across her waist. "The Regent could not have been more of a hero to me as soon as he heard of my plight."

Was that a trace of rebuke he read in her eyes? Jordan wondered. And why, for heaven's sake, had he begun feeling guilty as shc told him all this?

"He used his influence to stop my kin from pressuring me and helped me to gain a more favorable settlement. Thanks to His Royal Highness, Pierson's family will not gain more control over Thomas until he is of schooling age. So, you see, this is why I am indebted to him. After what he did for me and my son, I tell you, I'd walk through fire for that man—I don't care who despises him, or who claims he's just a buffoon. He's got a good heart, and for my part, I'll always be his friend. But I can assure you, I am not sharing his bed."

"Mara—" he started, chastened, but she cut him off.

"I don't care what they think of me out there, either," she added, nodding toward the door. "I cared enough about people's opinions when I was a girl. I can withstand their disapproval—but I do care what you think, especially after you risked your neck for my son and me back there in the park. I'm not the Regent's doxy. The truth is, I have no lover. Nor," she added pointedly, "do I want one."

He blinked.

"Thomas is all that matters to me now," she said.

"I see," Jordan murmured.

Beyond that, he did not know what to say. Taken aback by her preemptive rejection, he dropped his gaze, but he could still feel her watching him.

Well! It seemed he had just been told—politely, of course—but in no uncertain terms, that just in case he was even thinking about it, Mara's answer was already no.

Was he thinking about it?

If so, she had put that notion to rest.

Of course, when he recalled the harsh words he had said to her in the park, he could hardly blame her. Indeed, for a man who prided himself on his chivalry, he could only cringe at his uncivilized flash of temper back there by the Serpentine before they had parted ways. He had used finer terms, but had more or less called her a lying whore. *God.* And they thought the Regent was a bumbler?

"I apologize for accusing you unjustly, Lady Pierson," he forced out in a wooden tone. "I had no right to judge you. I should not have been so quick to believe the talk—"

"It's all right," she cut him off with an idle wave of her hand. "Believe me, the whole thing is already forgotten. I cannot possibly hold a grudge against anyone who would help protect my son."

Her magnanimity further confounded him as this was neither selfish nor vain; yet her clear smile told him she was sincere. As he studied her, it dawned on him that perhaps he had been more wrong about her than he had realized.

The Earl of Falconridge was not at all accustomed to being wrong. "Well, er—I should be going," he mumbled, eager to retreat and attempt to regroup. "I'll be back when I can to check on things here."

"I don't mean to impose on your time."

"It's no trouble." He gazed at her for a heartbeat longer, wondering if he really knew this woman at all. He had thought he did, but now he wondered if, over time, he had merely begun to believe in his own lies about her—the ones he had told himself so that he could bear having lost her.

"What is it?" she asked, watching him with curious amusement in her sparkly brown eyes. "You look confused."

"I am," he said.

"Why?"

"I'm not sure I deserve your forgiveness so easily. I acted badly in the park. Some of the things I said . . . well, I wouldn't have been surprised if you had slapped me."

She flashed a grin. "Can't say it didn't cross my mind."

Jordan couldn't help smiling back at her, ruefully.

It seemed his Mara was still as unpredictable as ever. Perhaps that was part of why he had always been so endlessly fixed on her. Unlike the enemy codes he was so fond of deciphering, he could never quite figure her out.

He shook his head to himself as he went to the door. "I'll be back later," he told her with a smile over his shoulder, already anticipating his return.

"We'll see," she replied with an arch smile, folding her arms across her chest.

He frowned at her over his shoulder, then he let himself out the front door. But as he strode back to the stables, suddenly, his heart was light. So, she was not the Regent's mistress, after all! Thank God. Not that she was interested in *him,* he reminded himself in amusement. Her Ladyship had made that very clear, indeed. Of course, as a spy, he had a particular talent for persuasion . . .

Don't even think about it.

With a nod to the grooms, he swung up into the saddle and rode off, still smiling like a fool.

Time to see what dark work Virgil had for him tonight.

From the window, Mara watched him ride away on his fine white horse. Still smiling to herself, she couldn't help wondering if perhaps there really *was* some Prince Charming left in him, after all.

But she wasn't getting her hopes up. Time would tell.

Maybe he'd come back, and maybe he would not.

For her part, she was still astonished at how he had single-handedly held off a mob swarming her carriage. And then could boast medical training, to boot? Her mild-mannered diplomat!

When he disappeared down the street, she turned away from the window shaking her head to herself, intrigued.

Where on earth did he learn to fight like that?

Chapter 6

TWO A.M.

The white winter moon in a black velvet sky turned the streets of London blue. The stars paraded over the equestrian statue of King Charles I at Charing Cross.

The familiar landmark crowned the broad, three-way intersection where the Strand met Whitehall and Cockspur Street. The normally busy crossroads seemed like a foreign place, deserted at this late hour; but, as Virgil had informed them at the meeting earlier in the day, it was the spot James Falkirk had designated for the exchange.

The Alchemist's Scrolls in exchange for Drake.

At any moment, Falkirk was expected.

Jordan stood at full alert, pistol drawn, his sword also at the ready, his foot resting atop the kingwood case containing the Alchemist's Scrolls. The dim streetlamps lit his dissolving clouds of breath as he waited in the stillness for the enemy to show.

Virgil was with him, a few feet away, leaning against the wrought-iron fence that surrounded the imposing monument to the murdered king. Meanwhile, hidden amid the shadows around the intersection's sprawling plaza, Max and Beauchamp waited with rifles to give them cover if needed: There were no guarantees this wasn't a trap.

Jordan continued scanning the dark streets through narrowed eyes, but his thoughts revolved around the rumored power struggle taking place among the Promethean elites.

The Order's sources indicated that Falkirk had begun quietly building alliances with other Promethean lords to make a stand against their current leader, Malcolm Banks.

Who, in turn, happened to be Virgil's brother.

Malcolm Banks was notoriously brutal; the Order viewed James Falkirk as the lesser of two evils. Therefore, Virgil had made it clear at the meeting that afternoon that their chief objective for tonight was to get Drake back.

Falkirk was not to be touched.

"*If he really means to overthrow Malcolm, we will not stand in his way,*" Virgil had instructed them earlier at Dante House. "*Falkirk can do more damage from the inside than we can from without. Even if he fails to take over the Promethean Council, all of them will be weakened by their internal struggle. We'll just stand back and let the two factions tear each other apart for a while. Then, when their strength is spent, we'll descend and finish the bastards off. But above all, first we've got to get Drake out of there.*"

Jordan suddenly tensed, hearing the distant rumble of a carriage. Virgil and he turned toward the sound.

As it grew louder, the Highlander sent him a dark nod. Jordan lifted the deep, shapeless hood of the black cloak spilling from his shoulders. Then he concealed his face with an expressionless black mask, like those worn by Carnival revelers. The Order had invested too much time and effort in every high-placed agent to risk needlessly exposing their identities.

Virgil did not follow suit, for his face was already known to their foes.

As the hackney rolled closer, Jordan's heart beat faster to think he was actually about to meet the second-ranking member of the Promethean hierarchy.

James Falkirk was something of a legend. Even some in the Order believed that the old eccentric could actually make the Prometheans' black magic work, as if he were some sort of latter-day sorcerer.

Malcolm's only interest in the centuries-old Promethean cult was as a means of gaining raw, worldly power, but Falkirk was a true believer in all their occult mumbo jumbo. Jordan wasn't sure which was worse.

In the next moment, the hackney rolled to a halt right in front of them, the moonlight sliding over its ebony surface. The driver kept his place up on the box, staring straight ahead, but the door swung open.

A small light glowed from within.

Jordan was keenly attuned to his watching brother agents posted in the shadows, covering them, as Virgil stepped up cautiously into the carriage.

Jordan holstered his pistol, picked up the ancient wooden box of scrolls, then followed the Highlander into the coach. He sat beside him, resting the wooden box on his lap.

Across from them, the coach held only one other occupant: a lean and patrician older fellow with a shock of pewter hair. "Welcome, gentlemen," said Falkirk. "No sudden movements, please. As you can see, I am armed."

Jordan had already noted the pistol aimed at them from amid the folds of Falkirk's black greatcoat.

"That won't be necessary," Virgil growled.

Falkirk smiled serenely. "I trust you brought my prize."

"It's here," Jordan said in a toneless voice from behind the mask.

"Good." Falkirk turned to his handler. "You must be Virgil Banks. Yes, I can see the family resemblance. By Lucifer," he said with a soft laugh, "did you know that Malcolm's grown son, Niall, has that same fiery red hair as yours? A Banks family trait, I presume?"

"Where is my agent?" Virgil answered dully.

"Let me see the scrolls first."

Jordan obliged him, opening the case.

Falkirk leaned closer; reaching into the box, he poked among the scrolls, examining them, murmuring to himself over certain symbols that must have confirmed to his satisfaction that, indeed, the documents were authentic.

His gray eyes lit up with incredulity as he met Virgil's stare. "Is this the full collection, on your honor?"

"This is everything we found," Jordan answered on his handler's behalf.

"But of course you made a copy for yourselves."

"Of course," he said.

"You were the one who did the translation?"

"I was," he said.

Falkirk smiled wanly, the lines of age in his bony face deepening. "Well, there are subtleties in these texts that your kind will never grasp."

Jordan shrugged, on his guard. "I did my best to decipher them in the limited time I had."

"Order whelp!" The old eccentric snorted. "You could study these Scrolls for a lifetime and still not penetrate their mysteries. Valerian the Alchemist was a brilliant thinker—"

"And a bit of a lunatic, what?"

"Nonsense, his genius rivaled the likes of Leonardo da Vinci's!"

"To the best of my knowledge, Leonardo was not a proponent of human sacrifice," Jordan said dryly, but Falkirk merely laughed.

"Ah, you disapprove of our revered Alchemist's writings? What would you say if I told you the bit about virgin sacrifice was just a metaphor?"

"I wouldn't believe you."

Falkirk's smile widened. "Then perhaps you're smarter than you look. But tell me, my fine scholar-knight, were you not at all tempted by the ancient knowledge you glimpsed in these papers?"

"Not really. At least now I know how to summon a demon if I should ever need one."

"You mock me!" Falkirk reproached him lightly. "Why do you dismiss what you do not understand?" He shook his head. "It is a sad thing to find such a lack of imagination in one so young."

"Where is Drake?" Jordan repeated Virgil's question.

"Nearer than you think." Falkirk nodded toward the intersection. "Just there, at the Golden Cross Inn. You will find him in Room 22."

Virgil nodded to Jordan, who jumped out of the hackney at once and stalked over to where Max was leaning against a building with his rifle in his hands and impatience gleaming in his silvery eyes.

Jordan quickly relayed the message, gesturing toward the nearby inn. "Let me know when you've got him," he said tersely.

They nodded, Max beckoned Beau over, then both agents dashed into the famous coaching inn at Charing Cross.

Jordan stalked back to the carriage. He was not about to leave Virgil alone in there; moreover, he was determined to pick Falkirk's brain while he had the chance. There was one problem in particular Jordan needed to solve.

Dresden Bloodwell had wandered the streets of London long enough, roaming through the shadows like a wolf, looking for those he could devour.

"What can you tell me about Bloodwell?" he asked Falkirk as he rejoined the two older men.

"I did not come here for an interview," Falkirk huffed.

"Come," Jordan insisted. "Is Bloodwell loyal to Malcolm, or have you persuaded him to join your little insurrection? Oh, yes, we know all about your plans," he said, bluffing as to the degree of certainty the Order had about Falkirk's scheme.

But when the old fellow raised his eyebrows, Jordan took it as confirmation.

"The Order has no plans to stand in your way," he assured him, determined to win a little of Falkirk's trust. "That's why we haven't taken you captive tonight," he added in a reasonable tone. "We easily could have."

The old man eyed him suspiciously. "You want to know about Bloodwell?"

"Actually, I want to kill him," Jordan said.

"Do you, indeed? To be sure, I would find that most convenient, myself. But can you? Dresden Bloodwell is as ruthless as they come."

"Well, Falkirk," he answered softly, "I can be rather ruthless myself when the occasion calls."

"Let me see your face, and I will tell you what I know," Falkirk challenged him.

"No," Virgil ordered, but Jordan weighed the risk against the possible gains and slowly lowered his mask.

Virgil growled his disapproval while Falkirk studied Jordan's face, looking pleased. "Well, you are brave, aren't you?" the old man murmured.

"What of Bloodwell?" Jordan prompted.

"Bloodwell answers to Malcolm for now. But I do not think his loyalty runs deep."

"Does that mean you intend to persuade him to your side?"

"No." Falkirk shook his head with a slight shudder. "I keep my distance from that creature. Malcolm believes he can keep control of his pet assassin, but if you ask me, Bloodwell is out for himself alone."

"Where does he make his headquarters?" Jordan pursued.

"He doesn't stay in one place for more than a few days. Bloodwell knows what he's doing. He is not a man whom I would lightly cross," he added with a warning look.

Virgil nudged him. "Go and see what's happening with Drake."

Jordan obeyed, leaving the carriage again. They could not let Falkirk leave until they were sure he had kept his end of the bargain.

He jogged across the square to the Golden Cross Inn, where Max and Beau were just now maneuvering out of the establishment's front door with a semiconscious Drake sagging between them like a drunk.

"Is hc hurt? What's wrong with him?" Jordan exclaimed as he opened the door of the Order's waiting carriage.

The other two carried Drake toward it.

"Drugged, I think," said Max. "Not sure yet." They hoisted Drake into the coach.

Beau turned around, standing guard, while Max stepped up into the carriage and checked Drake's pulse, listened to his shallow breathing, and pulled up his eyelids.

Drake mumbled incoherently and tried to brush Max off with a vague wave of his hand.

"His pupils are dilated. They've definitely given him something."

"Poison?" Jordan clipped out.

"Could be."

"I'll go find out," Jordan said in taut anger, dashing back to

Falkirk. *That bastard!* Wouldn't it be just like a Promethean to give Drake back to them with hours to live from poison in his blood? As soon as he reached the hackney coach parked in the shadows at Charing Cross, he threw open the door. "What have you done to him?" he demanded of Falkirk, then glanced at Virgil. "Drake is unresponsive."

"There is no need for alarm," Falkirk soothed. "I merely slipped a bit of laudanum in his drink—and I daresay, you should thank me. You'd never be able to control him otherwise."

"What do you mean by that?"

"I mean that when he wakes up, he is probably going to fight you."

"Why?" Jordan demanded.

"He does not know you anymore! He'll wonder where I've gone. Do not be surprised if the poor lad pleads with you to see me."

"To see *you*? After you tortured him?"

"I'm the one who made his torture stop," Falkirk clipped out. "You must understand, Drake has forgotten everything from his old life. He trusts me because I removed him from his prison cell and had our doctors nurse him back to health. He has become quite devoted to me, he looks on me like a father, and I'm warning you now, he is not going to like being parted from me."

"That is preposterous!" Jordan spat.

But Falkirk eyed the Highlander ruefully. "You trained him well as a fighter, Virgil. I'm told when he was captured, it took half a dozen men to bring him down. You spoke of summoning demons," Falkirk added with a glance at Jordan. "Well, Drake is like one himself, or a wild creature, at its most dangerous when cornered."

Jordan swore under his breath, shook his head, and turned away angrily, wondering what the hell the Prometheans had done to their brother warrior. He leveled a bitter glance at Falkirk. "So, you're saying he's out of his head."

"More or less, I'm afraid, yes. But he's really very dear, at least when he's calm. What can I say? I have grown fond of the boy. I wish him well."

"But the only reason you're giving him back to us is because he's of no use as a source of information without his memory! You're just using him as a pawn so you could get the Scrolls."

"It's nothing personal. Besides." Falkirk paused. "I owe the lad. He saved my life, as you've probably heard."

"Aren't you afraid of what he might tell us after you have gone?" Jordan challenged him.

"You are not hearing me!" Falkirk said with a burst of impatience. "The Drake you knew is gone! I cannot speak of the agent he once was, but the man he is today, well—you will soon find he has become—how shall I say?—like a child."

"A demon, a wild creature, or a child, Falkirk—why don't you make up your mind?" Jordan bit out.

"Fine. You'll just have to see for yourselves when the laudanum wears off in the morning." Falkirk glanced at the Order's chief. "Do not put him back in the battle, Virgil. He's already been through enough. Drake is finished as an agent. I only want him returned to his family so he can live out what's left of his life in peace."

"Oh, that's very big of you," Jordan muttered, shaking his head.

Falkirk suddenly lost patience with him. "Begone, both of you! Out of my carriage! And do not attempt to follow me," he snapped. "I must be on my way before I'm seen by any of Malcolm's spies. Especially Bloodwell."

Jordan stepped aside so Virgil could climb out, but the red-haired Scotsman paused.

"Falkirk, if my brother should learn of your plan, you know he will kill you. We can offer you protection, if you'll turn informant—"

Falkirk snorted in derision at this offer, pulling the door shut in Virgil's face. Jordan and he exchanged a cynical look as Falkirk's hackney pulled away.

They then ran over to the carriage where Max was still sitting with their unconscious fellow agent.

"Laudanum," Jordan confirmed. "If Falkirk is to be believed."

Virgil got into the carriage and began examining Drake. "Poor lad," the Highlander said gruffly under his breath. "Let's get him back to Dante House."

"Sir, if you can spare me, there's something I have to take care of now that the mission's complete."

"What is it?"

Jordan shook his head. Trusted agent that he was, his somber expression was enough to gain his handler's cooperation.

"Very well. You played your part in the exchange. We're unlikely to make more progress until this one wakes up." He glanced sadly at Drake. "We'll meet tomorrow morning, and you'll all receive your next orders."

"Aye, sir."

Max cocked a curious eyebrow at Jordan, but in answer, he merely sent his team leader a wry look as he cast off his cloak. He tossed it into the carriage along with his mask.

Beneath the cloak, he was clad all in black and armed to the teeth.

He shut the carriage door, nodded farewell, then watched them drive away. When they had gone, he cast a cold, speculative glance eastward toward the City.

It was time to pay a little nocturnal visit to the newspaper editors.

* * *

The next morning, Mara waited on tenterhooks as her butler, Reese, scanned the morning edition of the London *Times*.

She couldn't bear to look for herself.

While Thomas circled the breakfast table towing his wooden pull-toy pony after him, she watched in nervous agitation as her butler read the paper.

His spectacles perched on the bridge of his pointy nose, Reese stood by the window poring over each page by the golden morning sunlight streaming in.

"There is an article on the riot, my lady," he announced at length, "but it has no mention of you or Lord Falconridge."

"Really? Are you sure? Here, try this one." She handed him the *Post*—the newspaper notorious for its Society gossip page.

This was the hateful journalists' chance to tell the whole world that her carriage had been attacked because the mob had believed her to be the Regent's mistress. If the lie took hold, who knew if there would be more attacks on her, thanks to the people's dislike of the Regent?

Who could say, moreover, what damage the rumor's exploding like this could do to her reputation in Society?

What her mother would say, she could barely bring herself to imagine.

Her pulse pounded as Reese skimmed the second paper.

"'Tis the same," he confirmed a few moments later. "The rally was covered, but they made no mention of the attack on your coach. Not a word about His Lordship or yourself, ma'am. The report skips straight to the dragoons' arrival."

"It's a miracle," she breathed, slumping with relief.

"So it would seem, milady." Reese folded the paper neatly and set it down before her. "Perhaps a certain high-placed friend stopped them from dragging your name into it," he suggested with a shrewd look.

But she shook her head, puzzled. The Prince Regent had no success whatsoever in stopping the papers from lampooning him, so why would the journalists hesitate to throw mud at her as well? Especially when a whiff of salacious gossip helped them sell more papers.

Either they had somehow missed it, or something more mysterious was afoot. Jordan had seemed very sure it would not appear in the papers. Could he have had something to do with this, or was that just Jordan being right as usual?

Reese took off his spectacles. "Another thought, ma'am."

"Yes?" She glanced at him worriedly.

He took a delicate tone. "Perhaps they're holding it for the evening edition."

"Oh." Mara winced. "Perhaps you're right."

It was going to be a long day.

As soon as Jordan stepped into Dante House later that morning, he heard a commotion from upstairs: shouting, a loud bang like some large piece of furniture being upended, followed by the sound of shattering glass.

"Let me *go*!"

"Ah," he murmured to himself. *Drake's up.* He ran up the ornately carved wooden staircase to see if the others needed help with their returned agent, the supposed lunatic.

Striding down the upper hallway, he spotted Beau leaning idly by the wall across from one of the secure chambers, which had reinforced doors and iron bars on the windows. "I take it the laudanum's worn off."

"You could say that."

"Let me out of here!" Drake roared from inside the room. "I swear I'll kill you—"

"Calm down." Max's voice came from inside the chamber with him. "You're not going to kill me, Drake. We've been friends since we were ten years old. Don't you remember our school days up in Scotland—"

"I don't know you, man! Why are you lying to me? You let me the hell out of here! This is an asylum, isn't it? Why won't you listen to me? I'm not mad!"

"Damn," Jordan murmured, exchanging a grim glance with Beauchamp. He stepped toward the open door, leaning behind the butler to get a look into the room.

Poor Mr. Gray, with tray in hand, was standing uncertainly at the threshold of Drake's chamber, attempting to bring the wild-eyed earl some food.

Drake paused in his agitated pacing to lob another missile across the chamber with deadly aim and admirable speed.

Max ducked, smiling as the pewter candlestick slammed against the wall behind him, leaving a fist-sized hole in the plaster. "Ha! You see that? You've still got your skills, my lad! At least the bastards couldn't beat that out of you, could they? All your training. You may have forgotten us for now, but I know you're still you in there. It's going to be all right, Drake. Try to calm down. Why don't you have some breakfast?"

"Stay away from me," he warned, continuing to back away from Max. "You think I'm going to let you poison me?"

Jordan shook his head.

Drake, poor bastard, looked like hell. His coal black eyes were red-rimmed and full of quite tormented rage and confusion. Chest heaving with his efforts to attack anyone who got too close, he was flushed and sweaty, his black hair mussed, as though he had gone into this panic immediately upon waking.

He obviously did not know *where* he was—and did not look altogether sure of *who* he was, either.

"Don't give him any utensils," Beau muttered to the butler, who still did not dare venture into the room.

"Ah," said Gray with a blanch. "Good thinking, my lord. A spoon?"

"I wouldn't," Jordan said with a meaningful look. "No glass dishes, either."

The butler gulped. "Yes, sir."

All of them, including Drake, were trained to use whatever availed as a weapon. The handle end of a spoon could easily serve as a shank. A shard of broken glass from a perfectly innocent china plate could cut an enemy's throat or be plunged into his eye.

In short, it had been quite civil of Falkirk to warn them that Drake would not come back to them happily.

"If you don't let me out of here, I'm going to—"

"Drake, this is where you belong! You're one of us! Please, try to remember."

"I belong with James. Where is he?" he demanded, his expression turning even more frantic. "Please, he's an old man! If you say you are my friend, then let me go to him. He is in danger!"

"James wants you to stay with us, Drake. He drugged you and handed you over to us last night."

"I don't believe you! He wouldn't do that to me!"

When he abruptly hurled another object at Max's head, however, Virgil took command.

"That will do, sir!" the Highlander boomed, also inside the room with them. "If you cannot restrain yourself, then you will *be* restrained!"

Drake backed up a step at this threat, glaring at him.

"Now sit down and mind your manners, or you're not going to get any food! Understand?"

"I'm not hungry," Drake growled in defiance.

"Aye, then, no matter, Lord Westwood. Sooner or later,

you will be." Virgil dismissed the butler with a wave of his hand, then nodded to Max to leave the room.

He did so, then Virgil joined them in the hallway a moment later, pausing to lock the door.

"He'll be secure in there?" Jordan asked.

Virgil nodded.

But Max could only shake his head. "He's worse off than I thought."

"You just keep him from hurting himself," Virgil instructed their team leader. "Who knows what secrets about our foes are locked inside that head of his?"

Beau nodded. "Like what happened to his team? How did he get captured?"

"Beauchamp, stay here and send for us if he starts having another temper tantrum. You two, come down to the Pit, and we'll go over your assignments."

"Yes, sir."

With that, they repaired to the stone-carved meeting room in the Order's covert lair dug into the limestone under Dante House.

"Rotherstone," Virgil started, turning to Max as they took their places around the table, "you're in charge of finding a way to help Drake get his memory back."

Max nodded. "Once he settles down, I want to take him to his family estate, where he was born. The Dowager Countess of Westwood is still living there. If he's ever going to remember anyone, surely he'll remember his own mother."

"Good. Falconridge," Virgil continued, glancing at Jordan, "you're going to have to take over the project Rotherstone was working on, in addition to your ongoing efforts to locate Dresden Bloodwell."

"Yes, sir." He knew that Max had been assigned to monitor Albert Carew, a leading dandy, who had just inherited his brother's dukedom under rather mysterious circumstances.

Because of where and how the previous duke's death had taken place, Promethean involvement was suspected.

"Here, you'll need these." Max slid his file on Albert across the table to Jordan. "Good riddance," he muttered.

"Now, Falconridge, I'm not sure how much you already know about the case, but it's not his brother's death that rouses our suspicion," Virgil said. "Ever since Albert became the new Duke of Holyfield, he's been insinuating himself into the Prince Regent's inner circle."

"He's quite the toady to the Regent," Max agreed, "though, God knows, he's intolerably arrogant to everyone else."

"Has the Regent been made privy to our suspicions about Albert?" Jordan asked.

"God, no. I'm afraid His Royal Highness is an open book. He knows who his Order agents are, and he'll likely realize you're there because something must be afoot; but he knows better than to ask. He's familiar with how these things go, having been through similar threats to his security many times before. He trusts the Order. He'll wait for us to tell him when the situation has been cleared. In the meantime, if he knew our suspicions about Albert, chances are, his own behavior would tip the blackguard off straightaway."

"Aye, and if Albert were to realize we're onto him, he's likely to flee the country," Virgil chimed in. "Then we'll never find out what the Prometheans put him there to accomplish. That's why I want you on this matter, Falconridge. Albert has already decided he despises Rotherstone, but you've got a way with people. You'll have to overcome his wariness, make friends with him. Draw the bastard out. Win his trust. That would be ideal."

"I'll do my best. All I need is the opportunity. Is he a member at White's?"

Max snorted. "Haven't you seen him posing in the bay window there so the passersby can admire his clothes? Horse's ass," he muttered.

"Forget White's," Virgil said with an impatient wave of his hand. "More to the point, he's not only a regular visitor to Carlton House but now has also joined the Regent's weekly card game at Watier's."

"So I need to buy into that card game. How much is this going to cost me?"

"Ten thousand pounds."

Jordan laughed. "That's madness."

"Welcome to the wonderful world of Prinny."

"I take it you'll introduce me?" Jordan asked Max.

"No," Virgil interjected. "I don't want Albert drawing that strong a connection between the two of you. Rotherstone leaving just as you're coming in. It'll instantly raise his suspicions. If Albert's worming his way into Carlton House in order to aid the Prometheans, for whatever reason, he's already going to be on his guard. You've got a better chance of winning his trust and figuring out what he's up to if you join the Carlton House set from a completely different direction." Virgil gave him a hard look. "You'll use your contact with Lady Pierson as your cover."

Jordan stared at him in shock. "Come again?"

"Lady Pierson," his handler repeated with a no-nonsense look. "You were on very warm terms with her years ago, as I quite recall. These days she is the Regent's bosom friend. She's at Carlton House every week, as Max's file notes. You will pursue her as your cover," Virgil said. "That's how you'll gain access to the Carlton House set."

Jordan was already shaking his head. "Sir, no, with all

due respect. I am not dragging her into this. You cannot ask this of me."

"What makes you think I'm asking?" Virgil's bushy eyebrows drew together in a warning glower. "These are your orders, Falconridge. This is the best plan. You already have a connection, and no one in the palace will suspect her."

Heart pounding, Jordan cast about for some way out of this. "But she's thought to be the Regent's mistress! Why would I be following her around?"

"Actually," Max spoke up in a delicate tone, "all the Carlton House insiders know there's nothing going on between her and the Regent. Virgil's right, Jord. It is the best plan."

"Well, I'm not doing it." He rose from the table and started to walk away.

"You are not at liberty to refuse your orders, Falconridge!"

"When have I ever done *that*?" he bit out, swinging around to face them from a few feet away. He was shaking with cold fury. "How dare you ask this of me? You're the one, Virgil, who advised me to stay away from her all those years ago! Now you stand there telling me to pursue her?"

"I'm only telling you to *appear* to pursue her," he replied, without the slightest emotion on his face.

Exactly what Jordan had vowed never to become.

He shook his head. "You don't know what you're asking of me."

"Of course he does," Max murmured.

He shot Max a suspicious look. His team leader met his gaze matter-of-factly but said nothing.

Fuming, Jordan walked away.

He stalked out of the cavelike meeting room and down the dark tunnel hewn into the limestone, going to stand on the small dock that gave access to the river from underneath the house.

Heart pounding, he folded his arms across his chest and stared down into the murky water. He shook his head to himself again in silent fury. This was beyond the pale.

The sound of slow, deliberate footfalls approaching down the short tunnel to the docks heralded Max's arrival.

Jordan listened but did not turn around. "This was your idea, wasn't it? It's got Rotherstone written all over it."

"I thought it might suit your sense of efficiency," his brother warrior replied. "Kill two birds with one stone."

He turned to him. "What the hell is that supposed to mean?"

"You know exactly what it means." Max stared at him. "Stop lying to yourself. Damn it, man, I've watched you pine for this woman for twelve years. Now you have the chance to win her back *and* complete your mission."

Jordan huffed in angry embarrassment, looking away, but his friend was not through.

"Listen to me. I'm speaking to you as a brother now. Half the men in London have their eye on her. She's beautiful, available. If you don't pursue her while you have the chance, and she becomes involved with someone else, how are you going to live with losing her again?"

Jordan absorbed this, but the prospect of putting his heart on the line again with her rattled him more than Max could know. "This is none of your damned business."

"No, it's very much my business, you see. Because it was your loyalty to me and Warrington that did this to you. You never complained, you never said it aloud. You never had to. I know you wanted to quit the Order to be with her. But you stuck by us, and this is the price you've paid. It's not fair. Do you have any idea how guilty I feel, especially now that I have Daphne, and can finally grasp the full extent of what you gave up for us?"

Jordan stared at the ground, saying nothing.

"I was too young back then to understand what it meant that you had found her. You had found the one." Max shook his head pensively. "You were always so much farther ahead of Warrington and me. That's probably why you knew you couldn't leave us to our own devices out there. We just wanted to tear up the enemy; but you knew what really mattered in life. At least you used to."

Jordan looked at him.

"Now, you know I'm a man who always pays my debts," Max continued. "That's why, as your team leader, I fully support Virgil in making you do this—and yes, it was my idea. You've always been in love with Mara Bryce. But as detached from everything as you've become over the years, I figured you might need a nudge."

"So this is your brilliant solution—you and Virgil want me to use her?"

"Use her? Jordan, your lady is frequenting the same circles as a suspected Promethean spy. I would think you'd want to be there personally to *protect* her."

He eyed Max uneasily. But the conniving blackguard had a point. "Then, at least, let me tell her the truth."

"You know that you can't do that."

"Why not? You told Daphne. Warrington told Kate. Why am I the only one who ever seems to play by the rules?"

"I didn't tell Daphne anything until *after* I had married her. As for Kate, her grandfather was a member of the Prometheans. There were certain things she already knew. Moreover, Rohan didn't fill in the gaps in her knowledge until she was already devoted to him. This is in stark contrast to you and Mara, who are barely on speaking terms at present."

"We're speaking," he mumbled, dragging his hand wearily through his hair. "Yesterday, we reached a sort of . . . preliminary truce."

"Good, then you're halfway there!" Max exclaimed with an encouraging smile that rather annoyed Jordan. "Anyway, telling her the truth wouldn't stop her from going to Carlton House if I read her correctly. She's already proved her loyalty to the Regent even in the face of adversity. What she sees in him, I cannot say, but I understand he is her child's godfather."

Jordan nodded. "That is true."

"If you were to tell her there's a spy in the Regent's inner circle, you know it would only make her all the more determined to stand by His Royal Highness in a show of support. The less she knows, the safer she'll be. Telling her would only jeopardize the mission and put her in greater danger."

"I don't know . . ." Arms folded across his chest, Jordan stared down at the water lapping against the shallow dock. "Haven't I hurt her enough for the sake of the Order? I disappointed her twelve years ago, and now you want me to use her for my cover? Isn't that adding insult to injury?"

"Fine, then! Refuse the task and let your beautiful Mara walk into danger alone every time she goes to Carlton House. Why should you be bothered to protect her? I'll ask Beau to look after her instead. I'm sure once he lays eyes on her, he'll be more than happy to oblige."

"Ha. That pup," Jordan muttered, not appreciating the ploy. "She'd make mincemeat of him."

"Maybe so, but I daresay he'd enjoy it in the process." Max watched him shrewdly for a long moment.

Jordan sighed.

"So, we can count on you, then?"

"You're a bastard," he informed him.

"Anything for a brother," Max replied with a knowing smile. "You want my advice?" he asked over his shoulder as he began strolling away.

"Not in the slightest."

"Treat her like gold this time. Don't let her get away again, or you'll regret it for the rest of your miserable life."

Well, he was probably right about that.

Jordan stood alone in the dim torchlight for a long moment after Max had gone. Hell, maybe the conniving fiend was right. Maybe he'd never find peace until Mara was truly his. He took a deep breath and exhaled it in judicious measure. *Right. Best get moving, then.*

It seemed he had his work cut out for him.

After the long tense day, a celebratory mood lightened the Pierson household, for the evening edition of the London papers had made no mention the attack on her carriage and her rescue by Lord Falconridge.

Her dignity was spared!

Mara felt as though the weight of a blacksmith's anvil had been lifted off her back. She was free to enjoy the evening doting on her son.

Thomas opened his mouth, waiting for the next spoonful of applesauce as he sat in his high chair, cheerfully kicking his feet. He was covered in the stuff, having smeared it everywhere in his stubborn efforts to feed himself; but he was, as always, delighted by her attention.

Mara went on talking to him, trying to get him to practice his words between bites. For her part, she had barely touched her food, though tea and a light repast were laid out on the parlor table. Being on edge all day had robbed her of her appetite.

"Milady!" All of a sudden, as if to crown the day's triumphs, Mrs. Busby looked over from the window. "Your visitor's just arrived." She nodded toward the street.

Mara drew in her breath. "Lord Falconridge?"

"Aye, ma'am. I'll see to the boy." The old nurse bustled over and began wiping the applesauce off Thomas's face, making his sunny countenance more presentable for their visitor.

Mara glanced in the mirror over the sideboard, hurrying to smooth her hair and to brighten her cheeks with a few light pinches. "Reese," she said absently to the butler, "show Lord Falconridge in straightaway."

"Yes, madam." As her butler walked back to the foyer to receive the earl, Mara peeked out the window.

Jordan had just ridden up astride his white hunter, both man and horse lit by the ruddy brilliance of sunset.

He had scarcely reined in outside the crescent when Sergeant Parker strode out to greet him.

Mara watched her caller in blushing admiration, her pulse racing. Clad in a dark blue coat with nankeen breeches and black boots, Jordan dismounted from his horse with a graceful swing. As he alighted, a groom from her stables ran out to take his horse. To be sure, after his rescue of their lady and young lord yesterday, the whole staff had decided Lord Falconridge was their hero.

Mara's heart pounded as she watched him confer with her temporary bodyguards. When he nodded to the soldier and headed for the front door, she leaped back from the window to avoid being seen. Lord, what would he think to catch her ogling him like a seventeen-year-old!

A moment later, Reese returned to the parlor. "The Earl of Falconridge, my lady."

Mara lifted her chin and put her shoulders back, linking her hands across her waist in a graceful pose to stop herself from fidgeting with nervous excitement.

Jordan stepped into the room.

As he swept off his beaver hat, her heart skipped a beat.

"My lord." She greeted him with a modest curtsy.

He bowed, in turn, then he offered her a smile. "My lady. I am back, as promised, to see how you all are faring." He nodded fondly to Mrs. Busby.

He then raised an eyebrow when Thomas pointed at him with his little spoon and babbled a friendly but incoherent question.

Why, it appeared Thomas recognized him! Mara thought in surprise.

"And a fine good evening to *you*, Lord Pierson," Jordan answered the child.

Mara laughed, trying not to beam too much.

Jordan tossed her a sparkling glance. "I think he likes me."

"I do believe you're right."

"How are we all tonight, then? Recovered from yesterday's adventure?"

"We are," Mara answered. "And you?"

"Never better," he said lightly, setting his hat and riding gloves on the sideboard. That canny gaze of his never missed anything; it took in the open newspapers that she had left spread out there. He turned to her with a look of intrigue. "Parker tells me it was quiet overnight."

"Indeed." She gestured at the table. "May I offer you refreshments, my lord?"

He eyed the plate of cold cuts. "I could be tempted. How are you feeling today, Mrs. Busby? I was concerned about you yesterday. Any further chest pains?"

"No, thank ye, sir, I'm right as rain again." The old woman looked startled that a peer of the Realm should inquire after her health.

"And what of Thomas? Did he do all right last night after

that scare in the park? I trust our little master did not wake up crying with bad dreams."

"No, sir, he slept sound the whole night through," Mrs. Busby answered.

"Brave lad! You wait, Thomas. Someday you'll be big enough to protect your lovely mama all by yourself."

At Mara's polite gesture of welcome, Jordan sat down at the table. She could not take her eyes off him, mesmerized by his easy charm.

He turned as though he felt her gaze and gave her a smile that warmed her all the way down to her toes.

"So, what have you got?" he asked with a roguish twinkle in those blue, blue eyes.

"I could make you a sandwich?"

"Really?" He seemed surprised at her simple offer. Why? she wondered. Because she was a viscountess?

Surely the two of them had got beyond that.

She raised her eyebrows in amusement, waiting for his answer.

"That would be charming," he murmured, watching her oddly, as though this were the most fascinating operation in the world while she put a slice of the day's fresh rye bread on a plate for him and began building a sandwich for him out of thinly cut slices of roast beef.

"Mustard?" she asked softly, pausing.

He held her gaze a little too long. "Please."

Mara lowered her head, blushing she-knew-not why as she dipped a knife into the dish.

There was nothing sensual about a sandwich, she told herself, which did not explain why she had butterflies in her stomach. But she could feel him watching her with heated intensity as she spread the mustard across the slice of bread.

She flicked another cautious glance his way, pointing to the Swiss cheese on the serving plate in question.

He nodded, staring hungrily at her.

As she reached for a slice of the cheese to add to his sandwich, the strangest image came into her mind of Jordan licking the taste of the food off her fingers, a sudden, wild urge to feed him while sitting astride his lap.

A searing blush climbed up all the way from her throat into her cheeks.

Mrs. Busby cleared her throat and turned away. "I think His little Lordship is finished eating, ma'am."

"Er, yes." Blushing, Mara chuckled nervously. "He's wearing more of his supper than he ate tonight."

"Shall I take him up for his bath?"

"Yes, do—thank you. But let me know when he's ready for bed. I'll put him down myself."

"Aye, ma'am. If you'll excuse me, sir."

"Good night, Mrs. Busby," Jordan replied, as the old woman lifted Thomas into her arms and sped him away to the nursery to be cleaned up.

Mara wondered if it was as obvious to him as it was to her that the nurse had fled with Thomas in order to leave the two of them alone.

They exchanged a speculative smile.

She completed the sandwich and cut it in half, presenting it to her guest. "What would you like to drink?"

"Whatever you're willing to give me," he murmured, his gaze skimming the neck of her gown as she leaned near to set the plate before him.

"Tea, wine? Merlot might be nice with that. There's a keg of brown ale that was just delivered today. I thought your men might like it. I so appreciate them keeping watch over us."

"You know the way to a soldier's heart, don't you?" He smiled. "The ale sounds perfect."

She summoned Mary to fetch it for him, then looked over in surprise as Jordan's first bite of the sandwich evoked a near groan of pleasure from him. "Delicious!"

She chuckled at his hyperbole.

"No—I mean it," he vowed, swallowing. "This is the best damned sandwich I have ever had in my life."

She shook her head at him with a curious chuckle. Mary returned in short order and presented him with a pewter tankard of the dark ale on a tray.

He accepted it, and the maid retreated.

"I'm in heaven. Cheers," he added. "Aren't you going to have anything?"

She shook her head ruefully. She could hardly eat when her stomach was aquiver. As she sat watching him, she almost couldn't believe she was sitting here at the table with her idol, Jordan Lennox in the flesh. The man of her dreams. He was different now, but she still caught glimpses under that hardened, polished surface of the gallant youth she had known at twenty-two.

Before long, Mary returned to clear the few dishes on the table. Reese also made an appearance, lighting the three-armed candelabra on the table as the day's light faded.

When both servants retreated, the butler pulling the double doors closed behind him, they were left staring at each, smiling slightly in warm, savoring companionship.

"So," Mara murmured, resting her chin on her hand as she propped her elbow on the table. "Are you ready to confess?"

"Confess?"

She nodded over her shoulder at the broadsheets strewn on the sideboard. "Yesterday's adventure, as you called it, did not make it into the papers. Don't you find that odd?"

"Really? Yes, remarkable."

"I know! It's most mysterious, is it not? Neither the morning nor evening editions. You wouldn't happen to know anything about that, now, would you, Jordan?"

"Me? Heavens, no."

She narrowed her eyes, studying him as she smiled archly. "You did something, didn't you?"

"Maybe." He leaned back in his chair with an easy half smile, resting an idle arm across the back of hers. "I told you not to worry, didn't I? When are you going to learn to listen to me?"

"What did you do?"

"Don't you worry your pretty head about it."

She snorted at this blandishment and poked him in the waistcoat.

He laughed at her protest. "Somebody owed me a favor. Beyond that, it does not signify. As long as you are pleased."

"Pleased? I am utterly relieved! You saved my reputation."

"Ah, I'm not so sure you're out of the woods yet."

"What do you mean?" she asked in alarm.

"This rumor about you and the Regent." He shook his head. "It's got to stop."

"Yes." She sighed, nodding. The attack on her carriage certainly proved it had gone on long enough. "What do you suggest? I am sure you have some advice."

He smirked at her mild taunt. "Actually, the solution is quite obvious. If you want to discourage the gossips from talking about you and the Regent, then logically you must take care to be seen in the company of some other man."

"I see, so they can start a new rumor."

"Precisely. A less controversial one. At least, one that won't get you hissed in the streets." He took a swallow of ale.

She watched him, fighting a smile, but she had a feeling

she knew where he was going with this. "What sort of man do you suppose I should look for to aid me in this scheme?"

"Oh, I don't know, someone . . . universally well thought of, respected, and admired. Unfortunately, Wellington's busy, but if you wish to make do with me, I am willing to volunteer my services."

"How generous of you!"

"Yes, well, I am told I'm a capital fellow." He leaned back in his chair and regarded her in amusement. "I trust you see the practical benefits of this arrangement, Lady Pierson."

"I must admit I do. But . . . I also see the dangers."

"What dangers do you mean?"

"I told you I'm not looking for a lover," she said in a firm but gentle tone.

"Well, hell, neither am I! Don't worry. That won't be a problem. And if it is, there's always Delilah."

"But then Cole will put a bullet hole in you," she said with a mild wince of regret.

"Egads," he murmured softly. "Perhaps not one of my better ideas. No, but really," he said after a moment. "I have no intention of seducing you." *Unless you want me to,* his blue eyes seemed to say.

"Randy males have their uses, darling," she could still hear Delilah saying. *"You'll learn to enjoy them in time."* Mara lowered her gaze as a heated blush crept up her neck and blossomed in her cheeks.

"Ahem, would you like another pint?" she asked cautiously, remembering how many of those Tom could guzzle down in an evening.

Jordan shook his head as he set his empty tankard down, then, thankfully, changed the subject. "You know, you really impressed me yesterday, the way you handled yourself in the midst of that row."

"I did?"

"You kept a cool head in a bad situation."

"There wasn't much else I could do."

"Which is why I gave Jack an excellent new musket to keep under the seat inside your carriage from now on. You ask me, it should've bloody been there in the first place."

"A musket?" she exclaimed. "What, for me?"

"I will not have you defenseless if another such situation should ever arise. Don't argue, please."

"But Jordan, I could never shoot someone!"

"Even if they were threatening your son?"

Mara met his cool stare and remembered her determined vow to be both mother and father to Thomas. Mothers nurtured, but fathers generally protected. If she was going to do both, then maybe he was right. "I don't know how to shoot."

"Then I will teach you. It's not that difficult. We can't spare Sergeant Parker forever, and I may not always be there to protect you."

"You really think I can do it?"

"If illiterate farm boys of twelve can shoot a musket, so can you, love. Who knows? You might even enjoy it."

Mara still could not imagine herself firing a musket, but she shrugged, eyeing him with cautious interest. "I'll tell you one thing I did enjoy—your display of prowess yesterday in the 'manly art of self-defense.' "

He laughed.

"It's true! You quite deserved a headline. 'Lone Earl Holds Off Rabid Mob.' It's a pity the papers missed it."

"Why thank you, my dear. What is it?" he added when he noticed her studying him intently.

Mara chose her words with care. "Seeing you fight like that made me realize you must've been in more dangerous places while you were gone than I had any idea."

"Well, there was the small matter of a war going on."

She stared at him. "You saw action, didn't you?"

He just looked at her. No glib remarks forthcoming.

"So, that's why you were so sympathetic to the major at Delilah's." She shook her head, reached out, and laid her hand on his forearm. "My God, if I had known that, I would've been beside myself with worry. Were you ever injured?"

"Ah, bumps and bruises, can't complain. What of your marriage? How did that go for you?"

Smooth as silk, he turned the tables on her. Mara stiffened and withdrew her touch, instantly on guard. She dropped her gaze, not sure what to say.

"Hmm, suddenly quiet," he observed in a low tone. "Is this a widow's grief, or have we both been through a war?"

She met his gaze soulfully, mute with regret.

"How bad was it?" he whispered.

She lowered her head, but it was a long moment before she could speak. "Viscount Pierson gave me Thomas. For that—I cannot speak ill of him."

Jordan had tensed; now he stared at her. "Did he mistreat you?"

"It doesn't matter now. He's dead." She gave him a look that refused further discussion on this topic.

"So he is," Jordan said in a taut murmur, but dropping his gaze, he visibly strove to curb his anger.

She took a deep breath and exhaled it.

"Mara . . . I've been thinking," he spoke up quietly after a moment.

"Yes?"

Slowly, he reached for her hand.

Her heart pounded; his gaze remained fixed on their joined hands.

"I want to come back into your life . . . in whatever capacity you'll have me."

She held her breath, staring at him.

"You don't want a lover, and I can respect that. But you don't know how I've missed you. I wrote you so many letters."

"You did?" she asked, her eyes widening.

He nodded in regret. "But I couldn't send them."

"Why?"

"Turns out a junior diplomat's love letters don't rate very high as parcels for the few couriers who were able to get through the battle lines."

She stared at him in amazement. "Do you still have them?"

He shook his head. "I burned them when I heard that you had married Lord Pierson."

She winced and searched his face in pensive wonder. "What did they say?"

"I can't remember. Probably paeans to your eyes. That sort of nonsense. Most of all, they said how much I missed you. You don't know how many times I regretted trying to be so mature and responsible that night in the garden. Remember, when you proposed to me?"

She gasped, though his eyes twinkled fondly. "Oh, you are not a gentleman, bringing that up!"

"You were incredible—so sure about us. So passionate."

"You mean when I kissed you."

He smiled, holding her gaze until she was lost in his blue eyes. "I've thought of that kiss often."

"So have I," she admitted in a cautious whisper.

Jordan leaned closer and pressed his lips gently to her own. Mara shivered with desire, but when he started to deepen the kiss, she pulled away, her heart pounding.

"I can't do this! I can't afford to be hurt again. I have to be strong for my son—"

"I'm sorry." He sat back in his chair, his gaze lowered in chagrin. "I shouldn't have done that."

"You don't have to apologize—I'm not saying I didn't like it."

He eyed her in question, but just then, Mrs. Busby knocked discreetly on the parlor door.

"Milady, you told me to fetch you when Master Thomas was ready for bed?"

Mara lifted her chin, still blushing, and turned toward the door. "Thank you, Mrs. Busby," she called back, "I'll be right there."

Jordan offered her a taut, sardonic smile when she glanced at him again. "Then I shall bid you a fond good evening, Lady Pierson." He rose from his chair. "Thank you for the sandwich and the ale."

"Of course." Mara struggled with herself. *Oh, blazes. Say something.* She swallowed hard, gathering her nerve. "What about your plan—to help me start a new rumor?" she blurted out as Jordan started to turn away.

"Yes?" He glanced back again with interest. "What about it?"

She blushed harder. "Does your offer still stand?"

"What, to be your pretend paramour?" He shrugged. "Of course."

Her heart was racing. "Perhaps you're free tomorrow?"

"What did you have in mind?"

"Um, I don't know . . . shopping?"

"Ah." He winced.

She grinned. "Bond Street is a favorite daytime haunt of all the lady gossips. If they saw us there together, it would get our rumor off to a fine start."

"Very well, then. What time shall I fetch you?" he asked with a deep blue glow in his eyes.

She shrugged, biting her lip against a girlish smile. "Any hour in the afternoon that suits you, my lord."

"All right, I will be here at two. Do try to stay out of trouble until then, hmm?"

She beamed at him, suppressing a most unladylike giggle; he came over and took her hand in parting. He held it for a moment, gazing at her with a world of emotion in his eyes.

"What is it?" she asked softly.

"You were a charming girl, but you really have become a marvelous woman."

"Why, thank you."

He pressed a kiss to her knuckles; she did not object.

"Good night, my lady."

"Good night, my lord." Her heart skipped a beat as he released her hand with a sensual slide of skin on skin.

Then he collected his hat and gloves from the sideboard. Bowing to her, he left.

As her butler saw Jordan out, Mara's hand still tingled from the light caress of his fingertips across her palm.

Heavens, it was just as well that he had gone, she told herself, swept up in a rush of giddy sensations she had not tasted since her youth. If he had stayed a moment longer, she might have been tempted to do something unspeakably reckless. Like invite him upstairs with her.

Not to put the baby to bed.

Chapter 8

Any attempt at escape had proved futile, but Drake realized within a few days these men were not going to kill him. Whoever they were, they did not appear inclined to torture or abuse him. They really seemed to think they were his friends.

He quit arguing with them, as doing so thus far had got him nowhere. But uprooted once again from the brief security he had begun to settle into with his aged benefactor, James Falkirk, he felt himself holding on by a thread.

How could James betray him like this? Had he not saved the old man's life? Had he displeased him somehow, that he should hand him over to these strangers? But even stronger than his hurt, confusion, and anger, he was tormented with dread for the old man's safety.

Everything in him warned that James was in dire peril, but with them separated, Drake was powerless to help.

Now they were removing him from London, where James was, and with every mile they traveled, his agitation grew.

"Here we are."

When the traveling coach in which they had left London a few hours ago rolled to a halt, Lord Rotherstone—or rather, Max—sent him an assessing look askance, his eyes cool and shrewd, his tone all patient reassurance.

The marquess had insisted that Drake call him Max on account of their allegedly having been close friends since boyhood.

"Take a look."

Drake warily followed Max's glance out the carriage window. They had come to a halt on a pebbled drive in front of some large country estate.

"Recognize it?"

"Should I?"

"This is Westwood Manor. Your estate. Does it look familiar?"

Drake shifted uneasily on the squabs. "I-I'm not sure." He was supposedly the Earl of Westwood, but how could a chap forget something like that unless he had gone completely mad?

"Let's go and take a closer look. Come."

They got out of the coach, but for a long moment, Drake stood beside the carriage staring at his supposed mansion, feeling utterly depressed. If this was home, there was nothing in his heart to tell him so.

It was impressive enough, in the usual style. Portland stone. Great fat pillars in front holding up a classical portico. The usual rows of white-trimmed windows, slightly different in size and style on each story. Sculpted topiaries paired along the approaches to the entrance.

There were daffodils coming up between them as gray March yielded ground to April.

Drake scanned the tree line where the handsome green park and the horse pastures ended in peaceful woodlands.

The sky was cerulean behind the leafless branches, bare wood clacking on bare wood in the sharp chill of the breeze; but some of the boughs were studded with the start of bright buds.

"What do you think?" Max urged, studying him, his hands thrust into the pockets of his blowing greatcoat.

"Nice," Drake mumbled with a shrug.

"It's yours," the marquess answered. "Your ancestral home. Your inheritance. You were born here, Drake. And you grew up here, too—until you were recruited by the Order."

"Oh." He looked askance at him.

Max smiled sardonically. "Come, there's someone here whose one prayer in life has been to see your face again."

"Who?"

"You'll see." Max walked toward the house; Drake followed, the gravel crunching underfoot. Anxiety began balling up like a fist inside his solar plexus. He swallowed hard as he walked into the shadow of the great house. Ghostly glimmers of recognition danced ahead of him, just out of reach, like streamers blowing on the breeze.

His heart pounded as he forced himself up the broad, shallow stairs to the portico. His feet felt heavy with the reluctance of his arrival at the place.

He did not know for a moment which would be worse—to remain forever the blank slate that he was now, or to start to remember himself and his life at last. Perhaps it was better not to know. Maybe some things were best forgotten.

But then, suddenly, as he came up to the top of the entrance stairs, the front door opened. He stopped in his tracks as a thin, frail, bony, old lady flung open the door and stood there, staring at him, leaning on her cane. She wore a satin toque and two circles of pink rouge on her cheeks; but beneath her makeup, her face went paper white.

"Lady Westwood," Max greeted her with a slight bow, but she ignored him, her stare fixed on Drake.

She seemed speechless, then her rheumy old eyes flooded with tears. Drake glanced uncertainly at Max; the marquess sent him a discreet, encouraging nod toward the woman; but she was already coming toward him as fast as her hobbling gait would allow.

As she crossed the portico toward him, the sleeveless wool pelisse she wore over her gown blew about in the windy, warring drafts that swirled around the columns.

Drake watched her with a certain degree of wonder and curiosity, trying to coax his brain into remembering who she was. She seemed familiar.

He cast Max a startled look as she suddenly lurched forward and embraced him with a low cry. She sounded so distraught that he obliged her, returning her hug uncertainly. "Oh, Drake! Thank, you, God! My son's alive! You are alive! I knew it in my heart. Oh, my dearest boy, what have they done to you? I should never have let them take you away from me—my brave young warrior!"

As she broke down weeping his arms, Drake looked at Max in imploring bewilderment. Max's nod confirmed that this woman was indeed his mother, but Drake despaired.

If he could not remember his own mother, then for God's sake, what hope was there for him? It would have been better for him if the Germans had killed him.

But as his heart pounded, it all became too much. It overwhelmed him. Whatever he knew, he refused to remember now. It was too painful, and he had already suffered enough.

Nevertheless, as he returned Lady Westwood's hug as best he could, he caught a sudden whiff of her perfume . . . a faint hint of mingled lavender and rose that floated up to his nostrils and seized his complete inward attention.

It tickled something far at the back of his brain, but before he could sort out the sudden tangle of his internal reactions, she stepped away again with a sniffle, still clinging to his hand. "Come in, come in! My darling son, you are home at last. Now your mother is going to look after you."

Drake obeyed, Max following him, the stalwart Sergeant Parker bringing up the rear, ready to shoot him with that horse pistol he wore beneath his greatcoat if he made one false move.

When he stepped inside, a throng of silent servants stood around staring at him, marveling as he passed. Again, he was beguiled by another smell he knew as he followed Lady Westwood through the entrance hall. Beeswax polish with a hint of lemon . . .

He was escorted into a drawing room, where he paused, taken aback to find a portrait of himself hanging above the mantel. As they all sat down except for Parker, who stood in the wide doorway keeping watch on him, Max endeavored to answer Lady Westwood's anxious questions about his condition.

"We hope that being here for a while will gradually help to trigger memories of his old life."

"Yes, yes, he is most welcome, as are you, my lord, and your men. Home is best for him. This is where he belongs—"

All of a sudden, out beyond the drawing room, they heard the front door crash open, followed by the sound of swift pattering footfalls running across the entrance hall.

Someone was coming. Drake looked over.

Sergeant Parker whirled around to meet the challenge. "Stop! Who goes there—who are you?" he exclaimed.

A windblown girl with long brown hair flung into the doorway.

Parker grasped her arm, stopping her from coming any closer. With a fierce look, she pushed back against the sergeant, then frantically stared past him. She went motionless the second her gaze locked with Drake's.

"It's true," she choked out. "You're alive!"

"You're real?" he uttered softly, amazed.

"You know her, Drake?" Max asked at once.

He just stared. "I thought you were a dream," he whispered. She alone had been with him in his darkest hour, locked inside that Bavarian torture chamber, enduring hell on earth. A silent, tender presence watching over him, a woodland angel conjured by his madness. This lovely spirit seemed to have been with him forever, until he had supposed she was just a figment of his imagination. Yet now, here she stood, in flesh and blood.

The girl with the violet eyes.

Jordan realized over the next sennight that it was hard to "treat someone like gold," as Max had said, when you were keeping so much from her. Nevertheless, he had made up his mind to follow his friend's advice where Mara was concerned.

Life rarely gave a man a second chance. He would seize his opportunity and see where it might lead.

Before long, the talk about her and the Regent faded as the ton gossips began spinning a new thread: *What's going on between Lady Pierson and Lord Falconridge?*

They browsed the shops in Bond Street, took Thomas to see the trick ponies at Astley's, and had their first shooting lesson with a target set against a hillside well outside of Town.

On Saturday night, they attended the opera, where he introduced Mara to Daphne, Lady Rotherstone, and her auburn-haired companion, Miss Carissa Portland. The two ladies were escorted that night by Beau, since Max was still up north with Drake.

Beau looked Mara over, then sent Jordan a discreet look of approval; meanwhile, Daphne and Carissa quizzed the poor woman about herself until Jordan took pity and rescued her. His lady friends were rather protective of him—like doting sisters, he assured her in amusement.

Then the news arrived that the Regent had returned from Brighton, and the official announcement was made of Princess Charlotte's betrothal to Prince Leopold.

Now that all the world knew the happy news, Mara wanted to present the bride's proud papa with the Gerrit Dou before Carlton House was entirely flooded with congratulatory gifts. And she insisted on having Jordan's escort that day so he might carry the precious painting for her. The task of handling the masterpiece could not possibly be entrusted to a footman, or so she had claimed with a coy flutter of her lashes.

Jordan ignored the twinge in his conscience and assured her he'd be happy to assist. He got the feeling she fancied the notion of showing him off to her royal friend. Perhaps she wanted to see what "George" might think of him.

Therefore, the next afternoon, he found himself walking beside her through Carlton House. A top-lofty little steward marched ahead of them through cavernous chambers, his nose in the air.

Jordan carried the Gerrit Dou, now luxuriously gift-wrapped in peacock blue silk and tied with a white velvet bow. Treasure though it was, however, he feared it might be lost amid the opulence of Carlton House.

He studied the place with a cynical eye.

Though he had feigned surprise about the royal engagement, not even so skilled a liar as he could pretend that Prinny's ornate home was to his taste.

Indeed, "ornate" was too mild a word for such gaudy excess. There was no plain surface to be found. Everywhere, curlicues piled on arabesques, gilding, carved friezes, Corinthian pillars in every shade of marble, flowers enough for ten funerals, painted ceilings, patterned carpets, art treasures hung on every wall. It was astonishing. From room to room, the Chinese style warred with the Gothic, both vying chaotically with the Greco-Roman craze—but clearly, His Royal Highness saw no fun in Classical restraint.

Of course, Jordan could appreciate the size, the sheer grand scale of this monstrosity, never mind the war debt.

It was just the décor that could give a man a headache. "No wonder he has the gout," Jordan whispered to Mara. "I would, too, living here."

She pressed her lips together, then elbowed him and looked pointedly at the fussy little steward. *"Don't let him hear you!"*

Jordan could not resist teasing her some more, for one giggle from her in these marble expanses would echo for miles. "I should've brought supplies," he murmured under his breath. "You didn't tell me this was going to be a day's forced march."

"Behave, rudesby," she warned as they crossed the vastness, following the steward to the private wing where Prinny actually lived and received his friends.

But it was true. Jordan lost count of the drawing rooms and staircases they passed. He saw chambers and halls in every shape along the way, no mere squares and rectangles for their prince of pleasure, no, indeed, but a great, soaring Octagon and a few circular rooms, as well. Two libraries, five dining halls, including the famous Gothic conservatory, which alone could seat two hundred guests, as Mara had informed him in the carriage before they arrived.

"Honestly, I'm beginning to feel a trifle dizzy. Did you bring the smelling salts in case I faint?"

"Don't worry; if you do, I will revive you," she chided

in an equally playful whisper. Then: "Mind the painting, Jordan!"

He smiled broadly at her. "Yes, dear."

He rested the edge of the Gerrit Dou on a dainty golden console table when the steward held up a white-gloved hand and bade them wait.

The little man disappeared through the next door but returned a moment later, holding the door open for them. "His Royal Highness will see you now, my lady. My lord."

They walked into a drawing room of much more human proportions. Mara went in first and acknowledged her friend's status with a suitably formal curtsy; Jordan set the painting down to join her with a courtly bow to the future king.

The Regent greeted her with open arms and a wreath of smiles. "Lady Pierson! Come in, come in, my dear!" Beaming, the fifty-four-year-old prince rose in gentlemanly fashion to greet his friend.

Oddly, Jordan's first thought was that "Prinny" wasn't nearly as fat as the cartoonists liked to depict him.

The "first gentleman of Europe" was dressed in the fashionable uniform of the dandy. Jordan mused that Beau Brummell had done the nation a great service years ago in steering the Regent away from dressing in a manner that would have matched his home's décor.

Thank God, at least he didn't cover himself in diamonds like Napoleon. His Royal Highness's plain black coat was impeccably cut, his ruddy face beefy but clean-shaved, devoid of the white face powder and rouge that had been all the rage among the fops a mere decade ago.

Ah, the dandies versus the fops. An epic struggle. These foes had come to fisticuffs in the streets insulting each other's clothes back in the days when Jordan had first met the charming Mara Bryce.

"Congratulations to you and to your daughter. You must be so pleased," she was saying.

"I am glad to have the whole blasted business settled, in truth," he replied, lightly holding her gloved hands and gazing fondly at her. "I thought I'd never find a young man the headstrong chit would accept."

"Well, if a future queen cannot have a say in whom she marries, then what hope is there for any girl? You are a kind-hearted father to listen to her wishes."

He snorted wryly. "At least now if she ends up miserable, she won't have me to blame. Trust me, you are lucky to have a son. A daughter is a bird of another feather entirely."

"It's just her age."

"Yes, I suppose we are all intolerable at eighteen. But we shall see, shan't we, Lady Pierson? When Thomas is eighteen, you tell me *then* if you still consider him the eighth wonder of the world. How is my godson these days, by the by?"

"Perfection itself, as always, thank you, sir."

"Bring him to see me sometime soon. It's been months!"

"I will," she answered firmly.

"Now then, I see you've brought me something." He glanced past her with a curious glint in his eyes.

"And someone," she added, and she turned to Jordan, beaming.

For his part, when he saw how perfectly enchanted the Regent looked with Mara, he was rather touched, especially since it wasn't a look of lust.

With all his excesses, royal George was an easy target for mockery, but few men had the refinement truly to be just *friends* with a woman, and yet the prince's warmth toward her was obviously genuine.

This was a good man, Jordan thought, or at least a decent one, for all his foibles.

Privately, Jordan was relieved by this conclusion, considering the oath of loyalty he and his brother warriors had sworn to the Crown years ago as part of his induction ceremony into the Order.

Back then, it had been King George in power, and though His Majesty had already started losing his marbles, no one had ever doubted that the old king's heart was in the right place.

"Your Royal Highness," Mara said with a warm smile that belied the formality of her words, "will you permit me to present my particular friend, Jordan Lennox, the Earl of Falconridge."

"Aha, particular friend, eh? Interesting." Prinny furrowed his brow, studying him. "Falconridge. I know that name."

"Your Royal Highness." Jordan bowed low to him.

"Come closer." He beckoned with a chubby jeweled hand. "Your face is familiar, too. Foreign Office, what?"

"Yes, sir." Surprised that he remembered, Jordan raised his gaze to the Regent's and sent him a meaningful look, enough of a subtle warning, he hoped, for his current sovereign not to blow the cover of one of his own spies.

"Right! Well, then. Excellent." He returned his attention to Mara, eyeing her curiously about her bringing him along as her companion.

Actually, Jordan *had* met the Regent in at least one reception line at court and at Society events over the years, but he had always stayed in the background, never one to put himself forward with the royals. He had always feared he might give in to the temptation of an ill-advised witticism on the prince's spendthrift ways. Instead, he had opted to bite his tongue and mind his manners, and had thereby no doubt convinced the pleasure-loving prince that he was a very dull fellow, indeed.

Now that he had been ordered to join the Carlton House

set to monitor the Duke of Holyfield, Jordan was prepared to exert himself more to come across as a convivial chap.

Indeed, Max had warned him that he would have to act like an insolent prick to be accepted into the Regent's haughty set. Prinny liked his male friends rich, handsome, well dressed, and decidedly eccentric. Most were highborn; but there were a few colorful commoners, as well, dashing military types and the occasional artist on hand for variety's sake. Jordan bided his time, studying the situation.

"So, now, my dear girl, what's that you've got there?" the Regent inquired, nodding at the present with a barely concealed excitement like a child's.

"For you!" she answered cheerfully.

"No! You shouldn't have," he exclaimed.

"Of course I should! In honor of Princess Charlotte's engagement."

He bent and kissed her cheek. "You are too good to me." Then he gestured toward some nearby chairs. "Sit, please, both of you."

"Will you open it now? I can't wait for you to see it!"

"I thought you'd never ask," he jested, taking a seat across from them. He moved with considerable elegance for so large a man.

Jordan brought the present to him, then backed away again respectfully. "You really are too thoughtful, Mara," he murmured as he untied the bow.

"You know how much you mean to me and to Thomas."

Brushing aside the blue silk, he lifted the painting reverently out of his swaddling with a wordless exclamation of delight. He turned to her with childlike amazement. "A treasure! Mara! A Gerrit Dou! It is astounding."

"Oh, do you really like it?"

"I adore it!" He held the painting up, examining it. "Glorious! Look at the shading here. The way he has the light hitting her at an angle. Such a mood he evokes! She looks like she could step right out of the painting and sit down with us here, she's so alive."

"I daresay we might find her a trifle grouchy if she did that," Jordan commented, unasked.

The Regent looked askance at him. "But at least the expression in her eyes is real." He gazed again at the painting. "One grows so sick of artificial smiles."

Mara cast her royal friend a tender glance of knowing sympathy, but the look the prince sent Jordan was a veiled warning. *You might be on our side, but you watch your step with her.*

Jordan absorbed this, slightly startled. Perhaps the portly fellow was a bit cleverer than he was rumored to be. It seemed His Royal Highness had already realized there was more to Jordan's accompanying Mara here than was apparent to the eye.

Fortunately, just as Max had predicted, the Regent asked no questions but turned his attention back to this newest prize for his collection. "I must have this hung at once where I can see it constantly. And it will always remind me of you, darling creature." He kissed her on the cheek.

"I am so glad you are pleased."

"Entirely. Is it not a fine painting, Falconridge?"

"Indeed, sir."

"So." The Regent's attention now focused in on him. "What is your business with this lady, anyway?" he asked, blunt and breezy.

"Lady Pierson and I were first introduced many years ago, sir. Now that I am back from my post on the Continent, we have been enjoying . . . renewing our acquaintance."

Mara smiled at him, blushing slightly.

"I see," the Regent murmured, narrowing his eyes slightly. "Is he treating you well, my dear?"

"Very."

"Good. Take care that you do not cause this precious lady any unhappiness, my lord, or you may find yourself appointed the ambassador to some very remote and unpleasant location. You mark me, Falconridge?"

"Yes, sir, perfectly," Jordan answered, joining them in mild laughter though he got the feeling the Regent spoke not entirely in jest.

"You are very gallant, I'm sure," Mara teased the Regent, "but don't worry. I can take care of myself when it comes to him."

"You let me know if he gives you any trouble."

Jordan managed a taut smile. "I'm beginning to sympathize with Prince Leopold."

"At least you don't have to answer fifty questions from the Cabinet," Prinny said dryly.

"For Lady Pierson, I would be honored to endure the trial by fire."

"Ah, a good answer." The Regent nodded in approval.

"I daresay!" Mara took Jordan's arm.

Just then, the door burst open; they turned to see another renowned dandy striding in eagerly.

"Yarmouth!" Mara greeted him in surprise.

"Lady Pierson! Has he opened it?"

"I have," the Regent answered with a chuckle.

"Were you dumbfounded? I'm the one who helped her pick it out! Give credit where credit is due!"

"He does make a very skilled art agent, our Lord Yarmouth." Mara chuckled.

"Always happy to help, my dear. Especially when it gives me an excuse to pursue one of my *many* passions." The new arrival eyed Mara in a way that made Jordan bristle slightly. *Lud, does this one have designs on her as well?*

Jordan knew from his title that Lord Yarmouth was the

heir to the Hertford marquisate, and he had heard that he was probably Prinny's closest confidante. About age forty, the balding Yarmouth had a sly, lascivious air about him, perhaps a hint of decadence that he deliberately played up.

But apparently, this man, too, had an eye for beauty.

He regarded Jordan a tad suspiciously. "Who have you brought with you today, my dear?"

"This is the Earl of Falconridge. Jordan, Lord Yarmouth. The Marquess of Hertford's heir."

Jordan sketched a bow. "A pleasure, sir."

"Falconridge." Yarmouth furrowed his brow and tilted his head upward, scrutinizing him as only a dandy of the Regent's set could do. "Friend of Rotherstone's, aren't you?"

"We are club mates at Dante House, yes."

"Right." His sly smile grew approvingly. "The Inferno Club."

"Right," Jordan answered in kind.

"Oh, George, I meant to tell you—" Yarmouth said with a sudden snap of his fingers. "Rotherstone won't be playing cards with us next week. I'm not sure he'll be back."

"What, did we scare him away?"

"His new bride won't allow it. Play's too deep."

"Damn me!" The Regent slapped his thigh in astonishment.

Mara lifted her eyebrows.

"Forgive my language, Lady Pierson. It's just we're down a player now. Lud, I never would've taken Rotherstone for the henpecked sort. Falconridge," he ordered abruptly, sending him a keen look, "you will take his place at Watier's this week."

"Sir?"

"Watier's Club. The upper room. Wednesday night. We start at nine o'clock. You are free?"

It was not really a question. Jordan bowed. "Of course, sir. It would be an honor."

"Now, wait a moment," Mara protested. "Lord Falconridge is not the gambling sort!"

"Perfect!" Yarmouth grinned from ear to ear. "All the more reason to invite him, then. No head for cards, eh? Pity. No matter, you'll learn as you go on."

Mara huffed, holding on to him as she might have done to Thomas, but Jordan laughed at her attempt to shield him from the card sharps. "I can hold my own, Lady Pierson."

"But will you still be solvent by the time they're through with you? Oh, bother! Come along, my lord. I'm getting Lord Falconridge out of here before he begins to suspect I only lured him here to become your prey at the gaming tables."

The Regent and his boon companion laughed, but Mara and Jordan soon made their farewells and withdrew. She slipped her wrist into the crook of his elbow as they left the palace, returning to her coach.

Damn, he thought, that went better than expected.

The Regent apparently had a brain in his head after all.

As Jordan handed Mara up, he savored the light grace of her motion, stepping up into the coach and settling into the seat, all lace and pale muslin flounces.

He followed her in, taking the seat across from her; her groom closed the door, and immediately, Mara grinned at him, her dark eyes sparkling merrily. "So? What did you think of our Prinny? I'm dying to know."

He laughed softly as the carriage pulled away from Carlton House. "I think he liked the painting very much."

"Oh, come, you know that's not what I'm asking!"

"You want gossip out of me, is that it?"

"Of course!" she cried.

"But I don't approve of gossip, Lady Pierson."

"Hang your righteous airs, my lord Inferno Club! Now you *must* tell me what was going through your mind when you met him. I saw your face and would have given anything to know what you were thinking."

"Very well," he answered, laughing. "I was thinking that . . . well, how shall I say? Anyone who believes that you are sleeping with that man is a fool."

"Why, because he's portly?"

"No! Because he's not your type at all."

She grinned. "Pray, what is my type?"

"I am, of course." He stared straight into her eyes with a flirtatious smile that left her to interpret his reply as she preferred, either in jest or in earnest. But then he shook his head. "The Regent looks on you with a merely paternal eye. Which is fitting, since he *is* old enough to be your father."

"I suppose that's true."

"But I can see why you enjoy his company. He seems a capital fellow," Jordan concluded. *Much to my surprise.*

Quicker-witted than he had expected, to be sure.

Mara raised an eyebrow. "I can't believe they asked you to play cards with them. Please be careful. They play for ruinous stakes at Watier's."

"I've heard. Ah, don't worry. Once in a while such sport cannot be too damaging to a man's fortune—or his character."

"I suppose. But if it becomes a habit, our masquerade as lovers is through. A lady has her standards, after all!"

"No, anything but that! I will obey you, on my honor."

She smiled back at him.

At length, she glanced out the window and watched the streets rolling by. "I can see why you wanted to do something useful with your life," she mused aloud. "So many of them squander their best years in gaming hells and hideous bordellos. But that is how they seek excitement." She shrugged. "They brag about gambling themselves to the brink of total ruin and fighting their way back to solvency, as if they'd done something heroic. It will not end well for some of them, I fear. My late husband fit right in with them, and look at what happened to him."

"What did happen to him, exactly? If you don't mind my asking."

She shrugged and lowered her gaze, her expression darkening. "He was out late one night getting up to his usual antics with 'the lads.' On his way home in the wee hours of the morning, something spooked his horse and he was thrown. His neck was broken. He died in the street like a dog hit by a carriage . . . Alone, in the middle of the night. Probably too foxed to comprehend what had just happened to him, in those final moments."

Her blunt retelling of her husband's ghastly end rather chilled him—such a grim tale from such lovely lips.

"I am sorry. Truly. For both you and Thomas."

She gave him a dubious look. "Thank you."

"Do you ever miss him?" he asked softly.

Mara sighed, staring straight ahead in silence.

He took that for a no.

She sent him a guarded look askance that seemed to ask, *Does that makes me awful?*

Jordan gave her a gentle smile of regret, hating himself for whatever she had suffered being married to Pierson.

When Jack angled her carriage into the mews behind the terraced crescent, Mara turned to him. "Would you like to come in?"

"Unless you're bored of me."

"Don't be silly, I can't get enough of you."

He lifted an eyebrow, delighted by this flash of the coquette he had once known, tucked deep down inside the respectable viscountess, but still there. A playful smile curved her plump, tempting lips. "Come along," she ordered, then flounced prettily out of the coach.

As soon as they went in, Thomas came running, and the elegant court lady instantly turned back into the doting mama. She threw her arms open and bent down to catch her child up in her embrace. The boy was perched on her hip before she had even taken off her gloves. "Come, gentlemen, let us repair to the parlor. Mrs. Busby, would you go and tell Cook to fix us some refreshments?"

"Aye, ma'am." The old woman smiled at Jordan and bobbed a curtsy before hurrying off to her task.

"Ah, what are you building today, my little architect?" Mara asked as she set Thomas down amid his toy blocks scattered across the Persian carpet.

Jordan spoke several languages, but he could not decipher the tot's chirpy reply. As Thomas plopped himself down on the floor and began building again, Mara drew off her gloves, then gestured to Jordan to sit and make himself comfortable. "I'll be right back."

Taking off her bonnet, she went into the adjoining foyer to put away her hat and gloves, wrap and reticule. In the brief moment that she disappeared from view, Thomas turned and stared at Jordan; he raised an inquiring eyebrow and smiled at the tot, in turn.

The boy suddenly held up one of his blocks and babbled again, asking another not-quite-coherent question.

Jordan furrowed his brow as he searched the child's big, brown eyes, then he suddenly got it. "Oh! Right! I'd be honored to join you, Lord Pierson. I was a pretty fair builder of blocks in my day, I'll have you know." He took off his dress coat and settled onto the floor beside the urchin. "Now, then. Let's see what we've got here . . ."

Thomas stared at him in wonder and uncertainty as Jordan proceeded to build a small tower of blocks. When it was complete, he gave Thomas a smile and pointed to it. "Now comes the best part. Do you want to knock it over?"

Thomas toddled closer to the little tower, then leaned down and swatted it with a tiny hand. The blocks went flying, and the boy laughed uproariously.

Jordan laughed with him. "Your turn, now! Let's see how high you can build it." He pointed to the blocks, and Thomas got right to work with a serious air of industry.

Jordan was tickled by the boy's great focus on the task, when he suddenly noticed Mara standing in the doorway, watching them both with a dewy-eyed look.

She came in with a slight blush after having been caught staring. He held her gaze warmly as she fluffed her skirts and joined them on the floor.

Jordan found his own feelings in that moment curious. He savored an unexpected sense of home. But it was fleeting, interrupted by a loud knock at the front door, audible from the adjoining foyer.

Her butler, Reese, strode to answer, but the moment he opened the door, Delilah burst in with an anguished air of drama.

"Mara—darling!" she said with a theatrical sob, peering anxiously toward the staircase where the drawing room was situated.

Mara blanched, meeting Jordan's gaze as he arched a brow, but she quickly rose to her feet, hurrying out to meet her crying friend.

"I'm here! Delilah, sweeting, whatever is wrong?"

"Oh, Mara—it's Cole! I despise him!"

Jordan looked ruefully at Thomas. "Women," he whispered, man-to-man.

"I'm never speaking to him again! Oh, but it doesn't matter—he hates me, too. We had the most awful fight!"

"Again?" Mara answered sympathetically.

"Ahem," Jordan coughed, climbing to his feet.

Delilah recoiled. "Oh, no—I didn't realize you had company!"

"Mrs. Staunton," Jordan greeted her politely, pretending not to notice her tears or her indignant look that Mara might not be able to drop everything for her.

"I don't wish to interrupt," Delilah said with a martyred sniffle.

Jordan regarded her dryly, then glanced at Mara. "Why don't I take Thomas out to the stables to look at the horses? We'll have a nice visit with Jack."

"Oh, you don't have to do that—"

"He's no trouble. We'll be fine. I'm sure Mrs. Busby could use a break. Come here, tyke." He picked Thomas up with an easy motion. "Let's get you out of the nest and into the sunshine for a while." He sent Mara a reassuring look, but after hearing the morbid tale of how Thomas's father had died, he couldn't stop thinking of how unfair it was that this fine boy would grow up with no one to show him how to be a man, and, indeed, a lord.

"Just come and get us when you're through," he added. "Come on, lad," he ordered gently. He picked up his coat and tucked it loosely around Thomas. Then he carried the boy out, leaving both women staring, slack-jawed, after him.

"Well! It's good to see not *all* men are thoroughgoing mongrels." Apparently relieved to be rid of them, Delilah picked up her skirts and sailed into the parlor, angrily kicking a block out of the way with her toe before plopping onto the couch.

Still astonished, Mara lingered, watching Jordan carry Thomas off toward the back exit of the house. Over Jordan's broad shoulder, she could see her son's face; his expression was remarkable, eager for whatever adventure might lie ahead, perfectly at ease with his tall and protective new friend.

"That odious cretin tried to give me—me!—an ultimatum! He called me selfish and spoiled a-and a hussy! Can you believe that barbarian? I'm never speaking to him again!"

Mara fussed over her friend, but in truth, she was not overly concerned. Delilah's fights with Cole were routine by now. When her friend had vented all of her anger and frustration in the parlor, she perked up, visibly feeling better.

"I shall go to Bath to take the waters," Delilah declared, daintily blowing her nose on her handkerchief. "That would soothe my nerves—and then he would miss me, wouldn't he? That would show him!"

"I'm sure he'll come to his senses and beg your forgiveness when he's had some time."

"Well, I don't care if he crawls on his hands and knees. He's a devil. Men! They're not worth it, have you noticed? Pretending they care. All they ever do is lie!"

By the time Delilah bid her adieu with a kiss on the cheek, Mara was left entirely drained. With a low sigh, she hauled herself up from the sofa and went dragging out to join the boys.

She paused outside the doorway, besieged with a pang of tenderness when she spotted them together. Jordan was still holding Thomas, who was cautiously patting the neck of the tall, white hunter on which the earl had arrived.

Her smile grew as she walked out to join them. When Thomas saw her, he reacted with excitement, kicking his legs. "I petted the horsey, Mama!"

"Indeed, he did." Jordan let her son spill himself into her arms, but he kept his coat. Thomas clung to her neck, but he turned and kept staring at Jordan as though he didn't want to lose sight of him, either. "How's Delilah?"

"Oh, we go through this all the time," she whispered. "She'll be fine. They won't speak for a fortnight, then they'll make up, and the whole thing will start over again next month."

"Sounds exhausting."

She chuckled. "It is, believe me."

"Well, my dear," he murmured, his gaze skimming over her lips, "I should be going."

"Thanks for watching him. How did you get on?"

"Ah, he's easy. Calm boy, clever. He's got a cheerful disposition, doesn't he?"

"Yes." A frisson of happiness surged through her to hear her dream man compliment her pride and joy. "When will I see you again?" she asked, as he pulled on his coat and turned back to his horse, letting the stirrups down. They had been neatly run up against the saddle.

"Tomorrow?"

"Oh—I can't. I just remembered. I have to go to my parents' house. We go twice a month for dinner."

He looked at her in surprise. "Glutton for punishment, are you?"

"Now, now," she chided, fighting a smile. "You're welcome to come with me."

"I wouldn't want to intrude."

"Of course not. I understand. They're not the best of company."

He studied her. "Would it help you if I was there? Moral support?" he asked softly.

"Oh, would you?" she exclaimed.

He crooked a subtle, knowing smile. "What time do you want me here?"

"Oh, you are an angel! Isn't he, Thomas?"

"I don't know about that," Jordan said.

"If you're here by half eleven, we should be right on time

for the midday meal. Two o'clock sharp, every day for a thousand years."

"Right. Don't say I never did you any favors." He leaned closer and kissed her cheek, then he said good-bye to Thomas, running a light caress over the baby's head.

He turned away and swung up onto his horse.

Mara watched him with her heart lifting. "Say good-bye, Thomas." She nudged the boy into copying her in waving good-bye to the earl.

Jordan blew them a kiss in answer, then rode off.

She hugged her son as he cantered away astride his white hunter. "He really is rather wonderful, isn't he, Thomas?" she whispered. "What does Delilah know? Not *all* men are liars."

Chapter 9

Lady Bryce could not have been sweeter to their honored guest the next day, how ever appalled she might have been privately to find herself faced with the one person outside the family who had ever heard her verbally flaying her daughter.

No doubt she hoped the incident was forgotten and chose to focus on the fact that an earl at her table was a feather in her cap, especially a handsome, world-traveling sort of ambassador-at-large, who seemed so loyal to her daughter, even after all these years.

Mara, meanwhile, was a nervous wreck as usual in her parents' company. On the way over, she had given poor Jordan more pointers and instructions on how to manage them and more warnings about what not to say than he probably received from the Foreign Office before he was dispatched to some far-flung embassy.

Finally, he had laughed at her and told her to relax. "I am not devoid of all Town bronze, you know."

She had apologized with a sheepish wince. But now she saw she needn't have worried.

Though she was still braced to be mortified, either by her parents' embarrassing her or saying something rude to Jordan, his diplomatic skills served him well.

When her mother pried, and her father grumbled, he remained unflappable, amiable down to his gentlemanly fingertips.

With the keen eye and inborn patience of a herding dog steering a flock of difficult sheep away from danger, he used his seemingly endless supply of amusing anecdotes to redirect the conversation whenever her parents started to bicker or gripe at each other or showed early signs of starting to pick at her.

Mara could have kissed him.

Indeed, as the meal unfolded and he brought a calm into the storm that had always been her family home, she could no longer ignore the turn her feelings had been taking toward him lately.

He was so different from anyone else in her life. So sensible and sane. So easy and natural to be around.

Even now, sitting here, watching him distract and charm her parents, she was well aware this was his own quiet way of protecting her.

Whenever her parents started to attack, he parried with a nimble side-skip in the conversation, leading their attention away from her supposed flaws and failures with an innocent question on some other topic.

She marveled at his skill and realized deep in her bones that he was not going to let them hurt her.

Not today. Not while he was there.

She was not outnumbered anymore.

Gazing at him from across the family table laid with the usual roast beef dinner on the same bone china her mother had used since *she* was a bride, Mara knew that if she wasn't careful, her heart could run away with her again, just as quickly as it had all those years ago, like a wild horse breaking free of its paddock, galloping off down some moonlit lane.

Her lack of caution had led to such hurt and bitter disappointment that this time around, she had been taken pains to restrain her emotions toward him. After all, Jordan and she had agreed they were only friends. She was the one who had insisted on it!

Yes, but . . . look at him. Delilah was right. He was gorgeous. Impeccable. And smoldering more hotly every day.

When he licked his lips after taking a drink of the light wine that accompanied their dinner, Mara trembled and quickly dropped her gaze.

Of course he was handsome, with some strange charisma that riveted her despite his understated air. It was more than that. More than the manly elegance of his easy posture as he leaned in his chair with an intelligent half smile, listening to her father's bluster with perfect equanimity.

His appeal was far more than physical to her.

He made her feel . . . safe.

He had Sir Dunstan Bryce extolling the virtues of trout and grayling and the best places in these parts to fish. How had he discovered in less than half an hour one of the few topics that her father actually enjoyed?

He was terribly clever. More than that, he was kind.

Everything about him proclaimed solid reliability—a rare quality that any grown woman with a brain could not help but find devastatingly attractive. And yet, she had to remind herself, this was the man who had walked away from her. *Maybe we just weren't ready then.*

All she knew, as she lifted her gaze and watched him from across the table, was that she was ready now.

Ready for him.

The yearning desire gathering in her blood was so foreign to her. But surely she could not go the rest of her days never knowing what it would have been like to make love with him, this one man she had wanted all her life.

By the time they left her parents' house, she was feeling very peculiar, indeed.

With Jack up on the driver's box, as usual, Mara and Jordan slumped against the squabs as the carriage pulled away, both exhausted by the visit.

Mrs. Busby and Thomas sat across from them. They'd had the easiest time of it, for Sir Dunstan and Lady Bryce only enjoyed their grandson's presence until he began to act too much like a child. At the first sign of whining or tears, they frowned and began to criticize, which was Mara's cue that it was time to go. It was one thing for them to rail at her, but she did not intend to let them start in on the baby.

They waved good-bye as her carriage rolled off down the drive, but although Thomas seemed to be the only one who had any energy left, Mara noticed she did not feel anywhere near as glazed and battered as she usually did by the time she headed home. Perhaps because Jordan had borne the brunt of it this time.

"Blazes," he muttered at length, "I don't think I worked that hard at the Congress of Vienna."

"I'm sorry—"

"No, no. They're not so bad," he said with a weary laugh. "You're a godsend."

"How do you feel? That's the real test."

She searched her heart. "Intact."

"Good. Call on me whenever you need me." The intimate smile he gave her filled her with more robust gratitude for him than she could decently express in front of her child or Mrs. Busby.

Indeed, the heated wave of desire that moved through her body stunned her slightly. There had been no such feelings in all her years of marriage. She dropped her gaze, suddenly aware of every inch of the tall, strong, handsome man beside her. God, she had utterly forgotten this youthful and invigorating sensation.

Desire.

The flood of reawakening passion sprang to life in the core of her dormant body and spread with reckless speed, tingling along her every nerve.

Strangely, instead of confusing her, she suddenly felt like her old self again—a self she hadn't even realized had all but slipped away through the years. The real Mara. Flaws and strengths, passions, quirks, and all. It seemed like most of her life she'd been fighting for the courage to be herself. No matter who disapproved.

She reached over slowly and captured Jordan's hand.

He glanced at her in surprise as the carriage rolled homeward. Mara gazed at him in sober silence while Thomas babbled on.

Jordan furrowed his brow. "Are you all right?" he murmured in tender concern.

She gave a mute nod, her heart too full to explain. The heated jumble of emotions crashing through her could only be communicated by action.

He searched her face with a curious look, but he did not question her further. Not in front of Thomas. He just closed his fingers warmly around hers.

Mara bit her lip at the contact of his palm against hers; he began to realize then that she wanted him. Perhaps he noticed the swift beat of her pulse at her wrist where their hands touched.

His expression turned serious, and when he glanced at her again, his blue eyes had darkened. His immediate response, as naked as her own, made Mara catch her breath. Her respiration deepened; his hold on her hand tightened up a bit.

Mrs. Busby gazed politely out the window or kept her attention focused on the boy.

"Off we go, Master Thomas!" she said, when they arrived at last. Every moment had dragged on cruelly until the coach rolled to a halt in the narrow mews behind the crescent in Great Cumberland Street.

At once, Mrs. Busby collected Thomas and climbed out, as though she and the boy could not escape fast enough.

Mara blushed, feeling Jordan's sensual grasp on her hand holding her back, as though warning her not even to think about getting out of the carriage.

She wasn't. "We'll, ah, be along in a moment," she said mildly to the nurse, who had Thomas by the hand.

"Aye, ma'am. Come along, dearie boy."

Without even waiting for the groom, Mara leaned out and pulled the carriage door shut with a bang.

Immediately, Jordan tugged her toward him with a burning stare. "Come here," he whispered.

She obeyed, wrapping her arms around him. Then he was kissing her with explosive passion, caressing her hair as his mouth slanted over hers, over and over again, as though he could not get enough of her. Mara's toes curled in her satin slippers.

The taste of him spiraled through her senses as she clutched his wide shoulders in girlish thrill. He stroked her face with his fingertips and drank from her lips with a reverence that amazed her and sent her excitement climbing.

This man cared for her. He did not need words to tell her so. It was in the very way he touched her. With the carriage already parked in its place in the mews, they could hear the grooms disengaging the harness, the clip-clop of hooves as the horses were led away back to their stalls. No doubt the lads were grinning from ear to ear, and the servants' gossip would be all over the neighborhood by nightfall.

Mara didn't care. Certainly, Jordan didn't. As his fingertips on her cheek wisped down the side of her neck, inching down her chest until his hand expertly molded the curve of her breast, it was clear that he was ready for anything.

When her kiss faltered—merely from indecision—he paused. "Is this all right?"

"Yes, of course—but I wonder if we should go inside."

The smolder deep in his eyes leaped into flame as he stared at her in question. *Your bed?* his keen gaze queried.

Mara swallowed hard, her pulse racing, her cheeks turning scarlet. She glanced nervously toward the carriage window covered by the shade. "Maybe not. I can't face Mrs. Busby when you have me in such a state."

"I'm so sorry," he purred with a wicked smile.

It so charmed her that she had no choice but to grab him and kiss him again.

He let out a soft groan of amusement and delight as she plundered his mouth with her kiss.

"I take it I did something right," he panted, when she let him up for air.

She clutched his lapels tenderly, her chest heaving. "You do everything right, Jordan. It is your most maddening quality."

"What?" he retorted.

"You're practically perfect! How can any woman resist such a man?"

"I'm not perfect, Mara. You are."

"You see?" She laughed, dizzied with desire. "You just made my point for me."

"I adore you. That's all I know. I've dreamed of this forever."

"Oh, Jordan, so have I." She closed her eyes, leaning her

forehead against his in a surge of reckless longing. "I can't wait anymore," she breathed.

At once, his lips found hers. With a smooth motion, he turned her body away from him slightly, then guided her to lie back across his lap, holding her all the while. Her arms remained loosely draped around his neck, but this position freed his right hand to roam over her body, while his left arm still supported her back.

Mara kept her eyes closed in rapturous anticipation, yielding to his touch as he explored her body—until she suddenly remembered how unpleasant the conjugal act had been with her late husband.

Oh, dear. She froze. Maybe this wasn't such a good idea. Unbeknownst to Jordan—who was absorbed in kissing and petting her as if every inch of her was precious to him—old fears took off running through her mind. What if it all went wrong somehow? What if he, like Pierson, found her performance lacking?

She would die of embarrassment if she disappointed him when they both had waited years to be together.

What if she could not satisfy him? What if he got angry at her for not being any good at lovemaking?

Pierson couldn't even stay aroused the few times they had been together, and, of course, he called that her fault. It had always led to fights. God, she had hated lying there beneath him, the stale liquor fumes of his breath flooding her face. Those awkward nights had turned into naught but an unpleasant duty, an occasionally humiliating chore—for both of them. Their only motive had been to get a son.

Thomas was worth all the aggravation she had had to go through, but her scant experience of the marriage bed had left her with a barrage of anxieties that now taunted her.

It was one thing to know she had failed to impress her husband, but what if her ineptitude made Jordan lose all interest? Dear Lord, what if *laughed* at her? She knew his ironic sense of humor. But what man wouldn't laugh, pining away for a woman, finally having her, then realizing she was not so great a prize, after all?

Her fears stampeded on, half terrifying her, even as she tried to hide her inner turmoil.

On all those unpleasant occasions, Mara reminded herself, Pierson had never touched her like this. There was no reason to think it would be the same with Jordan.

His caresses glided over her body, down her thigh, awakening wonder over all her skin, but she suddenly found she couldn't relax. *You are taking a huge risk here.*

What if the beautiful new friendship they had salvaged from the past was ruined because of this momentous step?

No longer able to help herself, she reached down and suddenly stopped his hand. "Jordan, wait."

His fingertips had been sporting at her ankle and remained there, clearly intent on traveling north beneath her skirts. He lifted a curious, rather drugged-looking gaze to hers, his eyes blue eyes blazing hot with sensuality. "What is it, my darling?" he whispered thickly.

"Um—" Mara sat up, her chest heaving.

The haze in his eyes cleared slightly. "Something wrong?"

She held his gaze imploringly for a second, then she looked away, feeling utterly stupid. "I—it's nothing. Never mind."

His eyebrow lifted. "Come again?"

She winced. "I'm sorry."

He stared at her. "Did I do something wrong?"

"No! No. It's not you, honestly, it's me." She lowered her gaze with a wince. "I'm so sorry. I know I sound like an idiot. But I think I've, um, lost my nerve for this."

"Ah," he said slowly, the portrait of a man confounded—no, a gentleman. "I see. Yes, of course." He almost managed to hide his wince. He cleared his throat. Nodded. "As you wish, my dear." He took a deep breath and forced a wry smile. "I shall need a moment if you wish to go inside."

She searched his face, furrowing her brow. No disgust? No sign of anger or recrimination?

"I really am sorry," she said. "I don't know what's wrong with me."

"There's nothing wrong with you, I'm sure. A lady is allowed to change her mind. No questions asked."

"Oh," she said warily.

"If I frightened you somehow, I didn't mean to—"

"No! You didn't at all. It's just—I'm so terribly nervous," she admitted with a hapless shrug.

"Oh, sweeting, why?" he murmured, running his hand down her back. "You don't have to be afraid with me."

"I know. But, you see, I'm horribly out of practice." She was blushing as fiercely as any virgin. "I haven't—you know—in nearly three years, and the truth, I was never what you'd call an expert."

"Oh, there, there, darling," he comforted her in fond amusement. "I don't care about experts. All I care about is you."

"Well, there must be something wrong with me, because I never really enjoyed it in the first place."

He studied her for a long moment, his eyes gleaming with tenderness. "Mara, my dear, have you ever had an orgasm?"

"What's that?" she countered in a dull tone.

"My poor babe." He kissed her neck, and whispered, "This is a tragic state of affairs."

"You're telling me."

"You have needs, Mara. You're a grown woman."

"Yes, but what if I—can't?"

"Are you aware it's a skill one can learn? From the proper teacher, that is. Someone patient. Someone you trust. Do you trust me, Mara?"

She sighed as his lips skimmed the line of her throat. "Yes."

"Then don't worry. Just let go. If you tell me to stop, we won't do this. But in the meanwhile, you throw down the gauntlet like that," he murmured against her skin, "you make me want to prove to you that you *can* enjoy making love. Immensely."

A renewed jolt of awareness began unwinding the knot in her stomach. She could feel her tension easing, the heat returning to her cheeks again, though she lowered her lashes, watching her hands slide over his broad shoulders.

"Do you want me, Mara?"

"Oh, yes—so very much," she breathed as his thumb slid over her nipple through the fabric of her gown. "But what if it changes things between us?" She felt weaker by the second. "Now that you're finally back in my life . . . you make me so happy. I don't want this to come between us now."

He paused and gazed wistfully at her. "What an innocent you still are. So shy and nervous. I had no idea. Come here, sweet. Just let me hold you."

She wasn't sure how to take his observations, but when he smiled at her in reassurance, she accepted his invitation gladly. He put his arms around her in an embrace that offered safety, patience, kindness. The closest thing she had ever known to love. Mara slid her arms around his neck and closed her eyes.

They hugged for a long time in silence. He stroked her until a deep contentment gradually eased the anxieties that had gathered in her body—or rather, changed the quality of that physical tension, shifting its location . . . lower.

The tightness in her shoulders began melting away, dripping lower to become a tingle in her belly, a need that began thrumming in her blood.

Everywhere their bodies pressed together, she grew more

acutely aware of him as a man, all the hard, smooth contours of his muscled frame . . .

"So, what do you think?" he murmured at length, kissing her forehead. "Do you want to go in now?"

She was silent.

He pulled back slightly and looked at her in question; he arched a brow when he read the hunger on her face.

"Well, there's no hurry, is there?" she whispered.

He shook his head, staring at her in rapt approval. "Not at all. There's nowhere else I need to be. I'm all yours," he added, as the banked smolder in his blue eyes leaped back to full flame.

"Hmm, whatever shall I do with you, I wonder?"

"That is entirely up to you." He sank back against the squabs in a reclining pose that invited her do as she pleased.

His offer was more temptation than she could resist.

Heart pounding, Mara leaned in and brushed her lips lightly along his cheek, beginning with the utmost care. His skin was warm and smooth, his clean-shaved jaw strong and square; she kissed it, too, bracing herself against his shoulders. He tipped her head back against the squabs with a low sigh of pleasure as her light, nibbling kisses moved to his earlobe. "You're seducing me, Mara."

"I'm sure I wouldn't know how."

"Trust me, you're better at this than you know." He led her hand gently to the throbbing evidence of his desire.

Her eyebrows shot up, her blood leaped, and as she cupped the massive bulge in Jordan's trousers, she recalled her husband's lack of interest in her, and thought in wicked approval, *Now that is a cock.*

There was no question that *this* man wanted her. "Most impressive, my lord," she said faintly.

"Believe me now?"

"How can I not, with such . . . solid proof in hand, so to speak?"

He let out a husky laugh at her quip. To be sure, her shyness was definitely fading. It all but disappeared when he moaned softly, enjoying the taut squeeze of her hand as she stroked him through his trousers.

Though her cheeks still burned in a deep blush, all her skin felt tingly-warm.

"So," he resumed in a mild tone—such a courtly diplomat—"how may I be of service, my lady?"

"Hm . . ." She flicked a possessive glance over his muscled body. "Take off your coat," she ordered with a pleasant half smile and a quickening pulse.

"Excellent idea." In the close confines of the carriage, she helped him draw his arms out of the neat, tailored sleeves of his cutaway coat.

As they shifted positions, he stole a kiss on her neck. Mara quivered when his warm, silken lips lingered, offering several more in a delightful line that traveled down her throat.

She closed her eyes, a sigh of deepening restlessness escaping her when his lips parted against her flesh. She cupped his head against the crook of her neck, reveling in his open-mouthed kiss beneath her earlobe, raking her fingers through his short, soft hair.

He moaned in pleasure at her touch. She moved on, stroking his shoulders, running her hand up his chest—until she happened upon his well-starched cravat.

Without forethought, she plucked at one tidy fold of the square knot, freeing it. Jordan helped her; she slid it off his neck.

This was the first time she had ever seen him without his cravat. The deep V of his shirt fell open down to where his waistcoat remained buttoned. She pulled back to stare at him and was instantly entranced by the sweeping line from his bare throat down to his muscled chest.

Riveted by the wondrous new territory she had uncovered, Mara could not restrain her fingers from following her gaze.

As she touched him, his skin was hot and sleek; her fingertips skimmed the rough texture of his beard growth beginning to return many hours after his morning shave. She touched his Adam's apple and the vulnerable notch below it, that alluring dip between the masculine elegance of his collarbones. And then her hand trailed down the sturdy center valley between the sculpted swells of his pectoral muscles. "You are . . . a beautiful man."

"I'm all right," he replied with an all-too-charming half smile.

She gave him a sardonic look, then leaned closer and kissed his neck, just as he had done to her.

Jordan went stock-still, clearly savoring the soft pressure of her lips against his jugular; he swallowed hard. She could feel his pulse pounding beneath her kiss, but he did not move—he barely breathed—as though he were afraid of scaring her away.

He needn't have worried.

Long-dormant instinct was beginning to take hold, her body at long last responding as Nature had intended it to.

Hallelujah. Everything in her was coming alive again.

Her heartbeat was gathering strength as she slipped her hand eagerly into the now accessible regions of him hidden beneath his loosened shirt. In rapt admiration, she went exploring over his shoulders and partway down his chest, and after a moment, Jordan did the same, no longer able to help himself, it seemed.

He pulled her closer. Mara climbed atop him, straddling him on the carriage seat. As her attentions shifted from his neck to claim his mouth in a deep, consuming kiss, his hands clutched her hips through the layers of her skirts.

All of a sudden, they were on fire, two youths again, groping and fondling each other, all their supposed sophistication forgotten in a heightening fever of desire.

With her hands still inside his parted shirt, Mara continued marveling at the feel of his bare chest, warm, hard sinew beneath velveteen skin. Jordan's hands, meanwhile, slid upward, molding her waist.

When he clasped her breasts, he got her full attention. She paused in kissing him, waiting to see what he was going to do. Then through her gown, a few slow, forceful passes of his thumbs across her nipples teased her into a state of crazed arousal.

She shuddered with a torrent of fiery need.

Under the drape of her muslin skirts, she parted her knees to sit lower on him, until her very core was in firm, restless contact with the throbbing hardness concealed inside his trousers. She was shaking, kissing him wildly, fidgeting on his lap in the most unladylike fashion, until, half-out of her mind, her frustration broke from her in a whisper. "Jordan, please!"

He paused, cast her a wicked half smile. "Please what, Mara?"

"You're a devil."

"Who, me?" With one elegant finger, he began lifting the hem of her skirts.

Her chest heaved. The man had her in the palm of his hand in that moment, and she didn't even care. Sheer, unadulterated thrill raced through her blood as his hands disappeared beneath the billows of dainty fabric, reaching for the placket of his trousers.

His hips lifted slightly, a motion that roused an eager sigh from her. She stared at him in breathless anticipation as he freed himself from the constraint of his clothes. But when she leaned closer to kiss him again, a pained look of need flitted over his chiseled face.

"Oh, God, Mara, are you sure?" he whispered as he guided his long, rigid member to the drenched threshold of her core. "Is this what you really want?"

Her answer was a kiss full of trembling intensity. "I need you, my only darling, please. I've waited for you my whole life."

He pulled her closer. All speech, all thought, all rational capability fled as he slowly entered her. Naught but a whispered groan of bliss escaped him as he glided in gently, taking her to the hilt, rock-hard, magnificent in size.

She was amazed at the ease with which he penetrated her after all the trouble her husband used to have. It sank in then, truly, that maybe *she* had never been the problem.

Jordan was right. Maybe there was nothing wrong with her. She had simply married the wrong man, as a young girl under pressure to take a husband.

If she had waited for Jordan, the man she had really wanted, then she saw now she'd never have had such difficulties with sex. Indeed, she might well have had half a dozen sons by now, and daughters, too. The thought brought a wave of anguish amid the physical pleasure that enveloped her.

She let it pass. She had him now, as it always should have been, and her heart soared to know that, finally, this was the first time together.

By God, it would not be their last.

Meanwhile, after years of abstinence, she was as tight as a virgin, but there was no pain, only wonder.

And love.

"*Jordan.*" Pinprick tears sprang into her eyes as she wrapped her arms dazedly around him, still barely able to believe it was happening. A dream was coming true.

He whispered her name in heady tones, looking into her eyes with a world of emotion churning in his own, their blue depths haunted by loss but filled with the hope of renewal.

Yes, maybe this would change things between them, but for the good, not in any way they had to fear.

They belonged entirely to each other in that moment, the long account of bygone years swept away with the next kiss. The past did not matter anymore, for now they had the future.

She kissed him desperately, and in seconds, their fleeting sorrow had dissolved as passion overtook them.

His hips surged beneath hers as he began rocking her, holding her by her waist. She clung to him, and moved with him, arching, her breasts caressing his chest with every deep, rhythmic thrust.

So this is how it's supposed to be, she thought faintly, every inch of her aglow.

But after such long anticipation, their joining overwhelmed her senses quickly. Spasms of pleasure threatened from the innermost regions of her womanhood. But she did not want this to end. She tried to hold back, quaking with the effort. But she had no control.

He seemed to understand.

"Just let go for me, darling. Come to me," he breathed, his hands gliding up and down her back. "It's all right. You need this. I want to make you come."

She buckled at the slightest urging. With a small cry, she simply ravished the man on her knees, taking him greedily. Her whole body was shaking as she rode him to a triumphant finish, fairly screaming with release.

He joined her with a rough cry and an even rougher motion, thrusting into her. She gasped at the rod of hot iron pulsating within her. Trembling with passion, he was no longer the civilized diplomat-earl that she knew. Here was a rough and wild side of him she had never seen before—and she reveled in it.

Lost to all reason, his famous self-control nowhere to be found, he grunted with pleasure, gripping and squeezing her rear end in both of his hands, pumping with a fierce abandon that shook the whole coach. He bit her on the shoulder when he suddenly "let go," as he had put it. He clutched her hard, fairly growling with ecstasy, his breath hot against her ear, obscenities tumbling from him as feverish endearments.

She was fascinated as his feral groans faded to a disbelieving whisper. *"Oh, my God."*

"Yes." Trembling all over, she laid her head down on his shoulder. "Mmm."

Beyond that, neither of them moved. They remained joined, both dazed, but loath ever to be separated.

In that spellbound silence, Mara did not dare to say a word. She did not trust herself to tell him anything except, *"I love you,"* but neither of them was nearly ready for that.

After a long moment, Jordan finally spoke, still sounding slightly shaken and blissfully out of breath. "I hope I didn't leave teeth marks."

"Really?" Mara smiled in satisfaction and let out a sigh. "I rather hope you did."

Drake watched Emily feed the horses, unable to take his eyes off her.

The sky was bright, and the trees swayed over the meadow as she stepped up onto the bottom rail of the fence. Leaning over to shove away some of the greedier mares, she fed her handful of grain to a meeker chestnut filly who obviously did not rank as high as the others in the herd's hierarchy.

"There you are, girl," she murmured, her soft voice beguiling Drake right along with the animals.

Because he had remembered her on sight, his captors had started letting her take him outside.

Emily said it would be good for him, fresh air and sunshine. Max had finally conceded, for she was the only one who seemed to know where the devil to start with him.

"Here." She turned to him with a reassuring smile. "Let's feed them together like we used to. Give me your hand."

When he slowly put out his hand, she spilled a fistful of oats into his palm. "Go on," she coaxed him in the same soothing tone with which she had spoken to the horses.

Drake did not remember hand-feeding the horses with her, but that dulcet voice, as soft as breezes, could have given him any order, and he'd have obeyed.

Standing beside her, he reached over the fence and let an old bay gelding lip the grain from his hand.

Meanwhile, Sergeant Parker stood a few yards off, keeping a wary eye on him, his rifle hanging across his back. As the horse's velvety muzzle tickled his hand, Drake knew that his captors' suspicion of him was not unwarranted.

Even now, he was well aware of how easy it would be to vault over the fence onto one of the horses' backs and gallop out of their reach.

He mightn't get far without tack, but at least he would get a running start on the Order. He could escape, hide, survive—and make his way to London, back to James.

Dread for the old man's safety still moved like ominous storm clouds over the landscape of his mind—only now, a light had broken. And Drake found he could not tear himself away from her.

Emily.

He watched the gamekeeper's beautiful daughter in endless fascination.

Finding her, knowing that sweet, freckled face at once had

suddenly arrested the fear and rage that had been ruling him for an age. Near her, he felt at peace, his battered soul like a ship's crew resting in the clear eye of a tempest.

But somehow he knew this was only a brief calm, this country idyll. Despite all he had been through so far, the other end of the storm was bound to be worse.

For now, his fascination with Emily kept him here. Hang him if she wasn't as odd and wild as he was, in her way. Perhaps he sensed that if anyone could help him, she could. Perhaps he knew deep down in his marrow that if he could trust anyone, it was her.

Only her.

Acutely aware of the mysterious beauty beside him, close enough to touch—though he did not dare—he obediently stroked the broad, flat cheek of one of the horses, scratching away a little patch of dried mud.

Emily jumped down off the fence and turned to him. "Let's take a walk in the woods. Perhaps you'll remember the path—but don't worry if you can't. I know the way. I'd never let you get lost, Drake. Come."

He stared into her eyes, those eyes that had haunted his dreams for so long. Deep violet-blue with bright gold flecks, they entranced him even now. He nodded, abandoning his visions of escaping on a horse to follow her across the spongy emerald lawn into the wooded park surrounding Westwood Manor.

Sergeant Parker followed at a respectful distance.

Drake ignored him, contemplating Emily as she walked ahead of him. The slim, fey beauty did not appear to belong entirely to this world. With her freckled, sun-kissed complexion, her long, flowing hair, and her strange clothes, she made no bones about respectability. She was dressed more like a maiden of some Anglo-Saxon warrior tribe in worn leather boots, shin-length skirts of a dark, drab color, a leather belt around her hips slung with an odd assortment of the tools of her trade, attending plants and animals.

Her knife sheath, however, was empty.

Max had made her hand over her blade for fear that Drake might steal it from her to hurt himself and others.

Clever one, that Rotherstone.

Drake brushed off his annoyance and contented himself with watching the swing of Emily's skirts as she stalked over the ground ahead of him. Her long, golden brown tresses billowed on the breeze, slightly tangled, curling at the ends.

A woman of few words, she strode ahead of him in silent confidence, her very walk proclaiming her a free spirit who answered to no man.

Into the woods they went, the path opening before them. At once, Drake was struck by the familiar smell of earth flooding his nostrils, the smell of turf and soil and dormant things coming back to life.

A thick carpet of decaying wet leaves from the previous autumn cushioned their strides. Emily's footfalls made not a sound as she led the way, as much a woodland creature as any graceful doe. Even her clothes blended into the earthy scenery.

Sensing him falling behind, she turned and gave him a softly commanding look that brought him back into motion. Those deep, mysterious eyes could have summoned him from the other side of the world.

They matched the color of the bluebells on display at the feet of the barren trees and amid the still-leafless thorny brush. He followed her. Delicate sunlight filtered through the branches overhead and dappled the path before them while the bright springtime chirps and lilting warbles of flitting birds filled the woods.

Drake stared at the decaying beauty of a mossy old log that looked like it had lain there for a hundred years.

They wandered on, and vague traces of memory began to flash across his mind, chasing her in some childhood game, echoes of laughter.

He could feel the pent-up weight of memory building like pregnant clouds before a rain.

When they came to a brook, she crouched down at the banks and trailed her hand in the water. She nodded in encouragement to him to follow suit.

Drake splashed his face. The bracing cold water helped to clear his head.

I'm not sure I really want to remember. Doing so would make it all the harder to leave her again, and yet, he knew he would. He had no choice. All he lacked was opportunity.

It probably would not come today. He'd have to bide his time. He lowered his lashes, aware of Sergeant Parker several yards behind them. He did not doubt the trusty sergeant would blow a hole in him before he'd let him get away. Max might not do it on account of their boyhood friendship, but no such sentimental attachment would stop Parker from pulling the trigger.

"Come." Emily rose gracefully again and stole deeper into the woods.

Drake followed, his sense of familiarity sharpening with every second. She stopped a short distance down the path before a great, craggy oak tree whose gnarled ancient trunk rose from the forest floor like a ruined tower.

Her sideward glance beguiled him. "Race you!" To his surprise, she began climbing the tree. "Aren't you coming?" she called in a saucy tone over her shoulder.

"I don't think that's a—"

"Don't think, Drake. Just move," she instructed. "Your body will know what to do."

He frowned, but she was already well ahead of him, apparently unconcerned that he could see the stockings that disappeared into her boots. As her ivory petticoat swished, he even caught a glimpse of her unbleached cotton long drawers.

A remembered sentiment echoed to him from his boyhood. *I'm not about to be outdone by a girl!* At once he began climbing after her, chasing the past as much as following her. She was right—somehow, haltingly, his hands knew exactly where to reach to find the old woody knots in the trunk to grab onto, where to put his feet to ascend the massive oak, as if he'd done it countless times before.

In the next moment, Emily was settling herself into a cozy crook between two massive boughs some thirty feet above the forest floor. She looked like she belonged there.

Reaching the top of the trunk, Drake hesitated, assessing his situation.

She pointed helpfully to another thick juncture of the boughs across from her. "Your place is there."

Drake stared at it, ever so faintly remembering. The main trunk tapered upward, but the massive branch she had indicated offered a comfortable spot to lounge back with some security. He took his place across from her.

Ensconced in their tree, feet dangling, Emily smiled at him; but suddenly, Drake noticed the small scar on the back of her hand. "Your hand! I recognize that scar."

"Do you?" She leaned closer, studying him. "Then how did I get it?" she challenged softly. "Don't strain," she soothed when he swallowed hard, faltering. "Just let it come to you."

He closed his eyes for a long moment, then suddenly had the answer and smiled as he murmured: "My father's hunting falcon bit you."

When he opened his eyes again, she was grinning. "Indeed, he did. Prince Edward."

"Yes! That was his name. If that was not the haughtiest, most ill-tempered bird . . . and dangerous." He shook his head at her in wonder. "You were just a little girl."

"Eight years old." She nodded proudly.

"What were you thinking, putting your hand in his cage?"

"I wanted to pet him."

Drake scoffed, smiling, while Emily laughed.

"He was so beautiful! I didn't know he'd bite me."

"You also didn't know his favorite food was baby rabbits," he said, as another memory of those days came back to him without warning.

She wrinkled her nose at the reminder. "Do you remember the day we broke into the mews and rescued that clutch of coneys that were to be fed to him?"

Drake narrowed his eyes, amazed at the images of them together as children that begun to bloom across his mind. "Yes . . . we broke in and set those little rabbits free."

"You got in so much trouble," she teased.

"But you never did, did you?" he countered with a half smile. "You were the troublemaker."

"No, I wasn't. You were."

He shook his head. "You must have talked me into it."

"You just couldn't stand to see me cry."

Drake stared at her.

"Those baby rabbits were going to die a horrible death! We had to help them. But you were my hero that day," she reminded him. "You were the one who picked the lock."

"I don't remember that."

"Well, I do," she said. "I could never forget how you went against your father for me that night. And for those baby rabbits," she added.

He smiled at her, mystified. "I can't believe you still have that scar. But I'll bet you've never stopped trying to gentle wild creatures."

She smiled at him. Drake searched her face, hugely relieved that these small fragments of his life were starting to come back. It must be due to her. He had not felt so close to anyone in ages, so safe with anyone.

He knew in his heart that he had always trusted her. And that she had always loved him, even though his parents had warned him she was too far beneath his station.

Emily held his gaze for a long moment, her smile softening. "Do you know why I brought you here, Drake?"

He shook his head, mute with emotion.

"This is our Story Tree." She reached out and laid her scarred hand over his. "It's time for you to tell me what happened to you out there."

At once, he pulled his hand away, shaking his head. "I don't remember."

"Yes, you do. You're just afraid. But you're safe now. You must tell me. I know about the Order, remember?" she whispered, glancing down in the direction of Sergeant Parker. "You told me all about it when we were small. How you were going to go to a secret military school in Scotland, where you'd train to become a great warrior. I've never told anyone, just like I promised. But you don't know how I've worried for you. God, I thought you were dead. Finding you alive again, Drake, it's the best thing that ever happened to me, but this . . . what they've done to you—" She quickly looked away as her eyes filled with tears. She fought them back and turned to him again.

His heart was pounding.

"I want to help you. Please, you still trust me, don't you? You know I'd never hurt you. You cannot hold this inside. I'm going to take care of you, but I need to know the nature of the wound. Drake, tell me what those people did to you."

He just stared at her, refusing to talk now just as he had in that German prison, but for vastly different reasons. He did not want to remember. He just wanted to put it behind him. Besides, someone like Emily should never hear words like "torture."

She waited, then shook her head when he remained silent. "Don't be afraid. Whatever it is, you don't have to face it alone. I will make you well again, Drake. Every day I will tend you until you're strong again—"

"I am not one of your wild animals," he cut her off, unable to bear anymore. His voice was shaking, his throat tight. "If you love me, Emily, then you must let me go. Help me to escape these men."

"No. You need to stay here," she countered fiercely. "With me. Where you'll be safe. Where you belong. I'm not going to let them hurt you anymore. You can't ask that of me."

"You don't understand. There's more I have to do."

"You're not ready! By God, haven't they taken enough of you?" she cried. Then she shook her head stubbornly. "No. I will not hear of it. At the very least, you must regain your strength. You're not going anywhere until you've had a chance to heal."

"What makes you believe that's even possible, little Emily?" he murmured, eyeing her darkly. "Has it never occurred to you that I'm already beyond your power to save?"

She paled a bit at his answer, then shook her head again. "I don't believe that," she replied. "I will never give up on you, Drake, no matter what happens."

He dropped his gaze, seething. What a fool she was.

Beautiful, innocent fool.

Chapter 10

Making love to Mara had left Jordan with a delirious taste of happiness—and an uneasy conscience.

He was not at all accustomed to either sensation, and both made it difficult to concentrate when he sat down a few nights later to play cards with the Regent's set at Watier's. As the dealer flicked the cards to each player seated round the green baize table, Jordan forced himself to ignore his ever-growing concern over all Mara didn't know and focused instead on what he had come here to do.

His task that night was simple though it would require finesse: establish contact with his target, Albert Carew, the Duke of Holyfield, and begin to cultivate "Alby's" trust—this was the name by which his fashionable friends still called the duke from his days as Lord Albert Carew, a leading dandy but a mere second son, before he had come into his elder brother's title.

Once Jordan gained Albert's confidence, he would soon get to the bottom of his dealings with the Prometheans, who his controller was, and what the enemy wanted the duke to accomplish for them in his post among the Regent's innermost circle of rowdy male friends.

They were an odd lot, to say the least, Jordan mused, scanning them around the table.

Tonight he would also have to make sure the wild men of the Regent's set accepted him, so that he would be invited back and could continue observing the suspected Promethean traitor in their midst. That, in turn, meant he'd better play well at the tables—but not too well.

He did not want to outshine them, though he usually excelled at card games that allowed for a measure of mathematical play.

It seemed to be working. But he'd been doing so well all night at whist partnered with Lord Yarmouth that he figured he'd better take care to lose a bit when the gentlemen switched to macao in the wee hours of the morning.

Ah, macao, that infernal game for which Watier's was infamous. Losing money at the macao table was not difficult to do. Indeed, the youngest member of the Regent's set, "Golden" Ball-Hughes, barely twenty, had nearly perfected the art.

Having already squandered a greater fortune on the game than most people would ever possess, "the Golden Ball" seemed cheerfully determined to lose the rest of his still-vast inheritance before his thirtieth birthday.

Macao was a form of *vingt-et-un* where the house dealt each player one card to start instead of two, the aim, to reach the count of nine rather than twenty-one without going bust. Within an hour of play, Jordan had successfully divested the Falconridge fortune of some three thousand pounds. But he gave up the fish-shaped ivory chips representing the large sum with an idle smile.

"Well played, Holyfield," he offered, for Alby had done remarkably well that round.

The preening dandy feasted on the praise, which came at him from several directions as they all congratulated him.

"Born lucky," he declared, stacking up his ivory chips.

To be sure, Jordan thought, still smiling faintly. No doubt it was Alby's wonderful *luck* that had thrown his brother's dukedom into his lap and opened doors for him until he was dining with a future King of England. The Prometheans could not possibly have had anything to do it.

Of course, the Order knew better than that.

His elder brother's drowning death along with his newly pregnant wife while the couple had been on holiday in France, so near Malcolm Banks's territory, had instantly raised their suspicions that it was not the tragic boating accident it appeared.

It was possible that Albert might have paid someone to kill them out of his own dark ambition, but the Order doubted it. The dandy was a smug, scheming piece of arrogance but probably not capable of murder. Someone in his orbit might well be, however, someone who had a use for a man with access to the highest circles in the land. Someone with the ruthlessness to elevate the second-born son deliberately into the dukedom—for a price.

But for what purpose?

It was Jordan's mission to find out. At any rate, next came the refreshments. Considering it was three in the morning, Jordan had little interest in Chef Labourie's creations, but the other men's reactions were amusing to observe.

When the doors to the adjoining eating room were opened, a bevy of waiters welcomed His Royal Highness and his followers with a flourish.

After all, the Regent himself had initiated the founding

of Watier's upon hearing from his companions that the food at the other clubs was intolerably bland and monotonous. He had at once dispatched two of the royal chefs under his former page, named Watier, to create a new club on Piccadilly with an outstanding menu, worthy of London's gourmands and his own royal stomach.

As Jordan had rather expected, they proceeded to devour everything in sight. He hid his amusement as he took a plate—not to do so would have been rude—but truly, he had never seen a more colorful array of eccentrics, from the debauched to the downright strange.

There was one clubman called Bligh, who clearly belonged in an asylum, judging by his obsessive mutterings to himself. Even the other fellows gave him a wide berth.

Jordan had blanched and kept a wary eye on Bligh from the moment he had realized the unstable fellow had brought two pistols with him, right there in the Regent's presence. This was not a comfortable state of affairs for the Realm.

Prinny did not appear in the least concerned about his batty friend's Mantons, but Jordan had to restrain himself from leaping over the table to carry out a weapon disarm.

Most of the rest seemed harmless—though not to pretty young girls from the lower orders. Or boys. It was difficult to say. His gaze moved on. His Royal Highness might have an expert eye in choosing art, but with all the world at his fingertips, he had some rather strange taste in friends. Never had Jordan dined with such an exotic collection of giddy eccentrics.

The beaming boy, Golden Ball, kept bouncing about asking endless questions, blithely interrupting the literary man of the lot, Scrope Davies, who waxed poetic after each gulp of Scotch. Lord Yarmouth uttered shockingly lewd remarks about various ladies of the ton and what he'd like to do to them, scandalizing Lord Petersham, who lisped a comment of disapproval before pulling out his snuffbox to take a ritualistic pinch. Rumor had it Petersham owned a different snuffbox for every day of the year.

No one mentioned Beau Brummell, now exiled from the Regent's presence. He had ceased to exist. But his dwindling influence could still be noted in the great care all the dandies still lavished on their dress. Jordan wondered if His Highness ever missed his former friend and sartorial advisor, but he appeared content, holding court like a great, ruddy lump at the end of the table.

At his elbow was the even larger Lord Alvanley, with his nonstop witticisms—a great, fat, hilarious giant—currently making sport of the Honorable "Poodle" Byng for bringing his dog to the club.

"But he's good luck!" the doting pet owner protested as he fed his pampered poodle a bit of Chef Labourie's duck *à l'orange.*

Meanwhile, across the table, Colonel Hanger was making a private side wager with Lord Barrymore, known as Hellgate, on how long it might take the old "Drunken Duke" of Norfolk to fall out of his chair and pass out on the floor. His Grace already looked well on his way there.

All things considered, Albert seemed to be the most normal person there, aside from Jordan.

He seemed as perplexed by the rest of them as Jordan was. When Albert stepped out on the balcony to smoke a cheroot, Jordan saw it was the perfect time to approach his target.

"You have some skill at macao, Holyfield," Jordan congratulated as he approached, remembering how much Albert had enjoyed the earlier praise.

"Hmm, yes, thank you. I am not without my little accomplishments," he admitted, looking quite charmed with himself.

He was considered a handsome fellow by the ladies of the ton, and that, even before he'd got the dukedom.

Albert turned to look Jordan up and down. "Falconridge, is it?"

"Yes, Your Grace," he answered with a bow, but a wary sneer flicked over Alby's smooth countenance.

"Aren't you Rotherstone's friend?"

"We are club mates," Jordan allowed, well aware that Max and Alby, born on neighboring estates, had despised each other from boyhood.

And then there was their whole rivalry over Daphne.

"But I've seen you around Town with him," he persisted. "In Society."

"Not lately, I should think," Jordan said with a long-suffering look.

"Really?" Now he had Albert's full attention. "How unfortunate. Did you boys have a falling-out?" he asked as a gloating smile spread across his face.

"Well, not exactly." Jordan paused and looked askance at him. "Let's just say there are some men who are changed by marriage."

Albert stared at him eagerly. "How's that?"

"Well, you didn't hear it from me, Holyfield," he lied in a low tone, "but that bride of his keeps poor Max on a very short leash."

His eyes flared with glee. "You don't say."

"I fear he endures a considerable amount of nagging."

"My God! Daphne is a shrew? How delicious," Alby murmured. "I never would have thought."

"Women change with marriage, too, sometimes," he said sagely. "The most charming coquette can become a very harpy once the ring is on that finger."

Alby shook his head, savoring Jordan's revelations. "I am astounded. And yet, strangely pleased."

"Didn't you used to court her once? Daphne—I mean—Lady Rotherstone?"

Albert's short laugh was part wince, part sneer. "That was ages ago. But fortunately, I lost interest and abandoned the notion. She was not my type."

Ha.

"Well, from what I see, you are lucky to have been rejected."

The reminder of his defeat persuaded Albert to drop the subject of Lord and Lady Rotherstone altogether.

Meanwhile, Jordan could imagine his best friend's indignation if Max could've heard him describe the Divine Daphne as a shrew.

He suppressed a smile, recalling that he owed his team leader a report when he got home. Max had written to him yesterday, updating him on the progress Drake was making thanks to the influence of some mysterious servant girl called Emily.

Albert, meanwhile, had looked away, exhaling smoke from his cheroot while the night wind tousled his sculpted blond locks.

No doubt he had worn curl-papers for hours before coming out, the coxcomb. No man's hair should look that good. His next words, however, dissolved Jordan's mocking mood. "I hear you have made quite a conquest of Lady Pierson, Falconridge."

He sent him a sharp but guarded look askance. "On the contrary, it is Her Ladyship who has conquered me."

Albert snorted, taking his smooth-toned comment for idle gallantry.

Which was just as well.

Jordan hated feigning a cavalier attitude about Mara, but was not about to draw the attention of a suspected Promethean toward her. "One must amuse oneself somehow in this life, eh, Holyfield?" he tossed out.

Albert shrugged and bestowed his highest praise: "She dresses well."

"Indeed," he murmured, though he preferred her out of those fine Bond Street gowns she liked to wear.

"Doesn't it bother you, though—" Alby turned to him, "how she's always nattering on about that brat of hers? 'Sblood, the woman thinks her son is God's gift to the world! It annoys me to no end."

Jordan laughed softly. "I suppose she does. But you know, just because a woman talks, a man doesn't have to listen."

"True! And if there are benefits to be gained by pretending interest . . ."

"Precisely." Jordan held up his shot glass of whiskey to the lady, wherever she was, then sent it down the hatch.

Albert was regarding him with some amusement, a degree of cautious interest. "Will you be escorting Mara to the ball at Carlton House next week? You know, the unofficial celebration for Princess Charlotte's engagement."

"Yes, I will have that honor," he declared without concern. "Why do you ask?"

"There will be cards that night at the ball. I saw how well you were doing with Yarmouth." He glanced toward the eating room, then looked again at Jordan slyly. "Since we both seem to know what we're doing at the tables, perhaps we should partner at whist that night and give the others a thumping."

Jordan flashed a smile. "I like the way you think, Holyfield. That sounds very profitable."

"Excellent." Albert drew himself up and gave Jordan a princely nod. "We'll clean 'em out, then. I'm glad you've joined us, Falconridge. At least you're a vast improvement over Rotherstone. He never really fit in with our set. But you might."

"Why, thank you, Duke." Jordan bowed, not trusting himself to say another word.

Albert lifted his chin and took leave of him with a haughty

nod. Nose in the air, the duke sauntered off to rejoin the only man in the room he seemed to think truly worthy of him: the Regent.

Jordan eyed his retreating back with jaundiced humor. In all, a good night's work.

"Doesn't she look absolutely beautiful?" Mara exclaimed, watching Princess Charlotte and Prince Leopold greeting their guests in a receiving line that seemed to stretch for miles through the doors of Carlton House and beyond. "How proud you must be of your little girl, all grown-up," she said to the Regent, misty-eyed. "Look at the two of them together. They're adorable!"

"I suppose," the Regent murmured, though his eyes twinkled with fatherly pride.

"Oh, look at how he dotes on her."

The second that the chubby, slightly awkward Princess Charlotte dropped her fan, Prince Leopold rushed to pick it up for her and presented it reverently to his betrothed.

Mara sighed at their sweetness, so young and innocent. "Anyone can see they are in love. The prince can't take his eyes off her, and she is absolutely beaming."

The large royal looked askance at her. "So are you, my dear."

"Am I?" Mara turned to him with a deep blush and an irrepressible smile.

He lifted an eyebrow knowingly. "Just be careful with him. That is all I'll say. You know how protective I am of you and Thomas. If he hurts either one of you, I will throw him in the Tower."

"I'm sure that won't be necessary. He is the soul of honor," she declared. "We are thoroughly happy." She glanced toward the card room, where Jordan was engaged in whist, but beside her, His Royal Highness let out a disgruntled sigh.

"My God, the place is full of people in love. I can hardly stand it," he muttered wryly, but a wistfulness came into his eyes.

Mara wondered if he was thinking about his own first love—another widow—the unfortunate Mrs. Fitzherbert. He had been forbidden to marry her because she was a Catholic.

But he shrugged off sentimentality. "Enjoy, my dear," he advised with a smile as he left her company and went to mingle among his countless guests.

Mara watched the aging prince return to his hosting duties with a sadness to think that, for all the power and immeasurable wealth His Royal Highness controlled, he had been deprived of that treasure free to the lowliest peasant: love.

She looked up at the Gerrit Dou, now hanging over the mantel in the Blue Velvet Room, where it had claimed pride of place. Even the painting, dark as it was in the Dutch style, bespoke a man's love for a woman. Some elderly merchant had commissioned the portrait of his equally aged wife. What shone through was not the fresh-faced prettiness of a bride-to-be like Princess Charlotte, but the wizened beauty of an old woman's face, deeply lined, her looks long faded, but in her calm eyes, the inward light of love that had already lasted a lifetime.

Feeling herself growing foolishly misty-eyed once more with the drift of her thoughts, Mara shook herself, then went over to peek into the great drawing room where many four-man card tables were set up.

Here the noise of the ball gave way to the hush of the players' concentration. Mara fought a smile, seeing Jordan partnered with the insufferable Alby, duke of the dandies. Why, her *cher ami* must be a clever cardplayer, indeed, if the haughty Holyfield had condescended to pair with him at whist. Even as a second son, Alby had not been one to waste his time on losers. He did not even speak to men who bought their boots from the wrong maker, or, horrors—could not get in at White's.

The Earl of Falconridge, however, lived up to Alby's standards with ease, she mused, staring hungrily at her lover. His black and white formal clothes were simply masculine perfection. But that was Jordan for you.

As though he could feel her gaze perusing him, he looked over slowly toward the doorway and spotted her.

He sent her a smoldering smile from across the room, and Mara blushed, her heart skipping a beat as their eyes locked, a burst of gooseflesh tickling across her skin.

Oh, my. His plans for her that night were visible in his eyes' banked fire. Mara swallowed hard, her blush deepening.

Heavens, all she could seem to do was blush these days, and laugh at nothing, and hum inane tunes. Delilah had grown quite fed up with her.

She returned his smile in patient anticipation but did not begrudge him his card game. She'd have him all to herself later.

She sent him a little parting smile and tore herself away. Waving her fan to help cool her blood, she suddenly saw poor Cole, alone and brooding, leaning on the balcony that overlooked the Octagon below.

Mara followed his gaze, then winced with sympathy to see that he was watching Delilah throw herself at a mustachioed captain of the Blues.

Blast it, why is she being such a fool? But she already knew the answer. Cole knew it, too, but he certainly looked like he was running out of patience.

Mara set aside her preoccupation with a certain earl and went over to offer him some sympathy—and encouragement.

"Don't give up on her yet," she said softly, joining him at the railing.

"Why not?" he grumbled. "I'm a fool not to, the hussy. She is deliberately tormenting me!"

"Yes, but, in her own odd way, the hussy loves you," she said archly. "Believe me, she's just scared."

He turned to her with a look of abject misery. "Will you talk to her for me?"

Mara lifted her eyebrows. "I'm really not sure I ought to interfere."

"At least get her away from that blackguard, whoever he is! Please?" he added, looking so desperate that Mara smiled ruefully.

"That I can do." She patted Cole on the back as she moved past him, then she headed downstairs to try to talk her friend out of chasing her own destruction, or at least, to pry Delilah off the handsome officer.

At the victorious conclusion of their card game, Jordan rose and shook hands with Albert and their defeated opponents.

Even as they gave up their table to the next quartet of players, Albert was already gloating. "Well played, Falconridge! I'd say we did quite well for ourselves."

"Thanks to your skill, Holyfield," Jordan said without a trace of irony in his voice. "It was your play that carried the game."

"Maybe so, but you didn't make any major mistakes yourself."

"You are too kind."

Albert gave him a gratified nod, dismissing him, it seemed, then he went swaggering off into the crowd. Jordan gazed after him, wondering how Max had ever endured growing up next door to him. He had never met a greater jackass in his life.

In truth, he was surprised they had won, for once more,

he had spent the game uncharacteristically distracted. All he wanted to do was be with Mara.

His mouth watered at the thought of her in the plunging rose-colored ball gown that skimmed her curves, and the sultry heat that had warmed her dark eyes when she had smiled at him from the doorway.

Beyond an appreciative gaze, he had not chanced any outward sign of his passion for her. Not with his target sitting across from him at the card table. After all, he had told Albert that his interest in her was merely sexual.

This was for Mara's own safety, and Albert, a thorough cynic, was quick to believe it. But Jordan was well aware that the ploy could explode in his face if such words ever got back to her. *Where the devil is she, anyway?*

On his way out of the card room to look for her, he paused before the Regent, who came sauntering in just then, his ruddy cheeks aglow. "Falconridge."

Jordan acknowledged His Royal Highness with a courteous bow. "Sir."

The Regent apparently noticed his restless glance.

"Looking for someone?" he drawled, succumbing to a wry half smile. "She went that way." He nodded over his shoulder.

"Thank you, sir."

"Hmm." Eyeing him skeptically, Prinny moved on and was again surrounded by his guests.

Jordan went out to the balcony, nodded to Cole, and braced his hands on the railing, scanning the vast, airy space of the Octagon below, where the dancing would soon begin. *There she is.* A smile curved his lips as his gaze homed in on Mara. She was talking to Delilah.

He pushed away from the balcony to go to her, but on his way down the Grand Staircase, he glimpsed Albert from the corner of his eye. Jordan paused, registering some unknown, furtive mischief in the oh-so-casual way the duke was strolling along the wall below.

Albert enjoyed being the center of attention too much to stick close to the wall unless he was up to something. *Where's he going?*

Jordan knew better than to let the duke out of his sight. So, rather than going to see his lady, he followed his target, instead.

Some yards ahead, Albert nonchalantly took a glass of champagne off the tray of a footman and lifted a small painted cake off a table of sweets as he strolled past. Nibbling the one and sipping from the other, he pressed on, but Jordan sensed a calculated purpose behind the dandy's careless drifting.

As Jordan trailed him, he knew he was seeing Carlton House as it was meant to be seen, by the brilliance of its glittering chandeliers, a thousand bejeweled guests thronging its dazzling staterooms, gilded halls, and gleaming corridors.

The nude marble statues watched an endless paradc of Europe's rich and titled arriving in their best finery, the men in their elegant evening uniform of black tail coats and starchy white cravats like his own, the ladies blooming in every imaginable color, like the royal botanical collection at Kew.

Keeping Albert in sight, he heard snippets of conversation as he weaved among the crowd.

"The wedding will take place soon."

"On the second of May, isn't it?"

"Yes, at Westminster?"

"No, they're having it right here at Carlton House."

"Really?"

"It's to be a very small and private affair, mostly just the family, according to His Royal Highness. He thinks they're going to have it in the Crimson State Room."

"Isn't that lovely?"

The music also drifted in and out of his awareness, different groups of musicians posted here and there around the sprawling palace. Here a violin trio; there a harp and flutist. In through the window floated the strains of the Regent's favorite German brass band playing out on the terrace that overlooked the gardens.

All of them faded behind him as Jordan continued following Albert. Ahead, the duke was walking at a more determined pace now.

Twin antechambers with pristine marble floors flanked the first entrance hall where guests were still arriving beneath the great portico. Albert sauntered past it all, heading toward the Regent's private apartments within Carlton House, if Jordan recalled correctly. He was fairly sure this was the way they had come the first time he had visited, accompanying Mara to present her royal friend with the Gerrit Dou.

Taking his final swig of champagne, Albert went into a room off the far left corner of the antechamber.

Jordan made a cautious approach, sidling up to the double doors of the room. A quick glimpse around the corner revealed a grand Gothic library.

A number of guests were sitting around inside or chatting since it was quieter there.

Jordan furrowed his brow to hear Albert make an announcement to the others who had sought refuge there.

"Ladies and gentlemen, if I may have your attention," he said smoothly, "His Royal Highness will be making a toast on the Grand Staircase in a few moments to Princess Charlotte and Prince Leopold. Catalani is here and she has agreed to sing a song for the happy couple after the toast.

Not to be missed. Yes, that's correct," he answered an older woman who asked a question Jordan could not make out.

"You may wish to begin moving toward the Octagon, for directly after Catalani sings, I hear they are going to start the dancing."

The guests apparently did not dream that this might be some sort of ruse but took his advice to heart and began hurrying out of the library.

Jordan was bemused. With a stealthy glance around the corner of the doorway, he saw Albert momentarily distracted by a guest who wouldn't leave. As the duke repeated his announcements in a louder tone to an elderly couple, Jordan seized the moment to slip into the library while the rest were leaving.

At once, he stole behind the nearest large pillar, maneuvering out of sight.

A moment later, Albert passed nearby, elegantly shooing the last of the guests out of the library. Then he shut the library door behind them and locked it.

Immediately, Albert flew to the window, whipping the curtains shut. He moved from one to the next, then blew out the candles around the room, leaving only one small flame to work by.

Jordan welcomed the dark as an aid to his cover, while Albert, still unaware of his presence, strode to a small door at the far corner of the library.

Staring at Albert by the dim glow of the single candle he carried, Jordan saw him take a key out of his waistcoat.

He could feel the dandy's nervousness, could hear it in the way he fumbled with the lock.

What the hell is he after? Jordan crept closer, rounding the pillar—until Albert suddenly stopped, perhaps sensing another presence in the room.

He turned around and searched the darkness. "Who's there?" he demanded in a taut voice.

Jordan held his breath and did not move.

After a moment, Albert cursed under his breath and seemed to conclude it was only a figment of his own guilty conscience. Then he resumed his frantic scramble to open the door.

Waiting, his back to the pillar, Jordan listened until he heard the lock click, the handle turn, and the door squeak slightly being opened.

In a gilded mirror above one of the library's fireplaces, he could see that Albert had entered a small, private room with a desk and file cabinets.

Given that they were so near the Regent's private quarters, Jordan could not help but conclude grimly that Albert had just broken into His Royal Highness's personal business office.

Albert set his candle on the desk, again took out the key, and opened the top drawer.

Jordan watched in ice-cold patience as Albert rifled through the papers in the Regent's desk, his face a pale mask of dread by the flickering light of his candle. It was not the look of a man who was doing something he *wanted* to do but rather something he had been ordered to do, compelled. Indeed, what Albert was doing right now could get him hanged. He was looking for something, but what was he trying to find?

As the seconds ticked by, Jordan debated over whether to step out of the shadows and confront the dandy or to wait and see what he might do next.

All of a sudden, a knock sounded on the library door.

Inside the royal cabinet, Albert froze.

"Hullo? Is anybody in there?" a voice called.

Jordan looked over in horror.

Mara!

"Jordan, are you in there? I thought I saw you come this way." She knocked again. "Jordan? Open up! You promised me a dance. They're about to play the waltz!"

Good God, she followed me!

While Jordan cringed, he could practically feel Albert absorbing Mara's words. Suddenly, Albert was scrambling to put the papers back into the drawer, hurriedly locking it, and whisking his candle off the Regent's desk. He pulled the office door shut behind him and hastened to lock it, too.

This done, he took a few steps toward the center of the library and, with Mara still knocking, peered into the darkness in every direction; he held up his candle.

"Falconridge?" he whispered in angry demand. "Are you in here? Falconridge! By God, speak if you are here!"

Albert waited.

Jordan held his breath.

Damn it. This was exactly why he never mixed his work with pleasure. Whatever progress he had made with Albert, she had just unwittingly destroyed.

His only hope was that Albert would conclude that Mara was mistaken.

She knocked again. "Jordan?"

Albert sounded like he wasn't sure what to believe. "If you are in here, Falconridge, you will be sorry."

Jordan did not say a word.

He did not breathe.

He could feel Albert peering into the shadows, searching for him, but when Mara banged on the door again, the duke hissed a curse under his breath and left empty-handed, exiting by another door between a pair of columns on the other end of the room.

Jordan deduced that Albert would return to the party as

his safest option after all his sneaking around. He would want to be seen, to assure the world nothing out of the ordinary was going on.

Meanwhile, Jordan eased out of his place of concealment and went to answer the door before Mara drew any more unwanted attention.

Her knocking was beginning to sound more testy than good-natured. "Jordan, I know you're in there! Are you feeling ill?"

There was an ominous pause as he approached the door between them.

"I saw you come this way," she informed him through the door. "Jordan—are you in there alone?"

His eyes widened. She feared he had slipped away with another woman? Good Lord!

But he had seen her jealous before—at Delilah's dinner party. If Mara had indeed seen him come in here, then she was going to be suspicious about why she was being ignored.

And he could not have that.

"There you are!" she exclaimed the second he opened the door. "What are you doing in there?"

"Waiting for you." Jordan grabbed her wrist, pulled her into the room, straight into his arms, and kissed her heartily.

Change the subject . . . a favorite spy technique.

It never failed.

Chapter 11

With the Regent's cryptic warning to be careful with Jordan ringing in her ears, Mara had been alarmed when he had failed to answer the door. What exactly had the Regent meant by that, anyway? Did her royal friend know something about Jordan she did not—something that might've come out, perhaps, while the men were playing cards?

Good God, did he have another woman?

He well might, she had thought in sudden dread. After all, she did not see him all the time. They were lovers, but they each still had their own independent lives.

It was not simply that she did not trust in happiness to stay. It was that she could swear sometimes there was something Jordan wasn't telling her.

Fortunately, his smooth, deep kiss dissolved her fleeting doubts and left her feeling silly and relieved.

"Better?" he asked, his voice a husky murmur in the dark.

"What are you up to?" she whispered as she nuzzled the

tip of his nose with her own. "You looked so sneaky when I saw you passing through the Octagon."

" 'Sneaky'?" he echoed, arching a brow.

"You heard me." Still vaguely suspicious, she peered past him into the darkened room. A single candle glowed on a heavy library table several yards away. "When I saw you coming down the stairs, I thought you meant to join me. But you just ignored me and walked right on, as if you had something more important to do." She gave him a pout.

"No, darling, I had a better idea. That's all. It took you long enough to get here," he added with a wicked smile.

"Well, you could've told me you wanted me to come with you!"

"So everyone else could see us leave together? Think of the talk, Lady Pierson," he scolded in silken roguery. "Besides, I thought this made it slightly more exciting. You like excitement, Mara. Don't you? I know you used to," he whispered as he trailed his fingertip down her chest to her nipple through her gown.

She stared at him, her lips still moist from his kiss. "What did you have in mind?"

He smiled, looking every inch a true member of the wild Inferno Club. "Take a guess."

"Really, Lord Falconridge!" she chided rather breathlessly. "In the middle of the royal ball? There are a thousand people out there."

"So many, they'll never notice the two of usc are gone."

He kissed her again; she did not object.

"You look so beautiful, Mara. I've been wanting you all night," he confessed in a sensuous whisper, gliding his lips against hers.

Mara quivered.

But she still found his behavior slightly odd though she couldn't quite put her finger on it.

"*Be careful with him.*"

He tilted his head with a look of amusement, studying her. "What's the matter, darling?"

"I don't know." She stared at him. "Something doesn't seem quite right."

"Why did you ask me if I was alone? You did not seriously think I was in here with another woman?"

"Well—" As soon as he spoke her fears aloud, she realized how daft it sounded. But as her cheeks colored, she attempted to mount a defense nonetheless. "There are more than a few ladies out there staring at you tonight!"

"Really? I had no idea! Where?" he teased, glancing around.

"You rogue!" She smacked him lightly and he laughed.

"There's only one woman here that interests me, my pet. Now, are we going to stand here and squabble over nothing or take advantage of our hiding place?" he purred, capturing her elbow and drawing her close until her body cradled his.

His tall, hard frame against her had the usual effect, but she huffed at his teasing and turned her blushing face away from the soft, inquisitive brush of his lips. "Why did it take you so long to answer the door?"

"I couldn't find it after I'd blown out the candles."

"And why did you blow out the candles?"

"Why do you think?" He kissed away her slight pout.

She pulled back just a bit to look into his eyes.

He gazed so deeply into hers, so seductively. "You have no one to be jealous of, Mara. I'm all yours. Shall I prove it to you?" He captured her face between his hands and lowered his lips hungrily to hers.

As Jordan savored her mouth, he did not seriously expect Mara to let him ravish her in the Regent's library in the middle of a royal ball.

It never hurt to ask, of course, but he fully expected to be denied. Then he would take her back out to the Octagon like a good boy and dance with her, as promised.

When he kissed her, however, he got more than he bargained for. As she twined her arms around him slowly and opened her rosy lips against his, enticing him, he realized in shock the lady was game for it.

Amazement at her bold advance flickered in his brain, but when she pressed the back of his head, pulling him down to deepen his kiss, he certainly needed no prompting. He pulled her against him, molding the hourglass shape of her warm, sensuous body as their mouths joined in an intoxicating duel of tongues. His pulse slammed as she thrust her champagne-flavored tongue into his mouth; he savored it, then he did the same to her.

He could taste her passion in her kiss and the fierce claim she had laid on him as she ran her hands in high satin gloves all over him—possessively—his head, his shoulders, his arms and chest. Every touch was clearly meant to make him understand that, in her mind, he belonged to her.

Jordan had no problem with that.

Transported with delight at her aggression, he let out a low gasp of pleasure when her dainty, wandering hand suddenly cupped his already-swollen cock.

He let out a short, dizzied laugh, hardening instantly the rest of the way against her grasp. "I was not expecting that," he panted in amusement.

"Mmm," she responded as she rubbed him hotly through his trousers. In seconds flat, her fire had shredded and consumed all his cool calculation of a few minutes ago.

He dragged his eyes open and looked at her, her slave. "Where do you want me?" he whispered. "On the floor? On the couch? Standing up? Over there, perhaps?" He jerked a fervent nod toward the nearby pillar.

She followed his glance then flicked her lashes downward with a little smile; coyly demure, she turned away and sauntered toward the pillar, drawing off the long glove that he had started to undo.

With a naughty glance over her shoulder, Mara dropped her glove daintily behind her, a coquette's favor that he was clearly intended to retrieve.

Jordan stared, adoring this new, unbridled Mara, the lover he had freed in her. He was mesmerized by the sensual way she moved.

Then she leaned her back against the very pillar where he had hidden from Albert not long ago, her pose lifting her breasts as she offered herself to him with a sultry stare. "Come and get me."

Jordan was certain in that moment that without years of spy training to hide his emotions, his very jaw would have hit the floor. *Is this a dream?*

He went to her, a man in a trance, stepping past her glove to collect instead the delicate hand it had clad.

Lifting her bared hand from her side, he brought it ardently to his lips: first, a gallant peck on her knuckles, then he turned her wrist to press a more serious kiss into the soft flesh of her palm.

He closed his eyes and enjoyed a most exquisite feast, nibbling the fleshy curve at the base of her thumb and the tender lines of her hand that fortune-tellers claimed to read, tasting her wrist, savoring every elegant fingertip.

When she moaned, watching him, he moved closer, taking hold of her waist and shifting his attentions to the white, silky chest that had been tempting him all night.

Her daringly low-cut ball gown was in the first stare of fashion, to be sure, but what chiefly held his interest was the lush female flesh the gown adorned.

That tiny bodice in particular.

There wasn't much to it, a layer of rose satin stretched across little more than the lower halves of her breasts. Her nipples were barely covered, not even a necklace to mar that delectable expanse of milky skin. Just beneath her round, generous bosom, a sash marked the start of her skirts as well as the invisible corselet beneath it. The light stays nipped in her waist but, praise God, did not restrict her breasts, merely lifted them a bit for presentation, not that she needed any such help at all, he thought, devouring her with his stare.

One mere layer of fragile satin, and another, of even more delicate batiste—the requisite chemise beneath her gown—these were all that stood between him and the breasts he hungered for. Sporting with her nipples through her gown, he watched them swell behind the fabric, felt them harden eagerly, poking against his thumbs as they grew—like his craving to take them in his mouth.

"*Uh, Jordan, please.*" Her groan expressed the perfect echo of his lust-filled thoughts.

He slipped his trembling hand into her gown. He had to force himself to be careful. But by God, if he ripped that damned dress, he'd take up needle and thread and mend it himself if he had to. He would not be denied.

Whatever it took. He just needed a taste of those luscious nipples now. He sank to his knees; she relaxed against the pillar; and while a thousand people, royals included, milled about a few rooms away, he freed her breasts, one by one, and abandoned himself to his own private feast, fit for a king. He was soon so caught up in this splendid gluttony that at first, he barely noticed the naughty little foot in a satin dancing slipper that had crept up from the floor to caress his groin.

But one teasing pass of Mara's ankle, foot, and toe gently fondling his solid prick riveted Jordan's full attention. When she had played at this for a moment, taunting his member to giant, throbbing proportions, he could take no more and captured her foot in his palm, while a husky laugh escaped his lips, muffled by the silken curve of her breast. "Ever the vixen," he pretended to chide, though his tone was adoring.

She rested her head back on the pillar with a needy wince. "I shall perish of want if you don't make love to me soon, Falconridge."

"By all means, my lady." As he rose from his knees to oblige her, he registered increasing guilt for his lies, mingled with the wild lust driving him. He could think of nothing beyond joining his body with hers.

He picked her up with a sweeping motion and carried her over to the heavy Gothic library table, where the last remaining candle burned.

Mara closed her eyes as he laid her down on it and undulated against the hard surface in sensuous anticipation, waiting hungrily for him.

Standing by the edge of the table, Jordan swiftly unfastened his trousers. He knew they did not have much time. Someone could come along at any minute. But the element of risk only added to his arousal.

Without a moment to lose, he slid his hands up her legs, smoothly lifting her skirts. When he grasped her bare hips, he wasted no time pressing into her.

They both moaned in blissful relief at their joining.

"Oh, God, I've needed this." The low, breathless utterance escaped him helplessly.

She relaxed beneath him, her body softening, the sparkle in her dark eyes needy and hot as she gazed up into his eyes, taking him in more deeply. "Jordan. Did you mean it when you said you are all mine, or was that mere gallantry?" she murmured in a dreamy tone.

"It was true," he breathed. "It has always been true, Mara. Surely you know that."

She shook her head slowly. "I only knew that it was true for me. That I am yours." Then she wrapped her legs around him, her wet, slick passage greedily enfolding him, and he lost himself in the heaven of taking her.

By the single candle's glow, he watched her enjoying his lovemaking. The shine of her lips, her luminous skin flushed, her sumptuous gown straining below her heaving breasts as he possessed her. His already-raging hardness swelled with appreciation to even greater size at the glorious sight. In response, he glimpsed her white teeth as she bared them in the darkness, biting back a rapturous groan.

The sounds she made did wild things to some primitive part of him, deep within the civilized diplomat.

He longed to tear her gown apart, this delicious wrapping that hid the splendor of her naked body from him; but somehow, he restrained himself, for at least, the thin, delicate fabric proved little obstacle to his wandering hands. He cupped her breasts with pleasure as his hips pumped between her thighs.

At length, he linked his fingers through hers and leaned down, gently pinning her wrists over her head against the hard surface of the table.

"Oh God, Jordan, you satisfy me so deeply." She writhed beneath him, apparently thrilled by the light restraint. He fucked her harder. He heard a small, muffled noise of fabric pulled to the breaking point, expensive threads fraying like his wits, but the small noise did not pierce the thick fog of his passion. In that moment, he could not have adored her more.

In raw, ferocious tenderness, he could not take his eyes off her, this one, lovely, unforgettable woman who had taken his soul captive from the first time their paths had crossed.

He had to grit his teeth against the sudden bewildering urge to blurt out the truth, that he loved her so much he would die for her without a second thought. But the inward flash of these words took him off guard; he'd have to think about it. For now, he did not dare spoil the perfection of this moment.

Then the sweetness of her overtook him, and he closed his eyes, savoring every second. Time slowed, the rest of the world disappeared. There was only Mara.

She writhed beneath him, pulling him down to kiss her. Soulfully, she held his face and caressed his cheeks and neck and hair as she plied his mouth with her kiss. "Give me a child, Jordan."

Her breathless whisper shook him to the core. He literally shuddered, tears springing up behind his closed eyelids. He knew these were merely utterances born in the heat of passion, but they toyed with the deepest needs in him, needs that had gone unmet for too many lonely years.

No, he could not even let himself think about that possibility. It hurt too much.

But she was relentless, lifting her hips, raking her fingers slowly through his hair, fucking him, seducing him.

He knew she meant it. She wanted his babe in her belly. Jordan felt the room spinning. With each second that passed, his body begged for release like a tightly coiled spring.

"It's so good," she moaned. Too breathless even to sustain the kiss in which she had captured him, he rested his swollen lips against her chin and thrilled to the sound of her breathy gasps in time with his every stroke.

"God, Jordan, you know I can't resist you."

She was trembling beneath him, and he did not know how much longer he could hold back.

"Come for me," he rasped.

She required little further prompting, as wild with desire as he, but he touched her clit to heighten her pleasure, letting his thumb alight with a feather-soft caress on her rigid nub. It roused a frantic note of pleasure from her lips.

He closed his eyes, panting, determined not to lose control as he gave it to her as fast and hard as his passionate lady demanded.

I am going to lose my mind if you don't come soon, he thought, a marvel in itself, for he never lost control.

And perhaps that was his whole problem in life.

Determined to ride his quivering, wanton filly over the finish line before instinct mastered him, as well, he squeezed his eyes shut and began mentally reciting the emperors of Rome in chronological order, with the dates of their rule.

The old schoolboy trick didn't help.

She was afire beneath him, no demure passive female, but as hot and real and scarlet as any high-priced whore who had ever faked it for him in some foreign capital.

Her sudden wrenching cry of bliss was the signal he had been waiting for, holding back the tide; deep inside the warm, velvet grip of her body, he felt the slippery surge of her womanly release, and with that, it was all over for him.

Blinded by the sheer wave of pleasure crashing over him, he grasped the silken pillowed flesh of her sweet buttocks, driving in hard to impale and claim her.

Oh, yes.

She was molten flame beneath him, consuming him in undulating waves that flowed out from where their bodies joined, as though these seconds touched eternity.

Explosive charges crashed inside his senses, like so many mines laid for an enemy, dams bursting, walls crumbling under the onslaught of her love, towers blown to smithereens, leaving him nowhere to hide, no way to return to the old life he had known.

He wrenched out her name in a strangled whisper.

In the exquisite violence of surrender, he was utterly undone.

And after, awash in panting silence, in the deep, profound

calm, he knew, whatever happened, he could never give her up. Whatever happened, he could not lose her again. She must marry him.

She must. Because he could not live without her. He *would* not. Never again.

But with his mission still hanging over his head, he did not dare entangle her in this any more deeply. He must wait until the mission was over and the danger receded.

His heart protested, but he reminded himself he had already waited twelve years. He could survive a few more weeks without Mara for his wife. He held her, cradled her protectively, and made that promise to himself.

She captured his chin and turned his face to kiss him gently. They stared into each other's eyes.

You are a dream, he thought, flooded with gentleness as he stroked her hair. *My dream.*

She smiled at him. "Sometimes, Falconridge, you really quite outdo yourself," she murmured, joy shining from her dark, sparkly eyes.

He laughed softly; she joined him with the enchanting, husky laughter of a woman thoroughly satisfied.

"Thanks, I think," he murmured.

"No, my love, thank *you.*" She gave him a kiss, then pushed against his chest. "Off with you, now."

He withdrew from her body with a sigh. Then he fastened his trousers and helped her up.

While she drifted over wearily to the mirror to try to repair her appearance, Jordan took out his handkerchief and blotted away the sweat of passion. As he watched her, he found himself struggling with a small niggling doubt that cropped up in the back of his mind.

What if an offer of marriage was not what she wanted to hear? As much as she enjoyed her widow's freedom, he was not altogether sure she would give him the desired answer. Maybe she preferred their current arrangement as it was.

Well, if indeed he had planted his babe in her belly, as she asked him to, then he was not going to give her any choice. She would marry him and make a proper family with him whether she liked it or not.

Masking the fierce hunger deep in his soul for just that situation, he sauntered up behind her while she stood at the mirror fretting over her appearance. He laid his hands on her smooth upper arms and bent his head to kiss her shoulder from behind her.

"You are beautiful," he whispered.

"I am a tousled mess! And I'm afraid we've got another problem. You've torn my gown, you rogue."

"Hmm, I cannot say I am sorry," he drawled, his eyes dancing as he looked into the mirror at the two of them, he, standing behind her, holding her about the waist.

"How wicked you are."

"I'll take you home," he murmured, savoring the smell of sex that clung to both of them.

"Stay with me tonight," she whispered.

"Only if you'll make me a sandwich," he teased in silken innuendo. Lowering his head to kiss her shoulder, he shot her a smoldering stare in the glass.

"To be sure," she laughed with a hint of a delightful, girlish blush. She reached and cradled his cheek against her palm. "And then, my lord, once you've replenished your strength with some food, you can do that to me again."

"With pleasure," he growled, and squeezed her around her waist. "Mine."

"It would seem so." She accepted his hold around her waist serenely and laid her head back against his chest.

He planted another loud, hearty smooch of a kiss on her

neck and released her, moving toward the mirror to try to put himself back into order.

Mara gazed at him, smiling dreamily as he whisked his fingertips over his short hair and straightened his cravat; nevertheless, the lingering lover's flush in his skin, the glow in his now-heavy-lidded eyes all gave him a clearly sated look. By Jove, he had enjoyed this party more than the Regent would ever know.

"Somehow we're going to slip out of here without the whole world seeing us."

"Oh, we can take the Regent's private stairs. They're just through those doors and a short walk down the hallway."

"Ah." Jordan followed her nod past the pillars. The way Albert had gone. "Can we get out through there without being seen?"

Mara shrugged. "Only by a few servants. Better bring the candle," she added. "It's likely to be dark back there."

"What's that door over there, do you know?" he asked casually, nodding at the smaller doorway in the corner.

"Oh. That's the Regent's private office. Not that he uses it much," she jested. "He doesn't believe in paperwork."

"I second that." Jordan smiled back.

"Come on." She beckoned him over toward the exit by the pillars.

Jordan got the candle, then hauled open the heavy door for her; Mara slipped through first, then led him down the central hallway of the Regent's private apartments.

"I hope His Highness will not mind our intrusion so close to his personal chambers."

"Under the circumstances, I think he'd understand," she said dryly. "Our Prinny's had a few trysts in odd places, too, in his day."

"Thank you, I really did not need that picture in my mind."

She giggled as they hurried down the darkened hallway.

When they came to a side door, Jordan went first, opening it a crack. He could hear the party taking place in the antechambers a few rooms away.

Realizing they would no longer need the candle, he blew it out and left it in the hallway. Then he nodded at Mara, opened the door, and they both slipped out silently, hurrying down the Regent's private stairs.

Her skirts flowed out gracefully as they stole away down the steps, hand in hand, and arrived outside in the starry night.

Jordan told an attendant to bring his carriage. When he saw Mara shiver in the midnight chill, he took off his tail coat and draped it over her shoulders. She smiled at him. He sent her a look that promised he'd warm her up soon—under the covers.

As they waited for his carriage, he glanced back over his shoulder at all the glowing windows of Carlton House.

Countless questions still swirled in his mind after Albert's outrageous break-in. The first was obvious: What the deuce had the suspected Promethean been searching for?

But a second, subtler question still nagged. He shook his head to himself, pondering. Albert had *unlocked* the office door, and the Regent's desk, as well.

So, where the devil did he get the key?

What a bloody nerve-racking night.

Albert Carew, the Duke of Holyfield, was finding dukedom not at all what it was cracked up to be.

As his ornate carriage approached his brother's grand, ducal mansion outside of Town—er, *his* ducal mansion now—he scanned the moonlit property for any sign of the dreaded intruder.

Thank God, the place looked quiet, no strange vehicles or horses in the circular drive around the elegant fountain set before the house.

It appeared he was in the clear, at least for now, but one could never be too sure. Dresden Bloodwell might pop up at any moment like an outbreak of the plague.

No wonder my nerves are jangled. That devil breathing down my neck. Albert hoped at least he'd have some time to think up an excuse to explain why he had failed.

It was not his fault! Nothing ever *was,* really. That was Albert's policy in life, and it usually served him well.

A few minutes later, when his coach halted and his footman handed him down, he went striding into his giant home, drawing off his white evening gloves, his formal black satin cape billowing out handsomely behind him.

His butler let him in the front door with a sweeping bow.

"Any visitors?" he asked tersely.

"No, Your Grace." His butler removed the luxurious cape from Albert's shoulders and accepted his gloves. "Do you require refreshments, sir?"

He merely scowled at him. Who could possibly eat in this state of apprehension?

"Shall we draw your bath, then?"

Albert paused, took a deep breath, and ordered himself to relax.

His butler's civilized queries helped reestablish at least some sense of normality. It comforted him. "Yes. I'll have a bath. And use the lavender bath salts," he ordered. "It helps me relax."

"Of course, Your Grace." His butler bowed and went to tell the staff to wipe the sleep out of their eyes and start carrying the hot water up to His Grace's chamber.

Feeling rather better, Albert headed there himself. As he passed the pier glass in the cavernous entrance hall, he paused, attracted to his own reflection. He sent himself an approving glance, even as the ugly word "treason" slid through his mind.

Absurd! he immediately denied, though his innards recoiled. He ignored it. *I'm no traitor.* He hadn't meant any harm. It wasn't his fault, anyway. He'd had no choice.

He was merely trying to stay alive. *The devil made me do it,* he thought darkly, but at least the mirror comforted him, confirming that he was still just Alby, still himself, only better, a duke now, but still a Bond Street Lounger at heart, a pink of the ton, with a permanent place in the high court of White's bow window, where the ruling dandies like him sat on display for all the world to admire.

Traitor, indeed! Who would dare to say so?

Certainly he did not look the part of some skulking thief who would break into the Regent's desk to try to steal his private papers.

His mouth went dry as he recalled his failed adventure of this night. But, no. He must erase it from his mind. Every true dandy knew that life only counted when others were watching. If no one saw him do it, then practically speaking, it was the same as if it had never occurred.

Refusing to ponder the knowledge that he was completely out of his depth, he hurried on, leaving the entrance hall to jog up the staircase to his bedchamber.

He took the stairs two at a time, like a man trying to outrun his own folly. But even before he reached the upper floor and strode down the corridor toward his chamber, the memory of that darkened library returned to haunt his mind.

For a moment back there, Albert had briefly imagined he *had* been seen. What a close call that was! He thought he had sensed another person in the library—hiding, watching—and then Mara had come pounding on the door looking for her blue-eyed stud, but she was mistaken.

She had to be. Why the deuce would Falconridge bother to follow him? That didn't make any sense. No, his disturbingly appealing new whist partner had given Albert no reason to distrust him. Falconridge had a reputation for honor and a steady, earnest calm that put everyone at ease. It was absurd to think of the earl, of all people, lurking about like—well, like Dresden Bloodwell.

No one had been in the library besides himself: Albert needed to believe it for his sanity's sake. The eerie sensation of being watched was just a figment of his own increasing paranoia.

God knew, he was not made for intrigues. Constant, gnawing fear had him jumping at shadows ever since Dresden Bloodwell had first infected his life.

Even now, when he gained his large, shadowed bedchamber, he hesitated, like a child scared of the dark.

But he saw no signs of danger. He closed the door behind him in relief. Sauntering into his opulent haven, he pulled off the cravat that had taken his valet half an hour to perfect.

Drawn by habit to his vanity table, Albert tossed the cravat aside and watched himself unbuttoning his white silk waistcoat. But as he stood before the mirror, he suddenly gasped when the nightmare appeared behind him in the glass.

"Did you get it, then?"

He whirled around, nearly jumping out of his skin. "Christ, you scared the hell out of me!"

"Did you get the list?" Bloodwell asked in the same relentless monotone that sent chills down Albert's spine every time he heard it.

His heart beat so hard he could not quite catch his breath for a moment. Albert took a step back from Bloodwell, avoiding the penetrating gaze of the deadest eyes he had ever seen.

Bloodwell waited for an answer.

Albert faltered, scratched his temple, searching for courage, rested his hands on his waist, and braced himself. "No."

Displeasure radiated from the strange assassin. "You *were* at Carlton House tonight?"

"Yes, but I couldn't find it."

A silence.

"Was there a problem with the key I gave you?"

"No, the key worked fine, but the paper wasn't in there."

"Yes, it is."

"Are you sure it was sent—"

"Don't question me," Bloodwell cut him off. "My source on this is a hell of a lot more reliable than you. Of course, that isn't saying much." Dresden Bloodwell sat down where he pleased, right on Albert's favorite chair.

Did he plan on staying long?

Heart pounding with anger and humiliation at how thoroughly frightened he was of this man, Albert managed to lift his chin. "It's not my fault," he clipped out. "I was looking for it. But I was interrupted. Some woman came banging on the door. She didn't realize I was there."

Bloodwell looked at him for a long moment. "You really are a waste of oxygen, aren't you?"

"You ask the impossible of me!"

"That is not my problem. Time is short, Alby. When I ask you to do something, I expect you to carry it out."

He threw up his hands. "I tried!"

"Try harder. You owe me that, don't you? After all I've done for you . . . You are still enjoying your new station in life, aren't you, Your Grace?"

Albert checked his fury. "I'll get your damned list."

Bloodwell's wolfish smile flashed in the dark as he stood again. "That's more like it. When is the next time you'll see the Regent?"

"A few days. The weekly card game."

"Very well." Bloodwell nodded slowly. "I'll give you a fortnight to get back into Carlton House and try again. But the next time I call on you, Albert, you'd better have it for me. By Lucifer's beard, you'd better. If you don't produce results, I shall have no further use for you. Do you understand what I'm saying to you?"

Albert swallowed hard. "Yes—sir. Perfectly." Bloodwell's stare alone was enough to make him feel as though his own cravat was strangling him. His heart pounded so hard, he was feeling slightly faint.

He would've liked to believe he was too valuable for Bloodwell to dispose of, but there was no compromise in the killer's stare. "Good," he murmured at length. "Now, then. Anything else I should know? News from court?"

Albert shrugged and told him what he'd learned about the place and time of Princess Charlotte's wedding. At least it was something, enough to mollify the monster.

Bloodwell nodded. "Possibly useful. I shall bid you a fond good evening, Your Grace. See you in a fortnight."

Go back to hell, where you came from, Albert thought, his mouth dry, his heart pounding. His eyes wide with fear, he watched the tall, lean, black silhouette move toward the open window.

He slipped past the curtains billowing on the night breeze, exiting by way of the balcony. In the next moment, Dresden Bloodwell had vanished once again. Like a foul smell.

Two weeks. Albert let out a shaky exhalation and lowered his head, raking his hand slowly through his perfect curls. *Dear God. What am I going to do?*

Chapter 12

Drake had suffered an excruciating headache for two days, taking very little food, barely stirring from his room, where the drapes remained closed to shut out the light. On the third day, after the worst of his headache had passed, he had sat all day in a chair staring out the window, brooding and uncommunicative.

As strange and remote as he had been since the moment he had arrived, not until now had he gone completely silent.

Emily was worried.

She was not about to give up hope, but Drake was so different now from the man she had adored since childhood. Nor was he a very compliant patient. She had tended wild animals that were easier to work with than the earl.

All she wanted was to nurse him back to health, as she had done for a few wounded foxes, assorted birds with injured wings, and a baby fawn she had once rescued. It had been grazed by the same hunter's bullet that killed its mother. She had raised the deer and set it free, but it still wandered the parklands of Westwood Manor. It would still come to her hand if she offered food.

Unfortunately, the only treatment she had for Drake at the moment was a simple headache tonic. She wished she could do so much more to take his pain away, but at least this was something.

She wondered how he'd be today, on the fourth morning, as she stood at the potting table in the little greenhouse shed by the kitchen garden. For years, she had been growing a variety of needful herbs in clay pots under the glass, so they'd be ready for use in any season.

With her knife, she cut a few, fragrant sprigs of sage, the main ingredient of her trusty tonic, and put them in the bowl with the rosemary she had already culled. She savored the smells of the fresh herbs, moving on to gather a few peppermint leaves next.

All the ingredients would be boiled together. The old herbal country tonic smelled lovely. More importantly, it worked, at least on an ordinary case of the megrims.

Nothing about Drake's condition was ordinary, unfortunately.

As Emily put the peppermint leaves in the bowl, she couldn't help wondering not for the first time if his headache had more than a physical cause.

Now that he had been home at Westwood Manor for a fortnight, perhaps he was beginning to feel safe enough to let his missing memories return.

Lord Rotherstone had tried to draw him into conversation, trying to get him to tell if he had regained his memory or not. Emily had also tried to reach him, but he was not a man who wanted to be reached, preferring to stand alone as he battled the demons in his head.

It broke her heart to see him so damaged, all that roguish laughter fled from his black, flashing eyes. They were haunted now and filled with fear and deep, submerged rage. No, this was not the same Drake she had always known. But she was not giving up on him. At least he was alive. Anything was better than the torment of those dark months when he had gone missing, and she had feared him dead.

Now that she had him back, she would fix him, no matter what it took. And she didn't care anymore that his mother thought she wasn't good enough. Emily knew quite well that she could not marry Drake.

But no one had ever been able to stop her from loving him. As long as there was breath in her body, no one was ever going to hurt him again.

As she reached into the back row to cut off a small piece of the wood-betony stalk to add to her brew, she heard a sound behind her and turned to find he had just stepped into the garden shed.

"Drake! You're up." She clipped off the wood betony, put it in the bowl, and set her knife aside, turning to him with a beaming smile. "How are you feeling?" she greeted him as she wiped her hands on the work apron over her simple dun-colored dress.

"Much better," he murmured, gazing into her eyes as he joined her by the potting table. "Thanks to you."

She took his hands and searched his face. "I've been very concerned."

"I know," he said slowly. "But I think now everything is going to be all right."

"Is it?" she asked with a wistful gaze into his eyes.

He said nothing, but with a pensive smile, he pulled her into his arms. Emily closed her eyes, adoring him, as she savored his unexpected hug.

"You smell like peppermint and sage," he murmured fondly as he held her. He inhaled the scent of her hair.

"I was making more tonic."

"Thank you, sweet Emily, for your care," he whispered.

"It was nothing." His unexpected show of affection had her blushing.

"It means more to me than you know." He rested his lips against her hairline briefly, then he said, "Do you know you are the only good and pure thing in my life?"

Her heart clenched, but his startling confession left her tongue-tied. She hugged him back, a surge of protectiveness toward him flooding her heart. "I-I'm so glad you're feeling better," she stammered shyly.

Meanwhile, through the small dirty window over the potting table, she noticed Sergeant Parker standing outside waiting for Drake, his constant follower and guard.

Lord Rotherstone had been out for a morning gallop on his magnificent Thoroughbred. He reined in now, greeting Sergeant Parker. He leaned down to pat his horse's neck while the men outside the window exchanged a few words.

"Emily, there's something I want to tell you," Drake murmured.

"Have you got your memory back—" she started, but he hushed her. Gently gripping her shoulders, he stared into her eyes. "Whatever happens, my sweet, my innocent Emily, I want you to know how much you mean to me."

"Oh, Drake." She swallowed hard, wide-eyed. Was this a dream?

"I would never hurt you."

"Of course, I know that—"

"Good."

"Drake, is something wrong? You seem strange. Why are you saying these things—"

Again, he cut off her questions—this time, to her shocked delight, with a gentle kiss. Her heart reeled at the hungry caress of his silken lips against hers.

"I'm sorry," he breathed a moment later.

"It's a-all right," she assured him, as a bright blush suffused her skin. At last! She'd been wishing he'd do that for years. "I-I didn't mind."

"You might," he whispered. And in the blink of an eye, he grabbed her work knife, spun her about in his arms so that her back slammed against his chest.

To her horror, he held her own knife to her throat.

"I am so very sorry about this, Emily."

For half a second, she was still too much in shock to find her tongue. Holding her clamped against him, he started toward the doorway.

"What are you doing?" she burst out.

"Getting out of here. Don't fight me." He propelled her toward the door of the shed.

"Drake, please! Don't do this! They'll kill you."

"I cannot stay here. If I don't go now, James will die."

The moment they cleared the doorway of the potting shed, they were spotted. The yard broke into a clamor; Parker shouting, servants running. Emily saw Lord Rotherstone's face turn white.

He jumped off his horse. "Let her go!" he roared, marching toward Drake.

"Stay back, or I will cut her!" Drake snarled.

"Drake!" she wrenched out. It was possible in that moment that her heart broke quite into two pieces.

How could he do this to her? How?

"Shoot him," the marquess ordered Parker.

The sergeant's rifle immediately jutted from his shoulder.

Emily screamed: "*No!*"

Drake paused, but as the situation came into focus from her initial panic, she allowed him to use her for a shield.

He doesn't know what he is doing.

Rotherstone's hand came up, signaling Parker to hold his fire. "Drake, this is madness. Let Emily go. She's been nothing but good to you."

"I don't care. I owe you people nothing. Get back! I'm taking your horse. Don't try to stop me, or she dies," Drake warned, cursing under his breath as he dragged her over to the horse Lord Rotherstone had just finished exercising.

"He's mad, sir!" Parker shouted.

Emily whimpered, but clung to the promise he had made mere seconds ago inside the shed that he'd never hurt her.

At the moment, she was not so sure. But she was furious at him for doing this to her as well as for risking himself this way. She prayed Lord Rotherstone would be patient.

Against her back, she could feel Drake's muscled chest heaving; she tried to protest as he stepped up onto the stirrup, but knowing they'd shoot him, she let him pull her up in front of him onto the horse, taking her hostage.

She let him use her for a shield.

"You'd better let me ride away unless you want this girl to die," he warned. "Don't doubt me, Max. You know that I've got nothing left to lose."

"Drake, listen to me." Lord Rotherstone approached, his hands extended as if he could physically force Drake to be calm. "If you return to the Prometheans, the Order will have no choice but to treat you as one of the enemy."

"I'll take my chances," he spat. "Get out of the way, Max."

"Drake—"

He let out an angry whoop, spurring the horse forward.

The leggy Thoroughbred nearly trampled Max with its sudden spring. The marquess jumped aside.

Sergeant Parker bellowed for them to stop, but did not shoot for fear of hitting her. Drake ignored him, galloping hell-for-leather toward the woods.

The horse's speed and the threat of frantic tears blinded

Emily as they went racing down the footpath through the woods. With Drake's arm locked tight around her waist, she gasped as the Thoroughbred soared over a fallen log.

"Where are we going?" she cried, as they surged on.

"Not we. You are staying here."

"No, take me with you. I am not afraid."

"Typical Emily," he muttered grimly in her ear. "Don't be a fool. You're just a girl! You can have no part in what I have to do." His silence as they barreled on informed her there was no point in arguing with him or pressing for answers he wouldn't give.

Ahead, she recognized the boundary line of the Westwood property. When they reached it, he spilled her from the saddle; she landed on shaky legs but immediately went toward him again, trying to reach for his hand.

"You'll pardon me if I keep your knife."

"Drake, I'm begging you not to go. You need help! You are not well! You need *me*!"

"You've already helped me more than you know, my angel. Please forgive me for what I did back there. I'm sorry to scare you. It was just for show. You know that, don't you?"

"Don't leave me!"

"I have to."

"Please, I cannot bear it—"

"Let me go, Emily," he chided, as she clung to his hand with a sob. "You must forget me. I won't be coming back. Tell Max I've got to finish this. They're going to kill James if I'm not there to protect him, and he's the only one who can lead the others to stand against Malcolm."

"What?" she asked through her tears, bewildered.

"I know they think I'm mad, and maybe I am, maybe I am," he repeated, almost to himself, "but I can do more from the inside than they can ever accomplish from without."

"Please, Drake, I can't bear to lose you again."

"You have no choice. Neither do I."

"I could come with you."

He laughed bitterly. "What, into the belly of the beast? I think not. You are an innocent, and you must stay that way. Look at me, Em. I could only taint you now. Just know that it's for you and everything you mean to me that I have to finish this. You're the only thing left that's worth fighting for."

"Then stay with me! Don't go!"

"You have no idea what they have planned!" he barked at her, then began urging the horse away. "Good-bye, my Emily."

She lost her grip on him with a wild sob. He wheeled the horse around and bolted away down the road.

That night, before the news of Drake's escape had yet reached London, Jordan was engaged in playing cards with the Regent's set and carefully laying a trap for Albert.

The closer he and Mara became, the stronger his desire to complete the mission so he could concentrate on her.

He had indulged in one of his favorite spy tools: the artful lie. The rumor he had started worked its way in whispers through the room. It did not even require him to speak to Albert directly.

He murmured his little fiction to Colonel Hanger. Who told it to Barrymore, who told it to Norfolk, who told it to the Honorable Mr. Byng and his prize poodle, and so on, until it finally reached Albert—and by that time, no one remembered where exactly he had first heard this stunning piece of information.

If it were true, it would have been big news. Big enough for Albert to report to his Promethean controller.

Have you heard? The royal physicians are about to release a report that King George is on the mend. The King's madness is lifting again, just as it did a few years ago. If His Majesty continues to improve, he could be cleared to return to the throne. Then the Regent will have to step down.

The only one at the table who had not heard this shocking-yet-credible tale was the Regent himself. At the moment, he was lost in the ecstasies of an almond cheesecake. And no man there wanted to break the news to Prinny that he might soon be demoted.

What Albert might do with this choice morsel of information remained to be seen, but Jordan intended to find out.

As for the duke's behavior that night, Albert seemed to have decided that Mara must have been mistaken when she had come looking for him in the library; his attitude toward Jordan was only slightly warier than before. Perhaps his arrogance convinced him that he had outsmarted them all.

At any rate, by the time the gentlemen's final hour of whist wound to a close, Jordan had lost five hundred quid and won it back again.

The eccentrics of the Regent's set bid one another a weary good night as they drifted out of Watier's. Parked along Piccadilly outside, a line of expensive town coaches waited for them, their aristocratic coats of arms emblazoned on the doors.

The gamblers' grooms and footmen came to collect their drunken masters, both the dispirited losers, moping away, and the strutting victors, flush with their winnings.

Jordan's attention was subtly fixed on Albert as they stepped out into the wet black night.

"Must've rained," Albert remarked, pulling on his gloves.

Jordan nodded patiently. "That, or a fog."

The brick walls of the buildings, the shop signs, and cobbled streets were slick with a heavy dew and gleamed by the glow of the wrought-iron streetlamps.

When Albert's coach glided up to the entrance of the club,

the duke discreetly handed a small piece of paper to his footman. After murmuring an instruction, he climbed into his carriage. In the next moment, it rolled away.

Jordan's pulse beat swiftly as he considered his two options. The footman went one way and the duke went the other.

As the seconds ticked away, his vehicle pulled up next to collect him—the only one unmarked by a family crest. He had chosen a plain black coach that night for obvious reasons and had brought along two of the Order's trusty foot soldiers, Findlay and Mercer, to play the part of his coachman and groom. They were from Sergeant Parker's contingent.

When Findlay pulled the horses to a halt before the doors of Watier's, Mercer jumped down off the back and marched forward to get the door for him like a proper groom. Both men had donned the Falconridge livery, the better to play their roles.

"Your carriage, my lord." Mercer opened the door. "There's news, sir," he added in a lower tone as Jordan moved past him to step into the coach. "Master Virgil sent a messenger while you were inside."

He paused. "What is it?"

"Lord Westwood's escaped. He dodged Lord Rotherstone this morning by taking a servant girl hostage."

Jordan was amazed. "That Emily girl?"

"Wouldn't know, sir. They believe he's headed back to Town to return to the Prometheans. Every man we've got is out searching for him. Word's gone out that if he don't surrender, we're to shoot him on sight."

Shoot Drake? He absorbed this in shock, then shook his head. *I can't think about that right now.* The others would have to deal with their poor lunatic.

His concern at the moment was tracking Albert's footman. "Tell Findlay to follow that servant," he instructed, nodded at the liveried figure jogging down Piccadilly toward the intersection with St. James's. "But not to get too close. I don't want him noticing us."

"Yes, sir." Mercer nodded, shut the carriage door after Jordan, then went to tell Findlay what they were to do. Mercer returned to his place on the foot-bar in the back.

Pulling away from the corner of Bolton Street, Findlay turned the horses left down Piccadilly, then made a right onto St. James's. Inside the carriage, Jordan quickly changed coats, shedding the impeccably tailored plum merino wool that would mark him at once as a wealthy gentleman.

He replaced it with a plain drab jacket, then donned his weapons, buckling on a belt that had a sheath for a large knife on one hip and a holster for a loaded pistol on the other. He tucked an extra pistol into the waist of his trousers.

Out the window, he saw the premier gentlemen's clubs of St. James's rolling by, then they turned left into Pall Mall. Ahead, Albert's footman continued jogging doggedly down the pavement past the endless row of shops, unaware of the carriage following him.

At length, he went into the open lobby of a stagecoach inn not far from Charing Cross. Findlay stopped the coach, and Jordan jumped out, striding toward the entrance, with an order to the men to wait for him.

Because the London stagecoach service ran all night, even at this hour, weary, waiting travelers slumped in benches throughout the dimly lit lobby. Jordan prowled in, taking an inconspicuous seat in the corner. From there, he watched Albert's footman furtively hand the duke's message over to a weathered old clerk behind the ticketing desk.

The footman left, his part played, but from there, the message traveled on through a complex series of couriers.

Jordan shadowed each one to the next, until, at last, the path led him into the most unsavory part of London—Seven

Dials, the infamous haunt of London's hardest criminal gangs. White-chalked symbols scrawled on the grimy brick walls of corner buildings here and there proclaimed their territory and warned intruders away.

When the dark, dirty labyrinth of twisting alleys and winding lanes grew too narrow for a coach to pass through, Jordan got out again, left Findlay with the carriage, and beckoned to Mercer to come with him on foot. The sensible fellow paused to shed the Falconridge livery coat, which could've helped any Prometheans identify Jordan if they were seen.

Jordan took out his knife and sent Mercer a meaningful nod toward his weapons; the man drew his pistol. They trailed the final courier, keeping to the shadows.

Perhaps the cloaked man ahead had been born in Seven Dials, for he made his way through the London's most treacherous neighborhood with an unerring stride.

When he suddenly ducked into one of the dismal boardinghouses that crowded the street, Jordan halted Mercer at the corner several yards behind their mark.

"What do we do now, sir?" his assistant murmured.

Jordan scanned the place. "Let's try to get a better view." He gestured toward the grim, closed shops and other shady establishments, all crowded together and shuttered for the night. "I'll go round to the other side. If you happen across any of the locals," he added wryly, "avoid 'em. We don't need any more trouble tonight from one of these vile gangs."

"Aye, sir." Mercer nodded in full agreement, then Jordan stole off to explore the other sides of the ramshackle lodging house.

Given the hour, only a few windows glowed with light. He scaled a six-foot brick wall girding the property to glance into the first. A lowly and exhausted-looking seamstress was mending a pile of shirts.

Jordan moved on. He prowled atop the edge of the brick

wall until he reached a spot where he could jump onto the low, slanting end of a gabled roof above a rag-and-bone shop.

He sprang onto it in catlike silence and began climbing up its steep, angled pitch. As he neared the crest of the old, creaky roof, he heard a baby crying; feeble light glowed in the window above, where he spotted some poor woman who was up in the middle of the night, tending her squalling infant.

But he was in luck—for the noise bothered the neighbor above. At that moment, Dresden Bloodwell himself suddenly appeared in the third-story window.

Jordan froze as the Promethean assassin slammed the window shut with a look of annoyance, blocking out the noise. Then he disappeared into the lit room again.

Jordan's heart pounded. After all these weeks, he had finally located his primary target! But he exhaled with relief. If Bloodwell had paused to look around outside his window, Jordan would likely have been seen. To be sure, he would have made a very easy target exposed as he was on the roof.

Without a second to spare, he climbed to the apex of the gabled roof, but he still could not see inside Bloodwell's window. He had to go higher—and fast.

Balancing atop the slim apex of the roof, he walked to the end, then took a few running steps onto a fire-escape ladder affixed to the brick face of the next building.

He winced at the dull, metallic bang, but Bloodwell did not come to the window. Mounting the rusty ladder, he climbed in swift stealth until he reached the flat roof of the tenement house and immediately crossed it, creeping up to the back edge of the building.

When he peered over the side, he had a straight view into Dresden Bloodwell's shabby apartment, and what he saw confirmed beyond all doubt that Albert was indeed working with the Prometheans.

He could see the cloaked courier in the room, handing

Bloodwell the note that had originated with Albert, carrying Jordan's lie about the king's return to sanity straight to its intended recipient.

The courier bowed out immediately after accepting a few coins from Bloodwell. Bloodwell locked the door behind him, then turned around, opening the note.

Jordan saw him look up from the note and address someone else in the room. This surprised him. Bloodwell had a guest?

Determined to find out who else was there, he moved a bit to the left along the roof's edge, changing his angle to be able to see into the other side of the room.

It was then that he made the most astonishing discovery of all. A large, brawny, young man with flame red hair reclined in a lazy pose on the couch.

My God. Niall Banks—the Promethean heir apparent!

Malcolm Banks's son, second in power only to his father in the enemy's hierarchy. Virgil's nephew.

What the hell is he doing in London?

The Scottish-born Malcolm and his son had long based their operations out of France.

Jordan had to learn what was afoot. Clearly, Niall's presence in London was an even bigger find than the current location of Dresden Bloodwell's headquarters.

Damn, he mused as he stared at the next Promethean leader, James Falkirk was right. *That is quite a family resemblance.* Virgil and his red-haired nephew looked exactly alike, but thirty years apart.

Drawings that Jordan had seen of Malcolm, by contrast, had depicted a smaller man with spiky, white-blond hair.

From the rooftop, Jordan beckoned impatiently to Mercer. As soon as he got the Order guard's attention, Mercer joined him on the rooftop.

Jordan informed him of the red-haired man's identity, and

Mercer was duly impressed, but quick action was suddenly needed.

Niall rose from the couch and sauntered toward the door. Bloodwell moved to show him out.

"He's leaving." Jordan stared, not taking his eyes off them. "I need to follow him. We're going to have to split up. You stay here and keep both eyes on Bloodwell. We can't afford to lose track of him again. I'm going to follow Niall and try to find out what he's doing in London. You lie low here and don't try any heroics," he warned. "Bloodwell's too dangerous to take on by yourself. At the first possible moment, I'll return with Beauchamp or whoever I can find. We'll handle that Promethean filth."

"Aye, sir."

"Now, Mercer, I don't think Bloodwell will go anywhere, given the hour, but if he does, you'll have to follow him. Send word to Dante House of your location when you're able, and we'll come to you there. You can do this?"

The guard nodded uneasily.

"Good man." Jordan clapped him quietly on the back, already in motion, gliding away to the other side of the roof. In a trice, he was on the fire-escape ladder, descending as quickly and silently as he could move.

He dropped to the ground, then vaulted back over the brick wall below and ran through the darkness toward the front of the lodging house.

Jordan caught sight of the brawny, red-haired man just as he was leaving by the front entrance. As he walked away from Dresden Bloodwell's tenement house, Niall hid his distinctive red hair under a black hat and pulled the brim low to shade his face. Hands in his coat pockets, Niall strode southward out of Seven Dials.

Jordan shadowed him a stone's throw behind. When Niall came to the intersection at Long Acre, he approached the corner hackney stand and hired the only driver in sight. As soon as the carriage door closed, the hackney set off down St. Martin's Lane.

Jordan turned with a curse and cast about for any mode of transportation; but at that moment, Findlay came thundering along in his coach.

"Sir!"

Must have been keeping an eye out for me, Jordan thought gratefully. "Follow that hackney!"

"Aye, sir! Should I wait for Mercer?"

"No, go! He's keeping watch." Jordan pulled the door of his carriage shut, and Findlay cracked the whip over the horses.

Before long, Niall's lonely hackney was in sight again, continuing south toward the Strand, then turning west, back toward the wealthy section of Town.

To Jordan's bemusement, the night ended practically in the same spot where it had begun—in Piccadilly, in sight of Watier's, in fact.

But it was not the infamous gambling club on which Niall had set his sights, Jordan realized as the Prometheans' future leader got out of the hackney and carelessly threw the driver a coin.

Jordan remained concealed in his carriage, watching his every move as Niall paused on Piccadilly, his hands still in his pockets—as though concealing a weapon.

Then he began walking slowly toward the entrance of the opulent Pulteney Hotel.

Jordan narrowed his eyes. *Why's he going there?*

Chapter 13

James Falkirk always stayed at the Pulteney when he came to London.

At the elegant desk in his third-floor suite, he was absorbed in his studies on the Alchemist's Scrolls, ink stains on his bony fingers as he made more notes. His old eyes strained, bloodshot behind the spectacles perched on his nose, as the light from nearby candelabra flickered over the ancient symbols on the parchment. The candles' waxen stubs had melted into misshapen forms.

His lips moved silently as he savored each mysterious line. His mind seethed with the possibilities of power that this acquisition placed in his hands. Power to put the world the way it should be.

He did not question his own ability to know what that looked like. Instead, he puzzled over the terrible sacrifice that such potent spells required. When the time came, he would have to find a person of pure heart for it to work, an innocent, likely a virgin, untainted by the world . . .

Unfortunate, but it could not be helped. The price was always high. But whatever the cost, it would be worth it to bring about the great Promethean vision of one world united—before all hope of their recent near victory faded away.

They had been so close, working their way toward power through Napoleon's great reach. They'd have subtly taken it from him, too, eventually, their representatives stationed in advantageous posts woven all throughout the Emperor's ever-increasing bureaucracy. Empires did not run themselves, after all, especially gigantic holdings like Napoleon's that had stretched from sunny Spain to the very edge of Russia.

James shook his head to himself. Such an opportunity lost. He could kill Malcolm for botching it with his greed and feckless lust for power, his blind impatience, his lack of care. It would be a century before a chance like that came again, maybe longer . . .

If they had succeeded in establishing one united power ruling the world at last, there would be no more wars like the one that pulled Europe apart for the past twenty years, James thought sorrowfully. No more territorial squabbles, no more battles over gold or other resources for survival.

One day the Prometheans would ensure that everyone got what they deserved, merely what was fair. No more. No less. The savage beast, Mankind, would finally be brought to heel, its barbaric will broken by kindly masters whose control was that of an iron fist in a velvet glove.

Humanity would be made to stop causing so much trouble and finally learn to do as it was told. Those who would not see the light, well, they would simply have to be eliminated, wouldn't they? Regrettable, but once the unruly segment of the population was removed, then all would live in harmony under the wise rule of the enlightened.

To James and all the true believers in their creed, this shining vision was easily worth at least one innocent life.

But thanks to Malcolm, it had all unraveled, and now even the leaders of the Ten Regions were demoralized.

James knew that everything depended on him. The others were so disgusted with Malcolm that only he could bring the believers together again with renewed faith in their eventual success.

There must be a grand meeting, every one of their far-flung Perfected Ones gathered to reaffirm their bond. It would have to take place at one of their most powerful sites, where the old magic was strong. Rome, perhaps, James mused. Their undiscovered catacombs. Or their pyramid site in Egypt. Or their mountain temple deep inside the Alps.

All their scattered remnants banished from the courts of Europe by the cursed Order's onslaught would come together once more and be renewed at the time of the eclipse by the blood sacrifice of a virgin. It was a beautiful ritual. Beautiful and terrible. Together, they would be renewed. And then it would all start again.

If it took two hundred years, they would achieve it. They would never stop, and James would remind them all of this at the gathering he would call. They must be reborn relentlessly, like the phoenix from the flames, refusing to let their great obsession die. If Malcolm with his bestial nature could not inspire and lead them, but would sink into greed and corruption, then James had made up his mind that he would take the mantle. The old gods would simply have to protect him.

Just then, a subtle creak of the floorboards suddenly informed him he was not alone.

"Well, well, well."

He looked up and discovered Niall Banks leaning in the doorway of his sitting room, watching him in contempt, his massive arms folded across his chest.

James paled.

He was not surprised that Niall had picked the lock, only that he had failed to hear him do so. Then again, his hearing was not what it used to be.

"Aren't you happy to see me?"

"Niall, dear boy!" James forced out, rising quickly as his heart began to pound. "What brings you to London?" He hoped he sounded as calm and amiable as always.

"Father sent me to check up on Bloodwell. And—" he added, sauntering closer. "On you."

"To be sure," he jested mildly, his mouth gone dry.

"What's that you're studying, old man?"

Pinned in that flat, dead stare, James realized there was no way to hide the Alchemist's Scrolls. They were arrayed across the table in plain view.

His heartbeat hammered as he realized he was caught.

Niall flicked a withering glance from the ancient parchments to him. "Just as Father suspected."

"Pardon?" he asked hoarsely, still attempting to smile like some kindly old tutor.

"The Alchemist's Scrolls. All the way in France, we heard that they were found. So, you're the one who bought them."

"Er, yes."

"And when exactly were you going to let my father know you managed to procure this treasure?"

James could feel his patience wearing thin. "What would Malcolm do with the Alchemist's Scrolls?" he retorted crisply. "He can't read the symbols. He barely knows who Valerian was. Your father has only ever paid lip service to the old ways."

Niall appeared amused with his vexation. "It is true that Father and I are more concerned with the future than the past. All the same, you will hand those over to me."

"No, Niall," he said after a quiet heartbeat, "I won't."

Niall flashed a broad smile. "How quaint you are, Falkirk, with all your medieval superstitions. You actually believe in that nonsense, don't you?"

James stared at him, appalled by this sacrilege.

"For my part, I deal in realities," Niall said, drifting closer. "At least I can reason with Bloodwell, but you're just a funny old quiz, aren't you? Has it ever worked? Even one of your silly dark spells, hm?"

James looked away in fury, but he could not hold his tongue. "You are a disgrace to our creed. You understand nothing."

"Power, James," Niall said. "That is what I understand. Dress it up with all your ancient rituals if you like, but at the end of the day, it's like every other religion, isn't it? Nothing more than a pantomime men use for control. I'm going to have to take those scrolls from you now, old man. Hand them over."

James looked at him for a long moment. "I will not."

Niall's eyes narrowed. "My father wants them."

"He cannot even understand them! They're of no use to him!"

"But they're of use to you? How?" Niall studied him. "Just what were you planning on doing with these moldy old parchments? What sort of trouble are you up to . . . ?"

James glared at him; all of a sudden, Niall's eyes flashed. "Traitor!" he murmured, staring at James. "You mean to manipulate the others into going against my father, don't you? You think you would do better in his place?"

"And so I will," James vowed as he pulled out a gun.

But he wasn't fast enough. Niall leaped across the table and grabbed his arm, driving it upward, firing the single bullet into the ceiling.

Crystals shattered on the chandelier, and the next thing James knew, Niall had gripped him by the throat and slammed him back against the nearest wall.

Pain shot through James's frail, arthritic body.

Struggling for air, he fought to dislodge the red-haired giant's fingers from his throat, to no avail.

"You schemer," Niall snarled in his face as he towered over him. "You know how we deal with traitors in the Council."

"You're the traitor!" he choked out. "You and your father have betrayed the creed. You're only out for yourselves!" James closed his eyes, gathered all his concentration, and with what little breath remained, began to utter the most lethal curse on Niall he'd ever learned.

Niall laughed in his face. "What are you going to do, old man, summon a demon to kill me?"

At that moment, the French doors to the balcony exploded open in shattering glass, and Drake flew into the room. The black-haired agent crossed the chamber in a blinding streak of wrath, crashing into Niall; he slammed him to the floor.

James's neck was wrenched a bit as Niall lost his grip. He gasped for air, astonished, as the two large, muscular men launched into a battle that quickly wrecked the room.

Drake! James thought in amazement, rubbing his throat and still shaking. *Where the devil did he come from?*

They sprang up from the floor where they had toppled and turned against each other in rage. Then the weight of their warrior bodies collided in a savage mutual attack. With an almost animal fury, they battered each other, crushing furniture, denting walls—each meaty collision of fist or elbow to torso and jaw producing a thud.

When Drake grabbed Niall in a choke hold, his face turned even redder than his hair, but he seized the nearby desk chair and slammed it over his shoulder at his opponent. Drake released him, staggering back. He fell against the bedpost, where he steadied himself, blood beginning to trickle from a cut above his temple.

His eyes were slightly dazed for a second after the blow

to the skull. But as Niall spun around, he shook it off, and when the red-haired giant stalked toward him, bringing up his fist, Drake launched forward and delivered a huge roundhouse kick that swiped Niall's feet out from under him.

Falling flat on his back with an angry shout of pain, Niall flipped onto his stomach at once to get up, but Drake dove on him before he could rise, planting himself astride Niall's back to pin him to the floor and brutally wrenching both of his arms up behind him.

Niall grappled against the lock that Drake now held on him. "I'll kill you," he gasped out.

"Give me my knife, James!" Drake ground out.

James's gaze homed in on the knife slung on a weapons belt around Drake's waist.

"Give it to me!" Drake roared when he did not move fast enough. But there was no way James was going anywhere near the two of them.

Let them kill each other. He was getting out of here. He began quickly putting the Alchemist Scrolls back into their kingwood case.

Drake's eyes were mad and wild, fiery coal-black, his face darkening with the strain of holding Niall down. Both men's arms were shaking; they were two forces of brute strength pulling in opposite directions.

Niall plowed all his massive strength into trying to free himself, but Drake would not allow it.

All of a sudden, Drake let out a barbaric war cry and with a mighty jerk, dislocated Niall's right shoulder. The red-haired man's bloodcurdling scream was cut short as he passed out from the no-doubt-blinding burst of pain.

Drake immediately pushed to his feet and, crouched over Niall's oddly inert form, pulled out his knife with an evil hiss of metal to cut his throat.

"Drake, no!" James said sharply, stepping toward him.

Drake slowly looked over at him.

And James realized he had summoned a demon, indeed.

"*Why not?*" he growled.

"Malcolm will send an army after us."

Drake did not look concerned about an army.

"If they recapture you, they'll put you back in the dungeon," James added in a calm, cool voice, holding the demon's stare.

The warning worked.

How terrified he still was of that dungeon, James mused, as the Drake he knew gradually returned, flickering back to awareness behind the killer's eyes. His fingers flicked restlessly around the knife's handle.

"Here. Use these to bind him." James quickly found the manacles that his late bodyguard, Talon, had often used for binding Drake.

Maybe Talon had been right to do so, after all, James thought. Talon had always insisted that Drake was exceedingly dangerous, but seeing him for so many weeks in his helpless state, it had been easy to forget that.

After what had just happened, James thought this point well worth remembering.

His chest still heaving, Drake accepted his former shackles with a bitter smirk and put them on Niall's wrists as the semiconscious Promethean let out a groan. He slammed the manacles shut. James also handed him the leg irons.

Drake put these on Niall as well, then stood up and sheathed his knife. Then he looked at James. "Are you all right, sir?"

He waved this off impatiently. "Of course. What in the world are you doing here?"

"I escaped. There's not much time. The Order agents aren't far behind me."

"How did you get away?" James asked, a bit suspicious. This might be a trick, some wicked Order trap.

"No time to explain. We have to get out of here. Now. They've got half a dozen men on my trail."

James frowned. He handed Drake a clean handkerchief so he could wipe the blood off his face.

"Come, sir, we have to go now."

James hesitated, then decided to trust him. If Malcolm already suspected his plans of insurrection, then he had little choice. With Talon dead, Drake was the only one left who might protect him. "Very well. Fetch my coat, over there, be a good lad, would you?"

While Drake did as asked, daubing the handkerchief over his cut with a wince, James attended to the Scrolls.

When another low groan arose from Niall, still inert on the floor, Drake glanced coldly at the man he had thrashed. "Why don't you want me to kill him?"

"Leave him alive for the Order. Perhaps they'll stop chasing you if we give them Niall in your place." Shrugging on his greatcoat, James handed Drake the travel bag he'd already prepared. After all, he had intended to leave England in a day or so to journey to the other Promethean leaders' strongholds. He would show them the Scrolls and tell them of his plan.

He picked up the Scrolls' case, then nodded to his fierce young friend. They left his room, hurrying down the third-floor corridor of the hotel. Drake, with weapon in hand, hurriedly shepherded him down the back stairs, watching this way and that for any sign of the Order.

"Come, sir. Let us make for the river. A boat will be our fastest way to safety. Your coach is too fine to blend in—we must not be identified. I'll call a hackney."

James nodded, briefly scanning the ex-Order agent's face.

He had got so used to seeing Drake in a trusting, childlike state that after the lethal capability he had exhibited back in the room, James was unsure if this was all a ruse. Was it possible he had truly turned Drake into a Promethean?

It appeared so. He watched him, bemused, as Drake prowled out fearlessly toward the street. He lifted his hand to his mouth and let out a loud whistle, then waved his arm to be seen by one of the waiting hackney coaches down the dark street.

James winced, hoping the Order agents Drake had said were following him had not also heard his whistle.

Drake strode back to the wall where James waited in the shadows. When he began pacing with impatience for the carriage to reach them, James watched him. "You seem much better."

"Somewhat, yes."

He volunteered nothing more until James posed the question bluntly: "Have you regained your memory, my boy?"

Drake paused for a long moment, then turned to him. "Enough to know who I can trust and who I can't. They left me for dead," he added in a hard tone. "You're the one who got me out of the dungeon. Besides," he added in a low tone as he swept the dark streets with his even darker glance, "why should I remain in England? There's nothing for me here."

"If you join me, you will be a hunted man—and not just by the Order. Malcolm will send others when his son does not return."

"Which means you need me all the more if you wish to stay alive," Drake answered in a hard tone.

"I suppose I can't argue with that," James said dryly.

"Then let's get the hell out of here," Drake muttered, as the hackney finally rolled up in front of them.

They walked over to it; Drake got the door for James and

steadied him as he started to step up; but all of a sudden, a cool-toned voice gave an order from a few feet behind them. "Don't move . . . another inch."

Click.

James froze at the sound of a pistol being cocked behind him. He looked warily over his shoulder, then was filled with recognition. "Well, if it isn't the Order's resident scholar."

"Evening, Falkirk. Lord Westwood," Jordan greeted them coolly, a pistol in each hand. "Terribly sorry about this, gentlemen, but if either of you moves, I'm afraid I'll have to shoot. You. Put your hands up," he advised the hackney driver, who blanched and obeyed, taking his hands off the reins.

Jordan advanced, keeping them in his sights.

"Now, look here, young man," Falkirk spoke up, taking an oh-so-reasonable tone. "You and I are much too civilized for this nonsense. You are not going to shoot me."

"No, I am going to shoot him." Jordan pointed his left-hand pistol at Drake. "Step away from the carriage, Lord Westwood. You're a traitor to the Order, and however scrambled your wits may be, I think you know what that means."

Drake lifted his chin in defiance.

"Don't give me any trouble, Drake. I'd really rather spare you. You come peacefully with me, or else."

"Let him go," Falkirk said. "We left a prisoner for you upstairs in his place. Third floor, Room 32. The door is open."

Jordan eyed the old man suspiciously. "Niall?"

"Yes."

"Alive or dead?"

"Alive," said Falkirk.

Jordan nodded. "All the same, Drake is going to have to come with me. Let's go, now, move!"

"You're not going to shoot me," Drake murmured.

"Don't try me." Jordan aimed a pistol at his forehead, but in that split second in which even *he* wondered if he could pull the trigger and kill a brother agent, Drake's glance flicked past him.

His lips twisted in a cynical half smile.

And suddenly something smashed Jordan in the back of the head. He lurched forward, thrown off-balance, seeing stars, and tasting horror—for his first thought was that he had been shot in the head. He fell to one knee on the cobblestones. Amid those stunned, reeling seconds, he scarcely cared that Drake kicked the gun out of his hand, threw Falkirk into the hackney, and leaped in after him with a shout at the driver to go.

Clutching the back of his head, Jordan blinked hard, then looked at his hand.

Only a little blood. *What the hell?*

Squinting through the meteor shower of stars he was still seeing, he noticed the fist-sized rock on the ground beside him. A bloody stone? Some little David had just made a Goliath of him?

He cursed and straightened up, trying to shake off the cobwebs, and suddenly realized Drake was getting away.

He cursed again. The carriage was already too far down the road to chase—but who the devil had helped the lunatic escape by throwing that rock at him?

Furious, Jordan stalked into the darkness in the direction from which the stone had been lobbed. He faintly heard the echo of light, pattering footsteps, but no one was there.

"Hey!" he roared, running a few steps after them, but confounded, he soon gave up. He was chasing shadows—and beginning to feel like a damned fool.

All he knew was that it was no Promethean who had struck him, for they did not waste their time throwing mere rocks. It would indeed have been a bullet. Whoever had thrown it had not intended to kill him, but he shuddered to think they'd certainly had their chance. He spat another disgusted curse, then went back around to the front of the building to see if Falkirk's claim about Niall at least was true.

As he approached the entrance, galloping carriage horses barreling down the street to the hotel heralded his colleagues' arrival.

"You're too late," Jordan said flatly, resting his hands on his hips as Max jumped out of the coach. "He's already gone. That way. I believe they were headed for the docks."

"Parker!" the marquess ordered.

"Yes, sir!" Sergeant Parker and his men didn't bother getting out of their coach but drove on, following Drake, which, apparently, they had been doing all day.

"What are you doing here?" Max asked, but Jordan waited for the others to join him before he explained.

Virgil and Beauchamp got out of another carriage and came striding over, but Jordan lifted his eyebrows when Warrington jumped down from the other coach, six and a half feet of pure mean.

Rohan Kilburn, the Duke of Warrington, was the team's most formidable killer.

"Good timing!" Jordan greeted him. "When did you get back from Scotland?"

"Just today. What the hell happened?"

Jordan braced himself and told them.

"Niall's in London?" Rohan echoed.

But while Max groaned over how close Jordan had come to capturing Drake, Virgil pivoted and began marching toward the hotel entrance without a word.

"Sir?" Beauchamp jogged after him, casting the others a curious glance over his shoulder.

"I guess we're going in." Rohan's knife produced a soft metallic hiss as he drew it from its sheath.

"Virgil, wait for us!" Max strode after him.

They followed the old Highlander into the building and up to the third floor, and found Room 32, just as Falkirk had advised.

Jordan's jaw dropped when he saw their waiting prisoner.

"Thank you, Drake," Beau said wryly, leaning on the doorframe.

The men laughed a little at Malcolm's brawny, furious son spewing curses at them as he lay prone on the elegant carpet, manacled hand and foot.

Except for Virgil.

Without the slightest trace of a smile, he strode in and crouched down to check the extent of Niall's injuries.

"Give me a hand with him," the old man muttered.

"Can't we just drag him?" Rohan jested.

Virgil shot them a furious glance, and all of a sudden, the warriors quit laughing.

A stunned silence fell.

"Damn," Rohan murmured, one syllable sufficient to express the shock they all felt.

As the realization hit them, the men exchanged stunned glances.

Seeing Virgil and Niall side by side, the truth was as plain as their matching noses on their braw Scottish faces, and the thick, flame red hair on both men's heads. They were of equal size and build, as well. And the truth was suddenly obvious.

Niall Banks was not Virgil's nephew. He was his son.

Chapter 14

Virgil quickly masked his emotions behind his usual gruff exterior; Max rushed to assist their handler in helping Niall to his feet. One side of his face swollen, nose bleeding, and one shoulder hanging at an unnatural angle, Niall was apparently in too much pain to do more than snarl at them and plead for help by turns.

"Let's bring him in and get that shoulder set," Virgil muttered.

Max nodded to him. "I'll come with you."

The mood had gone awkward, all the men feeling rather like chastened boys in the face of their mentor's secret anguish. Still, Jordan had no doubt that Niall would have gladly slit any of their throats if he got the chance.

Beau stopped Max on his way. "Do you want me to go after Drake or ask some questions around here and see if the hotel staff or guests have got anything to share about Falkirk? Might prove useful."

"Good idea. Parker and his men are after Drake. Let me know what you find. Thanks, Beauchamp."

The younger agent nodded. Max and Jordan exchanged a grim look, then their team leader went to help Virgil with Niall.

When they had gone, Jordan turned to Rohan. "Fancy a trip to Seven Dials? I mean to pay a call on Dresden Bloodwell. Join me if you like."

He flashed a grin. "Thought you'd never ask."

During the carriage ride back to the seedy neighborhood, they had a quick discussion on strategy and checked their weapons. Jordan described the layout of the lodging house where their target was holed up and warned Rohan of possible gang interference. "Wouldn't be surprised if he hired some of the local thugs for added security."

Rohan nodded. Even someone with Bloodwell's abilities could not watch in every direction or stay awake around the clock.

"Best do this quietly, then. And if we can't grab him," Jordan added meaningfully.

"Mm-hmm." Rohan cocked his gun.

Recalling the narrowness of those rookery lanes, Jordan pulled the check-string to make Findlay halt the coach a few blocks away. They got out and left him to wait, guarding the coach with his trusty rifle.

They went the rest of the way on foot. The moment they stepped into the cramped, dirty street where Bloodwell's lodging house sat, however, Jordan instantly knew that something had gone wrong.

Dozens of people stood in the street, many in their nightclothes. More milled about between the lodging house and the building atop which he had left Mercer.

Rohan and he had stopped, but now exchanged an ominous glance. Then two uniformed Bow Street Runners came out from around the corner, carrying a corpse between them.

Mercer.

Jordan stared.

"What happened here?" Rohan demanded, marching over to get answers.

But Jordan could not even speak, stunned guilt choking off his voice.

The Bow Street officers recognized Rohan's air of authority, if not his face, and believed him when he said he was from the Home Office.

"Peepin' Tom here came to a bad end," one Runner quipped with jovial graveyard humor. "Took a nasty tumble."

"How's that?"

"According to witnesses, he was lurkin' on the roof up there watchin' some woman nurse her baby on 'er tit. Pervert." The officer scoffed in disgust. "Some of the local lads spotted him. He tried to run when they confronted him, but he fell off the building. Drunk maybe. Hard to say. But he was armed."

"Any idea who he is?" Rohan asked.

The other Runner shook his head. "Nothin' in his pockets to identify 'im. We'll see. Somebody's likely to show up at Bow Street sooner or later to report a missing person. It's a bad business, sir."

"That it is," Rohan murmured. "Carry on."

With a shrug and a respectful parting nod, the Bow Street Runner returned to his task of clearing the onlookers out of the street so the cart could take Mercer's body to the morgue.

Jordan and Rohan looked at each other but said nothing in front of these local "witnesses," any number of whom might be reporting to Bloodwell. Almost certainly, they were covering for him.

Jordan turned away with a furious curse under his breath

and rage building in his blood. "They threw him off the building," he uttered in a low tone of rage.

"Not necessarily. He might have jumped." Anger hardened Rohan's voice as well. "Mercer would've known he was more valuable to Bloodwell alive."

Jordan eyed him sharply.

The thought that Mercer could've taken his own life to evade capture by the Promethean assassin—and the sort of torture Drake had survived—only made Jordan more furious.

"Or," Rohan added with a cold shrug, "maybe it was an accident. Perhaps he did fall trying to escape. Whichever it was, Bloodwell's long gone by now."

Jordan glanced at him, then nodded toward the lodging house. "Let's go find out." Ice stole into his veins as he stalked into the building and began running up the stairs, his brother agent right behind him.

Jordan kicked open the door and lunged into the room, bracing his pistol with his left hand. He advanced into the apartment, Rohan behind him. Jordan moved to the right, Rohan swept to the left. But a quick search of the three-room suite only confirmed that their quarry was already gone.

Jordan's fury broke from him abruptly. With a low curse, he upended the table with a violent throw and sent it crashing sideways to the floor.

"Calm down!" Rohan barked.

"Why did I leave him alone out there?"

"You had no choice! Listen to me. This is not your fault—"

"Yes, it is."

"It could've happened to any of us! He let himself be seen."

"He died for nothing." Jordan shook his head and walked away again, his stomach in knots. He prowled from room to room searching for any clues to Bloodwell's purpose for sending Albert into the royal library.

But it was no use. The whole dingy apartment had been expunged of any telltale clues. No doubt accustomed to moving around constantly, just as Falkirk had described, Bloodwell had abandoned his latest hovel without a trace.

Once more, Jordan shook his head. "I'm going to get this bastard. So help me, God. If it's the last thing I do."

"How?"

He looked at him in seething anger. "I don't know yet."

"Where are you going?" Rohan demanded, as Jordan stalked out of the apartment.

"Home. I've had enough for one night."

Dresden Bloodwell loomed over Albert. "Who gave you this message?"

"I-I—no particular person! Everyone was talking about it. Why?"

"Because it was a trick!" he snarled. "Somebody's onto you."

"*What?*"

"I discovered a man tonight spying through my window," he bit out harshly. "Alas, the poor fellow took an unfortunate spill off the side of a building trying to evade me, so I was unable to question him and find out where he came from." Dresden continued pacing back and forth across Albert's opulent chamber. "I only had two visitors this evening—your courier and another man, whose name is not your affair. One or the other allowed himself to be followed straight to me. Now you tell me this flimflam tale of the King's wits mending—"

"Flimflam?" Albert cried, his eyes as round as saucers. "Why do you call it that? Hasn't His Majesty spent the past decade losing his mind and getting it back again? I thought you wanted to know any relevant news from court!"

"Well, yes, there is a small chance it could be true, and that it was my colleague who was followed, not your messenger. I don't yet know," Bloodwell growled. "But if this 'rumor' about the King turns out to be false, then it means you were deliberately fed the tale by someone who was trying to get to me. I will look into it, believe me. But in the meanwhile, you had better be more careful who you talk to—and you'd better get my list," he added coldly. "Because *I'm* running out of patience, and *you,* my fine Duke, are running out of time."

Mara awoke in the pre-dawn darkness to find a male silhouette in the chair beside her bed. He was staring down at her.

"Jordan?" She struggled to clear the cobwebs of sleep from her head as she pushed up onto her elbows. "W-what are you doing here?"

"Go back to sleep, my love," he whispered. "I just needed to see your face."

Something in his voice sounded strange, and it was too dark to see the expression on his face. But she instantly knew that he seemed—off. "Is everything all right? I didn't hear you come in."

"I was trying not to wake you. I'm sorry. I should've waited until tomorrow. I'll go now—"

"No, don't go. I'm always glad to see you, no matter the hour. Come. Lie down with me." She made room for him in the bed, pulling back the sheet in invitation, but he stayed where he was. She could feel his faint smile and his wistful gaze in the darkness. "What are you doing here, anyway?"

"I just missed you," he murmured softly.

"How sweet."

"I shouldn't have bothered you this late."

"I don't mind, truly." She stretched a bit and rolled onto her back. "Did you play cards at Watier's tonight?"

"Earlier, yes. You're very beautiful when you sleep, you know."

As Mara's vision adjusted to the indigo darkness in her bedchamber, the faint glimmer of starlight helped her to make out the lost look on his face. "Jordan, what's wrong?" she asked immediately. "Has something happened?"

"Oh—I don't want to bother you."

"Nonsense! What's the matter?" Alarm suddenly had her wide awake. She reached to light the candle by her bedside, but he stopped her, his hand closing gently over hers.

"I prefer the dark if you don't mind."

She tried to search his face, but the shadows hid him.

"What's wrong?" she whispered.

When he released her hand, she lifted it to cup his cheek, but he pulled away, sitting back in his chair for a moment. He rested his elbow on the chair arm in brooding silence, his fingers obscuring his mouth. When he spoke again, his voice was very low, and rather dark. "Those men I sent to guard your house under Sergeant Parker. You remember them?"

"Of course. What about them?"

"One of them died tonight." He paused, as though slightly bewildered himself that this could have happened. "Mercer. He was under my command."

Mara stared at him in shock. "Oh, Jordan," she breathed. "I'm so sorry." She barely knew what to say. "How did it happen?"

He shook his head. "I can't discuss the details. Suffice it to say he was a good man. Loyal. He didn't deserve what happened to him."

She could only gaze at him in shared pain, hearing the anger in his taut voice, the seething self-recrimination.

Considering his news for a long moment, she recalled that he had told her that those men sometimes protected foreign dignitaries and such. It must have had something to do with a mission like that.

But I thought he was playing cards with the Regent.

The misgiving that flitted through her mind seemed unimportant, however, when Jordan was obviously in pain.

"Did he have a family?"

"I don't know. If he did, I'll have to speak to them tomorrow." He got up and paced over to her bedroom window.

As he leaned against the wall, staring out the window past the light curtains, his back to her, Mara got out of bed, brushed down the rumpled muslin of her night rail, and padded over to him, the floor cool beneath her bare feet.

She caressed his back as she joined him by the window. Then she slid her arms around his lean waist. "I'm so sorry, my darling," she whispered. "Is there anything at all that I can do?"

He shook his head. "I shouldn't have bothered you."

"Nonsense, you were right to come to me. You're exactly where you belong. Look at me, darling."

Warily, he met her gaze. Mara stared into his eyes, read the haunted look in them, then lifted her hand and gently stroked his hair, trying to comfort him. She had never seen him like this before, so cold and shut down.

She could feel the pain in him and longed to reach him somehow. She knew he had come to her in his hour of need. He was full of seething emotion that he did not know how to release. She rested her fingertips on his chest, then lifted her chin to brush his lips with her own, a cautious invitation.

He accepted tentatively, holding himself back.

She gave him another; he returned it a bit more earnestly. She fingered the V-shaped neck of his shirt with a restless touch, and the next thing she knew, Jordan was kissing her for all that he was worth.

She wondered vaguely what she was getting herself into as Jordan gripped her nape and cupped the back of her head almost roughly, thrusting his tongue into her mouth. This dark, wild, dangerous current underneath his passion frightened her slightly and yet deeply excited her.

He began sliding her night rail off her shoulder with a desperate, shaking touch that bespoke his need. "Take this off," he ordered in a low voice roughened by desire.

Her heart racing, she stepped back a little to oblige him. His stare consumed her when she had lifted it off over her head. With nothing to cover her nakedness but her long hair, she reached for his hand and drew him toward her bed.

With fractured yearning in his eyes, he let her lead him in wordless acquiescence.

Beside her bed, he kissed her again, and there, they both undressed him, piece by piece, coat, weapons belt, boots, until, in moments, he was as bare as she. Mara delighted in the splendor of his body—tall and strong—as hard and muscled as she was womanly and soft.

Rather than lying down, she stood before him, getting better acquainted with all the marvelous parts of him that his handsome clothing usually concealed. But even Bond Street's finest tailors could not do justice to his athletic, sculpted body. Such a comely male form was surely meant to top a marble pedestal, she thought, kissing his chest and stomach, exploring his arms and his tight, chiseled waist.

She could tell that her ardent interest excited him. It was not just the quiver of lustful anticipation that confirmed it; the swollen evidence of his arousal clamored against her stomach, straining toward her breasts. She wrapped her fingers around it and caressed it as she pressed up onto her tiptoes to sample one broad shoulder with her kiss.

She flicked her tongue against his throat to tease him, but he moved suddenly, capturing her around her waist with one arm, hauling her up against his heaving chest. His mouth swooped down on hers in a hard, claiming kiss.

Mara yielded gladly, her heart pounding as he lowered her onto her bed. Her limbs were weak, sweet, and heavy with her desire for him. Surely there was one way to ease his pain.

With pleasure.

She reached down once more, taking hold of his engorged member. Jordan closed his eyes as she began to stroke him, with a tight but tender grasp, up and down the length of his shaft, rounding its pulsing head. Enjoyment began erasing some of the strain from his angular face, and that would have been reward enough for her; but then he moved closer, fully intent on giving her much more.

His velveteen skin was feverish, his eyes glittering with need when he dragged them open again, pressing her onto her back at the edge of her bed. Mara spread her legs, but bent one knee, accepting his touch as he took care to see that she as ready and eager for this as he was. But he pleasured her with needless self-restraint. She had wanted the man since she had opened her eyes and found him there.

The smell of him, the sight of him, his smile, the taste of him—all these things had become her addiction.

He heard the summons in her breathless groan and eased atop her. She welcomed him into her arms, her heart racing with the wild thrill of that delicious moment when he first mounted her.

"Ahh, God." He went perfectly still for a second, as though he could not trust himself. "You make me sane again."

She gazed wantonly into his eyes and wrapped her legs around him, joining him in the beautiful dance and the bliss of skin on skin. She felt so free with him, holding nothing back, in a trance as she slid her foot lovingly up and down the lightly furred side of his muscled calf.

He kissed her so deeply and already had her so aroused—neophyte that she still was—that she came in moments, but he wasn't nearly through with her, as she discovered when he rolled onto his back, taking her with him. Laughing, pink, and tingling all over with release, she found herself sitting astride the earl, their bodies still thoroughly joined, as though he had no intention of even giving her a break.

He held her in place atop him, luxuriously impaled.

"Now, then. You were saying?"

She beamed with a dazed smile from ear to ear. "I wasn't saying anything."

"Yes, you were," he taunted in a silken murmur. "You were saying, 'Jordan, make me come again.' "

"Oh, was I?"

"Mmm. Would you like to know my answer? Or would you rather I keep you . . . in suspense?" He tugged her down flat onto his chest and kissed her heartily, running his fingers through her hair.

Mara took note at once of the new sensations that this position awoke in her, a whole different series of pleasurable responses now that she was on top of him.

"I rather like this," she informed him breathlessly.

"So do I."

Aware that he had her full attention, Jordan licked her lips slowly, such a naughty boy, entrancing her, tracing her lips erotically with the tip of his tongue; she quivered violently and felt the way her breath rushed past her wetted lips into his mouth, and his into hers.

Both of his expert hands caressed her hair and made their way slowly down her back, gliding over the white contours of her derriere, spreading her wider, taking her to an even greater depth.

He had no qualms whatsoever about where he would touch her, she discovered. Then she closed her eyes in startled, wary, but blushing acceptance as his fingertip penetrated another orifice, one that had certainly never interested her husband.

Well! she thought. A decent woman really should protest, but everything he was doing to her melted will and rationality to naught. She was his, a toy to play with as he willed.

"So you like that," he commented. "Good."

Before long, she found that he was right, as usual: To her amazement, he reduced her to a state of mindless ecstasy once more, writhing with release, her whole body, her entire being, open to him.

She was sure she was utterly spent when she rolled off the man to try to recover her wits, panting as if she had just run a mile. But a wicked gleam had come into his eyes.

"Oh, Jordan," she said in a breathless tone of unadulterated praise, her admiring whisper partly buried in the pillow, for she lay on her stomach.

"Yes?" he murmured oh-so-politely as he crept up behind her.

"What are you doing?" She went motionless, scandalized and torn, half of her ready to beg for mercy, the other half eager for more.

"Pay no attention to me, love." He had the audacity then to nudge his way back into her womanhood without even asking.

"Aren't you *ever* going to come?" she exclaimed, laughing in delight.

"In due time."

"I had no idea you were such a bad man."

"I know," he drawled.

"Be gentle," she pleaded.

"With you, always. Does it hurt, my lady?" he whispered as he ran his hand up her body in the most beguiling silken caress. It made her aware all over again of the tingling hip he touched, and her side, and her shoulder, then he cupped his hand over her arm. His every touch made her feel like a treasure. "Does it?" he breathed.

"Oh, Jordan," she moaned, "you know I can't resist you."

"Nor I you, my beautiful one. My Mara. Do you know I'd die for you?"

Reaching back to caress his face weakly with her fingertips, she felt the sweat on his skin, his jaw in need of a shave. She savored the softness of his hair, and once more, she let him have his way.

She knew he needed it tonight.

"Come for me," he whispered.

"Again?" she panted. "I can't!"

"Yes, you can. Who knows when we may get another chance?"

"At the rate you're going . . ." Her cheeky quip dissolved on her tongue, however, for as it turned out, he was right once more.

There'd be no living with his ego if they continued at this rate, she thought, as he drove her to edge of wild release.

Good God, this man's cool control over her body was obscene. She was beginning to feel like she was no more than a violin in the hands of a virtuoso—made for him, fashioned to fit his hands alone, lovingly polished and perfectly tuned by a master, and only he could make her body sing.

"Oh, darling." Embedded deep within her from behind, he carried her gently with him when he eased onto his back.

Mara lay atop him, indeed, draped over him, her head resting on his chest while her breasts heaved, her whole body bared to the otherwise empty room as she gazed up at the ceiling, half-blind with rapture.

He held her in place with both of his large, strong hands splayed across her belly as he controlled her motions from behind. She rose and fell on the waves of his muscled, undulating body. She gasped in aching pleasure and writhed atop him in a sweat. Relatively helpless in this position, there was nothing to do but to enjoy her ravishment.

And so she did.

Especially when he rose a bit, bracing his hands behind him, so that she was more reclining on him rather than lying down, and still he pleasured her ruthlessly.

With his mouth at her nape, his fingers plucking at her nipples, she could not believe it when she felt the crest of climax start rising steadily again.

This is ridiculous, she thought. But the final straw was when she noticed the mirror of her dressing table and saw right there the shocking spectacle of their bodies entwined. A bed with twisted, tangled sheets, a room bathed in the deep blue of a spring night, the glimmer of moonglow in the mirror revealing a scene of unbridled eroticism.

Well, she was Lord Falconridge's mistress, after all.

And she refused to regret a moment of it.

Instead, she feasted on the victory of Jordan's long-denied release when he came at last. He clamped his arms around her waist and gave her everything he had—every wrenching pulse of his seed, every anguished moan of bliss, each ragged gasp—as though he were simply emptying himself into her, both physically and emotionally until he was wrung out.

Silence followed. They were both completely spent. They separated to their respective places on the bed and stared at each other, rather matter-of-factly.

Jordan grinned at her after a moment or two.

Mara laughed and let a doting hand fall on his shoulder. "Really, Falconridge," she chided with a pink-cheeked smile.

All of a sudden, her ears pricked up to an almost inaudible sound. She lifted her head off the pillow and swiveled a glance over her shoulder toward the door. "Did you hear something?" she murmured.

"No." Jordan's face darkened at once. He tensed and sat up. "What did you hear?"

"I think the baby's up. Listen—"

"The baby? Jesus, Mara, don't scare me like that. I thought you meant—never mind."

"You need to relax," she whispered.

He dragged his hand through his hair and muttered, "I'm trying."

They both listened, gazing intimately at each other.

Then they both smiled when a sweet little voice came very faintly from beyond her chamber door.

"Mama?"

When Jordan heard that innocent, querying singsong, his whole expression changed. Looking utterly disarmed, he began laughing softly. "You'd better go see what he wants."

"You don't mind?"

"As if I could stop you. Go on. I'm well aware I'm not your favorite male in this rotten old world."

"After that, you may be," she murmured.

He pulled her close again for a hearty kiss, which Mara soon ended with a guilty frown. "You don't think he heard us, do you?"

"We were quiet enough. God, you're beautiful." He brushed her hair behind her shoulder. "Stay. Maybe he'll fall back asleep."

"Mama!"

"So much for that," she murmured, smiling.

"Are you sure Mrs. Busby can't see to him?"

"She's not Mama. I'd better go put him back down before he starts crying." She hopped out of bed, unable to stop herself.

"I suppose you can't fight mother's instinct." Jordan folded his arms behind his head and rested back against the headboard, watching her in satisfied amusement as she quickly pulled on her dressing gown, tying the cloth belt.

"I'll be right back."

"I should be going, anyway—"

"Don't you dare leave!" She shot him a look of protest. "You stay right where you are. Do *not* leave. I mean it, Falconridge. Or you and I are going to have a problem."

"Yes, ma'am," he answered with a lazy grin.

She humphed. "You're half-asleep already as it is. You'll stay for breakfast; it's almost sunrise, anyway. For now, you're right where you belong."

He smiled faintly at her. "I know."

As she held his tender gaze, she had never felt closer to anyone than she did to him in that moment. Joy welled up in her so bright it made her feel lit up from within, like a candle set inside a lantern.

"Mama!"

"Going," she whispered hastily, then she slipped out the door and practically floated down the hallway, in her heart, a secret prayer that by this time next year, Thomas might have a new baby brother or sister.

Jordan's smile faded after she had gone.

God, he adored her. He had come to her in a moment of weakness, but he was already questioning the wisdom of that decision.

Things were about to get much more dangerous around his mission, and that meant it was best that he not see her again for a while.

He resented the duty that kept him away from her, but the safest thing he could do for her was to set her aside just temporarily while he completed his mission.

Mercer's death would *not* be in vain, by God. It was time to push harder, take more risks to see his task through to the end.

Now that the storm of his rage had cleared, he realized

that if Dresden Bloodwell had indeed spotted Mercer looking in his window, then he was likely alerted to the possibility that Albert had been compromised.

This meant that Albert was in danger, for if Bloodwell saw that he could no longer use the duke for his purposes, then it was almost certain that he would also kill Albert to bury the connection.

On the other hand, if Bloodwell confronted Albert and questioned him rather than killing him, Jordan knew that Albert already suspected *him* on account of the library incident, when Mara had come knocking on the door calling his name.

There was a possibility that Albert could point Jordan out to Dresden Bloodwell—in which case, he had no business being anywhere near Mara; however, if Albert realized that he himself was in danger, it might be the perfect moment for Jordan to push to win his trust. It would be best for everyone if he could just somehow get Albert to talk.

That was where he was going to have to start spending more time and earnest effort . . .

But what should he tell Mara in the meanwhile?

He was going to have to tell her something to make sure she backed off to a safe distance and gave him the breathing room he required to finish the job. He couldn't tell her the truth, of course, but he needed *some* sort of device to make sure she stayed out of harm's way.

With a sigh, he rubbed his eyes in aggravation, weary of the duty that would once more keep them apart. After what they had just spent the past hour doing, her complete surrender to him, it was going to make him seem like an utter cad to back off from her now.

You should have thought of that earlier.

But he couldn't, not in the sort of shape he'd been in when

he had first arrived. He had needed her too much. He had reached out blindly for her from his pain. And she had been there for him . . . so beautifully.

She really was one of a kind.

Well, there was no help for it now. He was going to have to lie to her and be done with it. He had already told her so many falsehoods and half-truths pertaining to his real work for the Order, what was one more lie at this point? The thought brought a bruised, jaded feeling to his soul.

But this lie was only to protect her.

In any case, expert liars like him knew your best bet was always to stick as close to the truth as possible.

Pondering his true feelings for her in the darkness of her chamber, he took stock of the fears that still did, admittedly, trouble him on occasion.

As they filled his mind, arriving all too readily, he slid down into the welcome of her bed, stared into the darkness, and waited for her to come back from tending her child.

Chapter 15

What a dismal week shc was having.

Mara attended a ball about a week later but was enjoying herself not a whit, despite her hosts having spared no expense for their daughter's coming out.

Once again, there was no sign of Jordan.

She flinched slightly when Delilah drifted over, fanning herself idly, and asked the obvious question.

"Where's Falconridge?"

Mara checked her impatience, however, sipped her wine, and did not reply until she could manage a tone of perfect nonchalance. "Don't know. Haven't seen the man all week."

Delilah's fan stopped; she looked at her. "Why not?"

She took a deep breath and managed a taut smile. "He's busy, I suppose."

"Busy! What does that mean?" Delilah turned and stared at her in shock. "Did you two quarrel?"

"No, no," Mara denied with a wave of her hand. "I am not the center of his universe, you know."

"Well, you should be! Oh, I knew the second I saw you that something was wrong. Tell me what happened!"

Mara shook her head with a look that conceded her bewilderment. "I'm not exactly sure. To be honest, I'm a little worried about him. He was acting so strangely the last time I saw him."

"When was that?"

"A week ago."

"A whole week?"

"He showed up in my chamber in the middle of the night," she confessed in a murmur. "He was troubled by something that had happened—which I'm not allowed to talk about—" she forewarned before Delilah could ask.

Mara shook her head, recalling it. "We spent an incredible night together, and the next day . . ."

Delilah waited, but Mara's words trailed off into silence as she brooded on Jordan's alarming words to her the next morning. Lord knew, she had been mulling them over in her mind from the moment he had walked out her door.

"I guess I'm feeling just a bit confused," he had said as they had sat at the breakfast table. His sated, smiling mood had turned more serious after Mrs. Busby had taken Thomas off to get the boy dressed for the day.

Mara had laid her hand over his. "What are you confused about, darling?"

"Us," he had answered, staring into her eyes. "Where all this is going."

She had stared back at him, motionless, in the cheerful brightness of the parlor.

She remembered his careful tone all too well as he had added, "Perhaps it would be wise if we took a few days apart. To think about the future."

Mara had set her teaspoon down uncertainly. "The future?"

"This is all happening so fast, don't you think? It's so strong." He looked a little awed by what they had found together.

"Is that a bad thing?" she asked cautiously.

"No, no—of course not. I crave your patience with me. I just think it might be prudent to step back just for a bit and take a little time to think this through. Make sure it's what we both want before we go any further."

Mara was taken so much off guard by his doubts that she barely knew what to say. "Isn't that the mistake that we made last time?"

"Exactly. We hurt each other so badly last time, I don't want to take the chance of that happening again." His tender stare had implored her to understand. "Please. I just need a little time."

She knew that Mercer's death had shaken him, and that he blamed himself. Maybe, somehow, that had something to do with his uncertainty. But she was nonetheless bewildered.

Time was the last thing she wished to give him, considering they had already lost twelve years together.

On the other hand, he didn't seem to be giving her much choice.

She had struggled to show patience and compassion. "I am glad you told me how you feel, Jordan. You're right, of course—this caught fire with a life of its own, between you and me. I can see how that could take you off guard. Especially after I vowed we would only be friends."

He nodded. "I've heard you say on several occasions how much you value your independence as a widow."

Her own words rang hollow to her. She should have known a day would come when she would have to eat them.

"As for me, I have the title to think of," he had said softly, and it was this point that had silenced her.

How could she blame a traditional, duty-minded man like

the Earl of Falconridge for harboring hopes of wedding a virgin in white?

It was every man's dream, indeed, the expectation of every noble lord—which made her heart sink lower.

She had willingly become his mistress and taken him for her lover, but that was not marriage.

Theirs was a highly passionate affair, but she suddenly wondered if he was telling her now, for both their sakes, that that was all that it could ever be.

As these thoughts promptly ruined her appetite, she suddenly thought that if he wanted time, he could have it, for these were words she was in no hurry to hear.

"There's also the boy to think of," Jordan had lastly pointed out. "He's already lost one father, and the more attached he grows to me, the more difficult it will be on him if we ever decide to stop seeing each other."

She had looked at him in a panic.

How could he say the words so calmly? Losing him was unthinkable for her. But amid the chaos he had loosed in her soul, her mothering instinct homed in on the validity of his warning. Forget her own heart breaking—Thomas must be protected at all costs.

Mastering her emotions, she had chosen her response with the utmost care. "Perhaps you're right," she had said with a cool control worthy of any Falconridge. "Maybe we both have some thinking to do. Thank you for bringing this up," she forced out, "not just keeping these misgivings to yourself. I truly appreciate your honesty. It's best to have all this out in the open between us."

He had nodded though he looked somewhat distraught.

She had reached out and touched his forearm. "Take all the time you need. You know how much I care for you. I'm not going anywhere."

If he had come back to her after twelve years apart, then

a few more weeks were not going to matter in the long run. And if he did not, it was best to have the hurt now and be done with it before she fell any more deeply in love with him. So she told herself.

If a little time apart helped Jordan clear his head, where was the harm? For her part, she was so sure deep down to her bones that their love was destiny that he must surely reach the same conclusion.

But with each passing day that she did not even hear from him, it grew harder to hold on to her faith.

". . . And I haven't seen him since," she finished telling Delilah about their difficult exchange.

Her worldly friend shook her head, looking stunned and appalled. "That's it. I'm giving up on men. If even Falconridge can turn out to be a bounder, then there's no hope for any of them."

"I'm sure he's not a bounder."

"Well, it sounds like it to me! I saw how hotly he pursued you all these weeks, Mara. He was like a bloodhound on the scent after you, no matter how he tried to feign that the two of you were only friends. Now that he's well and truly caught you, has he tired of the game? If so, that puts him among the most *odious* members of the entire male race—"

"No, no, he's not like that at all," Mara protested, though with uncertain conviction.

"Oh, really? And how do you know? I'll take a horsewhip to him if he thinks he can do this to my friend!"

"No, Delilah. I'm afraid he has a good reason for reconsidering our affair. He's probably just trying to spare me now from future heartache."

"What do you mean?"

Mara let out a small sound of distress, trying to think how to put it.

She wanted to believe his hesitation had been solely triggered by the death of the soldier under his command. She knew it had hit him hard, and she could see how something like that would make him feel compelled to reevaluate his responsibilities.

Unfortunately, she knew Jordan Lennox rather better than that. In her heart of hearts, the place where her deepest fears lurked, she worried there was more to it than mere male boredom or anything like Delilah had accused.

"He wants children," she confessed in soft-toned anguish to her friend. "He not only needs an heir, but actually wants to be a father. I know him. Family is highly important to him. The doting way he talks about his nieces and nephews, and he's so good with Thomas . . . he wants lots of babies. Daughters and sons."

"But so do you." Delilah stared at her. "You always say you wished you had more children."

"Delilah—I'm almost thirty years old," she forced out painfully.

"Still young enough to give him an heir!"

"Look how long it took for me to conceive the first time!"

"That was not your fault!"

"I can't be totally sure of that—and neither can Jordan. Even the accoucheur would not confirm it in any certain terms."

"That's because your husband was the one paying him," Delilah pointed out. "He's not going to come out and call a peer of the realm impotent if he's paying the bill," she whispered.

"Look at these girls," Mara said bleakly, shaking her head as a trio of bright-eyed debutantes in pastels went hurrying past, giggling to each other, all innocence and mischief, trying to find their sea legs in Society. "Beautiful, young, healthy."

Any of these fresh-faced little darlings would fall down

on their knees and give God thanks if the Earl of Falconridge offered marriage. They were born and bred to provide a noble lord with his expected brood.

"Oh," Delilah forced out abruptly. "I suppose I see what you mean. How depressing."

"Quite." Mara folded her arms across her chest and leaned back wearily against the wall.

At length, she shrugged, for what else could she do?

"I had my turn as one of them, and I ended up with Pierson. There's no going back now to change the past."

Delilah gazed sympathetically at her.

She blinked away a threat of tears at her cynical friend's rare tender look and summoned up a wry half smile.

Delilah put her arm around Mara's shoulders. "I'm sorry, darling. You were truly robbed."

"If only I had waited another six months back then, then maybe—"

"Don't do this to yourself. You had no hope that he was coming back, and that's his fault. Besides, if you hadn't married Pierson, you'd have never birthed that adorable little monkey of yours, now, would you?"

"True," she agreed with a low sniffle.

"Anyway, I don't see why you mean to take this lying down. This air of stoic resignation doesn't suit you, my dear."

"I have no choice but to accept his decision. It's his life."

"It's your life, too! I thought you were done letting a man tell you when to sit or stand or breathe after Pierson died."

Mara looked at her uncertainly.

"The Mara who came out of mourning was a free woman ready to fight for what she wants. You haven't lost your dream man yet," Delilah murmured. "You've still got him, it sounds to me. It's not as though he's ended your affair?"

"No, he said he just wanted time."

"Well, maybe it's *time* you remind him of where his heart

really lies. Hang convention! If he loves you, why should you not be his wife, as you should have been from the start?"

Mara bit her lip, considering the question. "It seems a lot to ask of him."

"Do you really think he could ever be happy without you? You'd really let him marry the wrong person like you did and end up just as miserable as you were with Pierson? Anyone can see you two belong together. For heaven's sake, if I were you, I would gird my loins for battle and fight for 'im!"

Mara couldn't help smiling. "You would, too, wouldn't you?"

"Sure as blazes!" Delilah took a drink of wine.

"I don't know. Don't you think it's better just to leave him alone until he's worked it all out in his head?"

"What, leave it to a man to figure out how he *feels*? You might as well ask him to knit you a stocking, darling."

"But I don't want to crowd him."

"Don't be daft! You need to manage him! Do you really think any male out there actually knows what he wants? No," Delilah answered her own question firmly. "They are babies in such things. They have to be *shown*. If you give him this 'time' he thinks he wants, and let him go off on his own for too long, it's going to seem like you don't care. Take it from me, Mara. I played it too cool with my love, and I lost him."

Mara looked at her in surprise. "No! Surely not. I know you two are still at war, but I can't believe that Cole is lost to you."

"He holds me in the utmost contempt now," Delilah informed her, looking away. Her shrug held only the thinnest veneer of nonchalance. "It's all my own fault. I pushed him away until he quit coming back. I suppose I just wanted to make sure he really loved me before I'd admit I cared for him . . . and by then, it was too late."

"Oh, Delilah."

"Just let him know he's in your thoughts. Please? That you miss his company? Just enough to remind him that he misses you, too?"

Mara shook her head. "I don't even know where to find him tonight."

Delilah gave her a pointed look, then scanned the room. "Ah! I see someone who very well might know! Leave this to me." With a naughty flare of her eyebrows, Delilah glided off into the crowd before Mara could stop her.

Across the ballroom, she could see her elegant friend sidling up to the beaming, smooth-cheeked "Golden" Ball-Hughes. That unlicked cub had no idea that the worldly widow was about to make him her toy.

But fifty scheming mamas in the ballroom looked daggers at Delilah—and not for the first time—as she led the young Midas back to where Mara still stood.

"Look what I found, Lady Pierson. Isn't he the most charming young fellow?" She flicked a piece of lint off his formal black tail coat and clung adoringly to his arm, while the Golden Ball completely missed her ironic undertone.

"What a relief to see you ladies here this evening," the rich young rakehell confided. "I can't endure all these giggling ninnies fresh from the schoolroom."

"Bless you, Mr. Ball-Hughes, for saying that," Delilah crooned, sending Mara a gloating smile.

"It's true," he vowed in heated earnest. "I've always found older women so much more enticing." He leered at them; Mara and Delilah both strove not to laugh at the cub.

"Tell me, darling, I see the Regent here, but where are the rest of your friends? Are they playing cards tonight? We thought it might be amusing to pop in on them."

"Er, ladies—" The lad began to color at Delilah's expectant look. "That will not be possible, I'm afraid."

"Why ever not?"

"Y-you cannot go to such a place as where they are this evening." He looked from one to the other. "It is not a-a suitable establishment—for ladies."

"Ah, they're at a brothel?" Delilah asked bluntly.

"Well, er, yes, to be quite honest," he stammered, turning red, while Mara absorbed this news, aghast.

"And Lord Falconridge is there?" Delilah pursued.

He nodded. "It was his idea."

"Really?" Mara uttered, frozen by this news.

"My, my," Delilah said, concealing her shared indignation from the Golden Ball. "What is this wicked school of Venus called, my love? Tell us where it is, hm?"

"Mrs. Staunton, you cannot mean to go there!" The lad was scandalized, glancing from Mara to Delilah.

"Why ever not? Do you think I've never been to one before?"

"You are jesting!" he whispered.

Still in shock, Mara hoped she was, but knowing Delilah, she probably wasn't.

"We are women of the world, Mr. Ball-Hughes. Do you not know we are free to do as we please?"

"You are serious?" he murmured, fascinated. "You really mean to see the place? Because if you really want me to . . ."

"Oh, would you? Unless you have some objection to being seen with us two ladies under your protection?"

"Well, not at all," he answered heartily with another schoolboy blush. "I was planning on joining the others there myself in a bit. Oh, why the devil not!"

Delilah laughed gaily, and suddenly the boy millionaire was beaming at the idea of walking into that notorious place, where all his friends were drinking and carousing, with two attractive worldly women on his arms.

Mara was feeling slightly sickened by the revelation of

Jordan's whereabouts. "Mrs. Staunton, this does not sound entirely wise to me."

"One moment, darling," Delilah said to the Golden Ball. She trailed a playful finger down his smooth cheek, then turned away and faced Mara's ominous scowl.

"I don't know about this. I might kill him if I see him with some harlot."

"It's still early, love. They're probably just making a party of it for now. You've got to show up and make sure he doesn't—do something stupid."

"He already has," she shot back, folding her arms across her chest. "That liar! Time, indeed! To think about his feelings!"

"Listen to me," Delilah whispered. "He's a man. That's what they do. You have to take control if you intend to keep him in line."

Furious, Mara growled under her breath, shaking her head.

"Come, Mara! It's bad enough to worry about losing your *cher ami* to some virgin bride, but for heaven's sake, don't surrender him to a courtesan! You don't want him catching their diseases, do you, darling? That would ruin all your fun. I say we go and ambush him! Oh, I can't wait to see his face when you walk in."

"I agree with you on that. I'm sure he'll feel quite sheepish. But after that," she added uneasily, "he could be furious."

"You're the one who should be angry! If he takes it badly, just pretend it was all a lark. At least you'll have your answer. Come on, let's get out of here. This ball is utterly dull, anyway, and I can't stand any more of these little debutantes tripping over their own skirts."

Mara still hesitated. "I don't know. I don't want it to look like I'm checking up on him."

"Mara, this man told you he needed time to sort out his

feelings, and now he's off at a brothel? What the devil is that? I'll confront him myself if you're too scared!"

"I'm not scared, Delilah, I'm just trying to respect his wishes."

"Oh. Like he's respecting you?" she retorted. "Mara, please, consider what I'm about to say to you, as your friend. If you are seriously thinking of marrying Lord Falconridge at some point in the future, of giving up your rare and cherished *freedom* for this man, then you had better take a frank look at how he spends his time when you're not there. You know I'm right! You married Pierson without truly knowing what sort of man he was, and how did that turn out?"

Mara pressed her lips together.

"Indeed," Delilah said pointedly. "Now, I'm not going to let you make the same mistake twice. We're going to that dreadful place, you're going to look right at your precious Falconridge knee deep in his mischief, and see for yourself if he is really what you want. I know you put him up on a pedestal; but don't forget, he is a ranking member of the Inferno Club. Something just doesn't add up with him! You know it as well as I. At the very least, find out who he really is before you pledge your life to him. Well?"

"Well!" she exclaimed, overwhelmed by her friend's dire warning. "What more can I say to that?"

It was either the best advice or the worst she had ever received, but Mara found she could not argue with a word of it. She thrust her misgivings aside and nodded, taking a deep breath. "Let's go, then."

Delilah sent her a hearty look of approval, then pivoted. "Mr. Ball-Hughes, my dear? We are ready!"

The handsome lad smiled slyly. "Ladies: Follow me."

The three of them slipped out of the dull, stultifying ballroom, then their cheerful young friend assisted them into Delilah's carriage.

As they set out for the school of Venus, the prospect of seeing Jordan at last, after so many days apart, made Mara's heart pound.

The news of his location was vexing, indeed, but she had to admit her life had been a dull, dry desert without him all week. Maybe Delilah was right. Maybe a little visit from her when he least expected it would keep him on the straight and narrow if he was thinking of straying.

When she recollected their erotic night together a week ago, she could not imagine he'd seek the embrace of some vile, diseased harlot over her to satisfy his needs.

For her part, Mara had need of him again as the thought of Jordan in her bed filled her with hungry yearning. It had been too long since her last dose of him.

Surely he missed her, too.

As the carriage rolled on through the dark streets of London, she found she really could not believe he was a bounder, nor would she assume so, unless she saw it with her own eyes.

He was probably just there enjoying the raucous company of his male friends. He must remain innocent until proven guilty.

"Here, put this on." Delilah handed Mara a black satin demimask that she produced from the folding compartment underneath the seat.

"What, you just happened to have these in your carriage?"

"Doesn't everyone?"

Mara laughed. "Why, Delilah?"

"Because that's how it's done! Oh, darling, you still have a lot to learn about being a merry widow." Delilah's eyes twinkled with mischief as she looked away, directing her gaze to their escort. "My dear Mr. Ball-Hughes, if this is one of those clubs where *particular practices* take place, you had better tell us now."

"Practices?" Mara asked with a curious glance from one to the other. "What practices?"

"Never mind, dear. He knows what I mean. Anything I'll need to explain to our pure little friend here?"

He laughed. "I've heard they've got an opium room upstairs, but besides that, nothing, er, out of the ordinary. How do you know about such things, Mrs. Staunton?" the young rakehell drawled, leering at her in thorough approval.

Delilah rolled her eyes.

"What practices?" Mara demanded.

Her friend just looked at her.

"Right," she murmured. "Maybe I don't want to know."

After a short drive, they arrived at a shabby brick building a stone's throw from the London docks.

The Satin Slipper.

Mara stared dubiously at it through the carriage window. "You're telling me some of the most powerful men in England are inside this low place?"

"Oh, yes. I daresay even the Regent has been here."

"No!" Mara turned to him in surprise. "Not His Royal Highness? I thought so much higher of him than this."

"Well, I could be wrong," he said. "But I'm certain every one of his brothers has visited here."

"Well, that I believe." The royal dukes were known as the most barbaric scoundrels.

"Shall we, ladies?" Mr. Ball-Hughes stepped down elegantly from the coach and turned to hand them down.

"This should be amusing," said Delilah, accepting his white-gloved hand first and alighting from her coach with a studied air of boredom.

"Or a nightmare," Mara muttered as she followed suit.

Her heart pounded as the Golden Ball led them to the entrance.

"It's all right. They're with me," he proudly told the pair of giant bullies at the door.

Mara pulled her cloak closer around her body, hiding her ladylike ball gown, while her face colored with nervous embarrassment behind her half mask.

"There you are, lads." Their young escort tucked a very large bill into the guard's breast pocket. The towering man stepped aside, and the Golden Ball led the way into the dimly lit brothel.

"Very nice," Delilah remarked, pressing the other gladiator-sized guard out of her way with a sensual caress on the man's chest. "Step aside, boys. I'll show your little hussies how it's done."

Mara scoffed at her saucy boast and followed Ball-Hughes into the large, gaudy, and surprisingly crowded parlor of the brothel.

I can't believe I'm doing this, she thought, slightly revolted by the unwashed stink of the place, which someone had tried to cover up by dousing it with horrid cheap perfume. Walking in slowly, she marveled at the half-naked women lounging languidly amid the men all about the room

But in a heartbeat, she was glad she had agreed to this adventure, for she suddenly spied Jordan on the far end of the room.

The moment she spotted him, a huge sigh of relief arose from the depths of her being, leaving her instantly reassured. He was simply talking to Albert Carew, the Duke of Holyfield.

The two men were engrossed in conversation at the bar.

You see? she told herself as a smile stole over her face, and the dread dissolved from her heart. How could she have doubted him? As soon as she saw him, everything felt normal again, and she feasted her eyes on the sight of his lean, hard frame.

Of course he wasn't off with some hired woman. All of her fears suddenly seemed as trivial as a gust of wind—and blew away. Their departure left her hoping anew that he wouldn't be angry she had come. He was bound to be more than a little surprised to see her there, but it was too late to turn back now. In for a penny, in for a pound.

Trying to drum up a bit of Delilah's flamboyant attitude, she squared her shoulders and sauntered in, heading for the oh-so-skilled seducer who had so ravished her just one week ago.

To be sure, if he had need of a woman tonight, it was going to be her, not one of these indifferent hussies. He wouldn't even have to pay her, she thought in wicked amusement.

Then Mara set her sights on him. She'd had enough of this separation. Delilah was right. She'd fight for him.

Time to go and claim her man.

Chapter 16

Albert was stone drunk, according to plan, and Jordan was as close to breaking him down in that moment as he was likely to get. "You have friends, Holyfield. If someone is threatening you, you don't have to face it alone."

Mara's interruption in the library still hung over their heads, making this an even more delicate operation: Jordan could not be entirely sure if Albert had decided she had come searching for him in error that night or if the duke was playing games, pretending to be friendly, when in fact, he saw Jordan as an enemy.

Jordan knew he had to be careful. More than that, he had to be patient. As much as he wanted to grab Albert by the lapels, throw him up against the wall, and beat the truth out of him, that wasn't going to help matters.

Winning Albert's trust was still the best way, at least for the moment. "If someone is blackmailing you—"

"If only it were that simple." Albert shook his head, soaked with gin and fraught with desperation.

"Are you being threatened with violence?"

"I'm not a coward!" he slurred.

"Of course you're not. Tell me what is going on."

"I can't speak of it."

"Why?"

"Because people will think that I'm the one at fault! They'll think—" His words broke off abruptly.

"They'll think what?"

Albert swallowed hard, then he looked over at Jordan with fear in his eyes. "That I killed my brother."

Jordan gave him a hard look. "Did you?"

"God, no! I was right here in London, at a ball, in front of everyone when I heard the news he had drowned! Ask anyone! Everyone saw me there! And yet, still some whisper, most cruelly, that I paid to have it done. Not true." He shook his head with a woozy swing. "I had nothin' to do with it. Somebody murdered him and now . . ."

"Now they're threatening you?" Jordan finished for him.

Albert's pleading stare confirmed it, but he was too scared to say it aloud.

"Have you seen the man making the threats?" Jordan pursued. "Could you describe him? Or has it all been through messengers?"

"I've seen him, all right," he breathed, nodding in dread. "Why else would I be in such a pitiful state? Look at me, Falconridge! I'm a wreck! My nerves are shattered. I look like hell—"

"Try to calm down, Holyfield. It's all right. I'm going to help you."

"How?"

"Tell me where he is. I'll get him for you."

"You and what army?" he retorted, for Jordan had not revealed his identity as an agent of the Order.

So far, he had merely prevailed on him as a concerned friend. "Just tell me where to find him."

Albert peered bleakly into his cup. "I don't know. He just pops up like a-a bloody shadow. He's pure hate."

"Fine. Then I'll set up an ambush for him at your house. You summon him by whatever means you would normally use, and when he walks in, I and a few of my colleagues will be ready for him."

Albert searched his face in trepidation. "You'd really help me?"

"My dear Holyfield." Jordan stood up from the stool and leaned his elbow on the bar. "Did you really think I was just a diplomat all those years I spent abroad?" he asked quietly.

Albert blanched. "It would only make it worse for me if you failed."

"I understand that. We can keep you safe. But you're going to have to cooperate. You can start by telling me what he wanted you to accomplish inside the palace."

Albert stared at him; Jordan stared back relentlessly.

The duke hesitated, took a deep breath—

Two dainty hands suddenly covered Jordan's eyes.

"Guess who?" teased a familiar voice behind him.

He flung her hands away. *This cannot be happening. Not again!* "What the hell are you doing?" he shouted, pivoting to face her.

Mara's eyes grew as round as saucers. She paled and shrank from him. "Surprise," she said meekly.

He glowered at her, too shocked and furious to find his voice for a second.

"Ahem, I'll leave you two alone," Albert said.

"Holyfield, wait—"

"Jordan! Don't you dare ignore me!"

"Leave me alone, Falconridge. These ladies over here need

my attention, and I can see this one needs yours." Albert slipped away to join the painted harlots on the sofa. They pulled him down onto their laps amid drunken laughter.

"Jordan! What is going on?"

He looked over slowly at his mistress, glaring at her.

Part of him wanted to throttle the woman. He could not believe she had just thwarted his mission again, ruined it for him, probably for good. "What the hell are you doing here?"

"I might ask the same of you!"

"You should not have come here. This is no place for a lady. Come," he said through gritted teeth as he took hold of her elbow. "I'll see you to your carriage."

"I'm not leaving!"

"Yes, you are," he said as he marched her toward the exit.

"You can't tell me what to do!" She shook her arm free, planted her feet, and turned to him in wrath.

"The hell I can't," Jordan growled. "You have no business being here!"

"Well!" She stared at him shock.

Seeing the hurt look in her big brown eyes, guilt began to overtake his fury. He dropped his gaze. "I told you I would call on you when the time was right."

"What a liar you are."

He glanced at her in cool surprise.

Mara folded her arms across her chest. "A brothel, Jordan, really? At least now I know where you learned some of your tricks."

He flinched. But of course, it was true. All those years without the woman he loved in his life, he had made do with whores.

She shook her head at him. "I thought you were better than this."

"It's not how it looks," he muttered, well aware he had already lost this battle.

"No, of course not. You just needed some time to sort out your feelings," she reproached him. "What a fool I was to believe you! Save your lies for your little virgin bride, my lord! You're going to need them."

He furrowed his brow. "What are you talking about?"

She just glared at him, then flicked a contemptuous glance around at the harlots. "So sorry to interrupt your fun. Enjoy yourself, you hypocrite."

"I will call on you tomorrow to discuss this—"

"Save yourself the trip," she shot back. "I can assure you, I won't be at home." She gave him an icy look, then stalked out, her head high.

"Mara!" When he tried to follow, Delilah blocked his path, stepping in front of him.

"Leave her alone. Haven't you already done enough damage?"

Jordan narrowed his eyes. "This is your doing, isn't it?"

"You had her fooled, but I knew from the moment I saw you that you were a cad, just like every other man. Stay away from my friend."

"You're no friend to her, Delilah. You dragged her here for the sole purpose of coming between us, didn't you?"

"I came here to show her you're a fraud. I don't trust you, Falconridge. You and your blue eyes."

"You just want her to end up alone and miserable like you. Misery loves company, Delilah!" he spat.

"I am hardly miserable, I'll have you know, and I'm certainly not alone! I could have any man here with a snap of my fingers."

"In your bed, no doubt, but they wouldn't love you. Not like I love Mara. That's what you can't stand for her to have when you're without it. Some friend."

He could see in her eyes that his words had struck home. She paled. "You don't know me," she ground out.

"Believe me, I know your kind all too well. Women like you don't have souls. I guess Cole finally figured that out."

Delilah stared at him in shock. She flounced out abruptly, leaving Jordan standing there fuming, at his wits' end, indeed, nearly ready to explode.

His life of secrets and the lies he had been telling Mara were suddenly intolerable. They were causing more problems than they solved. This was a debacle. Now both his mission and his love affair were strewn in pieces. He would fix them both, but at the moment, he had no idea how.

He shook his head, took a deep breath, and marched back to the brothel's gaudy parlor to finish this with Albert.

Unfortunately, when he arrived, he found his target passed out on the sofa. Albert was snoring, his head resting on the lap of some painted harlot, who was playing with the duke's hair and guzzling gin.

Jordan clenched his jaw and began to count to ten. He wanted to punch something, for even he had limits to his frustration.

Not only was Mara furious at him—understandably so—for he realized how bad this looked, but his mission tonight had proved a waste, as well. An unconscious Albert was useless to him as a source of information.

He turned to one of the waiters. "Fetch his servants to cart this idiot home, will you?"

"Yes, sir."

Before long, Albert's coachman and groom came in to collect their unconscious master.

Jordan shook his head in disgust as they carried the duke out. *Enough of the light touch on this.* He was through being nice to that damned coward, that treacherous fool.

He'd clear it with Virgil first, but tomorrow, after Albert had slept off his drunk, Jordan vowed to himself he'd descend on the duke's mansion in force and resort to more stringent measures to make the weasel talk.

He had just officially run out of patience.

There was a time for diplomacy, and a time to dole out a proper thrashing.

In a very rare, foul temper indeed, Jordan glanced down coldly when somebody touched him.

"Evenin,' handsome." One of the girls sidled up to him and caressed his back. "You look like you could use some cheerin' up."

It had been a week since he'd enjoyed a woman's touch, but he just stared at her, as cold and dark as January.

"Not interested." The edge in his low growl scared the whore away—but what scared *him* was the terrible thought that Mara might not forgive him for his lies.

If she banished him from her life, revoked her love, then he realized he might be making do with girls for hire for the rest of his dark, miserable life.

Albert awoke—barely—to a fiery headache and a raging thirst after a few deadened hours of gin-sodden sleep. Dried out from drink, his sudden panicked need for water was the only force strong enough to drive him into an upright position, then unsteadily onto his feet, shuffling across his bedchamber through the predawn twilight.

Still dressed in the fine clothes he had worn out the previous evening, even down to his shoes, he had no memory of coming home. He barely remembered being at the brothel.

Then again, not much about his life was worth remembering these days.

Seizing the pitcher of drinking water on his chest of drawers, he brought it up to his lips and, not bothering with a goblet, gulped water out of it directly.

It spilled over the wide mouth of the pitcher and ran down his chin, dripping on his chest, all over his rumpled attire. The former leading dandy of the ton was past caring.

Nausea followed straight on after guzzling the water. His stomach churned; his chamber swirled around him. He sank down heavily on the dainty stool before his dressing table.

Usually, he could not resist the nearness of a mirror, but this morning, he could not even stand to look at himself.

Escape.

He had tried to get back into the Regent's library at Carlton House; but they watched him all the time though no one accused him. At least not yet.

I should run away.

But what was the point? Even if he jumped aboard the next packet to Calais, Bloodwell's masters lurked in France, Belgium, Italy. No agreeable place was safe.

They were everywhere, and they'd get him.

Liquor was the last form of escape left to him, but God knew he had overdone it last night. And who could blame him? He was terrified. He still did not have Bloodwell's list. Which meant he was going to have to talk his way out of this somehow. At the moment, the thought of facing Bloodwell again made him feel sick enough to puke.

He lifted the pitcher again and poured the rest of its contents over his head in an effort to wake himself up.

The water splashed all over him, plastering his formerly perfect hair to his forehead, dousing his celebrated cravat, and wetting the floor beneath him as if a coward had lost control of his bladder.

"It's time, Albert."

He closed his eyes, but for once, he didn't jump out of his skin. No, he had been expecting this. At the sound of Bloodwell's footsteps sauntering closer, he opened his eyes again wearily.

"I'm here for my list."

Albert braced himself, then stood, and turned to face him. "I don't have it. I need more time—"

Bloodwell grabbed him by the throat. "What you lack is motivation, Albert." He pulled out a large knife. "But I have a notion of how to inspire you."

Albert cried out, struggling against his hold. He watched in helpless horror as Bloodwell flattened his right hand, splayed, across the top of his night table.

He secured Albert's thumb against the table, bringing up the knife to whack it off. "I warned you, Albert. Wasting my time is going to cost you."

"Wait! No! Please, don't, don't, please, wait! I-I know what to do. I have another solution," he begged him.

Bloodwell paused; his leery gaze slid over to him. "I'm listening."

"They don't trust me. They watch me all the time at Carlton House now," he forced out in a panic, cold sweat running down his face. "That's why I haven't been able to get in there again. But I know someone who can," he said with a gulp.

"Go on."

"Someone who has the Regent's complete confidence. A person they'd never suspect."

"Name?"

"Mara—Lady Pierson. V-viscountess. She's a cl-close friend of the Regent. A fashionable widow. She has far more access to Carlton House, a standing invitation! She can go in w-whenever she wants. She could get your list."

"One of the Regent's bed partners?"

"No. The tie between them is her son. Little wee boy. His name, oh, what is it—Timothy—no Thomas. Yes, Thomas that it. He's her entire world, and the Regent is his godfather. Take the boy, and she will do whatever you ask."

"This woman lives in London?"

"Near Hyde Park," said Albert with a gulp. "I don't know which street. I could find out!"

"Not necessary. I'll manage. This is good, Albert."

"Yes! You see, I-I told you I could be useful. I couldn't get the list myself, but I knew I could at least give you a good alternative, t-to help."

"If you're lying to me—"

"No, I swear! I wouldn't. Will you let go of my hand now, please? Please?"

Bloodwell released his hand with a sly smile.

Albert yanked it close to his chest, guarding it as he cowered before the shadowy man. "Why are you smiling?" he whispered, chilled. "You are pleased with my solution?"

"I could never condone failure, Albert. I'm just happy that I won't have to hear your whining anymore."

"What do you mean?"

"Get up," Bloodwell ordered. "You and I are going to take a little walk out to the woods."

Chapter 17

As the light rose over London, the dawn of the new day found Mara peaked and pale after a night of tossing and turning. Finally, she had won a few hours' respite from her insomnia, but then awoke late accordingly, and her whole morning routine was quite thrown off. To make matters worse, she was supposed to visit her parents.

It was now half past nine as she sat alone in the parlor, picking at her breakfast, her heart feeling like a bruised apple that had fallen out of the bushel basket and landed on the floor.

She couldn't stop thinking about Jordan. How she regretted hunting him down last night.

That's the last time I listen to Delilah.

He had spoken so coldly to her, had grown so irate.

She was glad, of course, that she had not found him dallying with a harlot. But it really wasn't much better to see him out carousing yet again with her late husband's friends from the raucous Carlton House set.

Something really was not adding up. And she was dashed tired of it.

Thomas came barreling into the parlor, banging one of his wooden blocks on the wall as he traveled, and aggravating the headache she already had from crying last night. "Thomas, stop that. You're going to dent the wall."

He sped over and tugged on her skirts, clamoring for attention. "Calm down," she ordered. "I'm trying to eat my breakfast."

When that didn't work, he resorted to whining. "Mama! I go outside!"

"Thomas, please—Mrs. Busby!" she called in tense impatience, catching herself almost sounding like her mother.

"There you are, little master! Sorry, ma'am, he got away from me. He's gettin' quick for these old bones."

Mara flinched with guilt as the old nurse hobbled in and collected the viscountess's rambunctious son. But Thomas didn't want Mrs. Busby. He began kicking about as the old woman lifted him. "No, no, no! Don't pick me up!"

Mara put her fork down with a sharp clatter. "That will do, young man! You don't kick Mrs. Busby, or anyone else, for that matter. Stop it!" She grabbed his little foot and stilled it firmly, giving him a scolding stare. "Behave yourself."

Thomas scrunched up his nose and pouted at her, but obeyed.

"That's better. You need to calm down. You're going to go see Grandmother today, and you mustn't vex her."

"Er, my lady, about that—I know we're all running a bit behind today," Mrs. Busby said tactfully, glancing at the mantel clock. "Do you know what time you'll wish to leave for your parents' house today?"

She was silent for a moment. "I'm not going. I'd like you and Jack to take Thomas there so his grandparents can see him, but I just can't—face them today."

"Of course, that's no trouble, but are you feeling ill, milady?" the old woman asked in concern.

"No, thank you. It's just—if my mother were to say one wrong word to me today, I don't know what I might do. She's sure to ask why I didn't bring Lord Falconridge with me again." Tears suddenly welled in her eyes to speak his name aloud.

"Oh, my dear mistress." The nurse put Thomas down on the floor. He ran off to play. The old woman eased into the chair beside her. "Do you want to tell your old Busby what's the matter?"

She succumbed to a sniffle. "Lord Falconridge and I had a falling-out last night."

"Dear me, no," the old nurse said with compassion wreathing her wrinkled face. "But all lovers quarrel eventually, my lady. If he hurt you, I'm sure he will apologize. Anyone can see the earl dotes on you. I'm sure he'd never knowingly do you any harm."

She looked at Mrs. Busby uncertainly, hoping she was right.

The old woman patted her hand. "There, there, milady. Jack and I will take Master Thomas today so you and your gentleman can patch things up."

Fresh tears rushed into her eyes at the old servant's kindness. "Thank you, Mrs. Busby."

Thomas had toddled back into the room. Seeing her tears, he climbed on her lap and touched her face. "Mama, you sad?"

"I'm all right, darling." She hugged him for a moment, then pressed a tender kiss to his downy head. "There now, off you go. Let's put your shoes on, Thomas. It's almost time to go see your grandparents. Try not to break anything while you're there, hmm?"

As she put him down, a knock sounded on the door with a firm triple beat that reached them from the foyer.

Mara's gaze flew to meet Mrs. Busby's.

The old nurse smiled reassuringly. "He's early."

Mara nodded and got up from her chair, glancing into the mirror over the fireplace while Mrs. Busby took Thomas away, mouthing a silent "good luck" over her shoulder.

Mara nodded in gratitude while Reese marched to the front door.

Another brisk trio of knocks resounded through the front half of the house.

Mara abandoned the thought of having her butler tell him she was not at home. He wouldn't believe it anyway. Quickly arranging herself in the yellow armchair by the empty hearth, she brushed the pale green skirts of her day dress neatly into place. She folded her hands in her lap so he would not see them trembling.

"My lady: Lord Falconridge," her butler announced a moment later, showing him into the parlor.

Jordan strode in with his shoulders squared and his chiseled jaw set at a resolute angle. He halted two steps into the room and offered her a very correct bow.

Mara greeted him with a dignified nod; Reese withdrew.

For a moment, they just stared at each other. Wistfulness and dismay seemed to fill the room, flowing back and forth between them.

"Thank you for seeing me," he clipped out.

She nodded, only wondering why the blackguard had to be so handsome. She could not help admiring his lean, athletic body in spite of herself as he turned around to shut the door.

It closed with a discreet *click,* and he faced her once more. Truly, his striking good looks made it all the harder to stay angry at him. Did he know how that indigo morning coat and the light blue stripe of his waistcoat beneath it brought out the ice blue beauty of his eyes? Or that the tight fawn breeches that clung to his thighs made her fight the urge to squirm in her chair with the memory of his body covering hers? His black boots gleamed as he paced restlessly into the room.

"I came to say I'm sorry."

She nodded with cool caution. "A good start. But you're going to have to do better than that."

A flicker of surprise passed across his chiseled face. Then he dropped his gaze and drew off his gloves. He seemed to search for words.

"What is going on, Jordan? Please. I'm not a fool. Whatever it is, just tell me. Is there someone else?"

"No!" he said in surprise. "Of course not."

Relief eased some of the tension from her posture. "Then what is it you've been keeping from me?"

He gazed at her for a long moment. "I want to tell you. I can't lie to you anymore. But I have to ask you first, do you love me?"

Mara let out a small, impatient sigh as Jordan searched her face. Now, this wasn't fair. Why should she be the first to make this profound concession when he was the one in the wrong? But looking into his blue eyes, she knew true love did not keep score.

"You know I do, you cad. Though not quite so much at the moment," she muttered wryly.

He stared at her in tender thanks, the trace of a smile softening his face. "I can see why."

She shook her head at him. "I gave myself to you completely, Jordan. Are you ever planning on doing the same?"

"I'd like to do that now," he replied with a taut nod. Then he began to pace.

Mara watched him avidly. "Very well. I'm listening."

With an array of tangled emotions visible on his face, he paused to pick up one of Thomas's abandoned blocks, which he placed gently on the table.

"Er, Mara?"

"Yes, Jordan?" she urged him softly.

He stopped and looked into her eyes. "I am not exactly a diplomat," he said. "I'm a spy."

Mara held her breath and tried not to look astonished. "I see."

"Do you?" He furrowed his brow, then glanced suspiciously toward the parlor door, as though he suspected someone of eavesdropping. "That's the real reason I had to go twelve years ago, and why I could not write. I couldn't tell you. I really shouldn't be telling you now. But back then, especially, you were so young, so reckless, indiscreet. You know you were." He paced again. "Given the danger, I didn't dare. I was afraid you'd make a mistake that could have had disastrous consequences."

Mara watched him in a state of shock—and yet she was strangely relieved. Finally, something made sense!

"I had to let you go—but I *did* mean to come back and see if you had settled down, in time."

She did not know what to say to that.

"At any rate, much of my agency's work was finished after Napoleon fell. I was called back to London. Some weeks ago," he continued, "we became aware of a possible new threat to the Regent. We had cause to believe that an enemy agent had infiltrated the prince's inner circle."

Her jaw dropped.

"I was tasked with eliminating the threat, and last night I was this close"—he held up his finger and thumb an inch apart—"to breaking down my target when you walked in."

"*Albert?*" she exclaimed.

He nodded. "That's why I got so angry. I'm not excusing

my temper, but frustration got the best of me, and I apologize for that. Getting to that point had taken so much effort, and when you walked in, the distraction provided him with an escape route. The chance was lost.

"It's not your fault, of course," he added. "You had no idea what you were walking into—and I can only imagine how bad it must've looked from your perspective. But it really wasn't what it appeared. Little is, in my life," he murmured ruefully. "I just hope you can understand. It's been so difficult, having to conceal this from you all this time. I knew it was wrong, but I didn't have a choice. Until last night. Hurting you like that." He shook his head with a hard look. "It isn't worth it. I don't want to lose you. When I saw your face last night after I yelled at you, I knew the time had finally come to trust you with the truth. And the truth is, I never needed time to sort out my feelings, Mara. I'm in love with you."

Her heart pounded as he gazed at her from where he stood by the fireplace.

He heaved a weary sigh and pushed his hand through his sandy hair. "I've been working like hell all week to complete the mission so my duty can *stop* coming between us. As soon as it's finished, then we can finally be together again, without any danger to you or anyone else. I've missed you every day we've been apart. But for your own safety, I've been trying to keep you removed from it all." He gazed at her with hope etched across his face and worry in his eyes. "At least now you know what's really going on."

"Oh, Jordan," she murmured, staring at him, scarcely knowing what to think. It was a great deal to take in. And though his declaration of love warmed her, the rest of his revelations brought a chill.

She got up from the armchair and crossed to the window, shaken as she contemplated it.

Good God, her lover was a *spy*?

He stayed where he was, keeping a respectful, or perhaps a wary distance, letting her absorb it. But when she glanced back at him, he was still watching her.

Mara tried to think what to say. "I am—appalled that I interrupted something directly concerning the Regent's safety. I'm truly sorry."

"It's not your fault. You didn't know."

She shook her head dazedly. "This is rather astounding."

"It's also extremely confidential."

"I can't believe it. Is Albert really—?"

"Oh, yes. I caught him breaking into the Regent's private office on the night of the ball at Carlton House."

"In the library?" She furrowed her brow, taken aback.

He gave a cynical shrug. "I'm afraid your arrival at the bordello was not the first time you scared Albert away."

She stared at him, the implications of his untruths starting to sink in. "You said you were waiting there for *me*."

His expression began turning grim at her uneasy tone.

"So, you made love to me while you were lying through your teeth. Under false pretenses . . ."

But she wasn't stopping there, and he knew it, for he closed his eyes as though to brace himself while she began piecing more of it together.

"You must know I care for you, Mara."

"Wait a second . . . I'm the one who introduced you to the Regent. The day you brought the painting with me to Carlton House . . . oh, my God!" She reached out to steady herself on the nearest piece of furniture. He moved forward with a stricken stare to steady her, but she warded him off. "Don't touch me!"

"Mara—"

"It was all a lie, wasn't it? A trick."

"No! Of course not!"

But how could she even believe a word out of his mouth?

Her heart was pounding. She felt ill. Tears of rage flooded her eyes as she stared at him in crushed betrayal.

"You need to leave. Get out of my house. And don't come back."

"Mara," he whispered, as an all-too-real sheen of tears also dampened his ice blue eyes, but his cold heart had melted too late. "I never meant to hurt you."

"You used me," she choked out, remembering that day in Hyde Park, when he had come over to admire Thomas. "Bad enough that you used me to get in with the Regent and his friends. Even *that* I could have forgiven. But you used Thomas to get to me," she ground out. "You used my son. You pretended to care about him!"

"I do care about him!" he cried.

She could not look at him. She could only shake her head. "I trusted you. And so did Thomas."

Jordan had turned as pale as if someone had just stabbed him in the heart. "I would never hurt Thomas, and I would never hurt you."

"*Then tell me the truth!*"

"I wanted to be with you!" he wrenched out. "You're right, it was my mission—but it was the only way I could let myself be near you again. You don't understand, Mara. There's something wrong with me," he choked out barely audibly. "I can't bridge the gap. I'm so cut off from everyone. Please. You're the only hope I've got. If you turn me away, I've got nowhere else to go."

"But I don't even know you!"

"You *know* me," he insisted in a low, strangled tone.

"How can I? You're a fraud, a liar! The smooth perfection, the gentlemanly front—it's all a façade! Who are you beneath it? Right now, I have no idea! And I'm not even sure I want to know."

He looked away. She saw that she had skewered him, but this did not lessen her hurt.

Reeling, she struggled for equilibrium. "I'm sure men like you have their own kind of honor—" She closed her eyes, swallowed hard, and steeled herself. "But I don't want to be around it. And I don't want it around my son."

He held her in an agonized stare. "You cannot mean this," he whispered.

"Go."

Jordan stood frozen for a heartbeat, staring at her, as though he half expected her to reverse herself.

She stood her ground, her chest heaving.

Visibly stunned, he lowered his gaze, then he picked up his gloves and walked stiffly toward the doorway of the parlor.

Mara willed herself to stop shaking, to no avail.

He paused as though to say something in parting, but he thought better of it and marched out of the room without a word, his shoulders rigid, his head held high like a good soldier. He stalked across the entrance hall and stepped out, pulling the door shut behind him with a quiet *click* that echoed through the house with a terrible finality.

The second he was gone, Mara crumbled. Sobs racked her frame. Tears poured from her eyes. It had all been nothing but illusion. Just a giant lie.

Her idol had used her for pleasure and convenience, the man she had trusted, looked up to, adored. She wept bitterly to have been so taken in, though he was an expert at such things. How many times had she assured herself that she could trust him? She felt like such a fool.

At least she had not been duped by an amateur. Nonetheless, she cursed herself.

Only the most naïve of fools could manage to lose her heart twice to a man who did not even have one to offer in return.

Chapter 18

The only thing Jordan knew how to do in that moment was to keep moving, focus on the task at hand.

That afternoon he arrived at the Holyfield estate dressed all in black, with his men in their battle gear ready to take Albert into custody.

Sergeant Parker, Findlay, and a few of the others who knew that Dresden Bloodwell was to blame for Mercer's death had joined him, hungry for revenge.

When they descended on the duke's estate, Jordan was the first off his horse, stalking to the front door with hellfire in his eyes. By God, his blood oath to the Order had already cost him more than he would ever have willingly agreed to pay at the outset if he'd known.

If Albert balked in the slightest, he was going to get a thrashing. He was in no mood for this today. Banging his fist on the door, Jordan sent a taut glance over his shoulder at his men and waved them into position.

When the door opened, a slim butler as fastidious as his master lifted his eyebrows. "May I help you, sir?"

"I'm here for Holyfield."

"His Grace is not available. You'll have to make an appointment—I say!" the butler exclaimed as Jordan planted his hand on the front door and pushed his way in, shoving the smaller man aside. "What is the meaning of this?"

"Fetch your master. Now." Jordan's glance swept the cavernous entrance hall with its checkerboard floor of black and white marble.

"His Grace is not at home! Who are you? How dare you intrude in this barbarous fashion?" he cried as Jordan's men followed him into the home, and contrarily, several of Albert's footmen came running into the hall.

"Stand down!" Jordan barked at them. Then he glanced coldly at the butler. "I am Lord Falconridge. I played cards with His Grace last night. I saw what sort of condition he was in by the end of the evening, and let's just say, I wanted to make sure he got home safely."

The butler eyed the line of Jordan's scowling, black-clad soldiers and clearly found his explanation less than convincing. "Of course he got home safely. I let him in myself!"

"Good. Then where is he now?"

The butler backed away with a pugnacious glare. "He has not yet arisen for the day! You must leave now, my lord. This intrusion is quite beyond the pale!"

Jordan nodded at his men. "Search the house."

As Parker and his mates advanced into the entrance hall, Albert's footmen yelled warnings for them to come no closer. The clamor grew louder as a few more arrived bringing weapons, ranging from an old blunderbuss to a handy shovel.

"Halt!" Jordan barked at his men as the threat of bloodshed loomed.

When his men paused, the footmen quieted as well.

"All of you, listen to me!" Jordan commanded, turning to the frightened butler. "The duke is wanted for treason. We are here to take him into custody."

"What?" the butler breathed. "This cannot be!"

"Oh, yes, it can. We have cause to believe the duke used his position close to the Regent to deliver secret intelligence into the hands of England's enemies."

His servants gasped.

"As deplorable as the charges are against your master, I am not wholly unsympathetic to his plight. Though I have orders to collect him, I intend to do my best to keep him safe. The fact is, there are worse men than me searching for him," Jordan informed them. "If you care for your master, you will tell me where he is. Unless you wish to be considered as being in collusion with him? Hiding him from justice at this point would be a crime."

The servants glanced uneasily at each other.

"Do you have any sort of official papers for your claim?" the butler attempted.

Jordan merely gave him an ominous look.

The little fellow swallowed hard. "He should be in his chambers. The footmen carried him up there last night when he arrived home in the, er, condition you mentioned, and he has not yet made his first appearance of the day."

"You will not object if we go and wake him, then."

"Er, no, sir, as you wish." The butler nodded to the footmen to let them pass.

Jordan strode toward the stairs, his men following. The butler hurried along after them, and directed them to a door off the third-floor corridor behind which, he said, lay His Grace's bedchamber.

With his weapon at the ready, Jordan laid hold of the door handle. Taking a deep breath, he opened it.

He advanced into the huge, opulent room, but at once, he saw that Albert was not in the great, canopied bed. He was not behind the corner screen or in the window nook. In fact, there was no sign of the dandyish duke, just a puddle of water near the stool before the elaborate dressing table.

A window was open; Jordan crossed to it and looked out, half-expecting to see Albert's corpse strewn out on the grass many feet below, but there was nothing there.

Suspiciously, he eyed the spikes driven into the stone, placed to allow the picturesque ivy to climb up the side of the housc.

"Sir?"

Jordan turned to Parker in question.

"He's not in here."

"Maybe he wandered off and fell asleep in another room," Findlay offered.

"Shall we check the rest of the house?" asked Parker.

Jordan nodded. "I'll come with you." With his men marching behind him, they began a systematic search of the sprawling Holyfield mansion.

The servants joined in, some of the calling out "Your Grace!" as they sought their missing master.

It took some forty-five minutes to conclude that Albert was nowhere in the house.

The butler was beginning to look very worried, too.

"Perhaps His Grace began feeling ill from drink last night and went out for a walk to clear his head. It was a fine evening. There are several places out on the grounds where he could have chosen to, er, take a nap."

"Like where?" Parker asked with a nod.

"Oh, there are many pleasant benches in the gardens. And a folly with a daybed by the pond. He likes to read the paper there sometimes."

"Maybe he's just not here," Findlay spoke up.

Jordan looked at the butler in question. "It's possible His Grace might have left on his own much earlier this morning. It would be unusual for him to leave without crossing paths with any of the staff, but it is not impossible. We are only servants, after all. The duke does not make us privy to all of his comings and goings."

"Are any of his carriages gone? Horses missing?"

"Go and check the carriage house," the butler ordered one of his underlings.

"Check the stables, as well." Jordan signaled to Findlay to go with him. "He might've gone off on horseback."

Jordan gritted his teeth, beginning to wonder if the little weasel had fled with some premonition of what he had coming.

Findlay nodded and marched off after the footman, who waited for him. "This way, sir."

"My lord," the butler said, "it could take an hour or more to find out if all the horses are accounted for. There are dozens in the stables alone, and many more that spend the night out in the pastures this time of year."

"Check," he answered.

The butler dispatched more footmen to the stables for this purpose, and another of Jordan's soldiers went with them.

"My lord, if His Grace did go into Town today without our noticing, then I would suggest you look for him at his club or his tailor's," the butler offered. "He could be taking tea with one of his lady friends, or perhaps he's even visiting the Regent."

Jordan nodded in response to his suggestions.

When the men came back a few minutes later and reported that none of the carriages were missing but that counting the horses would still take the better part of the next hour, Jordan called his squad aside.

"Let's split up to look for him. Wilkins, you stay here

and search the grounds. All those places the butler said, the folly, the benches, anywhere else that looks appealing. Report back to Dante House with any news.

"Parker, Jenkins, you two head back to Town. Look for him at White's and around some of the fashionable tailors' shops on Bond Street. Ask around if anyone has seen him. It could be that we're worried for nothing, and he's just carrying on as usual. Or," Jordan added grimly, "if he remembers the things he admitted to last night, it would not surprise me in the least if he woke up today and immediately made up his mind to flee the country.

"Parker, I want *you* to go down to the London docks and locate one of our contacts in the Customs House. Tell him you need to see the logbooks for this morning. Find out if he was aboard one of the packet ships heading for any Continental port."

"Yes, sir," Parker replied with a quick salute.

"I'll go to Carlton House and make sure he hasn't taken it into his head to try to break into the Regent's desk again."

"The palace guards know not to let him anywhere near it, though, right, sir?"

Jordan nodded. "They've been advised to keep a watchful eye on him whenever he visits, though, of course, they don't know why. Still, if he's desperate enough at this point . . ." Jordan shrugged. The men nodded, then they split up to carry out their separate tasks. "We'll be back again later tonight," he told the butler, "perhaps tomorrow, to see if there's been any word from him."

"Will you let us know if you find him, sir?"

"Yes, as much as I am able. In the meanwhile, I strongly suggest you keep the news of these grave charges against the duke to yourselves, for the sake of your own livelihoods. If I were you, I would protect the Holyfield name as long as possible. The status of the charges against your master could change if more information comes to light, and we should take steps now to preserve his reputation if we can. I know he'd appreciate that."

"Indeed, sir. Thank you, from the bottom of my heart."

Jordan nodded and took leave of them, but his thoughts were grim. *I have a bad feeling about this.*

As he walked out, an ominous foreboding from his deepest senses was growing stronger by the second. He pulled on his riding gauntlets as he walked over to his horse. Then he swung up into the saddle, scanning the landscape uneasily as he gathered the reins.

Everything in him clamored to get to Carlton House and make sure the Regent was safe.

Something wasn't right. He could feel it in his bones.

Later in the day, after her tears had subsided, Mara went out for a long walk.

The house was too empty without Thomas there—and without Jordan. She draped a light lace veil over the brim of her bonnet to hide her bloodshot eyes and to prevent her acquaintances from recognizing her.

She was in no mood for trivial conversation.

The lace covering blew in the balmy spring breeze as she passed burgeoning flower boxes, little manicured patches of emerald grass around some of the town houses.

She strolled to Hyde Park, where the fertile earth rejoiced in the lush, green luxury of May, all the world in full bloom—but in her heart, it was bleakest autumn.

Restless, she only stayed a moment at the park, gazing at the place where her carriage had been attacked weeks ago by that unruly mob. How handy Jordan had been with a weapon! At least now she knew why.

She moved on. Her ghostlike reflection was her only company as she drifted past shop windows with enough in her accounts to lay her hands on whatever she liked. But money could not buy her the one thing she desired.

All the while, his words haunted her. "*If you turn me away, I've nowhere else to go.*" As disillusioned as she was about him at the moment, as difficult as it was to separate the truth from his lies, once the shock wore off, her foolish heart began refusing to believe he did not care for her. For Jordan to come forward willingly and admit to such a terrible deception did not bespeak indifference, it argued, but the highest respect, trust, hope, esteem.

He was only doing his duty. Of course, he might as well have stabbed her in the heart, but if his mission involved protecting the Regent, then at least some good had come of it. Still, what a cold, heartless thing he was.

Perhaps that's what he *had* to be, in the hard life he had chosen. Mara let out another large sigh. At length, she decided to walk the extra two blocks to visit Delilah.

She was not going to say anything to her friend about Jordan being a spy—a spy, for goodness sake! She just wanted to let Delilah know she was not angry at her for instigating last night's debacle.

Before long, she arrived at her friend's elegant little jewel box of a town house. Mara lifted a white-gloved hand and knocked, her reticule dangling from her wrist.

In short order, the butler let her in and gestured her politely toward the music room upstairs, which Delilah used from day to day as an informal parlor.

"Mara!" Curled up on the sofa in her dressing gown, Delilah turned to greet her as Mara walked in, drawing off her gloves. "How are you? Oh, no," she said, needing no further answer beyond the red, swollen eyes and chafed nose that were revealed when Mara threw the veil back from her face. "You're a mess."

"Quite," she said wearily.

Delilah winced. "I would've called on you earlier, but I thought you would be visiting your parents."

She shook her head with a heavy sigh. "I just couldn't face the pair of them today. I sent Thomas on to see them with his nurse." She dropped into the plump, cushioned chair across from her.

"I've been so worried about you. I feel awful about what happened last night—"

"Don't. It wasn't your fault. I came here specifically to tell you that. I knew you'd be feeling guilty."

"Bless you." Delilah gazed sympathetically at her. "Let me send for tea."

"No, thank you. I don't intend to stay long. Thomas will be home soon."

Delilah did not appear to be listening anymore, having glanced toward the doorway, where her gaze remained transfixed.

Mara followed her stare, and to her astonishment, saw that Cole had just appeared, fastening his sleeves, then buttoning his waistcoat.

A bright beaming smile burst across Delilah's face. She held her hand out to him. "Darling!"

Mara's eyes widened. She sat up straight as Cole sauntered in, barely aware of her existence.

He walked over to Delilah and took her hand, then leaned down and kissed her in dreamy affection.

They gazed at each other in glowing intimacy.

Well! Mara dropped her gaze with a blush. "I see you two made up."

Cole laughed softly, glancing over at her. "Indeed. I owe your friend Falconridge a mighty debt of thanks." He took Delilah's hand between his own and smiled at Mara. "Whatever rebuke he scalded her ears with last night, I am happy to report, it brought my lady to her senses."

"Is that so?" Mara turned to Delilah in amusement.

"Very well, I admit it." Delilah began blushing like a girl. "Your 'Jordan' was horrid to me after you walked out. We exchanged *words*. But he made me realize that the love of a good man is too precious to risk losing."

"Really?" Mara exclaimed with a half-indignant smile. "I've only been telling you that for months, but you never listen to me. Jordan says it once, and it's suddenly Gospel?"

"It was the *way* he said it, darling."

"He did not spare her feelings like you do, Lady Pierson." Cole sent Delilah a doting look askance.

"I hated him at the time," Delilah agreed, "but within five minutes of leaving that place, I realized he was right. I was being a coward, pretending I didn't care, when the truth was, I was afraid of telling Cole how much he means to me."

"Until last night," he said softly, gazing at Delilah.

"Thank God, this wonderful man saw fit to give a fool another chance."

"You're not a fool, sweet."

"Yes, I am. You're just a very forgiving man."

Mara was astonished by this tender exchange between two of the greatest cynics in the ton. But it was obvious she was intruding. She cleared her throat. "Well, then! I'll leave you two in peace. I'm very happy for you both." Wishing them the best, she wasted no time in showing herself out. The visit had cheered her a bit, but, nursing a broken heart, she was happy to escape the lovestruck pair.

Now she knew how Delilah must have felt throughout all those weeks when she and Cole were at odds, while Mara had been falling in love with Jordan.

As for him, she thought as she sauntered homeward, he might indeed be a spy, but his diplomatic skills were proved by the peace treaty he had brought about between these two long-warring factions.

She could not help smiling to herself over Delilah's newfound happiness. Hopefully, this time her friend would not make a muck of it again.

Most of all, she thought, if those two could be reconciled, maybe there really was hope for her and Jordan.

This morning, she had ordered him out of her house and told him not to come back; she remembered with a pang the ashen color of his face at her words. She knew then that she had hurt him deeply. Likewise, her trust in him had suffered a serious blow, but as she walked up to her own front door, she mused that at least now her eyes were opened to the reality of who he was, what manner of man she was really involved with.

Maybe all was not lost, or needn't be. Perhaps in a day or two, she might feel ready to write to him and ask for another round of negotiations in the hopes of settling their unexpected war.

As she pushed open the front door, Reese did not appear as usual to attend her, but it was an informal day, and she assumed he must be busy at other household duties.

Tossing her reticule aside, she untied her bonnet, set it aside in a state of distraction, started to walk through the parlor—and stopped in her tracks.

"Hullo." A stranger, tall and lean, was seated in her armchair, his long legs crossed idly before him.

"I beg your pardon!" she burst out, clutching her hand to her pounding heart. "What are you doing in here? God, you gave me a fright! Do I know you?" She took him for a tradesman—one of the merchants or artisans that Reese made arrangements with for all the workaday household business and repairs.

She did not recall having any appointments, but—

"Lady Pierson, I presume?" His glance flicked over her. "You are more beautiful than I had expected."

And she realized abruptly that not even the wealthiest toadstool merchant in London would dare ogle a viscountess in such a vile manner.

Fear chilled her initial, blank surprise. "Your name, sir."

He rose from the chair. "Some call me Dresden Bloodwell. My true name, I fear, is long forgotten."

At first glance, he was utterly ordinary, though his height and muscular physique were impressive, the sort that one might hire for a footman or a carriage groom. He had hazel eyes, brown wavy hair that shone with oil, and a well-formed countenance with good, strong bones, but a sallow-tanned complexion faintly scarred with pockmarks.

It was his stare, however, that warned her "Mr. Bloodwell" was not quite right in the head. Good gracious, had this oddment simply wandered in off the street?

But he knew her name.

She backed away, holding his stare warily, as he advanced toward her with slow, measured paces. "Mr. Bloodwell, where are my servants? What are you doing in my house?"

He gave her a curious half smile, studying her with a lecherous gleam in those unsettling eyes. Then she noticed a faint banging sound coming up through the floor, as though someone were locked in the cellar.

Danger, whispered all her senses. She swallowed hard but refused to show her fear. "You'd better leave."

"Stay calm, Lady Pierson. And please don't scream. I trust a lady of your fine breeding will not resort to hysterics."

"Indeed," she agreed as she continued keeping a healthy distance between them.

"Good." He nodded, his stare fixed on her. "For you will need your wits about you to accept the deal I came here to make. And don't worry about your servants. They are quite unharmed. Believe me, they are not your main concern at the moment."

"What is this about?" she demanded, striving to sound calm.

"I came to propose an arrangement that I'm sure will interest you, my lady."

She edged toward the fire poker. "I doubt anything you say would be of interest to me, Mr. Bloodwell. I do not converse with trespassers in my home."

"Oh, I think you'll hear me out. I did not come empty-handed, after all. Here. You see? I brought you a present." He gestured to a small, flat box on the parlor table. "Go on. Open it."

She eyed the chipboard box warily. A common sort of box from any ordinary shop. "What's in there?"

"Well, if I told you, it would not be a surprise, my dear. Go on. Take a peek."

"Very well." She inched calmly toward the table, not taking her eyes off him.

He watched her reach over and slide the box toward herself. With trembling hands, she picked it up, untied the ill-made ribbon bow, and pulled off the lid.

Warily, she glanced down to see what was in the box.

She went motionless. The air rushed from her lungs, and horror turned the blood in her veins to ice.

Mr. Bloodwell folded his hands politely behind his back. "Now, you see, I have a little request for you, my lady. I don't think you'll find it too much to ask."

Her heart in her throat, she reached into the box in shock and pulled out the little multicolored jester's cap with bells that she had knit with her own hands for Thomas.

Mrs. Busby had put it on him that morning.

"Where is Thomas?" Pure terror made her head swim as she looked up slowly at Bloodwell. "What have you done to my child?"

"Easy—"

"What do you want?" she screamed.

"Just a simple favor. One little piece of paper. In exchange for your son's life."

The trip to Carlton House was a blur.

Please, I'll do anything you ask. Just don't hurt my baby.

She had run out of her town house in such a blindly frantic state that she had forgotten her bonnet altogether, only snatching up her reticule. With shaking hands, she had thrust into it the little piece of paper on which Bloodwell had scrawled the address in Seven Dials where she was to go afterwards.

She arrived presently in a hired hackney. Not the normal mode of transportation for any viscountess, but she had sent Thomas off today in her own carriage.

All the while, Dresden Bloodwell's instructions rang through her mind like a death knell tolling. *You will go to Carlton House. Enter the main library. Use this key to open the Regent's cabinet. It will also unlock his desk.*

If Jordan had not told her about the true nature of his work and what was going on in the shadows at Carlton House,

Mara would not have been able to hold herself together enough to keep putting one foot after another.

But thanks to the sketchy information he had shared just this morning in the midst of his apology, she recognized her instructions as the same ones that had been given to Albert.

Albert must have failed, and after meeting Dresden Bloodwell, there was no question in her mind now that poor, arrogant Alby was already dead—but apparently not before suggesting her as a useful alternative.

Part of her yearned to run to Jordan, fall into his arms, tell him everything, and beg him to save Thomas.

But she did not dare. Bloodwell's commands were very clear. *Do not stop anywhere. Do not speak to anyone. Do not attempt to go to the authorities. If you do any of these things or defy my instructions in any way, your child is the one who will pay for your foolishness.*

And if you dawdle, if I do not have that list in my hands by nightfall, the old nurse will be the first to die.

Mrs. Busby.

Dear God—please help me.

Arriving at Carlton House, Mara got out of the hackney, paid the driver with shaking hands, and walked numbly toward the private entrance she normally used when she visited Prinny.

The smartly uniformed guards, well armed and well trained, greeted her with warm, respectful smiles and a few looks of concern, noticing she was visibly upset. It took all her strength not to start screaming for them to help her, but somehow she refrained, and they, in turn, opened the gates without concern over such a familiar face.

Going through the motions, Mara thanked them with a nod. She managed a smile, then hid her relief when they told her His Royal Highness was not at home.

"I'll just wait for him, then. I just—really need to talk to him." Her lips trembled. "He's always been so good to me."

The tears in her eyes, though genuine, were apparently more of a weapon than the men were trained to handle.

"Of course, Lady Pierson. Right this way. Come, I'll walk you in," said their captain with the usual highborn chivalry of this class of soldier.

She followed him in a daze.

"Perhaps you should sit down," he said in concern, offering her his arm as though he feared she might faint.

Did she look that bad?

"Is there anything we can get for you?"

"N-no, I'm fine. Really. It's—it's just my little boy. A bit of conflict with my in-laws. Nothing new. I just need some advice from his godfather. If I could just sit somewhere out of the way and wait until he returns—?"

"Of course."

"Do you mind if I wait in the library?" she asked, steadying herself, though everything in her knew she would surely burn in Hell for this. "Perhaps I could find something to read to pass the time while I wait."

"Certainly, ma'am." The magnificently uniformed soldier showed her down the marble corridor.

When they stepped into the gleaming antechamber before the library, one of George's underbutlers spotted her on the guard's arm. He immediately furrowed his brow, noting her ashen countenance, and hurricd over with an equal air of concern. "Lady Pierson, are you quite well?"

"I'm fine," she forced out.

"She's just a little upset. She's here to see His Royal Highness."

"Ah. I'm afraid the Regent had an engagement earlier today, dedication of a new school out by Windsor. But he should be back quite soon, my lady."

"She'd like to have a seat in the library while she waits," the captain informed him.

"Of course. Would you care for tea while you wait, my lady? The kitchens just received an excellent new oolong."

"Yes, please—you're very kind," she choked out. *Get him out of here.* She felt horrible, on the verge of betraying them all, but she could not afford to have kindly souls hovering over her at the moment.

"I think Her Ladyship would like to be left alone," the officer commented discreetly to the underbutler as they headed across the gleaming antechamber.

"I understand. I'll bring your tea, Lady Pierson, and I will personally make sure no one else disturbs you."

"Thank you both, sincerely," she choked out.

"It's nothing, ma'am." The officer opened the library door for her and escorted her over to a leather club chair.

Mara sat down with a shaky exhalation.

"Here. Just in case," the captain murmured, offering her his own clean, neatly pressed handkerchief with a manly smile.

Fresh tears flooded her eyes. She nodded at him and blotted them with his folded handkerchief.

She did not want to think about what would happen to him or the equally good-hearted underbutler after her treachery was revealed. But neither of them had any reason to suspect her. Everyone here was used to seeing her on any given day.

"Would you shut the door, please?" she requested, as the captain took leave of her. "I'd rather not have the whole staff see what a watering pot I am today."

"Not at all, my lady." He bowed to her and stepped out, pulling the door closed gently behind him and leaving her alone.

To betray her country.

Mara closed her eyes, utterly nerve-racked. But time was

of the essence. George was expected back soon, and the underbutler would arrived in several minutes with her tea.

Mara reached into her reticule and pulled out the key that Dresden Bloodwell had entrusted to her. Gripping it in her fist, she turned and looked over her shoulder at the locked door to George's private cabinet. She swallowed hard at what she was about to do. *For Thomas.* She would do anything—anything—to protect her son.

If she had to betray every loyalty she held dear—her lover, her royal friend, her country—indeed, even if she hanged for this, which she probably would—then so be it. Jordan himself might be sent personally to arrest her for what she was about to do, and he'd probably relish doing so when he found out she had willingly aided his enemy, but the only thing that mattered in this moment was her child.

Heart pounding, she glanced once more at the library door, waiting to see if the underbutler was coming. But it was too soon. The minutes seemed to drag; each excruciating second seemed to take a month.

Inside the Regent's desk, you will find an official list of names, men who are being considered for a special commendation by the Crown.

She rose from her chair and walked with her heart in her throat to the locked door in the far corner.

Her shaking hands fumbled to fit the key into the keyhole, but then it entered, she turned it, and heard the bolt click.

She swallowed hard, again glanced furtively over her shoulder, then slipped into George's small private office and closed the door behind her in case the underbutler returned before she was ready.

Her pulse throbbed as she glanced around the little room. George's desk was just like him—ornate and oversized, with countless gilded flourishes.

Mara flew over to the huge royal desk and crouched, using

the key again to unlock the drawers. Swiftly sorting through the stack of the Regent's personal papers, she ignored invitations, schedules, a draft of a bill from the Tories, a report from the detail of soldiers assigned to his estranged wife, Princess Caroline of Brunswick . . .

A list! But, no, this was a petition signed by wool merchants asking for some change in the trade laws.

She kept looking until, near the bottom of the stack, she finally came to a simple piece of parchment. It bore two long lines of male names, about thirty in all, beneath the header, *His Majesty's Secret Services, The Order of St. Michael the Archangel.* Someone had scrawled, *Recommended for Commendation for Outstanding Valor and Service to the Realm.* Mara scanned the list uneasily.

Sebastian, Viscount Beauchamp.
Drake Parry, Earl of Westwood.
Rohan Kilburn, Duke of Warrington.
Max St. Albans, Marquess of Rotherstone.
Jordan Lennox, Earl of Falconridge . . .

The blood drained from her face as she read Jordan's name, but she recognized the other names, as well. Horror flooded her as she realized what she was holding in her hand.

These were his wild, rakehell friends from the notorious Inferno Club. And, standing there, it now dawned on her—the true purpose of their secretive gatherings at Dante House. It was not a gentlemen's club at all. Only a front for one of His Majesty's secret services!

So, this was what Dresden Bloodwell wanted, at the behest, no doubt, of whomever he was working for. With this list, all the agents' identities would be exposed.

The Order's enemies could come and pick them off before they even knew that they had been discovered.

The very world stopped turning as Mara realized Jordan could die if she went through with this and handed the list over to Dresden Bloodwell.

And if she did not, that fiend would kill her son.

She pressed her hand over her mouth, her pulse pounding with sickening force.

Surely there must be another way. *No, I can't take that chance.* She shook her head and quickly began putting the Regent's other papers back.

Her course was clear. Jordan and his friends were hardened spies. Thomas was a defenseless two-year-old, and she was his mother. She was all he had.

Locking George's desk again, she backed out of his office, glancing about to make sure she had put everything back properly. She pulled the door shut with a low *click,* locked it, as well, then rushed back to the table where she had left her reticule.

She paused, staring at the heavy, carved table.

Searing pain blazed in her heart as she recognized it as the very place where Jordan had made such passionate love to her on the night of the ball. Tears pricked her eyes; she squeezed them closed, her nerves frayed, her wits close to snapping.

I'm so sorry, my love. I have no choice.

He probably knew this feeling all too well.

She shook herself fiercely, flicking her eyes open again. *Keep moving!* The underbutler would be back at any moment with her tea.

She quickly put the key to the Regent's office back in her reticule, then folded the list up small and tucked it in there, too.

She calmed herself with the vow that she would warn Jordan and his heroic comrades of the danger as soon as she had her child back safely in her arms.

Until then, Falconridge was on his own.

She crossed to the library, braced herself, and pulled the door open, only to find the underbutler wheeling a tea cart across the pristine marble antechamber, heading her way. "Oh, forgive me—"

"My lady?"

"I no longer want the tea. I'm so sorry. I've come down with such a headache. I think it will be best if I just go home for now. I'll make an appointment to see His Highness later this week. But thank you. I am sorry for your trouble."

"It's no trouble at all, my lady."

She offered him a contrite smile. "I'll show myself out."

The underbutler bowed to her. "As you wish, ma'am."

Mara nodded to him, then turned calmly and headed for the nearest exit—the grand front doors beneath the famed porte cochere of Carlton House.

Just before she made a clean escape, however, a familiar voice called her name.

"Mara!"

She froze as that deep, cultured voice echoed off the sea of marble in the grand entrance hall of Carlton House.

The one person in the world she wanted to see even less than the prince.

Oh, God, please, don't make me face him now.

"Mara?"

She was unnerved. Half of her wanted to run, but she just stood there, paralyzed. In the next heartbeat, she managed to chase all emotion from her face and turned around slowly as Jordan came striding toward her, long and lean. He looked unusually formidable this way, dressed all in black.

"What are you doing here?"

Her defenses bristled with guilty defiance. *Don't let him notice anything wrong.* "I came to see the Regent."

"Oh," he murmured in chagrin, dropping his gaze as he stopped in front of her.

She could see by his pained look that he assumed she meant she had come to cry on her royal friend's shoulder over their falling-out. Of course, he had no inkling of her true purpose here. And he must not find out.

As a warrior, no doubt he could fight Bloodwell. But he was also a spy, and with his cold heart, he might see Thomas as a pawn in his mission, just like he'd seen her.

If she told him the situation, he might try to work out some sort of canny strategy to get his enemy.

Mara did not give one fig about strategy at this moment. Every maternal instinct in her only cared about getting her child back safely.

Jordan gazed at her, reading her taut expression with concern. "Are you all right?"

She took a deep breath, realizing she must be careful, or he could easily read her and guess that she was hiding something. She shrugged, and nonchalantly said, "I'm fine."

He flinched at her terse answer and looked away, scanning the gleaming hall briefly with that restless, piercing glance of his. "You haven't seen Albert here, have you? I've been trying to track him down all day."

"No."

He nodded, floundering. She waited, dying to go, but afraid of alerting him that anything was wrong, beyond their quarrel.

"Mara, about this morning, can I just say—"

"Please. This is not the time or place." She did not think she could bear it.

He dropped his gaze once more. "Of course. Just know that, if you should change your mind, I'm always here. You can call on me anytime."

She pressed her lips together, fighting the lump that had

risen in her throat. He was so beautiful and courageous—she could not bear to look at him.

Lying to him about something so huge in this moment was horrible beyond anything she could have imagined. At least now she knew what Jordan went through all the time.

It occurred to her that she was in exactly the same position he had been in twelve years ago. He had walked from her to protect his friends; now it was her turn to walk away from him in order to protect Thomas. Perhaps this love of theirs was simply not meant to be.

"I must go," she forced out. With a trembling farewell nod, she turned away.

"Mara?" He spoke her name like a caress.

She flinched. The memory of his touch, his kiss, making love to him in her bed was almost more than she could bear. But she could not refuse the irresistible summons of that voice.

She turned back carefully, warily, and looked at him in question.

"I really do care for you," he whispered.

Gazing at him through a mist of tears, it took all she had not to throw herself into his arms. She stood in silence for a moment, memorizing him.

But Thomas was waiting.

She steadied herself, tore her gaze off him, turned around, and forced herself to walk away.

Jordan watched her go in an agony of guilt. *God, what have I done to her?* He had never seen so much pain in her dark eyes. He was utterly deflated to know that he had caused her so much suffering.

Her feelings for him seemed to have gone completely cold. Just now, she had barely been able to look him in the eyes.

Determined to carry on despite the heavy burden in his

heart, he went into Carlton House and asked the little black-coated underbutler who approached if he could see the Regent.

"Oh, His Royal Highness is not here, Lord Falconridge."

Jordan furrowed his brow and eyed the man skeptically. "Didn't Lady Pierson just meet with him?"

"No, sir, she waited a while for him in the library, but then she wasn't feeling well and decided to go home. You might have seen her on the way out?"

"*The library?*"

"Sir?"

Jordan was already stalking back toward the door. The thoughts whirling through his mind were too dark, too shocking, too impossible to be true. It could not be.

He dashed out under the portico and glanced around until he spotted her out on Piccadilly. She was just climbing into a hackney.

A hackney? The elegant Viscountess Pierson?

His stomach twisted in a knot. At once, he called for his horse, keeping his stare clamped on the battered old carriage she had hailed.

He took note of the requisite hackney coach number painted on the back, "No. 145," it read, just as it disappeared into the traffic.

He cursed under his breath, but a moment later, the attendant brought his horse. Jordan swung up into the saddle without a word and immediately urged his white hunter in the direction she had gone.

He must not let her out of his sight.

Farther down Piccadilly, he spotted No. 145 again; he followed, keeping a wary distance.

She would not do it. She would never betray me.

He could never believe it of her. Still, hoping against hope, he intended to find out where the hell she was going. Why else would she want a few moments alone in the Regent's library?

The route her hackney took was beginning to look all too familiar—the busy intersection at Charing Cross, then the bend where it merged into the Strand. The knot in Jordan's stomach tightened when her hackney turned in at St. Martin's Lane and headed northward, up to Seven Dials.

Still, his mind refused to believe the picture that was coming clear.

A few minutes later, they were in London's seediest quarter, the realm of the criminal gangs, to be sure, no place where any viscountess should venture, especially alone. Still following, Jordan kept a wary eye out for any signs of trouble heading her way from the locals.

Fortunately, the worst criminal residents of these environs did not come out until well after dark, and at present, it was only teatime.

Nevertheless, they were not far from the place where Mercer had been killed. And more to the point, they were near the last-known haunt of Dresden Bloodwell.

Before long, Mara's hackney ran into the same dilemma Jordan had encountered the night he had tracked Albert's messengers. The coach could go no farther, unable to fit into the narrow, twisting lanes of the rookery.

Jordan jumped off his horse and ducked out of sight behind a corner, aghast to spy Mara get out of the halted coach to continue on foot.

What on earth was she doing? Had the woman lost her mind?

Reaching into her reticule, she paid the hackney driver; Jordan could not hear their exchange, but the coachman's gestures told him she was asking for directions.

She nodded, then, to Jordan's complete terror, she hurried away on foot into the shadowed labyrinth of London's underworld.

Something was terribly wrong. Something unspeakable.

There was no further question of it in his mind.

Leading his horse out from around the corner, Jordan approached the hackney driver. "That lady—where was she going?"

"Who are you?"

"Answer the question," he clipped out.

The jarvey scowled. "She asked me how to get to Neales Passage! What do you care?"

"I need your help. That woman is in danger."

"What?" the man scoffed.

"Guard my horse. There's a hundred pounds sterling in it for you if you stay right here until I return."

"Stay here? There's murderers about!"

"Double it then!" Jordan pulled his billfold out of his waistcoat. "Here's a hundred now. You'll get another one of these when I return. You dash off, I come and hunt you down."

The jarvey accepted the bills with a nervous glance around, then he nodded, "Aye," and took charge of Jordan's horse.

Then Jordan ran off silently in the direction Mara had gone. He found his way to the dark lane marked as Neales Passage, and just barely glimpsed her ducking into a wretched building ahead.

Luckily, she paused to glance above the door at the number on the dismal brick tenement building before stealing inside and closing the door behind her. Jordan narrowed his eyes but wasted no time in following her. He slipped into the building a moment after her.

Inside, he found a dim, cramped foyer from which a dirty staircase ascended. He could hear her light footsteps hurrying up the stairs. He followed silently, ignoring the claustrophobic stairwell with its greenish-painted walls that cast a sickly pallor over everything. The air reeked of urine and had a taint of squalor and disease.

God. Where was this leading? He had the sickening feeling he already knew, even though his brain refused to accept it. But it was the only explanation.

No wonder he couldn't find Albert. It appeared Dresden Bloodwell no longer needed him.

Jordan now considered it highly unlikely that his former whist partner was still among the living. But rage blasted through his veins to think that Albert's final act of folly, no doubt in trying to save himself, had been to point Bloodwell in Mara's direction.

As Jordan continued following her, everything felt so dreamlike and strange, for this was his worst nightmare come true. To protect Mara from this sort of horror was the very reason he had given her up years ago. But it seemed you couldn't run from fate.

Perhaps a part of him had always known somehow that it would come to this. *I'm so sorry, Mara.*

He cursed himself to Hell for ever agreeing to involve her in the first place, though admittedly, even before he had used her for his cover, she had already been a fixture in the Regent's social circles. Albert would have known about her with or without Jordan's being there.

As he heard her light, quick footfalls turn and hurry up another flight of stairs, the grim realization sank in that there was only one motive strong enough to have brought her to such a place.

Jordan closed his eyes against the gathering fury.

Bloodwell must have taken Thomas.

Why, Mara? Why didn't you tell me? Have you truly lost all your faith in me? Can you not trust me anymore?

With his heart nigh breaking in the silence to think that she had faced this on her own, he heard her footsteps stop above.

He ducked out of sight when she paused to look back. Perhaps she sensed that she was being followed.

Best to keep the advantage of surprise. If she spotted him, she might not be able to hide her emotions from Bloodwell.

Then, once more, Jordan could hear her footsteps running up the zigzag staircase. He continued shadowing her as his cold fury grew and hardened.

Her footsteps stopped.

Jordan looked up, peering over the angle of the stairs to see on which door she had paused and knocked. Three anxious raps.

At once, the door creaked.

"Ah, Lady Pierson! Well, consider me impressed. You made excellent time. Come in."

Jordan had never heard Bloodwell's voice before, but the sound of it sent icy hatred and almost primitive rage coursing through his veins.

When he heard the door close, he emerged from the shadows of the stairwell, his blazing stare fixed on the door to the apartment above.

"Were you seen? Were you followed?" Bloodwell demanded as he pulled her into his rooms.

"No. I got what you wanted. Now give me my son."

He shut thc door. "Givc mc thc list first."

"Where is Thomas?" she demanded in a shaky tone. "Return him to me, then you can have it!"

He smirked at her effort to make a stand and grabbed hold of her reticule, wrenching it out of her hand with a jerk of the leather handle that would have broken her wrist if she had resisted.

She stifled a small cry, watching in dread as he dumped it contents onto the floor. He ignored her money purse, the keys to her house, and her tiny appointment book, but bent to retrieve the folded piece of parchment.

Mara swallowed hard, staring with her heart in her throat as he opened it.

Bloodwell rose, laughing softly to himself as he scanned the list. "I knew it. Warrington! Rotherstone, as well," he mumbled more to himself than to her. He furrowed his brow with a introspective stare. "Hold on. This is the Dante House set!" He looked at her in distracted astonishment. "It's their fucking headquarters, isn't it? Bloody Lucifer!" He shook his head to himself in amazement. "Well, I'll bet that's where they're holding Niall."

He glanced at her though she had no idea who Niall was. "What a clever girl you are. It seems I have a lot of work ahead of me, but thanks to you, now it will be easy."

Mara swallowed hard this nauseating truth. "You have what you want. It's my turn now. Give me back my son."

"Cool your heels. You cannot imagine how much I'm enjoying this. Let's see, who else have we got? Beauchamp, hm. I think he tried to kill me a couple of months ago."

"Please! My child needs me!"

"*Shut your mouth!*" he roared without warning.

Mara jumped, startled, then backed away and dropped her gaze.

"Don't interrupt me when I'm trying to think," he advised her. Then he turned his attention back to the list with a gloating look. "Now then, here's a name I've heard before . . . Falconridge."

Her head down, Mara looked up fearfully.

"Hm, yes, Albert mentioned him a while ago. The newest member of the Regent's weekly card game, if I'm not mistaken. So, there's the Order agent in the Regent's set. Well, he's a dead man."

Unfortunately, Bloodwell heard her low gasp. She quickly looked away, but his cruel stare homed in on her.

"Aha, you know this man? Rather well, I wager, seeing these fresh tears. How touching. There, there. Are you sleeping with an agent of the Order, Lady Pierson? Now, that is a very interesting prospect for me."

Mara refused to look at him, but she had started trembling.

He laughed softly with hateful scorn, moving closer, and studying her, intrigued. "All you Society ladies are such whores. I hope he pleasured you well, this Lord Falconridge. I will enjoy killing him all the more for your sake."

"I want to see my son," Mara choked out, cowering from him.

"Yes, but, you see, it's only what I want that matters, my pretty viscountess." He lifted a stray lock of her hair. "You are too used to gentlemen, I think. You ought to sample plainer fare." She shrieked as he suddenly grabbed a fistful of her hair. "I know how to bring you down a peg."

Without warning the door suddenly banged open, splintering off its hinges. Mara looked over in terrorized bewilderment as Jordan lunged into the room. He charged straight at Bloodwell, who immediately pulled a pistol out of his belt and turned to shoot.

Mara saw Bloodwell's finger on the trigger. Jordan was still three paces away. Point-blank range.

Without any conscious forethought, she kicked Bloodwell's hand as hard as she could; the shot went into the ceiling, then Jordan tackled him.

They crashed to the floor, and Mara stepped back and watched in wide-eyed astonishment as Jordan's fist smashed again and again into Bloodwell's face. She was shocked by the brutal fury that had apparently been lurking all this time beneath the polished surface of her elegant, worldly earl.

What was he even doing here? He must have followed her from Carlton House. Which meant he knew she had taken over Albert's job as thief in the Regent's office.

While Jordan proceeded to beat the monster to a pulp, slamming Bloodwell's head against the floor, at least Mara had the presence of mind to retrieve the list of Order agents.

Barely daring to breathe, she picked it up as they grappled, but in the next moment, Jordan had battered his enemy into submission. Holding him down with his knee planted in the center of Bloodwell's back, he drew his knife to finish him off.

She gasped. "Jordan, no—he's taken Thomas!"

He paused, his chest heaving, wild fury in his eyes. He looked over at her with the diamond-hard glance of a spy who had no qualms whatsoever about cutting his enemy's throat.

"If you kill him, I will never find my son. He's hidden him somewhere."

He seemed to absorb this after several seconds. He looked down at his captive with a noisy inhalation through his nostrils. "You will take us to the boy."

Dresden Bloodwell let out a garbled laugh, blood trickling from the corner of his mouth. "The hell I will."

Jordan leaned closer and pricked the bottom of Bloodwell's eye socket with the tip of his knife. "You want to play nasty, eh? You will return the boy to us unless you want me to put out your eyes, one by one."

Bloodwell spat a curse at him.

Mara watched, appalled, as Jordan pierced the flesh of Bloodwell's face. *He's not really going to do it?*

Her jaw dropped as he slowly, inexorably, drove the tip of his dagger deeper into the skin.

It was enough to convince Bloodwell, apparently, for the man suddenly screamed out, "*No!*"

"Where's the boy?"

"Don't do it. Wait. I will take you to him."

When Jordan withdrew his dagger, only the barest tip was bloodied, but Mara stared at him in shock.

"Get to your feet."

Jordan exchanged his knife for his pistol and held the man

at gunpoint. Bloodwell whispered another curse but obeyed, clearly shaken by his opponent's remorseless attack.

Realizing they were about to leave, Mara quickly bent down and picked up her things off the floor, throwing the odds and ends back into her reticule, her hands shaking.

She perused the list. "This is what he wanted. I didn't want to do it. He made me. It's a-a list of names." She swallowed hard. "Yours is on it."

She showed him the paper. He glanced at it and let out a low, dark laugh, keeping his stare on Bloodwell.

"Should I burn it?" she offered in a shaky voice. "He's already read it, though."

"No. We're going to have to figure out who sent it. Give it here."

When Mara handed him the folded list, he hid it in his waistcoat.

"I'm so sorry—"

"It's not your fault. Don't worry, Mara. It's going to be all right."

Tears filled her eyes when, even now, he refused to blame her.

"Come, I've got a carriage waiting outside. You try anything," he warned Bloodwell, "you're going to lose more than your eyes. Now, walk."

Jordan half shoved, half dragged Bloodwell out to the waiting hackney, keeping the muzzle of his pistol thrust against the Promethean's temple.

When they reached the corner, he forced Bloodwell into the carriage, told the hackney driver to tether his saddle horse to the back of the coach, then ordered Mara to ride up on the driver's box with the jarvey.

She was looking at him strangely, but he supposed that should not surprise him after what she had seen him do.

He was not quite sure what had happened to him back there. He stayed focused on his task, but it had been very difficult to stop himself from killing Bloodwell.

They set off, Jordan riding in the carriage, keeping Bloodwell under control and his pistol pointed at him.

His threats, both spoken and silent, dragged each subsequent piece of the directions to the place where Thomas was hidden out of Bloodwell. Jordan called them out to the driver, and before long, they arrived at an abandoned shack in a wooded grove on the outskirts of Town. That Bloodwell had not tried to deceive them was proved when they spotted Mara's town coach parked nearby, hidden among the trees.

The jarvey had barely brought the hackney to a halt when Mara was already jumping down off the driver's seat and running toward the shack.

Jordan eased out of the back of the carriage, still holding Bloodwell at gunpoint.

"It's locked!" she called frantically to him, banging on the door. "Thomas! Mrs. Busby! Jack!" She began fighting with the weathered door to the shack as muffled cries for help began coming from inside.

Jordan suppressed another blinding jolt of rage when he heard the baby start to cry from inside the shack.

"It's all right, Thomas, Mama's here! Mrs. Busby! Jack? We're here to help you! Hang on, just another moment!"

"Walk," he ordered Bloodwell, moving closer.

The Promethean glared at him with a promise of retaliation in his eyes, though his nose and mouth were swollen from Jordan's blows, and blood still oozed slowly from beneath his eye, where the dagger had pierced him.

Still keeping his pistol trained on Bloodwell, Jordan went over to the door.

"Mrs. Busby, Jack, it's Lord Falconridge. Get back from the door!" he warned the captives inside. "I'm going to kick it in."

He gave them a second to move away if they were behind it, then he smashed the door in with a thunderous kick like the one he'd used at Bloodwell's. Mara immediately rushed in to save her child, but Jordan moved Bloodwell out of range.

Seeing the rescue under way, the hackney driver must have had all his nerves could stand. Abandoning the other half of his reward, he ran back to his coach, leaped up to the box, and drove away with a look of fright over his shoulder, no doubt wishing he'd never laid eyes on any of them.

Jordan felt a wave of deep relief but was still concerned as Mara carried Thomas out, hugging him to her, both of them weeping.

Mrs. Busby staggered out, her wrists still bound with rope.

"Mara! Go and get in your carriage!" Jordan ordered. "Mrs. Busby, you go, too. Jack can drive you all to Dante House—"

"He's been shot, my lord!" the old nurse burst out.

Dresden Bloodwell smiled. "Oh, yes, I forgot to mention that."

Jordan glared at him. "Mara! Put the baby in your carriage. Take my knife and free Mrs. Busby. Then go back in and see if Jack's alive!"

She nodded, looking grateful for such specific directions. Though still crying, she followed his instructions, placing Thomas in her carriage, then coming over to take Jordan's knife.

"Careful," he murmured, but she soon freed the nurse's hands and helped her into the carriage.

Mrs. Busby weakly took charge of the two-year-old once more.

As Mara hurried back into the dark, dingy shack, Jordan shook his head at the prisoner.

"You're going to pay for this, you know. A child? An old woman? You people never change."

Dresden Bloodwell said nothing, merely glared at him with a mocking smile.

Mara reappeared in the doorway to the shack. "Jordan, he's alive, though barely conscious. He needs a doctor, fast. He's been shot in the abdomen. I can't get him to stand up. Who knows how long he's been like this."

He nodded. "Very well. I'll get him. Come and take my gun."

"What?"

"Keep it pointed at him." He accepted his dagger back from her, sheathed it, then offered her his pistol.

Mara stared at it. "Me?"

"It's all right. You can do it. I taught you how to shoot, remember?"

"But what if he—" Her words broke off in dread.

"Right. Better safe than sorry," Jordan murmured. "Look away, my dear." She turned her head but saw him from the corner of her eye as he gave Bloodwell a faint, cruel smile and aimed his pistol at the man's knee.

"Falconridge—"

Boom!

Bloodwell howled and dropped to the ground. A stream of curses poured from his lips as he clutched his bloodied leg and rocked and writhed in pain.

"There," Jordan said politely. "He shouldn't be giving you any trouble now."

Mara gulped at her lover's cool control while Jordan quickly reloaded the pistol.

This done, he put it gently into her hands. "Just like that. Good. I'll be right back. In the meanwhile, if he moves a muscle, you have the Order's blessing to finish him off. He's useful alive, but we all know the world's better off with this filth dead."

Mara said nothing as they changed places. Both hands on

his pistol, she held Bloodwell at bay as she waited for Jordan to return.

Jordan stalked into the cramped, moldy shed where the boy and the two servants had spent the day. He found Jack in a bad state but was able to lift him to his feet.

The groaning driver leaned heavily on him, barely aware of what was happening, as Jordan half carried him out to the coach.

He smirked when he saw that Bloodwell had taken off his neck cloth and tied it around his leg for a tourniquet. The Promethean assassin was struggling back up onto his feet with a look of hatred.

"Jordan!"

"I'll be right there. Don't worry."

His back was turned only for a moment as he helped the wounded Jack settle into the squabs, then he nodded to Mrs. Busby. "Hold on, ma'am. We're going to get you out of here." Jordan laid his hand gently on the screaming toddler's head. "Shh, little man, you're all right now—"

And suddenly Mara shrieked from several feet behind him. The gun went off.

Jordan spun around to see Bloodwell charge, ramming her with a hard shoulder that would have knocked a man twice her size to the ground.

Mara went flying. Though she had pulled the trigger, the bullet had gone skyward; Bloodwell raced toward the carriage at a limping run, hellfire in his eyes. It was the only means of transportation out of here, and Jordan saw he meant to commandeer it.

Not bloody likely.

Eyes narrowed, he reached for his dagger as Bloodwell leaped for the driver's box with a grunt of pain. Jordan hurled it at him.

The knife bit deep into Bloodwell's thigh—same leg,

above the gunshot wound at his knee. The Promethean roared, and Jordan launched himself toward the driver's box behind the man.

Ignoring the knife in his leg, Bloodwell used the advantage of height to kick Jordan in the chest with his good leg. The blow set him back but did not dislodge him.

Bloodwell grabbed the carriage reins, but before he could disengage the brake, Jordan attacked again. They brawled atop the driver's box, Thomas wailing at the top of his lungs all the while.

Somehow, Bloodwell managed to get a length of the leather reins around Jordan's neck and began choking him.

Snarling and gasping for air, Jordan struggled against him.

Then Bloodwell reached down, pulled the knife out of his own leg, and stabbed Jordan in the side with it.

Jordan barely felt the wound at first in his heightened state of battle; reacting automatically, he flipped Bloodwell forward over his head with a roar.

The Promethean assassin slammed down onto the dusty road flat on his back. Unfortunately, as Jordan leaped off the driver's box to crush him under his weight, Bloodwell rolled out of the way.

Jordan cursed, landing on all fours in the dusty road; he held his side for a second as blood flowed through his fingers. Nearby, Bloodwell stumbled to his feet and hobbled off at top speed into the woods. "Damn it!"

Mara had regained her senses and was climbing dazedly to her feet. "Thomas?" she started.

"He's safe," he cut her off with a nod toward the carriage.

"Mama!"

She ran toward her child. "Where's Bloodwell? He hit me so hard, I think I lost my senses for a moment. What happened?"

"It doesn't matter. Just get out of here before he comes

back." Jordan pushed to his feet and saw her blanch when he swayed a bit unsteadily.

"You're hurt!" she said in horror.

"I'm fine. Listen to me—are you listening?"

She nodded frantically.

"Go to Dante House. It's on the Strand. Do you know it?"

"Yes."

"The old Highlander, Virgil—tell him I sent you to bring my team here, now. The Order's surgeons will attend to Jack."

"What are you going to do?" She paled. "Jordan, we'll go together! You're bleeding!"

"I've got to finish this. He can't live. He knows who we all are."

"It's all my fault," she whispered, staring at his side. "I'm so sorry. Sorry for the things I said to you this morning and—"

"Shh." He did not move closer because he did not want the blood to scare her. Instead, he just gazed at her with an ocean of feeling that there was no longer time to make her understand. "Just know I love you," he whispered, "and I always have. Ask the men at Dante House if I ever forgot you, and you'll know. Now, go. Get Thomas out of here."

"Jordan, I cannot possibly leave you—"

"You must. I'm hurt, all right?" he admitted quietly. "I need reinforcements. Go and get my team and bring them here. I'll keep Bloodwell contained until they get here. He won't get far with that hurt leg."

Mara stared at him, reading his face as though she understood that this was a lie, one told because he loved her. In truth, he had a strong premonition of his own impending death once he followed his nemesis into that dark wood, and he didn't want her to be there to have to watch him die.

He nodded at her.

He had always been willing to give his life in the Order's endless struggle against evil; if that was required of him now, then so be it. But one thing was certain. He was taking that bastard down with him.

Bloodwell could not be allowed to survive. Not when he knew Mara. Not when he knew names. If it cost him his last breath, Jordan vowed to finish this.

Then she and Thomas and his brother warriors would be safe. "Go," he ordered fiercely.

He turned around and began jogging into the wooded path by which Bloodwell had escaped.

Mara stood there, staring after him in shock, utterly at a loss. He had vanished into the shadows, but her gaze sank to the small pool of blood on the ground where Jordan had been standing.

She stared at it, hearing the echo of his words, "I love you," with their undertone of terrible finality.

And she knew there was no way that she could leave.

She had ordered him out of her life and out of her home this morning—it seemed like years ago—but now the real possibility of losing him permanently was unacceptable.

His life was in danger. The evidence of it lay there in a pool of crimson slowly seeping into the dust.

He was losing too much blood. If she took the carriage, how would he get to a doctor himself once he had finished Dresden Bloodwell?

He would never survive the wait for her to reach the Strand and find her way back here with his friends. He'd bleed to death first. Either he didn't know how badly he was hurt or had simply hoped she wouldn't notice.

Either way, Mara realized, it was up to *her* to help him. He needed her, even if the stubborn man refused to admit it.

Marching over to her carriage, she swept the surrounding woods with an uneasy glance, her jaw still aching from where that madman's shoulder had rammed her. With Dresden Bloodwell still in the area, she knew she was risking everyone's safety by lingering here, even Thomas's. Too much delay could possibly cost Jack his life, but if he had lasted this many hours, she prayed he would be all right a little longer.

Mrs. Busby looked at her in dread as Mara reached under the carriage bench and pulled out the musket Jordan had given her after the attack on her carriage in Hyde Park.

"Oh, no, my lady," the old woman whispered, holding Thomas on her lap. "His Lordship said that we should go!"

"I'm sorry. I can't abandon him. Just a few more minutes," she pleaded. "I know you've been through far too much already, but I can't leave him to die. Pray for us, Mrs. Busby."

She nodded with a pained look. "I've been doin' that all day."

"Thomas, you stay quiet." Mara caressed her son, not knowing where she got the strength to walk away from him again.

With a grim nod, she closed the carriage door, made sure the musket was loaded, then rallied every ounce of courage she had in her, and marched into the woods.

The gun felt so strange in her hands, almost as dangerous to her as it might be to her enemy.

But inside the woods, amid the leafy shadows, the birds had gone still. Not even the breeze stirred.

As she advanced, her swollen jaw thumping in time with her pounding pulse, she heard male voices somewhere up ahead.

"Come out, Bloodwell! You know it's over."

"Yes, but not for me. Falconridge, isn't it? Your wench betrayed your name, I'm sorry to report."

"Only because you terrorized her, and for that, I will make you pay."

"With what? That pistol? You're dying even now, and we both know it. How's your side feeling? Did I hit your lung?"

"Afraid not."

"Too bad I missed your heart. Come a little deeper into the woods, so I can finish you off."

"Show yourself!" Jordan roared into the brambles. "You're a damned coward! You and all your kind."

Cold laughter was the only answer that came back to him. Mara looked all around her, trying to figure out where it was coming from, where Bloodwell was hiding.

"You'd better make it a good shot, my lord! All that boyhood training for the Order . . . all for naught. It all comes down to this. You've only got one bullet in that pistol."

"Don't worry, Bloodwell. I have plenty more tricks up my sleeve. So, where did you leave Holyfield's body?"

She glimpsed Jordan through the trees some distance ahead, moving deeper into the woods, hunting Bloodwell. She realized the reason he was keeping him talking was so he could track him by the sound of his voice.

"What, Falconridge, just tell you and ruin the fun of leaving you to find him for yourselves?"

"You can address me as Your Lordship."

Bloodwell scoffed. "You might be interested to know that once I'm done with you," Bloodwell called from his hiding place, "I'm going straight back to that whore to finish what you so rudely interrupted—Your Lordship. I'm going to use her like a shilling whore. And when I've cut her throat, I'll dump her naked in the Thames. What do you say to that, my fine Order Knight?"

"Well, it's not very original, is it?" he replied crisply.

Mara shuddered, but she told herself that Bloodwell was only trying to taunt Jordan into making a mistake.

He, in turn, refused to rise to the bait, staying calm and fully in control. "You should never have gone near Lady Pierson or the child."

"Well, I—"

Boom!

Mara was not ready for the pistol's report when it went off. But Jordan had spotted him and taken his best shot. Bloodwell cursed, but when he stepped into view through the trees across from Jordan, the flesh along the top edge of his left shoulder was ripped open.

But even that was not enough to stop the likes of him.

Bloodwell charged at Jordan, wielding the knife he had pulled out of his own leg after Jordan had thrown it.

Mara trained the musket on him but hesitated. There were too many leaves and branches in the way. She could not see what she was doing.

She, too, only had one bullet in the musket. More ammunition waited back in the carriage, she was only just learning how to reload the stupid thing.

Then Bloodwell struck at Jordan with the knife, slashing him across his chest. She was too terrified to scream. Jordan ignored the fresh wound as though he did not even feel it, his icy, single-minded purpose: taking back his knife.

As Jordan struggled to wrestle the weapon out of Bloodwell's hand, Mara grimaced, debating, trying to aim among the trees, but she did not dare pull the trigger.

The men were too close together. Then her heart soared when Jordan came out of their clash brandishing the dagger.

Bloodwell took one look at him and ran.

Jordan did not make the mistake of throwing it at him again. He chased with eyes that glittered like the hardest, coldest diamond, surely giving everything he had left to go racing down the wooded path after Bloodwell.

He was unstoppable, leaping fallen logs, dashing past overgrown bushes, a warrior driven by divine forces, heedless of the fact that he was losing blood from both his side and the slash across his chest.

Mara trailed them and saw that just when Jordan was closing in on his quarry, Bloodwell came to an old woodpile, logs and kindling stacked waist high; he suddenly gripped an old axe that had been left there to rust.

He chopped wildly at Jordan, the longer-handled weapon nullifying the reach of the knife.

Mara gasped; Jordan ducked back; Bloodwell swung again and missed.

Coming up behind them, her heart banging behind her ribs, Mara brought the musket to her shoulder, praying for one clear shot. She did not yell to Jordan to move out of the way, for fear of distracting him.

She just got herself into position down on one knee some yards behind him on the path and waited for the moment when he would not be blocking her aim at Dresden Bloodwell.

Her pulse slammed as she held the musket at the ready like a good English soldier, waiting in the firing line for the commander's call.

Jordan bent and grabbed a hefty fallen branch, bringing it up to ward off Bloodwell's next crazed chop of the axe.

The heaving blow broke the branch in two pieces, but the wood saved him, absorbing the strike.

Mara saw Jordan look at the splintered spear that he was left holding. As Bloodwell lifted the axe high with both hands to split his skull, Jordan hurled it. The makeshift javelin plunged into Dresden Bloodwell's midriff.

He dropped the axe as he fell back against the woodpile.

Mara stared in shock as the assassin looked down at the

lance that had impaled him. Blood gurgled from his mouth.

A few seconds later, he was in Hell.

Jordan suddenly sank to his knees, his back to her, still unaware she was there. She could now see him shaking. Mara set the musket down and ran to him.

"Jordan!" At once she reached for him, holding him around the shoulders and the waist. She kissed his sweating temple and saw that he was covered in blood.

"What are you doing here?" he forced out.

"I couldn't leave you. I told you I'd always be here for you. Oh, my love," she whispered, appalled by all the blood.

"Help me."

Somehow she found her faltering courage and nodded. "That's what I'm here for. Come on. Let's get you back to the carriage. I'll take you to Dante House. You said they have surgeons there."

"I think—it's too late, Mara."

"No! You have to get up, Jordan, please! You have to try for me."

"I can't believe you stayed," he whispered. "Help me lie down."

"No. Get to your feet! You have to come to the carriage. Thomas needs you, Jordan. And I need you, too. I can't live without you." A sob escaped her as she strained to pull him up. "Come on. I told you, I'm not ever letting you get away from me again. Come on, Jordan, stand up. You can do it. You have to. For me. For us."

He set his jaw grimly, intense pain in his eyes, but he nodded, leaning heavily on her as she helped him to his feet.

"Hang on, now. Walk with me. It's not far. I'm going to get you straightaway to a doctor." She could not say more, for fear and grief suddenly swallowed up her voice.

But perhaps he heard her heart's plea by some other means, for he swallowed hard, nodded tautly to himself, and somehow found the strength to make it back into the carriage.

Mara closed the door, went to the horses' leader, and grabbed its bridle, pulling the team around until her carriage had rolled back out onto the main road.

She ran to the driver's box, climbed up, and took the reins, then drove hell-for-leather back to Town. Soon she was thundering down the Strand as though she had the devil at her heels.

She made straight for Dante House.

Chapter 21

Dreamy images filtered through Jordan's mind, a country house . . . he heard mischievous laughter, then he saw Mara at seventeen, as she had appeared to him in the ballroom so long ago.

He saw her making a quick little twirl to show off her rose-colored ball gown, her dark eyes sparkling more brightly than the chandelier above her.

Her silky sable curls brushed the tops of her white shoulders as she tossed her head, as though inviting his lips there. She was all scintillating charm, her hidden depths and sorrows veiled by playful flirtation. His heart clenched as he watched her.

Flawed she was, oh, yes, but her imperfections only made her more lovable to him. They meant she needed him, and Jordan had always been someone who longed to be needed. With all her lights and shadows, no wonder she had enthralled him from the start. A ravishing beauty on the cusp of womanhood, the object of all his desires . . .

As the past shimmered away into the painful present, he became aware of something squeezing him—bandages, wrapped around his chest and tightly hugging his waist where he had been . . . oh, yes. Stabbed.

Pleasant.

"Good morning," said a gentle voice. "Or rather, afternoon."

As his vision cleared, the blurry ovals above him turned into the concerned faces of those who knew him best.

Mara sat on the edge of his bed, studying him in tender anxiety.

He smiled faintly, warmed by the sight of her. "Am I going to live, then?" he mumbled.

"More than that." She took his left hand gently, tears in her eyes. "You are going to flourish. I intend to see to it personally. Though I'm afraid you're going have quite an impressive scar across your chest," she added, her soft voicc soothing him like a healing balm.

"Hmm, really? More impressive than Warrington's?" With a groggy half smile, Jordan glanced at the towering duke, who was standing nearby, staring down worriedly at him.

But at his low-toned reminder of their usual boyish rivalry, Rohan flashed a grin and clasped his hand. "Welcome back, brother. Nice work," he said in a low tone. "You finally put that bastard in the ground. Couldn't have done better myself."

"Well, coming from you," Jordan said.

"He's been here all the time," Mara said. "They all have." Jordan followed her smiling glance and saw Beauchamp leaning against a bedpost.

"You gave us quite a scare, Falconridge."

"Sorry about that. Didn't mean to cause a fuss." He started to laugh, but winced.

Laughing hurt, at least at the moment.

Mara laid her hand over his bandages. "Are you all right?"

Jordan nodded grimly in answer as his team leader, Max, sauntered over to his bedside. "Good of you to come back to us, old friend." The seriousness in his eyes belied his casual tone. "I suppose you must've realized we could never get on without you."

"Well, I've been telling you all that for years," he jested weakly.

"How are you feeling?" Max inquired.

"Like somebody tried to carve me up like the Christmas goose. Otherwise, right as rain."

Mara began to cry. She turned away, covering her lips with her fingers.

Jordan took her hand again. "I'm sorry," he whispered. "I was only teasing."

She nodded, avoiding his gaze as she wiped away a tear. He supposed he should not make light of it. That was just his way.

Standing near her, Max laid a comforting hand on Mara's shoulder, but he said to Jordan, "Virgil will want to see you. We've all been incredibly worried."

"I'll go tell the old man he's awake," Beau said. "He did your stitches himself, you know," he added, nodding at Jordan's bandages.

"Did he? That Scot was always handy with a needle. But I hope he didn't waste his favorite malt whiskey cleaning the wound."

"Apparently, he thinks you're worth it," Max drawled.

As Beau headed for the doorway, Max patted Mara's shoulder in approval. "Brave lady you've got here, Falconridge. Not a bad driver, either."

"Other than nearly running over one of the dogs," Rohan corrected sternly, though his eyes twinkled.

"He got out of the way," Mara protested.

"And so will we." Max sent Rohan a look.

The duke nodded. "Just let us know if you need anything, Jord. Good to have you back."

He nodded his thanks, touched by their concern for him. The men withdrew, leaving Mara and him alone.

For a long moment, they just held hands, gazing at each other. Her face was bathed in the soft daylight that poured in through the window, but her big, dark eyes were still haunted. At length, she let out a sigh of belated relief, shook her head to herself, leaned near, and kissed his brow. "Can I get you something to drink?"

He shook his head. "How's Thomas?"

The haunted look fled as the mention of her boy lit her eyes and made her chuckle. "He loves it here, I regret to say."

Jordan laughed—and winced again.

"Your friends have been keeping him so entertained that I think he's nearly forgotten all about yesterday."

"Yesterday? How long have I been sleeping?"

She glanced over at the mantel clock. "Just about eighteen hours."

"Blazes," he murmured. "No wonder I'm so hungry."

She smiled. "That's a good sign."

"I'm fine," he assured her.

She raised an eyebrow.

"But then again, if I'm going to get all this lovely sympathy . . ."

She tilted her head with a sardonic look.

He flashed a weary smile, but his expression sobered in the next heartbeat. "How is Jack?"

"Virgil says he'll have a long recovery, but his condition seems stable. Mrs. Busby is recovering from the shock of it all, as well."

"Good. And now, most importantly, my darling, how are you?"

She gazed at him with tears gathering in her eyes. "I'm wonderful," she forced out softly. "Just seeing you open your eyes and hearing you speak has already answered all my prayers."

"I suppose we'll have a lot to talk about."

"Not really." She shook her head and reached out lovingly to smooth his hair. "You don't have anything left to explain unless you want to. I want you to know I'm not angry at you anymore about the whole Carlton House cover story, either."

"You're not?"

She shook her head. "Now that I know firsthand what sort of evil creatures you and your friends have dedicated your lives to fighting, I could never begrudge your doing whatever it took to accomplish your mission." She shrugged. "I wish you'd have asked me straight out to help, but I understand why that would have been impossible."

He lowered his gaze, moved by her words as he held her hand. "You're a very generous woman, Mara."

"And you, my friend, are a bona fide hero."

He scoffed quietly and shook his head. "No. You want to see a hero, look at Rohan, look at Virgil and Max."

"I'm sure they are, my love, but those men were a wreck from the moment they saw you wounded." She gave him a fond smile, studying him. "Judging from what I saw, I get the feeling you're sort of . . . hmm, the glue holding things together around here."

The second she said it, Jordan knew exactly what she was talking about though no one had ever put it into words before, and besides, he was too well mannered ever to claim such a vital role.

"I'm glue?" he echoed dryly.

She nodded. "Warrington told me you're the one who's kept everyone sane."

"Well, look at them," he pointed out. "That's not saying

much." If not for the amount of blood he'd lost, he might almost have blushed.

She smiled knowingly. "We've had many interesting conversations while you were in dreamworld, by the by."

"Oh, dear. Lies, all lies."

She giggled. "I hear you spent the past twelve years, how shall I say, pining for me?"

"Pining?" he exclaimed with a wince. "They actually told you that?"

"Do you deny it, sir?"

"No," he muttered, trying to scowl, but he knew his eyes were sparkling as much as her own.

"According to Max, you could never seem to decide if you loved or hated me. Interestingly, though, the marquess claims there was never any question in *his* mind on the matter."

"Yes, well, Max always thinks he knows everything," Jordan attempted to jest, but Mara's gaze turned wistful.

"I'm glad I got to see how close you all are," she said as she caressed his hand. "How much you rely on each other. It relieves my mind to know you were not totally alone while we were apart. Now I understand what a sacrifice you were making, leaving me. Max said you were actually considering quitting the Order for me before you had barely got started."

"It's true."

"You had just completed years of training. And you were willing to give that up for me."

He nodded. "But I could not abandon them."

"Of course not. How could you? You're the glue, and you knew it—and Virgil knew it, too. That's why he put so much pressure on you to leave me behind."

"You talked to Virgil?"

She lowered her gaze with a pensive nod. "We were both

here through the night watching over you. He certainly looks on you, on all of you, like his own sons, and for that reason, I don't think he intended to deprive you of any happiness by advising you against me. He just wasn't convinced that what you and I had found together was real. He thought you were infatuated with, as he put it, a dark-eyed coquette. Would you believe he apologized to me?"

"Did he?" Jordan asked in amazement.

She nodded. "He admitted last night that when you came to him saying that you intended to ask for my hand, he told you to cool your heels and did a little spy work checking up on me." She smiled wanly, gazing down at their joined hands. "To no one's surprise, including my own, he quickly concluded that I was too impetuous and flighty to be trusted with the secrets you all had to keep."

Jordan shook his head in quiet anger at himself. "I should have fought harder for you. I should not have accepted his word as final—"

"It's all right," she soothed. "I didn't mean to dredge up the past. The future is what matters now. But I am willing to take responsibility for being a little rebel in those days."

"You had your reasons. Besides, I knew full well that your coquetry was only a façade."

"All I know is that I'm happy to have it confirmed that it was not a lack of feeling for me that pulled you away but your sense of duty to the Order and your loyalty to these 'brothers' of yours."

He shook his head. "Clearly, we misjudged you. Virgil and I both underestimated you, because yesterday, I saw with my own eyes what fierce mettle you are made of when those you love are threatened. Most impressive, my lady. There's no further question we could've trusted you with the Order's secrets."

"Yes, but if I had not married Pierson, I would not have Thomas," she replied. Her gaze sobered as she stared at him. "Thank you for saving my son's life."

"Thank *you* for giving me another chance," he murmured. "Mara?"

"Yes, my love?"

Jordan held both of her delicate hands in his own. "Nothing must be allowed ever to separate us again. I don't want to lose this chance. Whatever happens, wherever we go from here, promise me we're together from now on. I love you, Mara," he whispered. "I always have, and I always will."

"Jordan," she breathed, as he pulled her into his arms. She pressed a reverent kiss to his cheek and held him in her embrace.

Surely he had not survived the fight, but died, he thought, for this felt too much like heaven.

"I love you, too, my sweet man, so much," she choked out. "You've always held my heart."

His own was already overflowing, but he struggled to maintain a manly composure. "Does that mean you're finally willing to give up your freedom and marry me, you stubborn girl?"

She laughed through her joyous tears. "Yes, actually it does. And soon, or there could be gossip about the date on your heir's birth certificate."

He pulled back suddenly, his hands on her shoulders, and stared into her face. "My—my *heir?*" She smiled slowly until his eyes widened with amazed elation. "You mean—?"

"I'm late. Well, don't look so surprised!" She nodded, laughing, as he threw his arms around her. Then he claimed her mouth in a jubilant kiss.

* * *

As Beau made his way down to the Pit, the Order's subterranean lair carved into the limestone beneath the three-hundred-year-old Dante House, he savored the relief of seeing Falconridge rejoin the land of the living.

He had a deep respect for the earl's quiet strength, but even more than that, seeing Rotherstone's triad reunited had made Beau wonder for the millionth time that week about his own teammates.

Where the hell are they?

He thrust his gnawing worry aside, telling himself they'd be fine. Something had probably just come up. He was simply going to have to be patient, he told himself as he stalked across the torchlit chamber, but took care not to step on the ancient mosaic of the Archangel Michael set in a medallion on the floor of the main gathering chamber.

A lantern on the table flickered its reddish light on the white Maltese cross of the Order that hung against the dark, cavelike rock of their underground headquarters.

Beau crossed to the section of the Pit where he was fairly sure he would find Virgil—outside the holding cell where they were keeping Niall.

The old Highlander could scarcely seem to go two hours without looking in on the younger copy of himself, still safely contained behind the bars.

Nephew, indeed.

Beau could hear their terse exchange as he approached the rounded hollow of the holding-cell area. He shook his head to himself. Kin or not, surely their handler did not think Niall could be trusted in any way?

Was he the only one who could see the younger Banks would just as soon cut any of their throats, including Virgil's, if that was what it took for him to escape?

Virgil was leaning his hips on a tall stool across from Niall's cell when Beau stepped into the doorway.

"Sir?"

The older Highlander glanced over in question, his frustration with his "nephew" visible in his fiery eyes.

"He's awake," Beau informed him.

Virgil's posture lifted at once. He pushed away from the stool and left the holding-cell anteroom.

Meanwhile, Niall sent Beau an evil look, which Beau returned to him in silent warning.

Don't even think about it.

Virgil turned to Beau as he joined him. "How's he doing?" he asked gruffly.

"Better than expected. I think he had the proper motivation inspiring him to live."

Virgil almost smiled, then his eyes narrowed in question. "Have you made any progress on figuring out where that list came from or this key that Lady Pierson reported Bloodwell giving her?"

"The key—still no idea. The list—I might have, if Falconridge hadn't bled all over it. Unfortunately, it was in his breast pocket when he was stabbed. I'm afraid it'll be hard to trace beyond what the Regent's secretary already told us."

"Right. Just that it came from the Home Office. But we still don't know from which department, or by whose hand." Virgil shook his head. "It doesn't add up."

"Sir, is it possible we might actually have a traitor somewhere inside the Order?" Beau whispered.

"Hard to say. But who else besides one of our own could have known all these agents' identities? This could either be sabotage—or possibly, just somebody's stupid mistake, sending this to the Regent with the best of intentions. Either way, we need to know the truth. What's the matter?" Virgil demanded, noting his scowl.

Beau shook his head, exasperated. "What baffles me is

how the royal buffoon could've failed to grasp the danger of even keeping that piece of paper in his desk!"

"Lord Beauchamp," the Highlander chided with a frown that reproached him only mildly for criticizing their sovereign.

"Sir, you know it's true. How could he be so careless not to realize the peril he was putting us in by keeping this information so poorly secured? I know he likes to play at war and pretend he was actually there at Waterloo, but damn it, we dedicate our all to protect this man, and in turn, he's playing roulette with our bloody lives!"

"Believe me, I mean to talk to him personally about it," Virgil replied, though Beau had expected a scolding.

"Really? You have an audience with the Regent?" A smile spread over his face. "Please, can I come with you? I won't even say anything, I'll just sit there—"

"That will do, Sebastian," Virgil said wryly.

Beau scowled again. He hated being called by his first name.

"Give all your attention to that list, at least for now, while you're waiting for your team to get home."

"Yes, sir."

Virgil started to walk away, but paused, and glanced back at him. "Don't worry, lad," he offered in a low tone. "Your mates will make it back all right."

Beau gave him a rueful smile of gratitude. "Yes, sir."

Mara was holding Jordan's hand, and they were gazing at each other when Virgil cleared his throat from the open doorway.

They both looked over.

Jordan laughed, and Mara smiled as the big, weathered warrior came in with a fond lopsided grin to find his patient awake again.

Jordan dutifully answered Virgil's few gruff questions about his injuries and his overall condition. Then he told the Highlander their momentous news—wedding bells, a child on the way. "I wanted you to be the first to know," he said.

Virgil congratulated them with surprising warmth, even embracing Mara in fatherly fashion.

"Thank you," she was saying, accepting his well-wishes, when all of a sudden, little Thomas came barreling into the room in a state of giggling hilarity.

"Come back here, you wee rapscallion!" they could hear Rohan booming from the corridor. "Oh, where's he gone? Dogs, have you seen Thomas?"

Thomas squealed with glee at hearing Rohan ask the dogs this question.

"I hide!" he exclaimed, climbing in between Jordan and Mara, who had sat down again on the edge of the bed.

"Easy!" She restrained her son from jostling their wounded hero overmuch, but Jordan was just as pleased to see the boy as Thomas was to duck into hiding behind the man who would become a second father to him in the years ahead.

"Has anyone seen Thomas?" Rohan asked idly, appearing in the doorway.

A small giggle came from under the edge of the sheet.

"No Thomas in here," Jordan replied.

Mara poked the outline of a chubby belly. "Shh! He's going to see you," she whispered.

"You can't find me!"

"I wonder where he went. Guess I'd better keep looking," the duke drawled with a knowing smile at Mara. "Come on, dogs. Let's see if we can find him . . ."

When Rohan had gone with the pack of dogs following him, Thomas popped out from under the sheet, his hair sticking out in all directions, his newest teeth gleaming as he grinned.

Virgil chuckled at his antics, pressing the button of Thomas's little nose with his fingertip. "Reckon I'll leave you three in peace."

When he had gone, Mara scooped her son onto her lap. "I have something very special to tell you, Thomas—"

But he was not in the mood to stay on Mama's lap. He crawled over to Jordan, knelt before him, and stared somberly into his eyes.

"You still sick?" he asked in concern.

"Oh, I'm getting better," Jordan answered as his heart clenched. "Don't you worry about me. I'll be fine."

Mara and he exchanged a glance over the boy's head, but Thomas was already on to the next subject.

"I played with the doggies!"

"Did you? Tell me all about them," he invited, letting Thomas wriggle his way into a cuddly spot between the two of them. Careful of his wounds, Jordan put his arm around the boy he'd raise as his own.

Thomas proceeded to babble cheerfully about the guard dogs of Dante House, apparently mistaking his new friend, Rohan, for one of them.

"A common mistake," Jordan informed Mara in a low aside.

She laughed, but the more excited Thomas got about his subject, the less coherent was his speech.

Jordan had no idea what the boy was saying, but it didn't really matter. That chirpy little singsong voice was music to his ears.

As Thomas prattled on, Mara and he gazed at each other in tender amusement, eager to start their new lives together . . . a family at last.

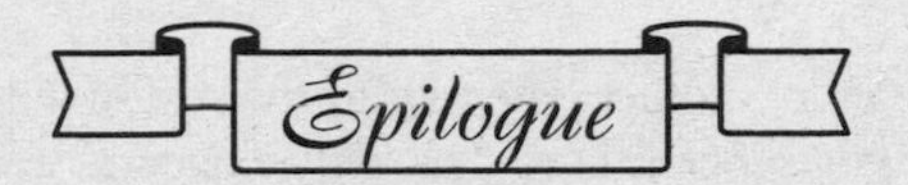

Epilogue

Far away across the Channel, Emily moved confidently through the Alpine forest, never letting her quarry stray too far ahead though she dared not let him realize she was following him.

Drake had gone into the castle farther up the mountain with the old man he now protected as staunchly as if Falkirk were his own father.

But soon, Emily thought, she would send a message to the Order and tell them where she was. She was rather sorry about throwing that rock at the one man, but it wasn't as though she could have let him shoot Drake. Still, she might need help in the future. It might prove too difficult to coax Drake home herself.

Meanwhile, in the castle's great hall, Drake stood behind James's chair in dark vigilance, eyeing each of the Promethean Council members who had gathered to see what James had to show them.

None of them could be trusted, but James was doing all he could to persuade the others to follow him in overthrowing Malcolm.

"Behold, one of the greatest treasures our forebears

ever created. I present to you, gentlemen, the Alchemist's Scrolls . . ."

Drake didn't bother listening to the rest, uninterested in their occult superstitions. His only concern was keeping James safe so he, in turn, could accomplish his goal of defeating Niall's father.

But after scanning the hardened faces of these powerful, shadowy men handpicked from among Europe's elite, Drake's gaze strayed toward the open window and the starry allure of the Alpine night.

Surely he must be at least in part a lunatic, for he could swear he felt her—as he always had—but no longer now as a mere angelic ideal, a private vision keeping him going. An innocent secret tucked away in his heart.

No, this time, she was out there—a flesh-and-blood woman with capable, healing hands and a level head and more courage in her heart than most men he'd ever met—and she was coming after him.

Drake was in some curious way afraid of her.

He had not actually seen her following since they had left London, that night he had saved James from Niall at the Pulteney Hotel. But although he had not laid eyes on her, he could still feel her, indeed, stronger than ever, could almost taste her on the wind.

The rustling of the night breeze through the pines, the scent of the mountain air, and sound of the brook outside the castle. All of it whispered her name to his deepest animal senses . . .

Emily.

AVON

At Avon Books, we know your passion for romance—once you finish one of our novels, you find yourself wanting more.

May we tempt you with . . .

- **Excerpts** from our upcoming releases.
- Entertaining **extras**, including authors' personal photo albums and book lists.
- Behind-the-scenes **scoop** on your favorite characters and series.
- **Sweepstakes** for the chance to win free books, romantic getaways, and other fun prizes.
- Writing **tips** from our authors and editors.
- **Blog** with our authors and find out why they love to write romance.
- **Exclusive content** that's not contained within the pages of our novels.

Join us at
www.avonbooks.com

AVON

An Imprint of HarperCollins*Publishers*
www.avonromance.com

Available wherever books are sold or please call 1-800-331-3761 to order.

FTH 0708